# CROSS INTENTS

## THE BAPTISM

# CROSS INTENTS

## THE BAPTISM

## S.R. WELLS

# CROSS INTENTS

## THE BAPTISM

This is a work of fiction. In some places where the story intersects biblical or historical canon, direct quotes are utilized. References to these quotes are included in the appendix.

The views and opinions expressed in this book are those of the author and do not necessarily reflect the official policy or position of Illumify Media Global.

Published by
Illumify Media Global
www.IllumifyMedia.com
"Write. Publish. Market. *SELL!*"

Library of Congress Control Number: 2022902765
Hardcover ISBN: 978-1-955043-69-4
Paperback ISBN: 978-1-955043-68-7

Typeset by Art Innovations (http://artinnovations.in/)
Cover design by Debbie Lewis

Sword and shield art by Phil Elsner
Author photo by Kimby Family Photography
www.facebook.com/kimbyfamilyphotography

*Printed in the United States of America*

*To the King and to His glory*

# 1

# THE END OF THE BEGINNING

## Rebellion minus 0 hours

A swarm of angels passed overhead in the King's Realm. One landed near Elric and shouted, "Come quickly! There is war!"

Elric raised his eyebrows. "What is war?" He turned toward the Mount of Assembly in the recesses of the north and gasped. Flashes of fire and lightning lit the heavens. Smoke billowed high.

"It's Lucifer. He is trying to ascend above the throne of the King and make himself like the Most High."

Elric shook his head and scowled. "But that is not possible. He can't possibly think—"

"We must go quickly."

They spread their wings and joined the rush toward the mountain.

Flapping and jostling amid the crowd, the angel called out to Elric, "His pride has deceived him. Now all light within him is gone. All reasoning of truth is lost. And worse, he deceived many of our own to join him in a rebellion. Michael has issued a call for all of us to join the fight."

"But I don't know how to fight," Elric shouted over the flurry of the flight.

"We will all learn," the other angel called back. He tucked his wings in and dove downward.

Elric hovered above the army advancing up the base of the mountain. Millions of angels pressed hard against a wall of defenders. Flashes of fire blasted up the mountain. The deafening roar of battle rang in his ears. Smoke burned his eyes, and he winced at the rank burning sulfur.

*How is this possible? None of this makes sense. There must be a third of the heavenly host fighting against the King. Why would they even want to . . .*

A sizzling hum approached from below. Elric glanced down. A pulsing ball of plasma energy hurtled toward him. He cut hard left, but the missile plowed into his chest. A shock wave of searing pain shot through his body. He gasped for a breath. Then everything went black.

Elric awoke face down on the ground. He shook his head and blinked.

*This is pain. A most unholy sensation I hope never to experience again.*

The pain subsided, and his strength returned. He pushed up with his arms, but a tromping foot on his back smashed him back down onto his face. He rolled. Another foot pounded down where he had just been. There, on the left—a rock formation jutting out from the cliff wall. He rolled again, clawed his way behind a cleft, and pulled his legs in out of the marching horde. He sat up and examined the faces of the attackers. Sinister and malevolent expressions twisted their faces.

*Their eyes!* Red. Evil. Devoid of all light.

A hand gripped his shoulder from behind. He turned with a jolt and looked up. The eyes? Brown and sparkling with life. The angel flipped back his long, flowing, jet–black hair and offered Elric his hand.

"New to the fight?" the angel asked, pulling Elric to his feet.

Elric nodded.

"I am Jenli, minister of records."

"Elric, choir director."

"It is a dark day," Jenli said.

"I don't understand it," said Elric.

"Neither do I."

"What are we supposed to do?"

"The King has already pronounced judgment. The rebels are to be stripped of four dimensions and removed from the King's Realm. They are to be cast down to earth into the Middle and Physical Realms. He has spoken. But we must cast them down."

"How do we do that?"

"Simply take hold of them and translate into the Middle Realm. Once you have them there, let them go and translate back here. They will not be able to follow. Watch me. This will be my third one."

Jenli waited and eyed each passing attacker. One passed that was about his size. Jenli pounced from behind and wrapped his arm around the rebel's neck. The rebel squealed. Jenli tightened his grip and lifted him off the ground. Jenli wrapped his wings around the two of them and disappeared.

Elric nodded and took a deep breath. He waited. He took another breath. Waited. *I am larger than most of these rebels. Surely, I will have the strength.* He took another deep breath. He pounced. He caught a rebel in a chokehold and jerked him upward. A surge of energy coursed through his frame—power from the Throne. He gritted his teeth, wrapped his wings around his mark, and translated into the Middle Realm.

In the Middle Realm, the rebel writhed under Elric's grasp and screamed. Elric released him and stepped back. The rebel fell in a heap and twitched and stretched. Elric covered his mouth at the horrific sight before him. The rebel's skin had become ashen black, as though scorched by fire. His hair, what remained of it, shriveled into sparse wiry tufts. The once–translucent white wings became leathery and bat-like. The rebel turned his face upward toward Elric, his red eyes full of hatred, and hissed. Yellow sulfur streamed through his jagged teeth. Elric turned away, wrapped his wings around himself, and returned to the King's Realm.

Elric hid behind the cleft in the rock, and the rebels continued to press their advance. This time, Elric didn't hesitate for a moment. When the first rebel passed by, Elric pounced.

* * *

## Rebellion plus 1 day

Elric pressed his shoulder against another angel's on his left. An angel on his right, about his size, pressed in from the right. Hundreds of angels of his stature stood in a straight line in the front. Behind them stood hundreds more with smaller frames. Tight ranks, grim faces.

A single angel, larger than all of them, paced on a raised platform in front. He stopped in the center of the platform, crossed his hands behind his back, and announced with a booming voice, "My name is Kai. I have been appointed as your . . . military . . . commander. As of today, by order of the King, we are all designated elzurim—warriors in the King's service. We will serve mostly in the Middle Realm, ministering to man and, as necessary, fighting against our new enemy."

The commander stopped and turned away from the ranks. He bowed his head and let his arms drop to his sides. Turning back around, he took a deep breath and raised his chin.

"We have entered a new time," he said in a low and pensive voice. "A day none of us could have ever imagined. But there is coming a day, hidden in the deep counsel of the King, when He will set all things right. Until then, we will fight for the Kingdom."

The commander stood at attention and gazed over the ranks. "You will be commissioned as officers. You will have warriors who will serve under you, and you will have regions of responsibility. As of this hour, I charge you—be valiant, be strong in the Lord. Rank number one, you will be my captains. The remaining ranks, you are lieutenants. Come forward now, line by line, and receive your new tools. By my own hand, I give to you a sword and shield. Learn to use them well. Captains shall wear two golden braids on your sleeves. Lieutenants shall wear a single silver braid."

Elric's line made a right face and filed up the platform. Commander Kai handed each warrior a sword and shield as he passed by. With each step, Elric's insides tied tighter and tighter into a knot. *I can't believe this is happening. How did it come to this? How long before the King vanquishes his foes and sets the Kingdom aright? One day . . . one day . . .*

# 2

# HEROD THE GREAT

## Birth minus 6 months

Two personal Roman guards of Herod the Great stood beside thick marble columns outside an arched doorway and wached the king talk to himself and make emotional gestures with his arms as if having a heated argument with someone.

"He is going mad," one guard said.

"Quiet, you fool. If you value your life."

The young guard lowered his voice to a whisper. "But look at him."

"Pressures of maintaining so great a kingdom," whispered the seasoned guard.

Still standing at attention, the young guard barely moved his lips. "It is more than stress. He is either mad or he has a demon."

"This is your first day in the palace, isn't it?" The older guard held his stance and kept his eyes forward.

"Yes."

"You will see many things. Remember your duties and do not speak of anything outside this court."

"Has he always been this way?"

"He has become worse over the years. It was a bloody rise to power thirty years ago. You weren't even born. There was a three-year siege against Jerusalem. Assassinations. Political maneuvering. Thousands were slaughtered. But he had the backing of the Roman senate and the muscle of our army."

"And now he controls all of Judea, Samaria, and Galilee. What, then, is the problem?"

"The Jews. They hate him."

The young guard waited a moment, then asked, "Why?"

"To begin with, he's not even a true Jew—his father was a descendant of a desert tribe that was forced into Judaism and his mother was an Arab. The Sadducees hate him because he executed the last of the old royal house—relatives of many of them. The Pharisees hate him because he is a murderer and carries out capital punishments without the approval of the Sanhedrin. The people hate him for his heavy taxes and taste for blood."

"Why does he not try to win them?"

"He did, at first. After the siege and a huge earthquake, he rebuilt Jerusalem with a new market, a theater, an amphitheater, a meeting hall for the Sanhedrin, and a new royal palace. He expanded Solomon's temple site and built all the colonnades and courtyards. But none of that helped. In fact, it only angered the Jews even more. The architecture is too Roman, and he erected a Roman golden eagle on top of the gate of the new temple."

"So now he keeps the peace with an iron fist. The Roman army, mercenaries, secret police."

"He doesn't care what they think anymore."

The guards stood at attention with mouths shut tight. Herod made a wide circle, passing near their post. Herod flailed his arms and shouted, "None! I can trust none of them!"

Herod turned his back and walked away again, and the older guard whispered, "This is his growing dread—his own family. You just saw Antipater, his oldest son."

"The one who told him that his sons Alexander and Aristobulus were calling him 'a shameless old man who dyes his hair'?"

"Yes. Antipater was banished with his mother when he was four years old because Herod wanted to marry a Hasmonaean princess named Mariamme. Now, eight wives and fourteen children later, Herod has no one he can trust. Seven years ago, he called Antipater back after thirty years of banishment. It appears to me that Antipater is trying to eliminate competition for the throne."

Herod paced close again, and the guards became like statues.

"Those insolent rebels," Herod grumbled. "They go off to Rome and get their Roman education and then come back here and try to lord it over me. They are nothing but Hasmonaean aristocrats with no idea of what it takes to be king. They hate me! I know it. And I know they are trying to gain the support of my armies. They scheme against me to overthrow my crown, and now they insult me in front of others." Herod raised his fist in the air and walked away from the two guards.

"I have heard of Mariamme. I heard he had her killed," the younger guard whispered.

"He loved her."

"What happened?"

"After Mark Antony's defeat by Octavian, Herod went to Rome to pledge his allegiance to Caesar. He received renewed support from Rome and gained new territories. But when he returned, there was a rumor that Mariamme had found another lover. The jealousy was too much, and he had her executed."

"Was the rumor true? Or did she love him?"

"She hated him. He had killed her grandfather to claim the throne back in the early years. Then, in an effort to placate Jewish leaders, he installed her brother Aristobulus as high priest. But Aristobulus's popularity grew, and Herod became jealous. Eventually, Herod felt threatened, so he had Aristobulus drowned in a pool at his palace in Jericho. She hated him."

Herod stopped in front of a pillar. He kicked it. "What should I do about these two insurgents?" He resumed his pacing and continued to rant.

"He is obsessed with maintaining his kingdom," the older guard said.

"I still say he has a demon."

\* \* \*

The great demon commander, Molech, peered out at the Physical Realm through the eyes of his human host, Herod, and threw his exasperated hands up.

"What should I do about these two insurgents?" he said.

The demon paced, using the legs of his human puppet. A company of beaelzurim attendants lined the royal court, watching their commander, waiting for blood.

"I cannot let this kind of disrespect go unchecked. I could take them out of my will. No, that is not enough. I know, I shall go ask *her*. She is the only one who understands, the only one who truly loves me. She will know what to do."

Molech walked his human puppet, Herod, out of the throne room and deep down to the secret place, the ultra–private chamber where he alone could go. The special place where he kept her.

The small square room had no windows. On the marble walls hung two iron sconces with torches that cast a dim and eerie yellow glow about the room and left many deep shadows. In the center of the room on a raised marble pedestal stood a large clay jar. In the jar, his Mariamme, embalmed in honey, preserved forever, waited for him with all her love.

The demon lord and Herod entered the secret chamber and closed the thick wooden door. It made a cold, thumping echo. On the stone bench by the pedestal sat a grotesque demon with wild, glowing red eyes, exposed blood–stained fangs, and massive studded arms. The two demons flashed fiendish smiles at each other. Herod's eyes saw the figure sitting on the bench—the lovely spirit form of his long–lost wife. She looked as beautiful as the day he took her for his own, and she smiled lovingly at him, the way she always did.

"Hello, my love," she cooed. "I have missed you."

He dragged himself across the room and slumped down beside her.

"What is it, dear?" she asked. "I can tell something is troubling you."

"Alexander and Aristobulus. They are trying to take over the throne. And they continue to malign me in public. What am I to do?"

Mariamme didn't flinch, "Kill them."

"I was afraid you wouldn't approve. They are sons we had together."

"Anyone who tries to usurp your crown is no son of mine. I say you have to execute them. In fact, I think you should take one of the golden cords that tie back the canopy of my bed—which I know you still keep untouched in the palace—and use it to strangle them before your eyes while you sit on your throne. Let this be a sign to all the glory–hungry sons who have an eye toward your kingdom."

"I knew you would understand. We have always had such a strong connection. I love you so much."

"And I love you. Now, go and do this thing. You must not delay."

Herod stood at the door for a moment and looked back at his love. He then went to her old room and retrieved the cord. After taking his place in the throne room, he summoned the two brothers. He presented the charges against them with cold composure. They denied all the charges and pledged their allegiance to him. He flung the cord down at their feet.

"Do you know what this is? This is a cord that belonged to your mother, whom I loved. But by it today you will pay the price for your treachery."

With a simple motion of Herod's hand, the executioner picked up the rope and strangled the life out of both of Herod's sons.

"Let this be a lesson to anyone who thinks they can ascend to my throne. Remove these dogs from my sight."

The demon from Mariamme's chamber stood over the bodies and laughed. The hundred other demons in the throne room cheered and shouted and flew around the room in a feverous frenzy. A small snake with knowing eyes watched from the dark corner. His forked black tongue shot in and out. The snake's glowing red eyes turned to slits, and he slithered off without a sound.

Herod retired to his bedroom, seething over who else might be seeking to betray him.

# 3

# THE MAGI

**Birth minus 4 weeks**

In the magi temple in Persia, a man with a white beard wearing colorful night robes rushed down the hall. The flickering lantern he held out at arm's length drove away the night shadows in the hall, and the *pad, pad, pad* of his leather sandals on the smooth stone floor passed by two . . . three unlit wall sconces. No time to stop and light them now. He veered left into a dark bed chamber.

With the lantern in one hand, Melchior nudged Caspar with the other. "Caspar, wake up. Wake up. You must come and look at this." Caspar roused at the sound of the excitement in Melchior's voice, scowled, and rubbed his eyes. He slipped on a robe, and the two hurried outside. They stopped in front of a wood table and chairs. Rolled parchments, layers of astrological charts, and measurement instruments lay strewn across the table. Melchoir pushed a stack of charts aside and set the lantern on the table.

Melchior pointed upward into the heavens. "There . . . rising in the east. What do you make of it?"

"It looks like the royal star, Hormoz."

"Yes, I agree. And with it rising in the east, we are entering a time most powerful to bestow a new king."

"True, but this is not remarkable."

"There is more. The sun is in Varak, where it is exalted."

"Hmm. A powerful king."

"And . . . notice that Keyvân is also present. That means the three rulers of the Varak trine are present."

Caspar eased into a chair. "This is amazing. We must be on the brink of the introduction of a great king indeed."

"And that is just the beginning." Melchior shuffled his astronomical plots on the table and moved his instruments out of the way. He pulled the lantern close to the parchment. "According to my calculations, we should see a conjunction of Hormoz and Keyvân . . . and the moon . . . within the next four weeks!"

Caspar jumped to his feet and looked at Melchior's charts with wild excitement in his eyes. For several minutes he kept checking the projections and muttering, "Incredible, incredible." He stepped back and gazed up at Hormoz with an enormous smile beaming from beneath his long mustache and beard. "An event like this would happen only once in several lifetimes. This is the most significant thing we will ever see. Go wake Balthazar."

In the main study, the walls were lined with open compartments containing rolled up scrolls. Balthazar examined the projected trajectories by lamplight. The three sat around the charts, looking at each other with childlike excitement.

"This will not be some ordinary king," Balthazar stuttered. "We are most fortunate to be poised to see this. An alignment like this is unfathomable. From where do we think the king will arise?"

Melchior didn't hesitate. "Hormoz is in Varak, the ram—which is the sign of the Jews. This king will have to come from somewhere in Judea, Samaria, or Palestine . . . but we have no way of knowing exactly where."

* * *

In the corner of the magi's study, a small demon named Nangar rubbed his hands up and down his spindly, ashen arms and licked his lips. The dim glow of the lamplight on the magi's maps could not reach into the dark corner where he kept his presence hidden from the men.

Nangar breathed a silky stream of smoke into the spiritual air. "Where? Where indeed. This is the question," he whispered.

*Marr believes he has the coming King surrounded in Egypt. What if he is wrong? What if they are all wrong? What if the King enters through a place in Israel, and none knows the location?* Nangar rubbed his hands over his smooth, bald head and smirked. *What if I could use these Zoroastrian priests to somehow lead me to Him?*

*These men—these wise, educated, sophisticated men—they believe all the lofty lies I have built up over the centuries. They sit here in their temple-observatory and study the stars while I combine their mathematics and mysticism to make them believe their lives are governed by the constellations. I have them. And now I shall use them to help me find the ultimate prize.*

The three priests double checked their star maps. Nangar smirked. *I need to move them to conduct a thorough search in Israel. It is a very long journey from Persia, though. They must be convinced that the king they seek is worthy of their homage. But I cannot have them start believing in the Creator King.* Nangar licked his lips again and nodded his head. *They are earnest and thoughtfully benevolent men. I will appeal to their intellectual curiosity and rely on their desire for enlightenment. They will make the journey. They will lead me to the hidden King.*

"We must learn more about this coming king of Israel." Nangar spoke into the smoky air of the Middle Realm. "We must conduct a search and find where he is to be born. We should search the archives for prophecies. Perhaps we can even go and honor the new king with gifts and well-wishes."

* * *

## Birth minus 6 hours

Four weeks of anticipation passed, and clear skies over Persia brought energized excitement to the magi temple. Caspar, Melchior, and Balthazar placed their measuring instruments and charts and scrolls on a table outside and prepared for the astrological event of a lifetime. Engrossed in a flurry of activity, they tracked the moon and the great traveling stars Hormoz and Keyvân. For several hours, they took measurements, recorded positions, plotted paths.

"It looks like our predictions about the triple conjunction are accurate," Melchior said.

"Truly, this is going to happen," Balthazar whispered.

The time drew close, all the activities ceased, and the three became silent. Closer and closer the heavenly lights drew together. All three men marveled with their awestruck bearded chins hanging down to their chests.

"Here it is! Here it is!"

The triple conjunction.

"The rest of the world sleeps, with no idea of this wonder."

"Historic. Amazing."

Their gaping mouths turned into enormous, satisfied grins, and their eyes twinkled back at the silent, starry performers in the sky. Silent. Distant. Well-ordered and . . .

*Flash!* Within a blink, the heavens opened up, and a multitude of angels appeared in the sky in front of the wandering stars. Rows upon rows of angelic beings came into view, all shining as bright as lightning and full of radiant colors. Trumpets started—loud, clear, and magnificent.

Each of the magi released a high–pitched yelp and flailed and jumped and fumbled around like startled rabbits. A faltering misstep knocked over the table with the scrolls and instruments, sending all the implements clattering to the ground.

The initial panic swept past them, and the spectacle overtook their entire conscious thought. Their legs became too weak to stand, and they sank to their knees with their eyes frozen on the heavens. Angels, or heavenly beings of some kind, sang about the birth of the Son of God. Trumpets, voices, regal majesty shook the heavens and pounded against their chests.

The music finished. A giant explosion of light. A dark, starry sky. Silence.

Flat on their backs, with streaming eyes and glowing faces, Caspar, Melchior, and Balthazar glanced across the ground at each other.

"What . . . was that?" Caspar stuttered.

"Never have I . . . " Balthazar slurred.

"In all our studies," Melchior stammered, "nothing could have prepared us for this."

They lay still for several minutes, breathing and gawking at the dark, empty sky. Balthazar sat up first. Caspar and Melchior followed. With all the stoic dignity he could muster, Caspar stood and righted the table. Balthazar gathered parchments and set them back on the table in a neat array. He spread the main tracking chart out in the center. Caspar relit the toppled lamp. Melchior restored the fallen instruments to the table.

Melchior cleared his throat and with a calm, analytical voice said, "We knew we were on the brink of the coming of a great king."

"Yes," said Balthazar, "but it appears we underestimated his importance. This is not just a great king. This is a King of kings. Could it be that this is the very Son of God himself?"

"That is what I heard from the . . . whatever they were . . . " Caspar said matter-of-factly. He set the lamp on the table next to the charts.

Balthazar said, "This would mean that there is one true God of all creation?"

They each stood in silence for several minutes, gazing into the heavens.

"What shall we do?" Melchior asked.

They grouped around the table and looked at each other with blank stares.

* * *

## Birth plus 15 minutes

Nangar stepped out of the shadows and stood beside the perplexed magi. They needed answers. He could guide them. "You must seek him out," he said. "This is, indeed, a thing of great wonder; and you desire to know all knowledge. For the sake of knowledge and understanding, you should make every effort to find the child and see him with your own eyes."

*I need to get them to take their focus off the touch they received in their spirits. Need to engage their intellect.*

"For the sake of knowledge and understanding," he repeated. His words shot like fiery darts and penetrated their spirits.

"We should try to find him," said Balthazar. "Seeing his star is one thing, but seeing him in person would be something altogether more interesting."

The other two nodded and stroked their beards.

Melchior said, "And how shall we find him? We know only that he is born in Israel."

Balthazar answered, "I said it weeks ago . . . prophecies in the ancient scrolls—there has to be something in there that—"

"Balthazar," Caspar interrupted, "we have looked. The only thing we have found is some vague reference to a king's star in the east."

"But there are many more scrolls. We need to continue searching."

Nangar whispered soothing words, "He is right. It is in there to be found. I will guide you. Together we can unlock the hidden secrets. Together we will find the child."

* * *

## Birth plus 8 hours

Daniel sprinted toward his base camp just outside of Bethlehem from the field where he had been watching the sheep. He had waited half the night for the shepherds to return from Bethlehem, and the news about the newborn King felt like it would explode within him. He had seen the angels in the sky. The other shepherds saw them, too—and they had actually gone to see the baby. Daniel couldn't wait to tell his father.

Out of breath, Daniel burst into his father's tent. "Father! Father! Wake up! The most amazing thing happened tonight!"

Jeremiah slept on a colorful rug bed mat, but roused quickly. "What is it Daniel? What's wrong?"

"Did you hear them? They were so loud!"

"Hear what, Daniel?"

"The angels! There were thousands of them! How could you sleep through it?"

"What time is it?"

"I don't know. Almost morning. I wanted to come straight here after it happened, but the other shepherds needed my help, and I figured you probably saw it anyway, and—"

"Daniel, slow down and start from the beginning. What are you talking about?"

Daniel rolled his eyes, took a dramatic breath, and said in his most grown-up voice. "I was out on the hillside with Jesse. We were talking, and then, all of a sudden, up in the sky I saw thousands of angels. They were all different colors and they filled the sky. They blew loud trumpets and sang an amazing song. They sang about the Messiah being born! The song said that He is coming to deliver us!"

"Angels?"

"Yes, I saw them! And I heard them!"

"Oh, Daniel."

"You don't believe me?"

"Well, it is not a matter of belief. It is . . . how long did you say you were out there with Jesse?"

"I'm not sure. It seemed like forever."

"Then that explains it—you must have fallen asleep and had a dream."

"No! This was no dream. I was wide awake. I know what I saw."

"But angels? I do not think—"

"Don't think they exist? Just because those Sadducees said that doesn't mean they're right. I saw them!"

"What about Jesse? Did he see them, too?"

*Just because Jesse didn't see it, it's going to be impossible to get Father to believe me.*

Daniel paused for a moment and answered in a dejected tone, "No. I don't think so."

"How do you explain that? If there were thousands of angels singing a song and making a great noise, do you not think he would have seen them?"

"But I saw them. I know I did."

"I don't doubt that you think you saw something, Daniel. But you must have been having a fantastic dream. It is the only thing that makes sense. I think you should . . . "

Daniel flung open the tent flap, ran to the edge of the hillside, and plopped down. Sitting all alone in the darkness, he fought back the tears and the lump in his throat. A nearby sheep bleated.

*Stupid sheep.*

The dew from the patch of grass seeped through the back of his tunic.

*Stupid grass. Stupid everything. This whole year has been stupid. First, I almost died, and then I lost my hearing. Father blames Levi, which is stupid. And Jesse . . . he's too much like Father. And those stupid Sadducees. No angels? Then what did I see tonight? No Messiah? Then what were those . . . whatever they were . . . singing about? It's all stupid. Am I the only one around here that sees that nothing in this stupid world makes sense? So what if some baby king was born last night? What's he going to do to help me?*

# 4

# A SON IN THE CITY OF DAVID

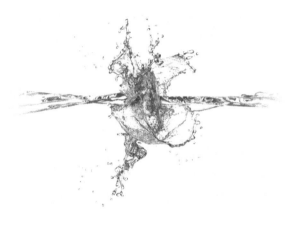

## Birth plus 1 day

In Bethlehem, early in the morning after Jesus' birth, a quiet, persistent rapping at the stable door behind an inn broke the morning silence. Elric stood by the door and watched. Jenli stood beside him. Inside, Joseph roused and peered from around the corner of the stable door at a bright–eyed lady of fifty, stepping side to side, wringing her hands.

"Yes," Joseph said, wiping the sleep from his baggy eyes.

"Good morning," the lady said. "I am Miriam."

Joseph answered with raised eyebrows and a puzzled look.

"Omer's wife." She paused. "The innkeepers."

The lights came on in Joseph's eyes. "Yes, yes, of course, good morning."

"Oh, my heavens, it's true then," Miriam said, peeking around Joseph into the stable. She squeezed in past him. "Omer told me this morning that he had set you up in here. Of course, if I had known last night, I would have done something about it. Sometimes I wonder about that man. Silly old goat. Sending a girl in labor out to a filthy animal stable . . . oh, the indignity! But it seems you made it through? And this is the little one? Oh, so precious. Is it a boy or a girl? Wait, don't tell me . . . I can usually tell just by looking at their little face—some of the ladies say I have a special gift for doing that. In fact, last week one of our neighbor's daughters had a baby—I took one look and I knew—'It's a girl, isn't it?' I said. And I was right. They all couldn't believe it. Except for my neighbor, of course. She has seen me do that for years. So then . . . let me take a look at you, darling." She paused for only a moment. "He is a boy?"

Mary nodded.

"I knew it," Miriam continued. "I can always tell. And a beautiful, healthy–looking boy at that. He even has some hair. It's so sweet— you know, sometimes they come out bald as can be. Two of mine did. Not a single hair. It grows in eventually, of course, but I think they are cuter when they have some hair to start with. So, you truly gave birth right here? Without a midwife? Oh, my, you poor thing."

She turned to Joseph. "That means you must have done the delivering? Well, you are a very courageous young man." She patted his cheek with her open hand. "I am very, very sorry that you had to start your family like this. If I had known last night, I could have done something. He's not a heartless man, of course—but he doesn't always think things all the way through. He actually thought he was doing you a favor. Imagine that! And then when he told me about you this morning, I had to come out here see how things were going. I was actually hoping you hadn't delivered yet so I could get you out of this animal shelter before the baby came. Well, I guess it is too late for that. But now, let me try to make things up to you a little. Come, my dear, we should get you into the house and get you cleaned up. A good bath and a real bed is what you need. Have you had breakfast? Oh, listen to me. Of course you haven't had breakfast. I will fix you something nice. And get you and the baby cleaned up."

"The blanket," Elric spoke to Miriam. "Wrap the Child in this blanket."

Jenli shook his head. "Better speak it again, captain. I don't think she . . ."

Miriam's fidgeting eyes passed by the special tunic on the shelf left by Elric the night before. She paused.

Elric smiled.

"Here, here," Miriam said, grabbing the blanket. "We should wrap him in this nice blanket before we take him outside. Ooh, feel this. It's so soft."

Elric motioned to Jenli. Jenli disappeared.

Joseph took the Baby, and Miriam helped him wrap the Baby in the blanket. Miriam pulled Mary to her feet, and they stepped out into the morning air. Miriam moved with quick, energetic gestures, but her pace remained patient and nurse-like for Mary's slow, tiny steps.

Elric took calm steps with his head straight forward, but his eyes darted all around the house and yard. The top of Jenli's head on the neighbor's roof . . . Brondor behind that corner . . . Kaylar's eyes peering through that wall—Jenli's team held a tight perimeter, each poised at the highest alert for the King's first movement out in the open. *With the Child wrapped in the tunic, the enemy should be unable to perceive His spirit. But I would prefer not to test that this early in the game.*

Miriam's voice prattled on in the background, but Elric's attention remained in the Middle Realm. "Keep moving," he whispered. "We need to get Him back indoors."

Miriam held Mary's hand and steadied her with each step. "What are you in town for? Wait, don't tell me . . . it's for the census, right? I knew it. That's why everybody is here. I have never seen so many people in this city. It is good for the business, of course, but I shall be glad when things get back to normal. So many strangers and so much commotion. Plus, it brings in extra Roman soldiers, and I think we all could do without that. They march around like they own the place and . . . oh, be careful, dear. Slow down, we are in no hurry. You are doing fine. What you need is a good hot meal, a nice bath, and a soft bed. I am going to set you up in a spare bedroom we have in our own house until you are feeling stronger. We will figure out the details later. For now, we need to get you in and cleaned up. If I had known last night, I would have had you in there already. It is unthinkable—having a baby in a stable. That man of mine. We are almost there, and you are doing well. You are such a sweet young lady. You don't talk much though, do you? That's fine, let's get you in and settled—then maybe you will feel more like talking."

The procession reached the back door of the house. Miriam opened it and gestured for Joseph to go in. "Omer, we have company," she called out into the house. "That's it, dear. We're almost there. Only a few more steps."

The door closed. Everyone inside. Out of sight. Elric nodded to Jenli, took one last glance around the area, and backed into the house.

* * *

With the morning meal done and the two women and the Baby in the back room, Joseph and Omer found themselves alone for the first time to carry the conversation on their own. Elric stood against the side wall and listened to the men's conversation. The incessant bubbling of Miriam's banter wafted in from behind the wall, and Omer gave Joseph a man–to–man see–what–I–have–to–live–with kind of smile and tried to get their conversation started.

"Joseph, you are from Nazareth, and you are here for the census?"

"Mm-hmm."

"Right." Omer looked around the room, down at his feet, and then back to Joseph. "Tell me, what do you do for a living back in Nazareth?"

"I am a carpenter," Joseph replied. "I like to work with wood mostly, but I can do any carpentry work—masonry, roof work, fencing."

"Ask him if he needs a carpenter," Elric said to Joseph.

The two men sat in silence nodding their heads. Then, a spark flashed in Joseph's eyes as though a thought had occurred to him. "Do you know anyone who is looking for the services of a carpenter?"

"You need a carpenter," Elric said to Omer.

Omer scratched his chin. "Why? Are you not headed back home after you register?"

"Well . . . no. We have no home back in Nazareth now, and I'm afraid everything we own is on those two carts out back."

The Baby's cry rang out from the back room.

A visible lump formed in Joseph's throat, and his eyes filled with tears. Omer looked toward the back room and then down at his feet. Omer cleared his throat.

"Where are you headed from here?" Omer asked.

"We don't know. Maybe Jerusalem. Wherever I can find work, I suppose."

Omer's eyebrows raised. He sat up and slapped his knee and announced, "We are both in luck! What a coincidence—I happen to have some carpentry work that I need done myself. Remember, I told you about the roof damage to two of our rooms and the broken awning? Do you think you could do those repairs?"

"I could take a look. I'm pretty sure I could take care of whatever damage is there."

"Would you like to take a look at it right now? The women will be busy for a while."

The two men excused themselves and headed out into the morning sunshine with a purposeful pace. They inspected the damage from the ground and from atop the roof and from inside the rooms. They discussed repair plans with much pointing and gesturing and nodding of heads. They discussed needed supplies and local vendors. They discussed a possible schedule. They discussed possible wages, including some ideas for barter. A full hour passed before the two men returned to Omer's house where the two ladies waited.

They told the women about the repair plans, and after more discussions, mostly led by Miriam, they reached a decision. Joseph and Mary would stay with Omer and Miriam until Joseph could complete the repairs enough for the damaged rooms to be habitable. Then he and Mary would move into one of the rooms. Omer would provide the funds for the needed materials, and for Joseph's labor the young couple could stay in the inn room rent-free. The room would be theirs for the full length of days for Mary's purification according to the law of Moses. At the end of those forty days, Joseph and Mary would make the customary journey to Jerusalem to present the Child to the Lord and offer a sacrifice at the temple. After that Joseph didn't know where they would live, and they would have to trust the Lord to provide something. If he could find work in Jerusalem and a place to live, they would stay there. If that didn't work out, he and Mary were welcome to stay in their room at the inn for a modest rent, and Omer could give Joseph some leads for jobs.

Elric smiled. *The details of life—how I love helping men weave their individual strands of thread into the great tapestry of the King. If only they could see the magnificent design they were a part of.*

# 5

# A CHANCE MEETING

## Birth plus 3 days

*J*oseph weaved his way through a large crowd at the census registration center. Jenli walked beside him and spoke to him while scanning the crowd. Local and Roman officials shouted orders and directed the movements of the assemblage. Roman soldiers stood at their posts with their menacing spear tips standing high above the heads of the milling crowd. Jenli shook his head and scowled.

*Look at these faces,* thought Jenli. *The familiar look of an oppressed people enduring yet another indignity under an iron–handed regime. They submit and follow directions like sheep. The sorrow in their eyes. Defeat. Hopelessness.*

Like the rest, Joseph set his course toward the center of the assembly area, straining for the instructions being barked out by an official.

Amid the crowd of people, dozens of elzurim and beaelzurim mixed and maneuvered. Other than an occasional shove or threat, they maintained their charges and kept moving.

*Stop looking at their faces and concentrate. Where is he? Where is he? He should . . . there!*

Across the courtyard, at the outer fringes of the crowd, Jenli's warrior Jerem pressed inward. Beside him, his charge. Jerem's eyes scanned left to right through the crowd. *Over here. Over here.* Jerem's eyes met Jenli's. The angelic link was made. Jerem leaned down and whispered to his charge, and Jenli did the same to Joseph. He stood back up and waited. Jerem spoke to his man again. The man's face lit up. He bounced up and down and craned his neck over the people's heads.

"Joseph! Joseph, is that you?" the man called over the commotion.

Joseph stopped and turned his head left and right.

"Joseph!" the man shouted. "Over here."

Joseph's gaze flashed from face to face. The man waved his arm and bounced with a broad smile.

"Rabbi?" Joseph called out, waving back.

Raziel, the rabbi from Nazareth—the one who had performed Joseph and Mary's wedding ceremony—waved again and shouted, "Joseph! What a surprise!"

Joseph gave up his quest to make it to the front and wound his way through the crowd toward Raziel. They met each other with a traditional kiss on each cheek and bright surprised smiles.

Jerem stepped up with a smile.

"Right on time," Jenli complimented.

"You too."

"Rabbi Raziel," Joseph almost shouted from excitement, "what are you doing here?"

Raziel laughed. "Master Zeev sent me out on some affairs of the synagogue. I am visiting the synagogues in several towns for the next month or so. This week, I am here in Bethlehem. I think I could be accomplishing more at home, but he was adamant that I take the trip. Sometimes I don't know where he comes up with some of his ideas." He laughed again. "But he is the master. So here I am!"

Jenli and Jerem smiled.

"But why come down here into this mess?" Joseph asked, motioning toward the crowd.

"Oh, I don't know. I had a feeling I needed to get out and mingle with the people. I knew the census was in progress, and I knew it was a major event, so I wanted to see it. I am a little surprised to see how many people are out here. It is amazing. Actually, I am grateful to have an opportunity to see it. What about you? What brings you here?"

"The census."

"Oh, yes, of course. Bethlehem for the line of David. How are you and Mary doing? I haven't seen you for a few months. Actually, she must be close to her due date?"

"As a matter of fact, she delivered the night before last."

"Congratulations!" Raziel burst out with an enormous hug which lifted Joseph off the ground. "This is wonderful news! Wait. How could you have found out so quickly unless . . . unless Mary is not in Nazareth."

"She is here, too. The Baby was born here in Bethlehem."

"Bethlehem?" Raziel shouted. And then in almost a whisper, "Bethlehem? Joseph, do you realize what this means?"

Raziel pulled Joseph out and away where they could have more privacy. They stopped beneath a stand of palm trees. Joseph looked around with a puzzled expression. Raziel looked like he would burst.

"Back before I married the two of you, you told me about some amazing signs. I didn't doubt the things you thought you saw, but I wanted see how things unfolded before I made up my mind about what it all might mean. I wanted to believe it, but there was one thing that did not seem to make sense. While there is a somewhat obscure reference in the prophets about the Messiah being called a Nazarene, it is commonly accepted that He would come from Bethlehem. It is in the prophet Micah: 'But as for you, Bethlehem Ephrathah, too little to be among the clans of Judah, from you One will go forth for Me to be ruler in Israel. His goings forth are from long ago, from the days of eternity.' I couldn't understand how He was going to be from Bethlehem when you lived in Nazareth. But now, here you are, and He actually was born in Bethlehem!"

Prickly bumps appeared on his arms and his eyes welled up. He rubbed his forehead. "This could actually be the Messiah. This . . . could . . . actually be . . . " He collapsed to his knees. The small cloud of dust that rose from his knees settled as he continued to rub his forehead. "How many people know about all this?" Raziel said, his voice low.

"There is Mary's family, but I don't think they believe it. You, of course. And then there were four shepherds who showed up on the night of His birth—they said they saw a vision and . . . "

"A vision? Of what? Angels again?"

"Yes, one spoke to them and told them where to find us, and then they saw a whole host of angels in the sky."

"Incredible, and then, what else?"

"I told them most of what we had seen and been through. They gave us a gift and then left. They are the only other ones we have talked to."

"Good. That is good. I don't know why, but something inside me tells me it is best to keep this to ourselves for now. It's not that I don't believe you—trust me—I am very excited about this. But, if this truly is the Promised One, He will take His place in the proper time without any promotion from us. I suspect it will be best to let Him grow without the distractions from a multitude of well-meaning, and not-so-well-meaning, religious leaders. Also, simply making the claim could bring down the unwanted wrath of a jealous king. Herod is ruthless and has a very long reach."

Joseph nodded.

"Tell me," Raziel said, "what do you have planned for His circumcision?"

"I hadn't gotten that far yet. I assume I will bring Him to the local synagogue."

"No, no, that will not be necessary. I shall . . . " Raziel stopped, as if pulling in the reins of a runaway horse. "Forgive me, I am presumptuous. If it pleases you, I would be very honored to perform the ceremony myself. And I will be most happy to come to wherever you are staying and do it."

"Yes, of course."

Jenli turned to Jerem with a smile. "This meeting went very well. Please send word to Elric. I will stay with Joseph while he finishes his business here."

"In His service."

# 6

## FIRST BLOOD

**Birth plus 3 days**

Elric and Jenli huddled in the corner of Omer and Miriam's house and spoke in low tones.

"This is the third time we have seen him," Jenli said. "First, he was turned away at the border of Bethlehem on the night of the King's birth. The day before yesterday, one of my warriors chased him out of the house next door."

Elric scowled. "How did he get inside our perimeter?"

"We don't know. And then today, we caught him trying to sneak through again."

"Is he a local?"

"No sir. I don't recognize him. He is a lieutenant. Blotchy red skin. And one eye that is half-closed."

"Luchek," Elric said with a grimace.

"Do you know him, captain?"

"Yes. I mean, I used to." Elric shook his head. "He is the one who attacked in Nazareth."

"Do you think he knows?"

Elric paused a moment. "He knows."

Jenli reached for his sword. "We must capture him before he gives away our location."

"I wonder," Elric said. "You said you caught him trying to sneak in today?"

"Yes."

"Why?" Elric rubbed his chin. "Why would he delay in telling his superiors?"

Mary and Miriam continued their own conversation in the Physical Realm. The Baby slept. Elric stared at the King in silence. *He looks so tiny. So human.*

"He's not going to deliver Him to his master," Elric said. "Not yet. He wants the glory of leading the attack. And he knows he can't launch an assault by himself, even if there are only a few of us. So, he will gather for himself a band of beaelzurim he can control. He will surround us and wait for an opportune time."

Jenli's hand went back to his sword.

Elric smirked. "And we are going to allow it."

"Captain?"

"You and I or a member of your team will always be present here to protect Him in case any of Luchek's team becomes too impetuous, but the rest of your team will form a loose outer perimeter and allow Luchek's team to think they are operating at will."

"A risky operation," Jenli said. He raised skeptical eyebrows. "What will this accomplish?"

Elric smiled. "Picture a dog with a bone he has found. What will happen if another dog tries to get close?"

Jenli smiled and nodded. "He will chase the other dog off. We are going to let the enemy do the job of providing a perimeter around us."

"Exactly."

"How long do you think this perimeter will hold before they attack?"

"I don't know, but I expect it will be a while. Gathering a team without the use of brute force will be a challenge for Luchek. It makes our timing with Zaben more complicated."

Jenli nodded. "Shall I brief my team?"

"Yes, and tell them to watch for my signal. When the battle does start, we are going to need every sword."

* * *

On the outskirts of Bethlehem, in a dank cave, away from the light of the sun, and away from the attention of everyone, three demons held a secret meeting.

The largest demon, the lieutenant Luchek, whispered his message. "And then, if all that is not proof enough, when the shepherds were worshiping, the two elzurim knelt and worshipped, too. You know they would never bow to anyone but the King." Luchek's words formed rank clouds in the stagnant air. One small demon trembled with excitement as another would–be recruit listened to Luchek's pitch.

"Yes, but did you actually see Him in the flesh?" the recruit said.

"Briefly, when they moved into the house."

"What did He look like?"

"I don't know—like any normal human infant. He was wrapped in a blanket."

"This is what makes your claim unbelievable. How is it possible that the King should look like a normal human? And what about the cherubim? They always go before Him."

"Do you not see? It's all part of His plan. He is treacherous and vindictive. He is making a mockery of Marr down in Egypt while He sets a trap here in Bethlehem." He paused a moment for the dramatic effect. "But He didn't count on *me*!"

"Do you think He doesn't know what you are scheming? There is nothing hidden from His sight."

"Are you so sure about that? How is it, then, that I was able to recognize Him, pinpoint His exact location, and almost get close enough to touch Him? I think there are shadows too deep for even His eyes."

"If you were that close, why did you not attack when you had the chance?"

Luchek squirmed and scowled through his good eye. "The captain who is guarding the child—I fought with him already, and I know he is too much for me. That is why I'm forming this team. We need sufficient numbers to deal a decisive blow and claim our prize for our master."

"For Marr."

"No! Not for that pompous sycophant. I hate him. I'm glad he is going to be humiliated by his grand campaign down in Egypt. We will deliver the prize to Satan himself and gain all the glory for ourselves." His blood–red eye bulged, and he clenched powerful taloned fists. "Think of it. We will be made mighty princes in the new kingdom, and I will take great joy in putting my foot on the back of Marr's neck and forcing him to serve me."

The recruit sneered with a wicked, jagged tooth, "Very well, I am with you, but I—"

"Good. Here are my terms. I am running this operation. You will do only what I say and only when I say to do it. You are to tell no one about our business. If any other demon starts to get anywhere near our center of operations, you are to divert him away without disclosing any information about what we are hiding. You are not to engage any enemy warriors until the day we make our attack. Let them come and go while you stay concealed as much as possible. We need them to think everything is normal and that they are in control. We cannot afford to raise any suspicions."

The new recruit fidgeted under the barrage of orders being levied upon him, and Luchek could tell he resented coming under his control. That subordinate resentment, though, only fueled his own sense of power and authority, and he continued his orders with long dramatic inflections.

"We are going to take our time. Maybe a year or more. I will do all the recruiting for the team, and I will build our numbers slowly so as to not raise any suspicions. We will be an ever–present shadow, hidden from the eyes of the King and those of His forces—until the time is exactly right, and then we will crush them when they least expect it."

The new recruit made an oath of allegiance there in the darkness, even though Luchek knew such oaths meant little between such self-serving creatures. It all gave Luchek a grand sense of power.

* * *

## Birth plus 8 days

Elric and Jenli stood outside Omer's home with vigilant eyes and crossed arms.

"Day eight," Jenli said.

"Mmm," Elric answered as he watched Raziel approach on the dirt street. "The shadows around us grow."

Raziel crossed the outer ring of shadows and the inner ring of Jenli's team with a bounce in his step and a large ceremonial pouch in his hands. He hummed a happy tune. He passed through Elric and Jenli and into Omer's house.

"Come inside. This is a very important day," Elric said to Jenli.

Jenli nodded, and they stepped inside.

All preparations had been made with care. Ceremonial candles sparkled throughout the room; the Chair of Elijah sat ready; glasses of wine stood by; and Mary held the Baby.

"A small gathering for an occasion as special as a Brit Milah," Elric said.

Jenli shrugged and replied, "With no family around and no friends in a strange city, there is no one to share this sacred event with besides Omer and Miriam."

"I am pleased we were able to have Raziel serve as the Mohel," Elric said.

Miriam floated and beamed like a grandmother.

"Miriam will serve as the Kvatterin?" Elric asked.

"Yes, and Omer is the Kvatter," Jenli replied.

Omer paced, wringing his hands and grinning.

Raziel began by reminding everyone that this sacred event had been observed since the time the Lord made His covenant with Abraham—the physical sign that distinguished the Hebrews from the rest of the nations. It represented a most solemn oath, and yet it was time of great joy and celebration.

"How many of these have you observed over the centuries?" Elric said to Jenli.

"Thousands. Every one sacred and full of hope."

"Every time I can't help but be amazed with how the King has fulfilled His promises to Abraham. Even during the darkest times when the enemy either nearly destroyed the descendants of Abraham or dispersed them into bondage, the King always preserved a remnant of His people. He has been faithful to His chosen people, and today He is going to fulfill another promise and become one of them."

Elric looked at the five simple humans in the house and shook his head.

"Without the backdrop of all the battles fought by men and angels since the beginning, these people can't begin to comprehend the event that is about to take place."

The air in the Middle Realm carried the sweet smell of the Spirit. *I wonder if the people can sense it.*

"I sense intense delight from the King," Jenli said.

"Yes," Elric said, "and the pride of the Father. How does this powerful love not burst the walls of this puny earthly dwelling?"

The official ceremony began. The Kvatterin handed the Child to the Kvatter, and all the people in the room recited the traditional blessing. The Kvatter then placed the Baby on the Chair of Elijah and the Mohel recited the accompanying prayer. Then, the Kvatter lifted the Baby and passed Him to the lap of Joseph, the Sandek. After another blessing, the Mohel performed the circumcision accompanied by the cries of the tiny baby Boy.

In that moment, Elric sensed a strange bittersweet emotion in the spirit. It surprised him. He thought he felt the Father wince as He watched His Son endure His first pinch of a painful world. At the same time, Elric felt a strong sense of satisfaction from the Father— not in the pain itself, but in the fulfillment of purpose that the pain represented.

Then, he saw . . .

*Blood!* Not just any blood. *This is the blood of the King of the Heavens!*

Elric's sword flew out of its sheath. He held it in the ready position with a trembling hand. His mouth hung open wide, and his eyes filled with tears. He dropped the tip of his sword downward and looked over at Jenli, who knelt with his face flat to the ground. "Until today," Elric whispered, "I have never seen the King's blood shed. And I hope to never see it again."

The rest of the ceremony—the various blessings, the passing of the Baby to the standing Sandek, the cup of wine—all passed before Elric like a dream as he tried to get over the thought of the blood, until it came time to give the Baby His name. As Joseph held the

Child, Raziel recited the traditional blessing and Elric's attention again focused on the ceremony itself.

"Our God and God of our fathers, preserve this child for his father and mother, and his name in Israel shall be called Jesus, the son of . . . " Raziel stopped.

All eyes turned toward him. *What is he going to say?* In earthly terms, they would all expect him to say "Joseph." But Joseph wasn't truly the father. The question was whether Raziel believed that, and would he be willing to risk speaking the truth?

Raziel looked Joseph square in the eyes and continued. "The Son of Yahweh. May the Father rejoice in His offspring, and His mother be glad with the fruit of her womb, as it is written: 'May your father and mother rejoice, and she who bore you be glad.'" Raziel continued on with the rest of the traditional blessing.

Omer and Miriam looked a little puzzled but never did ask anyone to explain. Mary and Joseph restrained little smiles and made a connection with their eyes too deep for Omer and Miriam to understand. Elric and Jenli didn't bother to subdue their smiles. They beamed and understood completely.

The remainder of the ceremony continued with all its traditions and joy. The baby Jesus became quiet again and rested, and a festive banquet filled the remainder of the day. One of the lambs from the visiting shepherds had been slaughtered and prepared, and they all enjoyed an enormous spread of food and wine throughout the day. Miriam floated about in top form, leaving little opportunity for others to run away with the conversation.

At the end of the day, Raziel pulled Joseph aside.

"Promise me you will seek me out if you ever come again to Nazareth," Raziel said.

"Of course."

"I would love to see Him grow, but you must, of course, follow the path that the Lord sets before you."

Jenli looked up from his ledger, stopped writing, and shook his head. "That path is not an easy one."

Elric crossed his arms. "The road through a battlefield never is."

# 7

# IN SEARCH OF THE KING

## Birth plus 10 days

In Persia, the magi convened to review their findings. Nangar lurked in the shadows.

"Ten days we have searched the archives, and this is all we have?" Melchior said. A dozen scrolls lay scattered atop a cluttered table. The faces of the three gray-beards that huddled around the table flickered in the warm candlelight. "Let's review them all together and see if an answer presents itself."

Balthazar unrolled a scroll and read from it. "'But One will come forth in those days whose goings forth are from everlasting to everlasting. Shout it in Zion, the throne of David shall be His seat forever.'"

The three nodded. Melchior stroked his beard.

Balthazar said, "This is an excellent prophecy, but it tells us nothing more than we already know."

"Agreed," Melchior said.

Caspar leaned over a scroll and pulled a candle closer. "' . . . and behold the star of the ram, whose coming calls forth the dawning of a new era.'"

"Again," Balthazar said, "a new king in Israel."

"Yes, but it does tie his coming to the appearance of the star," Caspar said.

"Here is one," Melchior said. "'Weep, o daughters of Zion, rend your hearts, o sons of Judah, for your King is cut off in darkness.'"

"Yes, yes," cackled Nangar. "And I will be the one who does the cutting. Keep searching. Find Him. Take me to Him."

"This does not seem to fit the other prophecies," Balthazar said.

"I concur," Caspar said. "This could refer to almost any of the ancient kings of Judah."

"And it gives us no direction," Melchior said.

"Listen to this one," Caspar said. "'Behold the sign, a great star of the great King. The wise will follow it carefully and see His face.'"

"Then," responded Balthazar, "we must follow the star to the King's location."

Melchior rubbed his eyebrows and shook his head. "How shall we do this? We all agree the King is born somewhere in Israel, and Israel lies to our west. The event we saw was in the eastern sky. From there all the stars track westward. Therefore, following the trajectory of any of the stars would only lead us west, which is something we already knew. There is no new revelation in this passage."

Balthazar raised a long bony finger. "But if we track the trajectory of one of the stars, say Hormoz, we see it disappears behind the horizon at roughly the same location in the west. We could perhaps use that point to chart our course."

"But that location changes by season. What season shall we use for charting the course? More importantly, the line between where we are and the spot on the horizon depends upon our current location. If we were in another country, our charted path would take us to a different place."

"We plot it from *our* location to the point on the horizon that the star disappears."

"Why our location?"

"The prophecy speaks to us."

"From what time?"

"From the time of the conjunction."

"Which star?"

Nangar spoke into the smoky atmosphere of the Middle Realm. "It doesn't matter. Plot your course and leave immediately. We must go to Israel and find this King." His words hung like clouds around the magi, but their spirits didn't seem to receive them. Nangar threw up his hands and snarled.

Rather than listening to him, the men had a long intellectual debate, and, in the end, all agreed that "following the star" meant "go to Israel" and that they didn't have any new information to pinpoint the King's location. They seemed encouraged, though, that the prophecy made reference to seeing His face. That meant that if they did make the journey, they might expect to have success.

"Go," Nangar muttered.

Balthazar unrolled another scroll. "Here is one I found today. ' . . . at journey's end, the star alights above the head of the King of stars. Wise is he who seeks it.'"

"Most intriguing," Melchior said while stroking his long beard. "'At journey's end.' To what journey might this refer?"

"It seems to imply the journey of the star," Caspar said.

"Perhaps," said Melchior, "but which one? We have three significant celestials in play right now."

The three mulled over these thoughts for several minutes. Balthazar offered his assessment. "I believe we can rule out the moon. It is not a traveling star like Hormoz and Keyvân. However, irrespective of the star, what does it mean by 'journey'? Surely, it cannot mean the daily journey from east to west. That would imply charting a course based on its intersection with the horizon, and we have already ruled this out as a viable interpretation. Besides, we have charted Hormoz and Keyvân carefully ever since the conjunction, and we have not observed either of them to 'alight above' any location."

After several more minutes of beard stroking, forehead rubbing, and foot tapping, Caspar had an idea.

"What if the 'journey' refers to something on a longer time scale? Something like the full journey between positions of opposition. For Hormoz, that is 399 days."

"Three hundred seventy-five for Keyvân," Melchior said.

"This is an interesting theory," Balthazar said. "Perhaps at the end of one of these stars' journey to opposition, we will see another event that will pinpoint the location. Of course, you realize this means waiting another 389 days to see if this interpretation is correct."

"Go now!" Nangar shouted. "We can't wait a year. We need to find Him now."

"There is something within me that wants to start our journey now," Caspar said. "The sight of those heavenly beings and the burning I felt within my heart is ever before me. Perhaps we do not need an exact location."

"That's right. That's right." Nangar wrung his hands.

"It is a very long journey," Melchior said. "I think we need to study further."

Nangar ground his teeth at his inability to get past the men's calculating intellects, and he seethed as they continued to debate. They all concluded the "journey" probably referred to the passage from one opposition to the next, and without a precise charted course, they agreed they would need to continue to wait for something that provided more direction—even if that meant waiting more than a year to find it.

* * *

## Birth plus 14 days

Tumur approached the town near Zacharias's house in Judea two weeks after the birth of the Son of Man.

*It has been six months and still there is no report. The girl Luchek followed must not have been the one. I'm not surprised. Luchek must have observed her long enough to realize this and was too proud to return here. Good.*

Tumur snorted a puff of smoke from his nostrils and ambled through town.

*The elzur lieutenant, Lacidar, and his team have the prophet John hemmed in all about. I'll never reach him directly. I don't care. It's not him I want. It's the One he will lead me to. Still, I hate the prophets of the King. I hate the word they bring. I hate the special favor they have with the King. I will sow thorns in his path. If it takes twenty years—fifty years—he will lead me to the prize, and I will make his way hard.*

Tumur stepped into the courtyard of the synagogue. No enemy guards stood by to prevent his access. He approached two rabbis who talked under the shade of a tree. They discussed the miraculous birth of John to Zacharias and Elizabeth.

"Miraculous?" Tumur interjected. "I doubt that. Remarkable, yes. But certainly not miraculous. Mothers and fathers have babies in their old age all the time. I wonder if Zacharias made up the story of his vision in the temple to exaggerate the significance of the birth and to make himself look more pious in your eyes. Think about it. In your lifetime have you ever witnessed a true miracle or seen a vision from heaven?"

Tumur breathed on them and watched the thoughts he'd seeded in the priests' spirits take root. He turned and entered the synagogue. He slinked down a hallway and poked his head into the archives. As expected, there was Zacharias, searching through the scrolls for messianic references. A warrior of the host stood by him. Three scribes worked at their tables with scrolls laid out and ink bottles at arm's length. Tumur pulled back and waited.

After some time, two scribes exited the archives and walked down the hall. Tumur edged up behind them and put a hand on each of their shoulders. He positioned his head between them and whispered, "Who does Zacharias think he is? How could his son be Elijah? He is shirking his other duties by spending all this time searching out the Messiah. He thinks he is so much better than you. His eccentric obsession is going to lead innocent people astray."

Tumur chuckled and melted through the wall on his left, into the private chamber of the chief priest. The priest studied a scroll and took a sip of water from his goblet. Tumur smiled and sauntered over to plant more words of division.

* * *

## Birth plus 35 days

Luchek and his team of fifteen demons met in the shadows of a house in Bethlehem.

"The days of Mary's purification are almost complete," Luchek said in a low raspy tone to his appointed officers. "I expect they will travel to Jerusalem soon to present Jesus in the temple and offer sacrifices."

"Excellent," said Deagos, a pernicious brute about the same size as Luchek. His leathery skin looked like the surface of molten lava with deep ashen-red crags cutting throughout a crusty charcoal black surface. His bulbous forehead gave the appearance of three–layered protruding eyebrows which hung so low into his hard–cut face that they almost concealed the tiny slits of his eyes.

"With them on the move, out in the open," said Deagos, "they will be more vulnerable, and we will be able to make our attack."

Luchek nodded. "Yes. It is an opportune time. We will wait until we are well clear of Bethlehem and have had the opportunity to assess the level of enemy protection."

Restless with anticipation, one of the other officers scratched at the dirt with the long talons of his bare dragon–like feet. "I shall take two of our team and prepare the location for the attack."

"Agreed," said Luchek with a small puff of sulfurous smoke. "The rest of us will travel with them while remaining undetected at a safe distance. If the elzur numbers are small enough and you have successfully prepared the area, we shall claim our prize, present it to our lord, and ascend to our rightful place in a new kingdom."

Deagos gave a *humph* and snarled. "If . . . this truly is the Promised One."

"Still you are not convinced?"

"I am less convinced now than ever. We all saw the child when Joseph finished the repairs and they moved into the room at the inn. There were no signs of deity. He looked like a typical human."

"He was mostly wrapped in a blanket!"

"We should be able to see the glory of His spirit."

"I've told you, it is impossible for human flesh to survive the glory of the King. He obviously has veiled His spirit."

"No cherubim."

"We have been through all this. He is the one. I know it."

"We shall see."

# 8

# ROAD TO JERUSALEM

## Birth plus 40 days

The clouds hung low from horizon to horizon, and the air felt still and foreboding as Joseph and Mary began their trip northward to Jerusalem. The trip wouldn't be a long one, two hours at the most, but Joseph set Mary and Jesus up on the cart behind their donkey along with provisions for several days. The dusty road was worn and well-traveled, but a sense of dread hung in the air that couldn't be explained by the sullen clouds.

After leaving the outskirts of town, Mary called out to Joseph, who walked in front of the donkey. "Joseph, I have a bad feeling about this."

Joseph rubbed the back of his neck and looked up and down the trail. His eyes darted from horizon to horizon.

"You are worried about what might happen when we get to the temple," he called over his shoulder. "We've talked about this. It will be fine."

"You know it could happen, don't you?" Mary said.

Joseph stopped the donkey and shuffled back to the cart, the dust rising and gathering around his leather sandals. As he walked, he rehearsed the significance of this trip.

The purpose of this trip was to dedicate Jesus in the temple, offer the required sacrifices, and perform the Pidyon Ha'Ben, the "redemption of the first–born son." Originally, from the ancient Scriptures it was the King's intent that every first–born Jewish male serve as a Kohen, that family's representative in the temple. But after the Israelites' sin with the golden calf at Mount Sinai, that privilege was forfeited by all the tribes except for the tribe of Levi, who alone had stood with Moses. Since all the non-Levite firstborns were technically still holy to the Lord but could not serve as Kohen, these firstborns had to be "redeemed" for the price of five silver shekels to permit them to be released from their bond. Mary and Joseph were not descendants of Levi, so in accordance with the requirements of the law, they were prepared to redeem their firstborn. However, considering who their firstborn was, they weren't sure what would happen when they got to the temple.

Mary said, "We are going to get there; one of the priests is going to prophesy about who Jesus is; they will bring Him to the high priest; and not only will we not be able to redeem him, but they will take Him away to be raised in the temple."

"You don't know that," Joseph said.

"It happened to Samuel in the Scriptures. His mother Hannah had to leave him at the temple, and we have Jesus, who is greater than Samuel. It only makes sense."

"Yes, but remember Hannah had made that vow before Samuel was even conceived. You made no such vow." Joseph paused for a moment and then proceeded in a slower, more contemplative tone. "Besides, even if it does happen, it would probably be for the best. He would receive the finest education. He would be well cared for. And look at us—I don't have a regular job and we have no home—He deserves a better start than we can offer."

Mary dipped her head and hid the tears welling up.

Joseph touched her on the cheek and wiped away a tear with his thumb. "Mary, we have already been given a great gift. No matter what happens when we get to Jerusalem, you will always be remembered as the mother of the Messiah. No one will ever be able to take that away from you." He chuckled. "Maybe even someday you will be written about in books. And I don't think we are going to have to leave Him at the temple."

Mary forced a smile.

"Mary, we need to settle this in our hearts before we get there. If the Lord requires us to leave Him to be raised in the temple, are you going to be able to do it?"

Mary's well of tears became flowing rivers that cut valleys through the dust on her face. She held her precious bundle close and rocked Him, staring into His sparkling eyes. She rocked for a long time without saying a word.

She shook her head slowly and said with a cracking voice, "Yes. Yes, I will do whatever the Lord requires." With a sad smile she added, "But I do hope He does not require it."

Even though a tiny glow of peace sparked within their hearts from having made their resolution, there still remained an uneasiness about their journey. Joseph tried to convince himself that it was only the anticipation of what might happen at the temple, but he couldn't shake the feeling they were being watched. He kept scanning the roadside and the surrounding hills as they continued, but he didn't see anything unusual.

* * *

Luchek's team scurried low like scorpions across the stretches of flat desert and took up hidden positions behind small mounds and rocky hills. They grouped into small pockets on the left and right and stretched out in front and behind. Several tracked from above, masked within the murky layer of clouds. Luchek had a simple and direct plan—on his signal, half his forces would engage any visible escorts while the other half would defend against any enemy that might appear from outside their perimeter. Meanwhile, he himself would make the assault on the Child.

They reached the place where his scouts had been waiting and preparing, and Luchek slinked up beside his officer.

"I commend you for your astute work. This location is perfect. The hills on each side of the road form an excellent trap. How about enemy forces? Any sign of the elzurim?"

"No. My scouts have been patrolling this entire corridor all last night and today, and there are no enemy warriors present. Also, we have been preparing the battlefield—speaking blindness and confusion into the air all around this region. If any enemy does show up, he will be lost in a fog of darkness."

"Well done. I will remember your initiative when we ascend to our places of power after this battle."

"Look at them," Deagos said with a sneer. "The only escort for the 'King' is a captain and a lieutenant? They are either mocking our power or this is not the King as you suppose." He drew his jagged black sword and moved from their hiding spot behind the hill toward the approaching travelers.

Luchek dug his talons into the bulging forearm of Deagos. "Or," he snarled, "it is as I have said from the beginning. This is the King in human flesh. And his warriors are purposely trying to not draw attention to his location in an effort to keep Him hidden. They could not be mocking us because they do not even know we are here. Be patient a little while longer. We will have our prize."

Deagos yanked his arm free. "I am tired of waiting. You disgust me. You used to be an agent of action. Now look at you, being 'patient.' You keep being patient. If that is the King, He is going to feel my blade today."

"No!"

Deagos unfurled his wings and shot straight up. He looped high enough for his bat-like wings to cut into the bottom of the cloud deck and then accelerated downward toward the unsuspecting travelers from behind. The remainder of Luchek's team turned to Luchek. He motioned for them to stay low and wait. This wasn't the way he intended for the battle to proceed; however, this brash move might play to their advantage by revealing the enemy's weaknesses or by drawing out any hidden forces lying in wait. With gritty anticipation, Luchek waited and watched.

The captain, Elric, walked in the very front. Following him, the man led a donkey which pulled a cart. On the cart rode the young mother and the One for whom they had come. Behind them all marched a lieutenant of the host. Both of the elzur escorts had their swords sheathed, oblivious to the onslaught about to be unleashed upon them.

*Deagos is wise to attack from behind, for the angelic escorts are both looking forward and unaware of anything coming from behind. It should prove effortless to cut through the lone lieutenant and reach the Child before the captain even knows what hit them.* Luchek didn't have to wait long for the initial clash. Deagos streaked toward the Child at a blurring speed with his sword outstretched, piercing through the unsuspecting stillness.

What happened next was too quick to fathom, even for the spiritual eyes that saw it. Without ever turning around, the lieutenant drew his sword. It became engulfed in an intense blue flame and made two powerful arcing circles at the speed of lightning. With precise timing, the first arc of his blade intercepted Deagos's thrusting sword in mid-flight and shattered it into shards at the exact instant that Deagos reached his position. With a continuous uninterrupted motion, the second circle of the lieutenant's blade cut Deagos in two and left nothing but a cloud of yellow smoke. Then with a third less vigorous swing, the lieutenant's sword gave up the blue flame and returned to its sheath, still glowing hot.

The lieutenant continued walking as though nothing had happened, although he did take a moment to turn his head each way and scan the horizon for any other would–be attackers. The entire engagement finished in less than a blink of an eye. The captain never even looked back. He opened his wings and shook them the way a hawk might flutter his wings to fling off unwanted dust. Joseph and the donkey continued plodding along while Mary and the Baby rocked in the back of the cart.

The officer next to Luchek looked up and waited. Luchek stumbled backward two steps and sank to his knees. Within moments the rest of his team gathered around.

"The flame of vengeance," one of the demons said. "You didn't tell us they would carry the flame of vengeance."

"And his sword wasn't destroyed," said another. "They must have special weapons."

Luchek rubbed his good eye with the back of his fist. "I don't understand. I fought with the captain, and he never—"

"I'm not going down there for a frontal attack," another demon said.

"I won't either," said another. "We may outnumber them seven to one, but that is of little consequence if we face the flame of vengeance."

"I'm out."

"I'm not going."

"No."

"No."

"I agree," Luchek growled. "We need another strategy." He shoved his sword into its sheath and crossed his arms. "Is there any more doubt about my claim about the Child? I think this display is proof enough."

The team members all looked around at each other and nodded their heads.

"This is the child King, and we will destroy him. But we will wait for another time. I will continue to bolster our numbers and devise a new plan of attack. You continue to hold our perimeter and keep unwanted rivals out. When the time is right, we will claim our prize."

# 9

# THE TEMPLE

## Birth plus 40 days

Jeremiah and his sons, Jesse, Levi, and Daniel, approached the temple at Jerusalem with awe in their eyes.

"Look at the size of these stones," Daniel said. He ran his hand along the outer wall of the temple.

Levi slid his hand over the flat face of the wall and traced the straight edge of a seam with his finger. "Every one was cut in the quarries and set in place here."

"This wall is wide enough to drive a chariot along the top," Daniel said.

Levi craned his neck upward. "If you could get one up there."

They both laughed.

Levi put his hand on Daniel's shoulder. "Prepare yourself to be amazed. You have never seen anything like what you're about to see. You were here when you were younger, but you probably don't remember. I'm glad Father decided to come and see it since we were so close."

They passed through the outer gate and entered a large open courtyard. Jeremiah and Jesse stopped, and Jeremiah called back to Levi and Daniel.

"Jesse and I are going ahead into the Court of the Israelites to worship. Levi—you stay out here with Daniel and show him around."

"I don't need anyone to watch over me," Daniel called back.

"It is for the best. Do as I say."

"Yes, Father," Levi answered.

Levi pulled Daniel to the side, out of the mainstream of the outer gate. "Look around," Levi said, motioning with his arm. "This is called the Court of the Gentiles."

Grand colonnades with hundreds of stately marble columns supporting the porticos lined the outer courtyard area. Daniel's mouth hung wide open and his eyes darted everywhere. "It's amazing."

"This is a sacred place built on sacred ground. Solomon's temple stood right here in ancient times. It was rebuilt after the exile, but Herod came in and expanded the temple grounds and built up everything you see here. He did it to buy the favor of our people, but I'm glad to have such a majestic place to worship and perform our religious duties."

"It's amazing. Everything is so tall. And huge."

"This outer court is the only place non-Jews are allowed."

Daniel's attention turned inward toward the bustling crowds of people. Rows of vendors stretched in each direction, and the colors and sounds swirled around in continuous motion. The mixture of smells—sheep, bread, perfume, sweat, incense, roasting meat— created a disjointed stew of emotions. It was as though they had stepped onto a fast-moving cart, racing through an atmosphere full of energy. Over in the corner, under the shade of the colonnade, sat a rabbi teaching a small group of interested pupils. A choir of skilled Levite singers lifted hallowed harmonies above the shouts of vendors to would-be buyers while doves and pigeons flapped and cooed inside small wooden cages. A handful of foreigners milled about, admiring the architecture and pointing out artistic features to each other while devout worshipers stood, knelt, and paced, offering up prayers to an unseen God. Hundreds and hundreds of people filled the courtyard, each one going about their own business.

"What are all these people doing?" Daniel said.

"Some are worshipers on pilgrimages. There are foreigners on tours. Of course, all the women and children. Do you see all the priests in the white linen robes and tubular hats? They help direct traffic and advise worshipers about the kinds of sacrifices needed and where to go. See those rows of tables over there? Those are the money changers. The temple has its own currency, and those men will exchange people's regular money for temple money. The vendors over there sell animals used in the ritual sacrifices. There are vendors who sell food. Vendors who sell souvenirs."

"Doesn't all this seem like a business?"

"It takes many people to keep everything running. But remember, this is only the outer court. The temple areas become increasing holy as you move from east to west into the inner courts. Behind that big stone wall is the Court of the Women, where both Jewish men and women are allowed. In this court, there is always dancing, singing, and worshipful music. Beyond this is the Court of the Israelites, where only the Jewish men can enter. The very inner court is the Court of the Priests, and it's there the sacrifices are offered. Father can't even go in there. Finally, there is the temple itself."

The radiant white marble of the temple soared above the rest of the complex. Stark. Majestic. Unapproachable.

Daniel looked at the bustle of the outer courtyard. He looked up at the temple. He looked back at the crowds.

"What's the real purpose of all this? All these people running around. They'll never be able to get up there. It's like God is trying to keep us away."

"The Lord is holy."

"I suppose. I keep thinking about the angels I saw in the sky. And those men who convinced Father there aren't any spiritual beings. No life after this. It makes all this seem useless." He stared at the temple. "I feel like there's something more. Like there's a whole other world. I don't know. I don't understand."

\* \* \*

The mighty senturim stood guard in the Middle Realm around the temple grounds, with one senturi stationed at each corner of the outer wall. The human-like forms of these angels towered fifty feet tall, and they had four wings like the cherubim, although they rarely used them. Their primary station was to stand guard over sacred or strategic places on earth. They carried flaming broadswords that were always ablaze with pure white flames, and the huge blades were so substantial that even the mightiest of the elzurim could not wield them. Though not as powerful as the cherubim, the senturim could certainly defend any earthly location against any beaelzurim, and they were a most formidable presence at the temple gate.

Accompanying Joseph, Mary, and Jesus, Elric and Jenli started up the path leading to the temple steps. The senturi at the southern temple wall dropped to his knee, bowed his head low, and laid his sword in front of him with open hands. Elric muttered, "No, no, no." and shot forward toward the senturi. He reached him in a single wing beat.

"Stand up! Stand up!" Elric said. "In the name of the King, stand up and hear my word."

The senturi stood, but kept his gaze fixed on the young couple approaching the temple grounds accompanied by an angelic lieutenant. "But that is—"

"Do not speak it," Elric said. "Please, look at me."

The senturi turned toward Elric.

Elric felt dwarfed by the senturi—his own entire frame no larger than one of the senturi's legs. He lifted off and hovered near the senturi's ear. "Thank you, I will explain," Elric said.

Elric kept his voice low enough for only the senturi to hear. "Our mission is to keep the King hidden until the appointed time. Please do not do anything to draw attention to Him. We must enter here today to fulfill the requirements of the law, but His risk of exposure is extreme. We must not allow any enemy to escape who has knowledge of who He is. Therefore, allow no beaelzurim to enter until we depart, and watch closely all those who are already within the walls. If circumstances require it, you are authorized to send any of them to the abyss."

The giant pillar of power nodded. "Fortress of the King," he said with a low rumble.

Elric continued, "By your leave, I must deliver these orders to the other guards."

The senturi nodded, and in a blink Elric visited the other three outer wall guards. Like a hummingbird darting from one blossom to the next, Elric moved to the inner court where he gave word to two more senturim who stood at the entrance of the temple. From their position they could survey the entire Court of the Priests as well as the outer court. They would be critical to the success of this mission. Elric briefed them, and by the time he returned to the outer court gate, Joseph and Mary had climbed all the steps up the temple mount and prepared to pass through the southern gate of the thick stone outer wall.

They entered wide eyed, flanked by Elric on the right and by Jenli on the left. With the one–month–old Jesus wrapped in the blanket Elric had left in the Bethlehem stable, they passed under the portico and then past the ranks of marble columns.

The Middle Realm in the Court of the Gentiles had as much activity as the Physical Realm. A demon perched on a money changer's table and helped the man justify in his mind his own personal right to inflate his exchange rate and pocket the extra profits. An angel ministered strength and comfort to a widow who poured her heart and tears into a desperate prayer. Another demon fueled fires of discord among a group of Pharisees and Sadducees over some detail of doctrine of which neither side had correct understanding. Several dozen beaelzurim worked their evil plots within the outer court walls, and an equal number of angels with their own assignments performed their duties. With so many opposing spirits in such close proximity, the palpable friction charged the air, but each spirit kept to his own sphere of authority.

Jenli's team, who each stole in without raising any attention from the preoccupied enemy forces, mingled amongst the crowds. None of Luchek's team made it past the senturim, even though each made an earnest attempt. They retreated, hid outside the walls, and waited for their prize to reemerge.

# 10

## DEDICATION

**Birth plus 40 days**

$\mathcal{E}$lric and Jenli continued into the temple grounds with Joseph and Mary, who held Jesus close in her arms. Elric scanned the crowd for both enemy forces and suspicious humans.

Across the court, one of Jenli's team gave a nod. "My team is in place and all is clear so far," Jenli said to Elric without turning his head.

Elric kept scanning. "With this many people and so many enemies in open contact, this is by far the most dangerous operation we have faced. Extra vigilance."

They weaved their way into the open courtyard. Elric stopped cold. That man over there. The Holy Spirit glowed all around the man, and he had a full suit of spiritual armor. Although deep in prayer, he kept looking over at Mary and the Baby. Elric motioned to Jenli. Jenli nodded. The man focused an intent, persistent gaze at Mary with a knowing, insightful look.

Elric whispered, "He looks like he might have a revelation about . . . " Elric paused. "He's headed this way! Have your team form a buffer zone around us. The Spirit of the Lord is heavy upon this man, and we cannot let enemy ears hear anything he might say. Also, prepare two of your warriors to intervene and break up the conversation on my cue."

In an instant Jenli disappeared, and an inconspicuous circle of angels formed.

Joseph and Mary exchanged startled glances when a stranger approached them from across the courtyard as though he knew them. He appeared unthreatening, being somewhat frail with long years etched on his face and beard. His eyes twinkled with joy, and his trembling hands showed his excitement about something. He walked up to Mary and stared at Jesus.

"It is true!" his voice crackled. "It's Him! Praise be to the God of our Fathers; my eyes have seen Him!"

Joseph and Mary exchanged glances again.

Elric glanced all around. No enemy close enough to hear.

"I'm sorry," the man said, "I have startled you. Please let me explain. My name is Simeon, and I have been praying for the consolation of Israel my whole life. Years ago the Lord told me that I would not see death before my eyes had seen the Lord's Christ. My remaining years are few, and I wondered if I would ever see the fulfillment of that promise. Today, I was praying in the Spirit, and when I saw you, He revealed to me that this little one is the Promised One. You know this, do you not?"

Joseph put his arm around Mary. "Yes, well we—"

"I know this may seem forward, but please, may I hold Him?"

Mary flashed an apprehensive look to Joseph, who gave Mary a shrug and a nod.

Elric's hand moved to his sword handle.

Simeon took Him into his arms as though he held the greatest treasure imaginable, stared down into His face, and said, "Now, Lord, You are letting Your bond-servant depart in peace, according to Your word; for my eyes have seen Your salvation, which You have prepared in the presence of all the peoples: a light for revelation to the Gentiles, and the glory of Your people Israel."

He blinked through a flood of tears and held Jesus for what seemed like a long time. Finally, he handed Him back to Mary and blessed the young couple.

With a quiet and earnest tone, he spoke to Mary. "Behold, this Child is appointed for the fall and rise of many in Israel, and as a sign to be opposed—and a sword will pierce your own soul—to the end that thoughts from many hearts may be revealed."

Time to cut this meeting short. Elric gave Jenli the sign. Jenli lifted his left arm, and two priests in white linen robes approached Joseph, Mary, and Simeon from behind.

One of the priests tapped Joseph on the shoulder. "Sir, it appears you are here to dedicate your son and offer a sacrifice. Come, let me show you where you can purchase a pair of turtledoves. Do you have the five shekels required for the Pidyon Ha'Ben, or do we need to visit a money exchanger?" Before Joseph could answer, the priest led him and Mary off to one of the vendors to their left.

At the same time, the second priest put his arm around Simeon's shoulder and turned him toward the right. "Sir, is there something I can help you find this morning?"

"No," rattled Simeon. "I've already found Him. That was the Messiah! I saw Him!"

"Yes, I understand. We should let that nice young couple tend to their business. My name is Jennidab. May I buy you something to eat? You look hungry."

"That was Him!" he said, looking back toward Jesus. "The Lord revealed to me that He was the Christ—I have been praying for this my whole life."

Jennidab turned Simeon away with his hands on his shoulders. "You have been given a great gift. Blessed is the man who sees the salvation of the Lord. But it is not yet the hour for Him to be revealed to the world. Come, let me get you something to eat." He dropped several coins on the table of a food vendor and said, "My friend here is hungry. This should cover his meal. Thank you."

One of the coins rolled off the table and fell to the ground. Both the vendor and Simeon looked down. Simeon retrieved the coin. They looked back up, and the priest had disappeared. Jennidab, now unseen to the Physical Realm, stood beside the perplexed Simeon and smiled. He reached forward and touched Simeon's eyes. "See Him not," he said.

Simeon turned back toward Joseph and Mary, his anxious eyes searching everywhere.

Joseph finished purchasing a pair of turtledoves, and he turned toward the priest. "Thank you for . . . " He looked at Mary. "Where did he go?"

Mary shrugged.

"The priests are always so helpful here," Joseph said.

They headed toward the fourteen steps leading up to the Beautiful Gate into the Court of the Women.

"I was beginning to get worried," Mary said. "I knew someone would prophesy over him, and I was right. What if he had told one of those priests and they brought Him to the high priest?"

Joseph stopped walking and took Mary's hand. "But he didn't. I told you, I do not believe it is God's will to leave Jesus to be raised in the temple. We should not let that be a worry. It was amazing, though, hearing another confirmation, was it not?"

Mary nodded but kept a nervous eye toward everyone.

Elric smiled and also continued examining the crowd. He whispered to Jenli as they walked, "There should be less chance for entanglements with enemy forces in the inner courts, but we must also avoid revealing the King to the priests now. The time is not right."

Jenli whispered back, "If there are any more prophets present who truly know the word of the Lord, it will not be possible to keep them silent."

"Keep your team close."

Up fifteen more steps to the porch leading to the Gate of Nicanor, beyond which lay the Court of the Israelites and the Court of the Priests, Joseph and Mary presented their sacrifice and completed all the requirements of the law. They offered dedication prayers, and the priest holding Jesus completed the ceremony for the Pidyon Ha'Ben. He handed Jesus back to Mary.

"The Messiah!" a woman shouted.

Elric spun around and pulled his sword. An old woman pointed at Jesus from across the court.

"Anna," Jenli said. "A prophetess of the tribe of Asher. Widowed sixty years ago, she never leaves the temple, serving day and night with fastings and prayers. I should have known she would—"

"Praise God, the Messiah has come!" Anna yelled. "Look everyone, it is He!" She pushed against the crowd toward the place where Joseph and Mary stood. "The redeemer of Jerusalem. This is the One. This is . . . "

Every demon eye in the Court of the Israelites drilled in on Jesus. Elric swallowed hard. *Oh, no!* He gritted his teeth.

At least fifty demon swords rang out as their blades slid from their sheaths. With a roar, they all exploded inward. Like a flash of lightning, Jenli's team formed a tight circle around Jesus. Elric leapt in front of the ring. A wall of demonic steel, frenzied red eyes, and bared teeth closed in. *Smash!* With his left hand, Elric blocked the blow of one demon; with his right, he thrust his sword through the chest of another. He spun, clipped the leg of the attacker on the left, and cut down two more with a horizontal power slice. The wounded attacker on the left dropped to one knee. Elric finished his spin and drove his sword through the demon's back, who collapsed amid a cloud of sulfur. Elric smashed the face of an attacker with his shield, sending him faltering backward. A slash, a thrust, a spinning slice. Four more demons fell. A wounded beaelzurim at his feet regained enough strength to rise to his hands and knees and grope for his sword. Elric pierced him through again. He wedged his foot under the incapacitated demon and, with a lifting kick, flung him into three more attackers. A thrust to the left. A quick glance to the right. Jenli was spinning, hacking, pounding back the enemy.

A demon leapt over Elric's head toward the inner circle. Elric shot up his left hand and snagged his ankle. A defender from behind drove his blade through the demon's neck, and Elric hurled him back over the heads of the incoming forces. Leaving a trail of yellow smoke, the demon landed in mid-court—a court embroiled in chaos. More demons rushed in from the outer courts. The other angels in the temple had joined the fight. All across the court, steel crashed and sparks burned through the Middle Realm. Most of the combatants didn't know what they were fighting for, but the furor of every engagement burned hot.

Elric brought his blade straight down and rent an attacker from top to bottom. He blocked an incoming fireball with his shield.

"They are gaining in strength and numbers!" he called out to Jenli.

"I don't know how much longer we can hold out," Jenli shouted back. "Why are we not granted the flame of vengeance?"

Elric leapt to avoid a waist–level swing. He flipped, blocked a fireball, and landed behind the attacker. He thrust his blade through the attacker's chest and withdrew it in a wide arc, cutting down two more assailants. *Why indeed?* He glanced quickly at Joseph, Mary, and Jesus. Unharmed, but dangerously vulnerable. *These beaelzurim aren't our only problem. If the priests get their hands on the King . . . I need to get Him out of here. I wonder what is happening in the Physical Realm.*

The Physical Realm churned with growing chaos, shadowing the struggle in the Middle Realm. The crowds stirred, and stories flew around about something happening in the inner court. In the excitement, the message became twisted as it passed from one group of people to the next. By the time news made it out to the edges of the Court of the Gentiles, people relayed different messages: "the Messiah has come to deliver Jerusalem," or, "the high priest is calling on all Jerusalem to revolt against Rome," or, "a Roman soldier has murdered the high priest," or some other combination of these ideas. The priests, including the one who had dedicated Jesus, shouted over the clamor for the people to remain calm. The last thing they needed were Roman soldiers storming in to quell a full-scale riot.

Elric blocked a sword strike and answered with a disabling thrust. He looked back toward the two temple senturim who remained motionless. *What are they waiting for? Why don't they—*

"Aughhh!" Jenli's voice rose above the noise.

*Oh, no! Jenli!* One demon pinned Jenli to the ground with his sword through Jenli's chest. Two other demons catapulted over him and pounded one of Jenli's warriors with rapid, repeated blows. The warrior blocked the blows with his shield, staggering backward with each strike. A third attacker launched over all of them on a direct trajectory toward the King.

"No!" Elric shouted. He leapt toward him but stopped in mid-lunge. Some vile creature had a hold of his leg.

The attacker frothed at the mouth and dove toward Jesus with his wicked sword held high. His massive arm muscles tensed in preparation for a powerful downstroke. With a haunting squeal, he swung his blade toward the King.

*Shhhh-boom!* An immense ball of scintillating white fire blasted the demon on his chest, sending him careening backward until he disappeared in a flash of white light followed by a pale, yellow vapor.

*The senturim at the inner court! They have joined the fight!*

The once motionless statues of restraint now demonstrated their power, and they moved even faster than the elzurim. With their flaming broadswords outstretched at their foes, they spoke a single word, "kaleesh," which in their tongue meant "righteous in judgment." The energy from that word flashed like the explosion of a star, traveled down their arms, through their swords, and out the tip toward their targets. The intense ball of energy sizzled the spiritual air as it traveled to its mark. In an instant, less time than it took Elric to complete a swing of his sword, the two senturim vanquished five of the attackers within the inner court.

The other four senturim leapt over the outer the walls with a single unfolding of their wings. They each used a blast of fireballs to announce their arrival into the fray, but after that they imposed their huge swords directly onto the heads of the enemy. Unlike the elzurim, there was no thrust-and-parry, give-and-take when a senturim swung his sword. They simply lowered the flat side of the blade down on the head of the enemy faster than the enemy could respond and pressed the demon into a puff of yellow smoke. The elzurim had never seen one of the senturim use the sharp edge of his sword, and there were only wild imaginings about the kind of devastation that could be carved by that edge. In less than five seconds, the senturim cleansed the house of enemy forces. The Middle Realm fell silent.

The senturim returned to their posts without a word. The elzurim stood dazed. The wounded regained their strength and rose to their feet.

The crowds of people, still in confusion, milled around. The initial excitement died down, and it appeared the priests had prevented a riot.

*This is our opportunity to get the King out, but even with all the confusion and pushing, there will be people who might see the King and recognize Him.* He spotted Anna, still looking for the Messiah. He spotted Simeon wading through the crowd. *I can't take the chance. This calls for drastic measures.*

Elric held his sword out horizontal to the ground and spoke the word, "blindness to the King." Without a sound, a horizontal blue disc of light exploded outward and expanded like a circular wave in a pool of water until it reached every person within the temple complex. *Now I need to get Joseph to move.*

"Joseph, it's time to go," Elric said. "Take the Child and leave the temple now. You have fulfilled the requirements of the law. Now you need to leave. Do it quickly."

Joseph turned to Mary, who watched all the surrounding commotion with a confused expression. "Mary, I think we should leave. I don't know why, but I sense we should not tarry here any longer."

"I agree," she said with a quick response.

Elric pulled Jenli in close. "You and your team explain to these other warriors what happened. Then meet us outside. I'm taking the King out."

Joseph and Mary pressed their way out to the outer courtyard. They passed hundreds of people, all straining toward the inner court. The people bumped and shoved and shouted a dozen different things they heard about something they thought had happened.

"They are all looking past us as though we're not even here," Joseph called back to Mary, pushing through the crowd. "There's the outer gate. We're almost there. Are you all right?"

"Yes, fine," Mary called back, holding Jesus close.

They kept a quick pace until they jostled all the way out of the temple grounds. They scampered down the steps to where their donkey was tied.

They stopped and looked at each other, breathing hard. Joseph panted a nervous laugh. "What just happened?"

# 11

## ROAD TO BETHLEHEM

### Birth plus 43 days

Three days after visiting the temple, Joseph shuffled into their rented room in Jerusalem and slumped onto the stool by the door to wash his feet. He looked haggard and discouraged.

"Still nothing?" Mary said.

"It's strange," Joseph answered as he swabbed his foot with the sponge, "it's as though every door is closed. Nobody in Jerusalem needs the services of a carpenter. I can't even find any small temporary jobs."

He wrung out the sponge and started on the other foot. "Actually, that's not completely true—there are plenty of opportunities for work if I wanted to be a part of one of Herod's big construction projects. He has dozens of them going on, here in Jerusalem and all over the country. But I can't see doing that kind of work. Supporting any project of his seems . . . wrong. I do not want to have to do that."

"I agree," Mary said. "We will find something else."

"But what? And when?" Joseph said. "We can't stay here like this much longer. The cost of a room here in Jerusalem is much higher than in Bethlehem, and we only brought provisions for a few days."

Elric watched the emotional edges unravel the way they always seemed to do with humans under situations like this. He whispered to Jenli, "If only they could see how much work your team has done to close all those doors."

"Not only my team," Jenli said. "The King has hundreds of individual seemingly unrelated circumstances all throughout the city working together to drive them back to Bethlehem. Even I have to marvel at the intricate details for which we only know a small part."

Elric's eyes sparkled. "The ways of the King are infinitely more meaningful and interesting than we can ever imagine, and they are always intended to lead man to a deeper relationship with Him. I do love being a part of the play, even when it means watching these poor humans scratch their way through. All we can do is help mold the circumstances and reinforce the things the King is already speaking to Joseph's heart."

"I sense it's time for some additional nudging," Jenli said. Elric nodded.

"The Lord does not want you to stay here. It is time to return to Bethlehem." Elric spoke the words into the air so both Joseph and Mary could hear. The words rolled up into tiny spheres of light and penetrated into their spirits. He waited to see if the seeds took root.

The two humans continued pondering their circumstances for a while longer, trying to figure out what they should do, and the discussion simmered all throughout dinner. The Baby slept, and the flickering glow of the lamp cast a rosy warm glow on His puffy little cheeks.

"It's strange," Joseph said. "In my mind, it makes the most sense for us to be here in Jerusalem. The temple is here. The palace is here. This is the seat of power and the place we know Jesus is going to rule from. I don't know when or how it is going to happen, but at some point, Jesus is going to have to take his place in the royal palace. It all makes sense in my head, but for some reason my heart is telling me something else—like we are not supposed to stay here. But still, I am having a hard time letting go of Jerusalem. Am I crazy? Maybe we should give it a few more days. Maybe I should take a job as one of Herod's laborers so we can settle here."

"Maybe you should follow your heart," Mary said. "I can't explain it, but something inside also tells me we don't belong here. At least not now. What if the reason you have not found anything is that the Lord is trying to guide us to another place?"

"I don't know. I suppose."

"I have to admit," continued Mary, "I am a little surprised about how things are turning out. I was sure I was going to have to watch Him grow up in the temple—and I do think I was ready for that. But now, I have a feeling we should go back to Bethlehem—and not because I'm afraid of losing Him to the priests. Bethlehem feels right."

"I feel it, too," said Joseph. "Have you had any dreams?"

"No, have you?"

"No. Sometimes I wish the Lord would tell us directly what we are supposed to do." He paused a moment. "Maybe we should sleep on it. Perhaps He will give one of us a dream tonight. Hopefully, things will be clearer tomorrow morning."

Elric smiled. There would be no dreams tonight.

\* \* \*

## Birth plus 44 days

Joseph and Mary slept well—deep and dreamless. But the morning light did bring the unspoken clarity they hoped for. After only a short discussion, both Joseph and Mary knew they should return to Bethlehem for now.

They finished the morning meal, loaded the cart, and headed southward. Mary wrapped the Baby in His blanket, and He looked as human as usual. A captain and lieutenant of the host provided a conspicuously inconspicuous escort while a silent shadow surrounded them at a safe distance.

Two hours later, after an easy and uneventful trip, they knocked at the door of Omer and Miriam, who appeared more than happy to see the young couple back.

"I don't understand it," Omer said. "Even though we still have booming traffic from the census, your old room is still open and available for you. You can move back in right now. And, I have leads on some potential jobs for you."

After moving into their room, stowing the cart, and tending to the donkey, Joseph went straight out to see about work. He returned a few hours later shaking his head and smiling with amazement.

"I guess we are meant to here," Joseph said. "I have found enough work to keep busy for a year!"

\* \* \*

## Birth plus 7 months

Six months after returning the Bethlehem, Elric squatted low next to Mary on the floor and shook his head. He wiped the corner of each eye with the back of his hand.

"What is it?" Jenli said.

"I . . . still struggle to comprehend."

Mary helped Jesus push up and stand on His chubby little legs and doughball feet, His tiny hands wrapped around her index fingers.

Elric continued. "He spoke the universe into existence. And now this young girl teaches Him to stand." He shook his head again.

Jenli rubbed the stubble on his cheek and jaw.

Elric stood and walked to the other side of the room. Jenli followed.

"What is the condition around our periphery?" Elric said.

"Luchek's numbers continue to grow."

"Are they keeping their distance?"

"Yes, after the attack on the road to Jerusalem, they are all very cautious. They are doing an excellent job, however, at keeping all other enemy from getting close.

Elric nodded. "Good."

"And, whenever Mary takes Jesus to the marketplace, He always wants to be draped in and holding onto His blanket. In fact, He does that whenever they are outside the house."

Elric smiled and looked back at Jesus who bounced up and down and babbled like a happy child.

"It is only a matter of time before Luchek believes he has sufficient numbers—or his team becomes impatient," Jenli said.

"Either way, we are in for a difficult fight, and the timing will be critical."

"Zaben's plan did not include this additional complication."

Elric rubbed his chin and raised his eyebrows. "No. No it didn't."

# 12

# INTO THE SEAT OF DARKNESS

## Birth plus 10 months

The relentless midday sun roosted over the burnt–out rubble of Rachael's old family home in Egypt. Timrok surveyed the ten–mile perimeter around the property from outside the shell of the house. His team stood guard around the perimeter, enforcing the no–entry zone he had pronounced over a year before. All was quiet. He stepped into the roofless remains of his command post and sat on a spiritual stool he had fashioned for himself.

He formed a small energy ball in his left hand. With his right hand he drew the energy out into a thick strand. He rolled it between his fingers, molded it, breathed into it. Moments later he had a tiny trumpet, no larger than his thumb, silver and perfect. Timrok held it by the bell between his fingers and gave it a gentle flick into the air, where it floated at eye level. He blew on it. It sounded a tiny little tone, clear and bright, and floated away. Timrok nodded and smiled. He formed another energy ball for another little trumpet.

From far over the horizon the sound of a mighty battle wafted through Timrok's command post. The muffled roar of thousands of spiritual combatants rose and fell like ocean waves crashing on a rocky shore. Timrok looked up in the direction of the sound, looked back down at the tiny trumpet between his fingers, and gave the trumpet a flick.

"One," he said to himself. "In over a year, only one enemy has strayed into our perimeter."

He smiled and shrugged. "We did send him to the abyss, though."

He looked off toward the distant battle and caught a glimpse of a high-swooping swarm of demons diving onto Zaben's fortress. He took a deep breath and released another tiny trumpet.

Timrok had just sent his eighth trumpet into the atmosphere when a flock of gray doves took off from the northern field. Their chirping flight caught his attention, and he turned in time to see two white lights approaching low and fast. Within seconds, two angelic visitors alighted inside the command post.

Timrok jumped to feet. "Greetings, my captain," Timrok said to Elric. He bowed his head to the commander with Elric. "And greetings to you, Commander Kai."

The commander, who was almost twice the size of Elric, nodded once as Elric said to Timrok, "It's good to see you, my friend. It has been a long time."

"A very long time," Timrok said, looking across his silent, eventless post.

Elric smiled. "Jesus is ten months old now, and it is time to prepare for the next stage. I have a new assignment for you."

Timrok palmed his sword handles. His bright eyes darted back and forth between the captain and the commander.

"The battle is going well at Zaben's stronghold," Elric said. "The enemy is fully engaged there and is still convinced they have the Lord trapped within. However, their command center is completely open—their warriors and messengers are free to come and go at will. It is time now to cut them off. I need you to take your team and attack their command center."

Timrok's jaw fell slack and his eyes widened. "Sir, the Prince of Persia is in command there. And I would suspect that Satan himself has set up a throne to oversee the battle."

"He has indeed," Elric said.

"I love a good fight, but, sir, this fight will be short and fruitless. We are no match for that kind of power."

"Agreed," answered Elric. "That is why you are bringing Commander Kai with you."

The commander smiled and gritted his teeth. He had the same kind of dogged spark in his eyes that Timrok himself always had when facing overwhelming odds.

"And," continued Elric, "your mission is not to defeat them but to distract them and prevent any outside communication. Commander Kai will keep Marr busy while you and your team deal with all the peripheral warriors and messengers."

"And what about Satan?" Timrok fidgeted and his voice cracked. "He is not a mere beaelzur like the others. A cherub is not one to be trifled with."

"He will either stay for the fight or will try to escape. I suspect he will break away. And there is little you can do to restrain him if he does. This is fine, as it will divide the leadership. Let him go and seal in their command center. No word comes in or out."

"And if he stays to fight?"

"Then I'm afraid it will be a very short engagement." Elric's tone then changed from calm and factual to grave and serious, "Do not expect to receive power to vanquish any of the enemy in this battle. Simply pin them down and cut them off."

Timrok stood tall, raised his chin, and clenched his fists. "Yes, captain. For the honor of the King we gladly accept this task. Is there a specific strategy you have in mind for the attack itself?"

Elric smiled, cocked his head, and said, "You . . . just attack."

Timrok remembered their first conversation a couple of years before on the cliff in Africa, laughed a deep hearty laugh, and answered, "In His service."

"Look," Elric said. "Your replacements are here."

Four senturim descended and took up positions at each corner of the property.

* * *

Timrok expected to see turmoil over Zaben's stronghold, but the spectacle that came into focus as he, his team, and Commander Kai approached the engagement area was far more expansive than he could have imagined. Not since the Rebellion had he seen a concentration of demonic warfare this large and this intense. A boiling black cloud of evil blanketed the Middle Realm for miles, and it touched everything.

"Heartrending, is it not?" Kai called out to Timrok. He tightened in their flight formation.

"I had no idea."

"You have been insulated in your remote post," Kai said. "In my command center, the reports have been horrendous. Over the last ten months there has been a sharp rise in illnesses—everything from the common cold to blindness, cancer, and leprosy. Strange accidents which leave people lame and suffering are increasing. Infant mortality is up. Life expectancy is down. The fertility and health of the herds and flocks in the region are at an all–time low. Crops are failing from months of drought. A scourge of snakebites and wild animal attacks fill people's hearts with fear and despair."

"What about the prayers of the righteous? Surely the people must be calling out to the Lord."

"In the face of all this calamity, instead of calling for help from the King, the people have embraced the darkness and help fuel it. In fact, most of the people blame the Lord for all of it. There are conflicts all throughout the region. Even gangs of children from one neighborhood band together to fight children from other neighborhoods to assert their power. People take other people to court over petty differences to satisfy their greed and spite. Divorce is on the increase, and assaults against young girls are rampant. There are some who recognize the spiritual void, but instead of turning to the King, they look to man–made idols, divination, and witchcraft."

"What about inside Zaben's stronghold?"

"The situation inside the palace grounds is better. The presence of the host provides a buffer; however, there is still unrest and a sense of dread. Those who live within the complex aren't experiencing the misfortunes of those in the surrounding areas, but everybody is always on edge and suffers from restless sleep."

"Benjamin and Rachael?"

"Our chief treasurer is having some difficulty meeting budgets due to falling revenues. His faith remains strong, though. Their ten-month-old boy, James, is generally healthy, although he fights colic. Benjamin rarely ventures outside the palace grounds because he can sense the darkness around them. And with all the stories of wild animal attacks and roadside robbers, Rachael prefers to keep herself and James within the safety of the palace walls."

Timrok and his team approached the command center at the outer rim of all the devastation. The battle itself swirled high into the sky a short distance away, but everywhere he looked, he saw the far-reaching effects of evil on every living thing.

"This is why I fight," Timrok said. "To destroy the works of the enemy, and to defend the honor of the King."

"You will get that chance today," Kai said.

Timrok felt like they were a flock of tiny hawks dispatched to stop the raging winds of a hurricane. He picked up his pace, gritted his teeth, pulled out his two swords, and began their final dive onto the command center.

* * *

Timrok's team of commandos pounced on the seat of darkness from behind, and the audacious appearance of the dazzling elzurim sent the dozen demons in the makeshift throne room jumping like startled cats. Mostly lesser spirits filled the command center, messengers for the higher–ranking ones on the front line, and Timrok's team bound half of them before they knew what hit them. The other half met the brawl with bared fangs and swinging swords.

At the same time, Kai breached the room feet first through the roof and landed a massive blow on Marr's chest before the evil prince could draw his sword. The two tumbled to the floor, and both of their swords clanged to the ground, landing together in the corner out of reach. The two giant spirits locked arms and tried to overpower each other as they struggled back to their feet. The touch of one immovable power on the other caused a spontaneous release of energy, and the places where their hands, arms, and thrashing torsos made contact sizzled with searing flames and blinding sparks. The two brawns grappled, and a surging cloud of energy and smoke enveloped them. None of the other spirits dared to even approach their dangerous sphere of conflict.

Timrok pulled his sword out of the chest of a stunned demon, bound him in a cord of light, and dropped him to the ground. Timrok leapt back behind the throne out of the fray to take stock of their situation. His eyes went first to the throne itself. Satan had disappeared. Timrok scanned the entire command center. No sign of the mighty cherub. Timrok grimaced and nodded. *It's just as well. We would not have stood if he had stayed for the fight.*

He turned his attention to Marr and Kai. They stayed locked in an arm hold, well matched, with sparks and fire and smoke shooting from their embrace. The whole room filled with smoke, the smell of burning sulfur, and the sounds of war cries and shrieking demons. Timrok surveyed the rest of the battle. His team fought with their usual prowess—wrangling multiple demons at once, flipping, spinning, bounding downward from the ceiling—every movement fluid, purposeful, and lightning fast. The beaelzurim pinged and darted in a frenzy. Some purposed to drive the elzurim out, fighting and thrusting and releasing bound comrades. Some demons tried to disentangle themselves from the skirmish and escape the control room, but they could not escape the speed of Timrok's team.

Timrok jumped up and stood on the armrests of the throne to oversee the fight. The battle settled into a rhythm. With the large number of demons in the room, his team couldn't bind them all. As soon as they could bind one, another would be released by a comrade. His team had sufficient numbers, however, to keep the command center contained. And from his position Timrok could see if any enemy might break away. He watched and waited.

A new demon messenger appeared from outside. He stepped in through the front wall, saw the battle, and bounded upward toward the ceiling. Timrok shot from his position and caught the demon by the ankle before he escaped. With one hand he slung the demon downward and with the other he sliced the demon in half with his sword. He whipped bindings around the surprised spirit before he hit the ground.

Timrok returned to his position on top of the throne and stood with his blades ready.

# 13

## STEP OF FAITH

### Birth plus 12 months

The mysterious child King of Israel was now 375 days old by the calculation of the Persian magi, and with great anticipation the three gray-beards gathered outside their Zoroastrian temple for some great revelation from the heavens about the location of the King. Astronomy instruments and charts littered their table, along with a modest clay bowl filled with figs and a carafe of lukewarm water.

"Tonight could be the night," Melchior said.

Caspar and Balthazar nodded.

Caspar rehearsed the prophecy from the scroll. "'At journey's end, the star alights above the head of the King of stars . . . '"

Melchior answered, "'Wise is he who seeks it.'"

"Keyvân completes its journey to opposition tonight," Balthazar said. "So, hopefully we will see some celestial body stay in a fixed position over the place where the Child is to be found."

"I expect it to be bright and obvious," Melchior said.

Caspar stroked his long beard. "It would not surprise me if we see a sky full of celestial beings singing a song."

"That would be most enlightening," Melchior said.

A year of anticipation had brought them to the very edge of their perseverance, and they met this night with high hopes.

Until the clouds rolled in.

Before any of the heavenly lights could become visible, a thick layer of clouds piled in. The starry panorama became obscured by an impenetrable wall of darkness. The three men slumped into their chairs and stared into the black sky. All the excitement and expectation fell from their faces, dripped off their sagging shoulders, and evaporated into the starless night as it became obvious that the clouds were going to stay.

After several hours of sitting in speechless darkness, Melchior stood up, pulled a fig from the bowl, threw it toward the chirping crickets, and announced, "I am going to bed."

Caspar replied with a defeated voice, "I shall stay here and continue watching, just in case."

"As shall I," said Balthazar.

"As you wish. These clouds are not going to clear tonight." Melchior stopped and turned back toward the table, "But if they do, be sure to wake me."

"Of course," replied Caspar.

Caspar and Balthazar tried to maintain their vigil, but after another hour of dark inactivity, Balthazar fell asleep where he sat. Caspar lasted a little longer, but eventually sleep overtook him, too.

Melchior woke the two the next morning. "Did anything happen after I went to bed?" he asked.

Thick clouds still covered the sky. Caspar and Balthazar rubbed the sleep out of their eyes, looked up at the gray clouds, and kneaded their stiff necks.

"Not a thing," answered Caspar. "I can't believe we waited a year for that."

"Now what?" Balthazar asked.

"Perhaps it doesn't matter," said Melchior. "I think Hormoz is the one we need to be watching anyway, and it does not complete its journey for another 24 days. I say we wait and see what happens then."

"We have no other choice," Caspar said. "We know nothing more now than we did a year ago."

Balthazar stood. "I'm hungry. I'm getting something to eat."

\* \* \*

Nangar sat atop the astrological charts of the magi and watched them trudge back into the temple. He rubbed his forehead and brooded.

*How do I get them to step out? They have contemplated searching for the newborn King of Israel for a year now. I prod them and prod them, and still they delay. Intellectual interest and mystic curiosity aren't enough. They feel too safe and familiar with their temple, their ancient scrolls, and their research. The trip to a foreign country is too far and too hard, especially with little hope of actually finding something only intellectually interesting.*

*But I can't turn this into a spiritual quest. For years I have blinded them to the one true King. The last thing I want is for them turn to Him now. It was a close call last year when the heralding angelic host announced His birth. They planted a seed that almost took root.* He chuckled. *But I stole the seed. I replaced it with intellect and reasoning. But that doesn't help me get them moving.*

He hopped down from the table and ambled inside. The three magi sat in sullen silence around a table, eating a barley loaf and a bowl of grapes. Nanar slinked back into the corner shadows.

"You don't need another sign," he cooed. "Go. Strike out for Israel now. Twenty-four more days is too long to wait." His words floated through the spiritual air and blanketed the three men. "Think of the knowledge you will gain by seeing the Child," he continued. "Seek Him now. No more delays. Go to Jerusalem and start your search. You are clever—and very wise. Surely you have the ability to . . ."

Balthazar stood up. "I'm going to the library to search through more scrolls."

"No!" Nangar said. "No more delays."

Caspar dropped his piece of bread onto the table. "I'll go with you."

In the library, the three magi rummaged through piles of scrolls. Nangar wrung his hands and muttered, "There's nothing more here. It's no use. Get out there and search for the Child."

Melchior rolled up a scroll and placed it back on a pile of scrolls on an inset shelf in the wall. "Sometimes I think we search in vain."

"Keep looking," Balthazar said.

"Here," Caspar said. "This might be something."

"What is it?" Balthazar asked without looking up from his own scroll.

"Ancient Jewish manuscripts, left by exiles. They appear to be sacred writings. There are probably a dozen books here."

"No!" shouted Nangar. "Do not read those! There is nothing of value there." He wrung his hands faster. *Aarrg. I kept those hidden all this time. How did he find them?*

Melchior slid another scroll from the shelf across the room and spread it out on a table. "I have read portions of those before. There is nothing of value there, only religious rituals and strict moral code."

"Still," Caspar said, "we seek a Jewish king. It is logical to investigate Jewish writings. Since we are looking for specific clues, perhaps something new will present itself." He sifted through the stack of parchments and laid one on top. He whispered aloud, "'In the beginning, God created the heavens and the earth . . . '"

Beams of light shone down through the Middle Realm onto Caspar. Most reflected off his helmet of darkness and floated away into nothing. Some beams hit the parchment, and the parchment gave off a warm glow. Tiny waves of light reverberated from the glowing page and pulsed against Caspar's spirit. Light completely surrounded him.

"No, no, no," mumbled Nangar.

Caspar kept reading—all afternoon and late into the evening.

The next morning, Caspar handed Balthazar a pile of manuscripts. "You should read these Jewish writings."

"Why? Have you found an instructive prophecy?"

"No, but I'm beginning to think that . . . I wonder if . . . well, read these and we'll talk."

"No, no, no," droned Nangar.

Balthazar read. Caspar read other Jewish scripts. Beams of light gleamed down.

At midday, Melchior rolled up another fruitless scroll and placed it back on its shelf. He shuffled over to the table where Balthazar and Caspar sat, engrossed in their reading. "You two have not said a word all morning. Are these writings providing direction? What have you discovered?"

"Caspar is right," Balthazar said. "These books require more study. I also have read portions of these manuscripts over the years, but presently, I am seeing more here than I ever had."

"More? More what?"

Balthazar shook his head. "It is hard to explain. But these writings are more than moral code. More than religious ritual. Behind it all is—"

"One true God," Caspar said, just above a whisper. "The true creator of the universe, the giver of life."

"And," Balthazar said, "He is not a mystic, unknowable power—but a personal entity, with intellect, character, and desire for fellowship."

Beams of light radiated down on all three magi. Caspar and Balthazar's words entered the Middle Realm and spiraled like sparks through the air. Their helmets of darkness eroded with each strike of a spark, and their dark breastplates became thinner and thinner. Nangar huddled in the corner.

Caspar added, "Enough of a desire for fellowship to come to earth and live amongst men."

Melchior sat with eyes wide and took a long, deep breath. "Like we heard in the vision last year."

"I believe they were angels," Caspar said.

"No!" Nangar shouted. "There are no angels! Enough of this. That vision wasn't even real. We should leave now. Let us find this child King—the King foretold in the stars. You will see that He is nothing more than a normal baby. He is surely not God." His words shot from the shadows, passed into the rays of light, and dissolved before they could reach the men.

"Here," Balthazar said. He dropped a stack of parchments in front of Melchior. "Read for yourself."

All three read for the remainder of the day amid a shower of light from the Throne.

The next morning, the magi rose and returned to the Jewish manuscripts. Nangar paced. *I must stop this. The King is drawing them away. These men are mine.* He stopped and smiled. *I know—this will slow them down.* He opened the palm of his hand and spoke, "Sickness. Influenza." A ball of flaming plasma formed in his hand. He spun it with his fingertips, and it swirled and divided into three balls. With a sneer on his lips, he flung the fireballs at the magi. The flaming darts sank deep into their spirits. Nangar chuckled.

Midmorning, Caspar said, "I have developed a headache. Perhaps I have been studying too hard." He rubbed his throat and sniffled. "Perhaps I should rest for a while." He rose and left the library.

Not long after, Melchior said, "Actually, I'm not feeling well myself." He stepped out.

Only minutes later, Balthazar coughed, rubbed his throat, and left.

Nangar sat on the table and let out a long sigh. "That's better."

The next morning, Nangar sat alone in the library. The following morning, Nangar remained alone. The third morning, each of the men came and read for a few hours. The light from the King beamed strong, but the weakened flesh of the men filtered most of it out.

"This is what becomes of those who seek God," Nangar jeered. "He is punishing you for your unworthiness. He strikes you down with sickness."

They returned to bed.

The next morning, all three returned to the library, looking stronger. They went straight to reading. Through sniffling noses and raspy coughs, they studied all day. The intensity of the light from the Throne drove Nangar to the farthest side of the room.

They studied again the next day. Nangar crouched in the corner. *I'm losing them . . . I'm losing them. I only hope that eventually they will search for the Child and lead me to Him.*

Two more weeks passed.

"We approach day number 399," Balthazar said.

"I can't wait to see the message the God of Heaven has prepared for us," Caspar said.

"Answers," said Melchior. "Soon we will have answers."

The day finally arrived. Once again, the magi had their table set out with all the requisite instruments and scrolls. Once again, they fidgeted and looked to the skies.

Once again, the clouds rolled in.

\* \* \*

## Birth plus 13 months

"This is unbelievable," Balthazar said. The three magi collected their equipment from the table. "How can it be that there is a cloudy night on two of the most important nights in history? Every day for the last two weeks has been perfectly clear!"

Melchior, with hands full of instruments and parchments, wrestled the door with his elbows. "Personally, I don't think it is a coincidence."

The three stepped inside and walked toward the library.

"Probably not," said Balthazar, "but we did not foresee anything like this in our horoscopes. In fact, all the signs seemed to indicate the opposite. We should have seen something remarkable on one of these two nights. Something tangible with which we could work."

Melchior dropped his instruments on the library table. "I think this is something bigger than the stars. I think the God of the Hebrews is trying to tell us something. What if these clouds are meant as a sign to us?"

"But I thought a star was supposed to be the sign," said Balthazar.

"We have been working under the premise that a guiding star would appear at the end of the journey of either Keyvân or Hormoz. But the prophecy does not specify whose journey is made. What if the 'journey' refers to *our* journey? What if we are supposed to begin our search without full knowledge of his location, and at the end of our journey, He will guide us with a star?"

"It makes sense," Caspar said. "From all we have been reading in the Hebrew Scriptures, this God of Abraham rewards those to move forward in faith."

Melchior rubbed the back of his neck. "I can't explain it, but I have a sense deep within me that this God wants to be found by us. And I want to find Him. And not because I think it is an interesting thing to study, but because I am beginning to believe that He is—"

"Truly God," Balthazar finished.

"Exactly. And I want to see Him and offer Him my worship."

All three men's eyes shined with wild excitement.

Nangar crouched in the corner. *The presence and work of the Holy Spirit is too strong in the room. I am powerless to speak.* He snorted a puff of yellow smoke. *It is no matter, though. I have already lost these men. And I concede these three insignificant men for the chance to find the Child. Perhaps they might actually, finally, begin their search.*

"I say we leave as soon as we can put together provisions for the trip," announced Caspar.

"I agree," said Melchior.

Balthazar nodded. "We still don't know where to even begin the search," he said.

"We should head toward Jerusalem," said Melchior. "Surely the Israelites will know where He is. After all, He is their king. We will go directly to the capital and make inquiry there. Who knows, maybe He will already be in the palace. Or in their temple."

The trek from the magi's far eastern home to Jerusalem would take at least two months, and the three magi made lengthy and involved preparations for the extended desert passage. Part of the preparations included a gift for the King of Heaven.

"We clearly should present Him with gold, and I have set aside a good part of my treasury to dedicate to Him," Balthazar announced.

"I have also," said Caspar. "How about silver?"

Melchior shook his head. "Definitely not. Silver may be a sufficient gift for an earthly king, but this King is worthy of only the finest. Nothing less than gold."

"Spices and incense?" Caspar said.

Balthazar nodded. "It is a customary gift. I believe it would be expected. But which ones are precious enough?"

Caspar said, "Cinnamon? Cassia? Pepper? Cardamom? Ginger? Cloves?" Each spice earned a wrinkled nose and apathetic shrugs from Melchior and Balthazar.

Nangar sat in the shadows shaking his head. *I grow weary of this banter over the King.* "How about frankincense and myrrh?" His words floated through the Middle Realm and rested on the magi. He laughed to himself at the rich irony of the suggestion. *He is going to need them when I get finished with Him.*

Caspar paused. "Frankincense? Myrrh?"

"Burial spices?" Balthazar shot a surprised glance with raised eyebrows. "Does that not seem a strange gift for a baby?"

Melchior stroked his beard. "Why not? They are the most expensive of the incenses and spices we could offer. He would certainly have no immediate use for them; however, they are highly valuable—gifts worthy of a king."

Caspar nodded. "None of the other spices are right. They are simply too common."

"Very well, frankincense and myrrh will be part of our gift."

After three days of preparation, they loaded several months' worth of packs stuffed with tents, food, water, and necessities onto a good-sized caravan of camels. Wooden chests carried gold, silver, and precious spices—some for restocking their supplies for the return trip, and some to present to King Herod as the customary gift when seeking an audience with a foreign dignitary. And they carried the gift specially prepared for the King of Kings.

\* \* \*

## Birth plus 14 months

With every plodding step of the camels along the dry, dusty trail to Jerusalem, steady streams of light rained down on the magi in the Middle Realm. Nangar followed but kept his distance. He reached a hiding spot and waited for the caravan to cross the next valley.

*I'm beginning to think this might actually work. Look at that. The King is constantly speaking to them. They have torn down most of the strongholds I have built up all these years, and the words of the King are penetrating. Actually, this is better than I had planned. If they can hear Him, He will lead them. I don't care that I've lost them. I would gladly trade the souls of these three men for glory that awaits me for delivering the Son of Man to destruction. Keep speaking. Keep leading.*

Two months of gritty travel passed—six camels, three men, and a skulking spirit. Finally, in mid-evening, the city of Jerusalem appeared in the distance. The shining gold dome of the temple glowed like a beacon in the setting sun. The magi decided to set up camp for the night, being too late to cover the remaining distance and still obtain an audience with Herod. They would start out at first light with fresh, brightly colored garb to honor the royal court. Tonight, they would spend under the stars again, still anticipating some kind of star to guide them the rest of the way. Tomorrow they would stand before Herod.

# 14

## DARKNESS UNLEASHED

**Birth plus 16 months**

Timrok stood on the armrests of the dark throne and tracked every movement of the battle inside Marr's command center. For three months, not one of Marr's minions had escaped Timrok's grasp, and no messages from the outside had penetrated with news from the main battle. Above him hung a thick cloud of smoke. Below him, strewn across the weathered stone floor, lay over a dozen bound beaelzurim, writhing and shouting curses at his team. To his left, his team of five warriors had their hands full.

Prestus, one of his warriors, blocked a blow from one demon with his shield while thrusting his own blade toward another. His thrust missed its mark, and he sprang upward and somersaulted over a swinging blade, landing behind his first attacker and clipping the demon's leg with his sword. The demon squealed.

Chase, another one of Timrok's warriors, had one demon beaten and flat on his back, but before Chase could bind him, the demon rolled to his right and sliced through the bindings of light of a captive. Chase now battled two.

Another demon cut another captive loose. Kylek shot up toward the open ceiling and caught the escaping demon by the waist. The two spiraled downward. They crashed on the ground, and Kylek blocked the sword of another attacker while on his back. Sparks flashed from the colliding steel. He bounded to his feet and met the attack, but lost track of the escaping demon. That demon lunged toward Kylek's unsuspecting back.

Micah disengaged from the two demons he fought and leapt toward Kylek. He hacked through the arm of the attacker just before his blade reached Kylek's back. The demon's sword clanged to the floor, and sulfurous smoke belched from his severed arm. Micah bound that demon in a blink and re-engaged the other two.

Nalyd locked in a grappling match with a demon larger than himself. They rolled and tumbled as all the other fighters jumped over and around them.

Timrok turned his attention to his right.

Marr and Kai fought a fierce sword battle. The crashing swords of these two giants made the others look like child's play. Their swords hummed with energy. The blades roared as they severed the air. They exploded with power on impact—rending the air like thunder. Both combatants stood solid as stone at the collision of their blades, but the shockwave of their contact sent nearby warriors reeling.

Marr made a spinning lunge toward Kai. Kai deflected the blade downward and somersaulted over Marr's head. He landed and made a power swing toward Marr's turned back. Marr spun with a roar, and their blades met with a crash. They locked in place. The energy from their touching blades crackled and created a fireball with searing sparks flying everywhere. Marr jabbed his other hand toward Kai's face. Kai caught Marr's hand in mid-thrust and locked arms. Using the momentum of Marr's fist, Kai pulled Marr forward and flipped him over backward.

The two giant spirits flipped across the room, and Timrok jumped straight up to avoid getting plowed over. The fighters on the left side of the room didn't see them coming, and half of them were trampled like unsuspecting insects. The two brawns' swords collided again and sent the other half flailing from the shock. The battle of the lesser spirits shifted the right side of the room. One demon made a break toward the front wall.

"No, you don't!" Timrok shouted. He shot from his position and caught the demon outside the stone ruins. Timrok seized his ankle with one hand and flung him downward. With his other hand, Timrok drove his sword through the demon's chest. The two spiraled downward through a cloud of yellow smoke. The demon hit the ground with Timrok's blade still protruding through his chest and out this back, the tip of the blade pinning him to the ground. Timrok bound him and pulled his blade back. He hoisted the captive by the back of the bindings and tossed him back into the command center.

Timrok paused and looked across the plain toward Zaben's stronghold. The battle still raged. *Why has there been so little traffic from the main battle to the control center over the last three months?* He imagined the generals on the front line commanding their hordes and exercising their control. He shook his head. *The generals are too arrogant to seek direction from the control room. And they're reluctant to send a messenger with news for fear that the messenger would return with directives.* He shook his head again and returned to his position back on top of the throne.

Marr and Kai battled on the left again, and Timrok's team fought on the right. Three frenzied demons attacked one of Timrok's warriors with their backs to the battling giants. In a defensive move, Kai leapt backward in a tight back flip. He landed near the sparring warriors and swung his blade in an upward full–circle motion toward the pouncing Marr. Kai's blade smashed into the three demons on the backswing and catapulted them out of the building. Marr brought a crushing blow down on Kai's ready blade and thundered orders to the three.

"Escape, you fools! Take word to the front," he roared. "Release the generals! Tell them all to attack. Hold nothing back!"

The three messengers bolted toward the main battlefront, and Marr pressed his blade toward Kai with a low, guttural growl. "I am tired of waiting for my master to authorize the use of my strongest forces. Today your puny stronghold will be crushed by my word."

Timrok shot out of the command center. The messengers were already halfway to the battlefront. Timrok blazed forward. *Faster! Faster! Aha!* He snagged two of them by their heels and dragged them to the ground. In two quick strokes he subdued and bound them, but the third streaked onward with an evil, high–pitched shriek. Timrok launched forward and flew with furious speed, gaining on him with every stroke. His focus zeroed in. *This one cannot deliver his message. Almost there . . . almost there . . . now I have you . . .*

*Zzzz-whump!* A force hammered his back from above. He gasped for air and spun around, face up. *Oh, no! I've gone too far into their . . .*

Twenty enemy warriors pounced on him. Two grabbed one wing. Three seized the other. Timrok thrashed—both blades whizzing and carving clouds of yellow smoke. *There are too many!* The writhing mass plummeted downward. An enemy sword slashed through his left arm. "Aughhh!" His sword tumbled away. "Arrghh!" Light burst forth from a wound on his leg. He gritted his teeth and swung the sword in his right hand with all his waning strength. His blade crashed against an attacker's blade, shooting sparks through the sulfur cloud. At the same instant, an attacker from behind clipped his right arm, and his sword flew off into the air. Dazed and disoriented, Timrok clenched his teeth. An attacker landed his feet on Timrok's chest. Timrok blinked. The jagged demon sword drove straight into his chest. Everything went black.

Timrok opened his eyes. From the flat of his back, he watched a rabid pack of beaelzurim swarm around him on the ground. He jerked upward but couldn't move. Bindings constricted him from his neck to his feet, and an enemy warrior's foot held him to the ground.

He looked back toward the headquarters where his team was fighting. None emerged to help him. *They are too disciplined to deviate from their orders and too outnumbered to rally a rescue.*

He looked into the seething darkness. *Yes, the escaped messenger completed his task.* Besides the thousands of attackers already swarming the fortress, lines of massive beaelzurim now pressed in around Zaben's stronghold from all directions, their red glowing eyes burning holes through the thick darkness. The largest of the enemy, the generals who had been held in reserve, hurled flaming balls of energy into the lines of angelic defenses.

To Timrok's right, a nearby general formed a pulsing sphere of energy in his palm until it became a huge, blazing red and orange ball of flame. The general released it, and the energy ball cracked through the air at the speed of light and blasted through the first two layers of fortification. The inner layer of defenses deflected the bombardment, but it tore open dangerous holes in the outer layers. The swirling hordes of attackers pressed their advantage through the openings, and the defenders barely kept them from penetrating into the center of the stronghold.

Timrok let his head drop to the ground. He took as deep a breath as the tight bindings would allow. *This is it. Zaben's forces might be able to hold off the enemy for maybe a day, but certainly not two.*

# 15

## KING'S QUEST

**Birth plus 16 months**

*E*arly the next morning, Molech, the demon commander who ruled from the human palace in Jerusalem, manipulated his puppet, Herod the Great, with his usual words. The court was quiet and idle for that time of day, but Herod's mind was active with the dark torments that filled his troubled days and fitful nights.

*And what about the Primus pilus?* the familiar voice in Herod's head jabbed. *How do we truly know where his loyalties lie? Maybe Caesar hand-picked him to overthrow my rule to bring in a Roman governor. Maybe he intends to lead a coup and take the throne himself.*

A demon captain entered the court. "Master, a visitor from the eastern region."

Molech's eyes tightened, and he nodded once. He would have to let Herod's mind meander off unguided into the irrational dark alleys of suspicion and treachery. But he had been down that path so many times, he knew the way all too well.

Nangar stepped forward and bowed. "Master Molech," he said, "I bring to you a gift from the east that I think you will find most interesting."

Molech stepped out of Herod's body and stood on the elevated platform above Nangar. With a sneer he answered, "What is it?"

"I have three men who are seeking the Christ child."

Molech laughed a loud, mocking laugh and sat down on his spiritual throne. "Then your men have come to the wrong place. Marr has the Child surrounded in a stronghold in Egypt. While I am left here in this miserable place with only a handful of worthless malcontents, Marr's special forces are poised for a glorious victory in which I will have no part."

Molech blew a snort of sulfurous smoke through his nostrils and opened his right palm where a fiery red ball of energy formed. He crushed it within his closing fist and swatted the residual smoke toward Nangar. "Take your men to Egypt."

"I have reason to believe the Child may be here in your region," Nangar pressed.

"You are a pitiful fool. Marr's armies scoured this entire region for months. There is nothing here. What makes you think you know more than everyone else?"

Nangar scowled and took a step toward the door. He stopped and looked around at all the spiritual power standing in the court. He paused and returned to the throne. "Because I am convinced they are being directly led by Spirit of the King. His presence is strong in them—I cannot even speak to them anymore. I assure you he wants these men to find Him."

"But why would He lead them here? I have already told you the Child is in Egypt."

From behind the shadows came a small spirit in the form of a snake. His deep red eyes glowed with wisdom, and his voice echoed with smooth intrigue as he slithered toward the throne.

"What if Marr is wrong?" the snake said. His black forked tongue shot in and out. "What if the Child is actually hidden somewhere here in your jurisdiction? Think of the glory that could be yours if you—"

"Perhaps you may be right," Molech said to Nangar, "this is a most interesting gift you bring. Have these men appear before Herod."

"They are already on their way. They should be here any moment."

"Good. And if the Spirit of the King is with them as strongly as you say, it would be best if we clear the court of all the beaelzurim but me, lest the King suspect our intentions and lead the men away."

All the demons stood still and silent, looking toward the throne with questioning eyes.

"You heard me," Molech blasted, "clear the court! All of you."

The attending spirits filed out, but Nangar lingered. "Surely you do not also mean me? After all, it was I who brought them—"

"I alone will stay with Herod. I will call when I am ready for you."

The snake glided across the marble floor in a southward direction without another word.

* * *

Minutes later one of Herod's attendants approached the king with a message. "Your highness, three magi from the far east seek an audience with you. They have brought these gifts to honor you and your kingdom."

Four other attendants entered. They carried boxes and set them before the throne. They raised the lids and revealed gold, silver, and many precious spices. The gold and silver glistened in the morning sun beaming through the arched windows, and the rich smell of the exotic spices filled the room with captivating warmth.

"What is their business in Israel?" Herod asked.

"They seek . . . " The attendant paused a moment, looked around at the guards, swallowed hard, and said, "To see the newborn king of Israel."

"The newborn king of . . . " Herod's fists clenched. He sat upright to the edge of his throne.

Herod relaxed and sat back in his chair and replied, "How interesting. These must be men of surpassing wisdom if they have knowledge of a new king that I have not heard of. Please show our guests in."

The magi appeared regal in their brightly colored robes and turbans. They carried themselves with great dignity and took their place in front of the throne.

With his head bowed, one announced, "Mighty Herod, King of the Jews, your fame and greatness is known throughout the world, even in Persia, our country from which we have traveled these two months. Thank you for granting an audience with your humble servants. We are indeed honored to stand in your presence. I am Balthazar."

"Thank *you* for your kind gifts. I do love receiving spices from the east. Please, step forward and tell me what brings you on your long journey to Jerusalem."

Another said, "I am Caspar. Where is He who has been born King of the Jews? For we saw His star in the east, and have come to worship Him."

The third added, "I am Melchior. We mean no disrespect to your highness, but we believe this Child to be the King of all kings, the very Son of God. We honor you and your nation for being the one to whom this great gift has been given."

Herod stroked his beard, "Very interesting. Word of this child had not reached my ears until now. How did you come upon this great revelation?"

They explained their journey had started with the appearance of the king's star and the triple conjunction, and they gave a brief lesson on astrology and the significance of the event. They told about the amazing display of the angelic host and the message they brought.

"The problem that remains for us," Caspar continued, "is that we do not know His location—only that He is here in Israel somewhere."

Balthazar said, "Naturally, we assumed that you would have already known about this and would probably have Him here in your great palace."

Herod shook his head, "Unfortunately for all of us, that is not the case. Not only is he not here, this is the first news of a new king that I have received. You were wise to come to me first, though, for even though I know not the location of this new king, I will not send you away empty-handed. I shall call for all my wisest counselors and priests to see where the king was to be born. It will take several hours before I can gather everyone. Until then, please enjoy the hospitality of the palace."

Herod called to one of his attendants, "Show my honored guests to our finest quarters. See to all their needs and the needs of their beasts."

Then turning again to the magi, he said, "I will call for you after my council has convened."

The magi bowed and left the court followed by several attendants.

* * *

The summons for all the chief priests and scribes went out, and word about the magi's quest filtered throughout Jerusalem. Troubled questions filled the streets.

"Could it truly be that the Messiah has been born?"

"What will Herod's reaction be?"

"Are we to have more war and oppression before the Messiah is old enough to deliver us?"

The word also reached the ears of the beaelzurim in the city, and they had questions of their own.

"What if Marr is wrong and that the Child is right here?"

"What will Satan's reaction be?"

"Who will be the fortunate one to find the Child and strike the fatal blow—thus earning the most honored position in the new kingdom?"

The buzz within the spiritual world reached such a level that Molech called all the captains of the city and issued an edict.

"No actions shall be taken to either find the Child or to attack Him until I give the word. If He is indeed here, the elzurim have been able to keep Him hidden from us until now, so there is no reason to believe that we will be able to find Him on our own. Instead, we are going to use these men. For whatever reason the King is guiding them to Himself, so we must not disrupt their quest. If they do find Him, we will know it. And then we will mount our attack. Send the orders. Go now."

The demon captains flew from the palace court.

A large group of chief priests and scribes filed in. They milled about for an hour, talking, sharing ideas, waxing philosophical, and trying to impress each other with their extensive knowledge of the Scriptures. They discussed the messianic references about Egypt and Nazareth, but after only a small debate, they reached consensus that Bethlehem was most likely the birthplace of the promised messiah. They reported to the king.

"The Christ is to be born in Bethlehem of Judea, for so it has been written by the prophet, 'And you, Bethlehem, land of Judah, are by no means least among the leaders of Judah; for out of you shall come forth a ruler who will shepherd my people Israel.'"

With the magi absent, Molech allowed the regular contingent of demons to stay for the council. The demons responded to the chief priests' report with incredulous looks and remarks.

"Bethlehem? These men are mistaken."

"Of course, we know of those prophecies, but there is no palace in Bethlehem worthy of the King's Son."

"We scoured all of Bethlehem for months and found nothing."

"This prophecy could mean that the Son will live in Bethlehem when He is older."

Molech silenced the court with an upraised hand and spoke through Herod to the men. "Bethlehem, you say? This is very good information. Thank you all for your excellent wisdom. Tell me, do the Scriptures indicate exactly where in Bethlehem He might be found?"

The council muddled around with this more difficult question for several minutes and reported they knew of no clear references to an exact location.

Herod followed up, "What about the time of His birth? Do the Scriptures indicate when He is to be born?"

This sparked considerable debate. Some believed they could pinpoint the time; some opposed such presumptuousness; and others weren't sure. In the end, they reported they could not specify a date with any confidence.

"Is it possible the time is now? Is there anything that precludes His birth from taking place during our time?"

On this point the council had nearly unanimous consensus. It was possible that the Christ could be born during their time.

Herod thanked them all again and sent them on their way. With the court empty again except for Herod's attendants, Herod's dark thoughts took over.

*This newborn king will mark the end of my kingdom if I do not do something immediately*, the voice inside his head prodded. *I must find the child and kill him before he becomes known and powerful. But I must not allow the people to know. If they find out that I have killed the one whom they believe could have been their messiah, they will surely revolt. This will be a most delicate matter; the whole city is already talking about him. I must accomplish this quickly, and I must accomplish it secretly. His identity must never be known to the people. I cannot send troops out to find him because the people will know the order came from me. I know—I will use the magi. They are already on a quest to find him. I shall tell them to return here and report his location once they have found him.*

Molech dismissed his attendants. Herod dismissed all his attendants but one.

Herod called the remaining attendant forward. "I will see the magi in private now. Fetch them discreetly."

Within minutes the magi stood before the king again.

Herod greeted them. "Thank you for waiting. I trust your stay has been pleasant?"

The three nodded and bowed before the king.

"I sought the counsel of my most learned priests, and I am happy to report they all agree the king you seek is to be born in Bethlehem of Judah. They could not give an exact location, but I am confident men of your great wisdom will be able to find him, if he is indeed there. How long ago did you see the star?"

"It has been nearly a year and a half," Caspar said.

"This is a long time," Herod said. "We can only hope the child is still there."

"We believe in our hearts he is," Melchior answered.

"Go then to Bethlehem in peace with my blessing," Herod said. "Go and search carefully for the Child, and when you have found Him, report to me, so that I too may come and worship Him."

"You are a wise and gracious ruler." Balthazar bowed. "Thank you for your hospitality and kind help. We will certainly find the Child and return here as you request. Now, if it pleases the king, we will take our leave."

The magi left the court, and Molech called for Nangar and a beaelzur captain.

"The men are headed to Bethlehem," Molech said. "My hope is they truly are being led by the King and that they will find the Son of Man." To Nangar he said, "You may continue following your charges, but see to it you do not give the enemy reason to change course." To the captain he said, "Form a detail and follow behind at a safe distance. If you make contact, report back to me immediately so we can prepare an offensive."

# 16

## THE SIEGE

**Birth plus 16 months**

In Bethlehem, a stealthy snake weaved its way through every dark shadow in the city. He crossed an unmarked territorial line, and Luchek's blade smashed down onto the ground in front of his nose.

"What are you doing here?" demanded Luchek.

"I am merely passing through," replied the snake. His forked black tongue shot in and out.

"Are you on some particular mission? For whom do you work?"

"I work for no one. I merely wander the world seeking opportunities."

"There are no opportunities for you here. This area is under my control. Turn around and continue your work elsewhere."

"Well, well," said the snake in a smooth, low voice, "a warrior of position and influence. You must be very powerful to control an entire area of the city."

"Not only is this district mine, but I command an entire team."

"A team? It requires great power and wisdom to hold a team together. A team, you say? Then are you on some special mission yourself?"

"It is a secret mission, and you are asking too many questions, little one. Be gone now before I have you forcibly removed."

"A secret mission? A dark and treacherous one, I presume? I live for missions like that. Do you have room on your team for one more?"

Luchek eyed him with suspicion. "You don't even know who our target is, and yet you wish to join my team?"

"Hmm, so there is a specific target?" the snake cooed. "This must be a very important target to warrant an entire team, led by a great warrior like you. Now I am even more intrigued."

"Why should I let you in? What could you possibly offer that would strengthen my position?"

The snake glowered and answered, "I am quite effective in a fight, and I know many things from my travels."

"Then," Luchek shot back, "tell me something useful that I do not know . . . something 'from all your travels.'"

The snake became very quiet. "There is word that Marr has made a fatal mistake—that the Christ child may actually be hidden somewhere here in Judea. And . . . " he paused.

"And what?"

"It would not concern you. You have your mission here. As a matter of fact, I think I shall move along. I would rather find a more significant operation than . . . this."

"Wait! You must tell me more of what you know."

"No, it is not relevant to you. I will be going now."

"Wait, wait. You can join my team. Tell me what you know."

"You first. What is your mission here?"

Luchek said, "It's true." He looked all around and whispered. "The King's Son is here. I have Him surrounded."

"How remarkable. How do you know it is Him?"

"It's a long story, but trust me, I know with no doubt that it is truly Him."

"Why have you not told anyone? Our lord would want to know about this."

"He will. When the time is right. This is my prize. I found Him. I have Him trapped. I will be the one who receives full credit for delivering Him to our lord."

"How many seraphim and cherubim are guarding Him?"

Luchek chuckled. "It would be most difficult to sneak into the world and remain hidden if He was escorted by those giants, do you not agree?"

"None? Then how many elzurim stand guard?"

"A captain, one lieutenant, and an additional warrior, plus several more who work around the periphery and pretend to be tending to other business."

"Then why have you not attacked? If you have such a strong team, you could easily overwhelm them."

Luchek squirmed and fidgeted with his hands. "They wield the flame of vengeance."

The snake's eyes widened. "Interesting." He smiled.

"I have already lost one of my team to the abyss from a premature strike. I am building up my forces and waiting for an opportune time. Now, tell me what else you know."

"Your time has run out," the snake said.

"What do you mean?"

"There are men headed this way right now who seek the King. Molech knows of their quest and will certainly be sending his own team to investigate. They will probably be here within an hour."

The snake slithered away toward a nearby bush.

"Wait," Luchek said. "Are you not going to join my team?"

The snake continued without turning his head. "And face a sword of vengeance?"

Luchek swallowed hard. *An hour? That means we must begin our attack immediately. Are we ready? Do we have enough forces?*

The image of Deagos being dispatched so effortlessly by the elzur lieutenant on the road to Jerusalem made him shudder.

*I have no choice. The time is now.*

One of his officers stood at his post on a nearby roof. Luchek flew up and stood close, with his mouth next to the officer's ear. "Gather the other officers," Luchek said. "Meet at our secret cave. I have urgent news, and we must meet immediately."

Luchek gazed in the direction the snake had disappeared. Just then, an enormous spirit in the form of a fearsome dragon heaved into the air on terrible leathery wings with a dreadful screech. It headed south toward Egypt.

In his secret cave on the outskirts of Bethlehem, five demons gathered around Luchek with anxious expressions.

"The time has come for us to make our attack," Luchek announced.

"Why now?" one of the officers asked.

"Molech has dispatched a team to search Bethlehem. They will be here within the hour. If we hope to claim this victory for ourselves, we must move now."

The officers breathed fast and heavy, and their heads twitched as Luchek laid out his battle plan.

"You all saw what had happened to Deagos," Luchek said. "We can assume the enemy still possesses that same fatal power. Avoid direct contact with the elzurim's blades at all costs. Through a series of sharp swooping maneuvers, we will distract the enemy with superior numbers and draw them away from the Child. All we need to do is divert the guards' attention away long enough for one of our team to reach the Child."

Luchek met eyes with each of his officers. "It is a dangerous mission. A single swipe of the enemy's sword will mark an instant end to your time on earth. However, the glory of the prize makes the risk more than worth it. I believe one of us will be fortunate enough to strike the final blow that will usher in the beginning of a new kingdom."

They all palmed their sword handles and looked at each other with wide eyes.

"Go brief your teams," Luchek said. "We attack on my signal."

* * *

Jenli looked out the window of Joseph and Mary's room into the waning afternoon sun. "The darkness closes in," he said.

Elric pulled his sword. "I sense it as well."

Jenli's warrior pulled his sword and stood in the center of the room.

Elric moved next to Jesus, who played on the floor. "No word from Zaben's stronghold in days. The timing of this will be—"

Four beaelzurim swooped in through the roof, swords drawn, shouting terrifying war cries. The three angels swung their swords at the attackers, but the demons dodged and spun and shot out the back wall. Before Elric could turn his head, a second wave flew through the front wall. Again the angels swung their swords. Again the demons evaded the blades and shot out the back. A third wave blasted through without engaging.

"They are trying to draw us away," shouted Elric. The next wave plowed through the wall and out through the roof. "Stay close to the King. Don't let anyone near."

Four more of Jenli's team jumped into the room from behind. Elric met them with welcoming eyes, and the seven expanded their defensive circle outward, forming a larger buffer zone around the Child. Another wave swooped through. For half an hour, wave after wave swept through the room.

"Why do they not engage?" one of the warriors called out between attacks.

Another wave crashed through.

"They fear the sword of vengeance," Elric answered.

"None of us have it," Jenli said.

Another wave crashed through.

"They don't know that yet," Elric said.

"This seems like a good time for it," Jenli said.

Another wave. This time, one of the elzurim's blades found its mark on one of the more careless attackers. The surprised demon squealed and flew away.

The attacks stopped. Every angelic eye darted toward the ceiling, the wall, the ceiling.

A new wave burst in, drawing a little closer, and two of the demons purposely made minor contact with their swords. They encountered no blue flame, and they were not vanquished.

The next wave brought a few more cautious contacts.

The next wave brought more contacts.

The demons continued swooping in and out, but many of them stayed, thrusting their way inward. Elric and Jenli's team found themselves embroiled in an all-out battle.

Elric struck down an attacker, bound him, and shoved him aside with his foot. He raised his sword and blocked two incoming blades. *We are outnumbered. The skill and power of our warriors is sufficient now, but we need more reinforcements. It's time to send the signal.*

He motioned to Jenli to take charge, and Elric bolted straight up above the house and raised his sword high above his head. He spoke a single word, and his sword burst forth with an intense white light. To a human who might have eyes to perceive it, it looked like a brilliant star. To the angels who watched for it, it became a shimmering signal to come to the King's aid.

With his sword ablaze as a flashing white beacon, he made a flight across the region to call the rest of his team. He flew from the hills of Judea and made a wide sweeping circle as far south as Egypt and then around the far east side of Jerusalem. He remained there for a brief time and then flew back down to Bethlehem where he took up a position directly above the house. The battle below him grew in numbers and intensity, but he held his position, calling for reinforcements with his radiant light.

# 17

## THE BREACH

**Birth plus 16 months**

In Jerusalem the three magi finished repacking their camels' saddlebags with fresh provisions from King Herod for the relatively short trip to Bethlehem. Balthazar began to mount his camel but stopped and gazed into the eastern sky.

"Look at that," he called to the other two. "What star would be rising in the east in that position at this time of day?"

"And with such brightness?" said Caspar.

"That is no star we know," Melchior said. "Most curious."

The three stopped fussing with their provisions, congregated, and stared at this interesting star. Calm, but intrigued, they stroked their long beards and rubbed their chins.

"It's moving!" Caspar squeaked. "Look, the star is moving!"

The other two nodded with their mouths hanging wide open. The unusual star carved a path from the east to almost overhead and then due south toward Bethlehem.

With a crackling voice Balthazar recited the words they had pondered over a year ago, "'At journey's end . . . '"

Melchior finished the quote. "'The star alights above the head of the King of stars.'"

"The King's star!" Caspar shouted. "The King's star!"

The three old men jumped up and down like excited young boys, hugging each other, slapping each other's shoulders, and laughing out loud.

Out of breath and full of life, Melchior said, "Quickly, we must follow it. Hurry! Hurry!"

The other two had already mounted their camels. In a fast–moving cloud of dust, their small caravan blazed southward as fast as the magi could drive their beasts. They covered the two–hour walk less than a single hour. With every step, the star became nearer, sharper, distinctly stationary. And so the star, which they had seen in the east, went on ahead of them until it came to a stop over the place where the Child was to be found.

* * *

One of the defending angels at the inn in Bethlehem nicked Luchek's shoulder with his blade.

"Argh!"

The angel stabbed his sword into the ground, used it as a vault, and planted both feet on Luchek's chest. The kick sent Luchek tumbling out of the house.

Luchek jumped back to his feet and grabbed two of his officers about to re-enter the fight. "This was supposed to be a swift, precise strike," he railed. "But because of the incompetence of this team and your lack of leadership, this is turning into a full–scale protracted battle—one in which we're probably not strong enough to prevail. Look around."

Most of his team had been pushed out of the house and now engaged in open warfare in the air and on the ground surrounding the house.

"But the captain's beacon," one the officers said. "He has called in five additional warriors."

"We are losing our numerical superiority," the other officer said.

"I don't want excuses," Luchek shouted. "We still have them outnumbered. And they do not have the flame of vengeance. Get our warriors in there and penetrate the inner defenses!"

* * *

Daniel and Levi sat on a quiet hill south of Nazareth and watched over their flock of sheep in the meadow. The day grew dark. The bustle and noise of the day gave way to a gentle breeze and a cricket's song.

"Why can't Father agree that it's possible for there to be angels?" Daniel asked.

Levi laughed. "You're still thinking of the vision you saw, aren't you?"

"I can't help it. I know what I saw."

"That was a year and a half ago." Levi shook his head. "I don't know about Father. Ever since he started listening to the teaching of the Sadducees, he has been—"

"Hey! Look at that!" Daniel said. "Do you see that light?"

"Yes."

"What is it?"

"I don't know. It looks like a star."

"I've never seen a star like that. It's so bright, and low." Daniel said.

"I suppose you're going to tell me it's an angel."

"Now you're making fun of me, too?"

Levi laughed and gave Daniel a playful shove. "No, of course not."

\* \* \*

The magi approached the outskirts of Bethlehem. They slowed their camels to a brisk walk. The star still shined before them and remained low enough in the sky to pinpoint the area in the city they should travel toward. With excitement high and anticipation brimming, it took all the stoic discipline they could gather to keep from sprinting this final stretch.

\* \* \*

The team of demons from Jerusalem followed close behind the magi.

"Look at that," Nangar said to Molech's captain when they reached the outskirts of Bethlehem.

"That looks like a battle," the captain said.

"Somebody found the King before us," Nangar said.

"But they haven't defeated Him yet, or the battle would be done." The captain turned to his team of ten lieutenants, each a powerful hulking brute. "Get in there. Destroy Him."

Nangar grabbed the captain by the arm. "Are you not going to report this to Molech?"

"After my blade cuts off the head of the Man of Flesh." The captain yanked his arm free and took off toward the battle.

"These warriors," Nangar said to himself. "They know nothing of subtlety."

He fumbled with a sword and made a few feeble swings.

"I was the one who brought them here. I am the one who should receive credit for finding him. I will be glorified for this victory."

He swung his sword again sped toward the battle.

"I will have my piece of this fight!"

Nangar approached low and fast. By the time he arrived, Molech's team already had the elzurim on the defensive. They pressed them inward, and it looked like they had the superior forces. Nangar picked the nearest defender, extended his sword, shouted, and made his attack.

* * *

In Egypt, Timrok twisted and tried to stretch, but the bindings held tight. He lay flat on his back with a dark warrior's foot on his chest. *Out of the fight. How could I have been so careless?* He lifted his head and looked toward Marr's command center where his team had Marr pinned down. To the north, Elric's beacon shined in the distance.

*The situation in Bethlehem must be dire. I wonder if my team has noticed Elric's beacon.* He held his head up for several moments. *There!* Five lights shot out of the command center and headed north. *Good.* Another light shot upward and disappeared. He let his head drop back down with a thud.

He strained his neck the other direction. *Zaben's stronghold is in trouble.* The power of the heavy beaelzur forces, combined with the relentless pressure of thousands of blood–hungry demons, wore down the angelic defenses. The outer defenses broke down, and the middle defenses became increasingly vulnerable. More and more assaults penetrated all the way to the inner line. *It won't be long now before the stronghold is breached.*

Timrok closed his eyes and clenched his fists.

* * *

The magi dismounted and stood with their mouths open and their eyes wide. The star that led them from Jerusalem stood right above a house, and in the waning dusk its light illuminated that house—and only that house—with a magical glow.

Melchior said, "If we are to believe that the God of Israel is leading us by this star, there is no mistaking to which house it leads."

They stepped up the door, rather out of place in their foreign, bright, and regal garb.

"What now? Do we simply knock?" Caspar said.

"This is why we have come," Balthazar said. He tapped on the door.

A young man cracked the door open, revealing only the warm lamplight from inside.

"Yes?" the man said.

Balthazar bowed his head. "Sir, we are travelers from the far east. We are seeking the newborn King of Israel. We have followed His star to this place."

The man behind the door paused a moment, looking them over, then opened the door.

"Please come in. My name is Joseph. This is my wife, Mary."

"You are very kind. My name is Balthazar. These are my companions Melchior and Caspar."

Caspar looked around at the austere single-room accommodations and the plainly dressed young toddler on Mary's lap, and asked, "Is this child the One whom we seek?"

Joseph and Mary smiled at each other. Joseph answered, "I believe so. This is Jesus. I will tell you our story and you can judge for yourself. But first, please tell us your story and how it is that you came to find us."

The three retold their story as they had done for King Herod. Joseph and Mary sat, smiled, and nodded with understanding expressions. None of the fantastic things they said seemed to surprise Joseph and Mary who took it all in and never showed even a hint of disbelief. The magi finished recounting all that had happened to them, and Joseph laughed aloud and slapped his knees.

"Yes, I definitely think you have found what you were looking for," Joseph said. "Now, let me tell our story."

Joseph began from the very beginning and left out no details. The magi sat with sparkling eyes as he told of the shepherds and their experience with the angelic host in the heavens. They gasped at each fulfillment of prophecy. They hung on every word, and the excitement on their faces couldn't be contained.

* * *

With Timrok's team now in the fight in Bethlehem, Elric dove back into the center of the fray. The room swelled with the sweet smell of the presence of the Holy Spirit as the magi and Joseph shared their stories, and the power of His presence gave strength to Elric's team, who were on their heels from the frenzied onslaught of the growing numbers of enemy attackers. *Even with my extra blade, and those of Lacidar and Timrok's teams plus the additional strength from the King, it will probably not be enough.* Elric shot a desperate glance at Jesus. *Why? Why would the King be willing take on such vulnerable flesh?*

While the humans talked quietly, the chaotic melee in the Middle Realm boiled all around them.

* * *

The great dragon blasted into the command structure in Egypt and exploded in a colossal fireball of energy. The heavy black smoke sank to the ground and rolled outward like a boiling waterfall, and Satan emerged from the smoke, motionless in front of his throne. He waited for Marr and his warriors to climb back to their feet.

He roared at Marr with his eyes blazing, "You fool! The Child is not here. He is in Bethlehem! While you press this meaningless battle here in Egypt, He has remained hidden and undisturbed in Judea. A small band of pitiful warriors has Him surrounded, but they need real power to complete the job. Redirect all your forces to Bethlehem immediately!"

"But lord, I—"

"Immediately!" he blasted with more flames and smoke.

\* \* \*

The battle reached a peak in Bethlehem.

Elric slashed and spun and kicked. *There are too many!*

The attackers pressed fatally close, and Elric now stood as the last single point of defense for the King. He held off four raging demons, but a demon captain slipped through and raced toward the Child.

Elric couldn't reach him.

All time ground to a stop.

The demon raised his awful, jagged black steel high above his head and released the most terrifying, evil screech Elric had ever heard.

Every spirit in the room froze, and every eye turned inward— every demon eye, wild with anticipation of sweet imminent victory; every eye of Elric's team, heavy with dread and bewilderment.

In the stillness of that split second, one of the magi's voices broke through into the Middle Realm. "This truly is the King whom we seek."

Another magi stood and extended his arms with his palms upward. He bowed his head. "The God and Creator of the universe has taken on human flesh to dwell among us"

Luchek laughed and shouted, "And that human flesh will be His undoing! Do it!"

The demon brought his sword crashing down toward the Child's head.

Elric cried out, "Nooooo!"

Too late. The course of the demon's blade could not be stopped.

*This is it!* The event that would forever change the entire universe.

# 18

# A LIGHT IN THE DARKNESS

## Birth plus 16 months

*f*lash!

The beaelzur blade reached the Son of Man, and an ear–splitting crack and a brilliant flash of heavenly white light exploded in the Middle Realm. Elric staggered backward. *Blind! I can't see!* He blinked, straining through the fog of the moment. *Did the demon truly vanquish the King? What will the Godhead look like with part of Him destroyed? Did all that power transfer to the spirit who crushed Him?* Slowly, the blindness became a hazy white blur. Finally, obscure forms came into focus.

All the spirits stood around the room, squinting and rubbing their eyes.

The young Child bounced happily on Mary's lap.

Joseph and the three magi talked calmly.

No sign of the demonic assailant. He had vanished.

"They can't touch Him!" shouted Elric. "He is still the Almighty King, even in human flesh, and they can't touch Him! Drive these traitorous creatures out of here."

*Crash!* Swords collided, sending sparks sizzling through the spiritual air. Mayhem erupted—war shouts, flashes of light, clouds of sulfur.

Through the roof, dodging a blur of enemy swords, Grigor burst in and alighted in front of Elric. "The time has come," Grigor shouted. An enemy sword sliced through the air toward Grigor's neck. He ducked, and Elric drove his sword over Grigor's head and through the forehead of the attacker.

"Yes!" Elric shouted. "Finally!"

Elric withdrew his sword. Grigor was gone. Elric smiled. *Faster than lightning, this one.* Elric shot straight up with one powerful burst from his wings to a height much higher than before—high enough to be seen well over the horizon. With two authoritative words from Elric's mouth, his sword erupted again in dazzling light—this time, blue. The signal surged across the sky as far away as Egypt.

* * *

Zaben hovered at the top center of the angelic stronghold in Egypt. All around him, the circle of beaelzurim pressed their frenzied attack. Thousands of fiery missiles blasted inward. Sparks and flashes of light glowed through the sulfurous cloud that stretched from the top of the stronghold dome to the ground. The cloud hung like death in the spiritual air for miles around the stronghold and shrouded the movements of the advancing hordes. The never-ending tumult— shrieks, exploding fireballs, war shouts, clanging steel—climbed to a deafening level.

The outer layers of defense had fallen. Thousands of elzur warriors and lieutenants lay in heaps around the perimeter, bound and unable to fight. The captains and commanders in the middle ramparts now bore the increasing pressure, and they were being smothered by the sheer numbers. The inner ring of generals held their line, but not for much longer.

Zaben raised his eyes above the battle and gazed again across the northern horizon. *Come on . . . come on . . .*

A general to his left fell. Two beaelzur generals, three dark commanders, and a dozen demon warriors took hold of the mighty angelic general. They tore at his wings, pierced and slashed him, and immobilized every limb. He tumbled downward in the center of a writhing mass of flames, light, and smoke.

An earsplitting shriek from the left rose above the clamor. Zaben spun around toward the sound. There, from the direction of Marr's headquarters, came two additional awful shadows. Marr. Satan. *Oh, no! This is the end. We only have seconds . . .*

Zaben turned again to the north. *Come on . . . we can't hold on any . . .*

A pulsing blue beacon appeared in the dark sky. Elric's signal from Bethlehem.

Satan and Marr reached the edge of the battle, barking orders to call off the assault.

"Now!" Zaben shouted. "Now! Now! Now!"

Zaben's five warriors blew a battle signal on crystal clear silver trumpets. The pure tones rang out over the noise of the battle, and at the sound, every angelic warrior shot straight up into the sky. Fallen elzurim, loosed by their comrades, freed the other fallen warriors and joined the others high above the citadel. Within a single breath's time, all angelic resistance from the stronghold disappeared.

*Crash!* The spiritual dome of the stronghold imploded. Like a wall of water bursting through a shattered dam, the momentum of all the attackers smashed inward. Marr and Satan tumbled in amid the tidal wave, and their orders to pull back were drowned in a sea of confusion and chaos.

The trumpets sounded again. In an instant, the angelic host dropped like a curtain over the beaelzurim horde. The host formed a new dome, this time with the enemy trapped within. The elzur generals lined the innermost layer and concentrated their efforts on Satan, Marr, and the enemy generals. The elzur commanders and captains made up the middle layer of defenses. The remainder of the warriors formed the outer shell. The entire momentum of the battle shifted in a single instant.

Zaben hovered over the dome with a glint in his eyes. Confusion, disarray, and shock rumbled from within the dome. *It will be hours before they realize what happened. Probably a day before they can counter with any kind of organized attack. I hope Elric can keep his timeline because I don't know how long we'll be able to keep them contained.*

* * *

In Bethlehem, the surge of light from Elric's blade subsided, and he lowered it with a smile. He stared in the direction of Egypt. He took a deep breath. *Time is now my enemy. We must move quickly.* He glanced down at the melee below. *But first, I need to separate the King from this battle.*

Grigor appeared, hovering face to face with Elric. "The King's position has been compromised," Grigor said, "and none of the enemy who knows His location can be allowed to go free." Grigor smiled. "'Vengeance is mine,' says the Lord of Hosts. Speak the word."

Elric's eyes grew wide. He raised his sword high above his head and shouted, "Vengeance! Vengeance for the King!"

His words rolled up into a ball of blue light and shot up the blade of his sword. It reached the tip, and the ball of light exploded and surged back down. A sapphire–blue ring of glowing energy burst from the bottom of Elric's sword's handle. It started as the size of a man's fist and shot downward and outward in an ever–expanding disk. It swept through the air of the Middle Realm, and every elzur blade it touched burst into intense blue flame.

Elric laughed and dove into the center of the fight.

His team came to life with renewed purpose. With the blazing authority they now wielded, he and his team decimated the enemy who had possessed the upper hand moments before. One by one, they reduced the beaelzurim to wisps of dissipating sulfuric vapor. Many of them tried to escape, but Elric's team apprehended each one and dispatched them to the abyss. Not since the days of the Nephilim had so many beaelzurim been confined to the abyss in a single day. The victory was complete and the battle decisive.

One demon remained, and Elric pinned him between his glowing blade and the blades of Jessik and Kaylar inside the room where the battle had begun.

"Luchek!" Elric rumbled.

Luchek stood limp and trembling.

Elric's whole body shimmered with a white–blue aura, and the flame of vengeance pulsed and danced between the floating blade components of his sword. He raised the blade to Luchek's bare neck. "You dared to try to strike the King?" He pressed his blade close, and Luchek stretched his defiant chin upward out of reach. Elric paused. He growled. He snapped his blade back with discipline and purpose.

"You deserve the abyss," he said through clenched teeth. "But I have other plans for you. I want you to bear the shame of your defeat before your master. Report to him everything that happened here today. Tell him the King cannot be touched. Tell him what happens to anyone who tries."

Elric said to Jessik and Kaylar, "Escort this traitor to Jerusalem. Make sure he stands before Satan."

The two shoved Luchek out of the room, and Elric turned to Jenli. "I need you to go with them and lead this detail. Hold him someplace hidden between here and Jerusalem for three days. Then take him all the way into Herod's palace."

"Shall I walk directly into the enemy's stronghold?" Jenli asked with raised eyebrows.

"The flame of vengeance will remain on your swords for the entire mission until you have delivered the prisoner. The enemy will keep their distance. The Lord will be with you."

Jenli smiled and looked at his blazing blue sword. "In His service."

"Our quest has taken a new turn," Elric said. "We now know the enemy cannot touch the King directly. However, the sword of man is still a threat. Now, the enemy will concentrate on working through men. We will continue to keep the King hidden, but we must watch for enemy movements among men."

* * *

Jenli marched out of the room and left Elric alone with the humans. For the first time since the battle began, Elric turned his attention to the Physical Realm.

The magi filed out the front door and left Joseph and Mary alone, looking at each other with shrugs and raised eyebrows. Moments later, the magi filed back in, laboring under the weight of carved wooden trunks. Joseph and Mary looked down at their feet, up at the ceiling, over at each other, and smiled silly, awkward grins.

Elric chuckled.

Bowing low before Jesus, the three magi each opened their trunks. The warm aroma of the spices wafted through the room, and the gold treasure glistened in the lamplight. Joseph and Mary gasped. Mary covered her open mouth with both hands.

"This is . . . more money than we have ever seen in one place," Joseph said. "We can't accept this."

Balthazar said, "This is our gift to the King. You would not dishonor our service to Him, would you?"

Mary put her hand on Joseph's shoulder. Her eyes filled with tears.

"No," Joseph said. "Of course not. We are humbled by your generosity and honored by your gift. Thank you."

The magi lingered for almost an hour, taking turns touching and holding the Son of Man, giving thanks for the amazing opportunity, and worshiping Him as though He was literally God on earth.

Elric smiled and breathed in the wonderful fragrance of the worship rising out of the room toward heaven. *They actually understand. Of course, He is God in the flesh on earth.* He glanced around the room—the room that was a battlefield an hour ago. He shook his head. *How is it that I was surprised by the inability of the enemy to directly touch Him? He is still the King regardless of the form He might take. He doesn't need the elzurim help to protect Him physically from these spirits. Even after all we have been through so far, I still have much to learn about our role in this amazing plan.*

He took in a deep breath and let it out slowly. The unfolding of the great mysteries of the King made this whole adventure rich and satisfying beyond anything he had imagined.

# 19

## FLIGHT

### Birth plus 16 months

The magi stepped out of Joseph and Mary's room into the quiet of the early night. Their faces glowed, and their eyes sparkled. The stars twinkled in the heavens.

"Now what?" Caspar said.

"It's too late to travel back to Jerusalem," Melchior said.

"Shall we find a room in one of the inns?" Caspar asked.

Balthazar looked up at the stars. "No," he said. "I think I should like to sleep under the stars tonight."

Melchior nodded. "The lights of heaven. I agree."

"Under the stars," Caspar said.

They led their camels out of town on foot at a contemplative pace. They walked without talking, not sure how to put into words all that stirred within their spirits. They found a suitable place outside of town and set up camp. They didn't erect tents but laid their bed mats out in a row on the ground. Then they lay on their backs and gazed at the stars.

After several minutes of silence, Balthazar said, "After all the years of studying the stars and looking for meaning in them, tonight the heavenly expanse seems completely different."

Caspar said, "We saw, and touched, the very One who spoke all those stars into existence."

"I almost feel a personal connection with them," Melchior said.

They each lay awake soaking up the majesty of the heavens and thinking about the great Creator. The entire journey, starting with the original appearance of the King's star, had left them forever changed. Eventually sleep overtook them and they slipped into peaceful dreams.

Elric waited there for them. He spoke to all of them in a dream, his words floating like a sparkling white cloud over the men in the Middle Realm. "Today the King has made Himself known to you. Blessed are you among men. Now receive this word from the Lord— do not return to Jerusalem and report to Herod, for he seeks to kill the Child. Do not fear. Return to your home in peace for the Lord is with you." The cloud hovered over the magi until it seeped into their spirits and flashed onto the backdrop of their minds.

He leaned down low and touched each one on the forehead. "Receive the word of the Lord," he said. With each touch he spoke. "Peace. Joy. Strength."

* * *

Elric imparted peace, joy, and strength to the last magi and stood up straight. He opened his wings, looked back at the three sleeping men for a moment, smiled, and flew back into Bethlehem. He entered Joseph and Mary's room. The lamp had been put out, and everyone slept. Timrok's warriors stood guard.

"Time is short," Elric said to the team. "We need to get Jesus out of Bethlehem before the enemy can regroup. By morning there will surely be additional scouts from Molech to check on the status of Nangar and the other scouts, so I need to speak to Joseph directly in a dream. And the message needs to be direct and unambiguous."

Elric stood over Joseph and placed his hand above Joseph's head. His hand began to glow. He spoke, "Get up! Take the Child and His mother and flee to Egypt, and stay there until I tell you; for Herod is going to search for the Child to kill Him."

And then, somewhere between the misty dreamlands and consciousness, Elric gave Joseph a shake.

\* \* \*

Joseph awoke with a start. *Who nudged me?* He turned toward Mary—sound asleep, with her back to him. *There is some kind of presence here.* He strained his eyes into the dark room. No one there but Mary and the Baby.

*What a dream. Wait. Was it a dream, or was it real?*

An angel—shining white—with an urgent message. *It seemed real. As real as if the angel was standing right there.* He squinted again into the darkness. *He looked different from the one I saw before we got married. But everything else about it felt exactly the same.*

He sat perfectly still, his heart thumping in his ears. He forced himself to take slow, deep breaths.

*That was real. It was more than a dream. I received a message from the Lord.*

He grinned in the darkness and rubbed the prickly bumps on his arms.

*A message from the Lord. How amazing that He would send a messenger to tell me . . . wait . . . he said Jesus is in danger! Jesus is in danger, and we need to flee the country immediately!*

He turned to Mary and woke her with a gentle shake.

"Mary, I had a dream from the Lord. An angel told me that Herod is going to search for Jesus to kill Him. We have to flee to Egypt."

Mary wiped the sleep from her eyes and mumbled, "Flee to Egypt? When?"

Joseph jumped up and reached for his tunic. "Tonight. We need to pack up and go right now." His voice carried resolve, and he moved with urgency.

Mary sprang out of bed.

"You pack in here," Joseph said, lighting an oil lamp. "I'm going out to hitch up the cart and pack my tools."

Mary slipped on a robe. "Should we wake Omer and Miriam and tell them we are leaving?"

Joseph stopped. *Omer and Miriam have been so good to us—we can't disappear without saying goodbye. On the other hand, if Herod's soldiers were to interrogate Omer or Miriam, we'd all be at risk.*

"No," Joseph said. "It will be too dangerous for both them and us. It's best if they don't know anything. Leave enough money on the table to cover next month's rent." His tone softened. "I don't like leaving like this, but we have no other choice."

It took little time to pack all their meager belongings onto the carts and begin trudging off into the unknown darkness. Joseph estimated they were in the second watch of the night and determined to put as many miles between them and Bethlehem as he could before sunrise. While Mary and the Baby slept in the back of the donkey cart, Joseph pulled the hand cart and pressed hard down a southward trail under a partial moon.

\* \* \*

Elric walked with Joseph, giving him the physical strength to bear the load and keep the pace swift. His words of strength and energy penetrated Joseph's spirit and brought vitality to his flesh. They needed to put distance behind them—more distance than would be physically possible for Joseph and the donkey.

He sent Lacidar and his team back to their place in Judea. Jenli's team stayed behind to deliver Luchek to Jerusalem. Timrok's team went ahead of him to clear their way. He remained the lone visible escort. Low profile, nothing to attract attention. *Even though the enemy can't touch the King directly, we don't want to get caught alone in the middle of the desert by the horde of angry beaelzurim that could be raging toward Bethlehem from Egypt at any moment.*

"Hurry," he spoke to Joseph. "We must hasten the pace."

*The boldness of this plan is beyond me. Behind us, the anger of an earthly king and a powerful demon commander will chase us like wildfire. At the same time, we run toward Egypt, directly into the largest confluence of enemy forces ever amassed on earth. The timing will be critical. The success of this journey hinges on how long Zaben can keep the enemy contained. The pressure building under the lid of the cauldron Zaben has created must be incredible.*

"Faster," he said to Joseph. "Faster still."

\* \* \*

Morning light brought intriguing tales of nighttime dreams of the magi. They compared their dreams, and the three wise men from the east were amazed by the vivid reality of the visions of the angel. And the message delivered to each of them was exactly the same. There could be no doubt they had received guidance from heaven, and the experience only helped to strengthen their newfound faith in the living King. And so, having been warned in a dream not to return to Herod, they departed for their own country by another way, full of joy, full of faith, and full of anticipation for what the child King would do for the world.

\* \* \*

Morning light brought two of Molech's scouts to Bethlehem. They scoured the streets from north to south, but they found no sign of the original team Molech had sent the day before. In fact, the whole town seemed quiet. Too quiet.

\* \* \*

The morning found Joseph at the end of his strength. They had covered a good distance during the night, but he needed to stop and rest. He parked the carts under the shade of some trail-side trees. He set out a bucket of water and some of the barley straw from the supply in the cart for the donkey, and they all ate under the warmth of the morning sun.

"I am going to try to sleep," Joseph said. "Let Jesus run around and play. But watch for soldiers, and don't talk to anyone who might pass by on the trail. We need to keep moving, so don't let me sleep long."

Mary nodded.

Joseph pulled off his sandals and lay down in the back of the cart. He took a deep breath, and by the time he had let the air out, sleep overtook him like a crashing wave.

Joseph's eyes popped open. He blinked and squinted from the light. He sat up and looked at the position of the sun in the sky. *It's not yet midday. Good. I didn't sleep too long.* He hopped off the back of the cart and looked for Mary, who he found playing with Jesus under the shade of a tree.

"You're awake already?" she called out. "You didn't sleep long."

"I feel good," Joseph answered. "Strong, rested. I am ready to go."

Mary folded up the blanket she was sitting on, hoisted Jesus back into the cart, and climbed in after Him. Joseph drank from a water skin and popped a date into his mouth. He walked over to the donkey and stroked its neck with one hand while holding a handful of straw in the other.

"How are you doing, girl?" Joseph said to the donkey. "Did you get some rest? We have another long trail ahead of us today."

The donkey munched the straw and shifted her hooves with quick, energetic movements.

"It's strange," Joseph said to Mary. "After a hard night of travel, and with so little sleep, I don't understand why I feel as strong as I do. My feet aren't even sore."

"Maybe the Lord is strengthening you," Mary said.

"Maybe." Joseph lifted the handles of his hand cart and pushed it toward the trail. "We're going to need it. I still sense we are in great danger."

With a constant inner urgency driving him, Joseph pressed onward for three days. Little rest, unexplainable strength, and no signs of Roman soldiers.

* * *

It had been three days since Zaben received Elric's beacon and trapped all of Marr's forces within his stronghold. At first the containment of those forces presented little challenge. The trap had stunned and confused the enemy, and the spirit of the King empowered all the elzur forces. Over the last day, though, the pressure within the stronghold built, and to Zaben's dismay, he could feel the cloud of heavenly strength lifting.

At the center of the tangled mass of beaelzurim stood Satan, huge and dominating with his flaming arms stretched upward. Molten fire shot out of his mouth and hands and fingertips like lightning, and a shroud of thick black smoke billowed around him. The bolts of fire blasted through the beaelzurim from one to another and infused them with unnatural strength. The generals' fireballs became larger and more devastating; the dark warriors' blades burned with red–hot flames; and their fury blazed out of control. Instead of the chaotic mayhem of selfish individual efforts, the bolts of fire from the dark master brought the demons under his control resulting in more unified and coordinated attacks. The mounting pressure could not be contained much longer. Without direct intervention by the King Himself, Zaben's stronghold would burst soon.

The first of the beaelzur generals blasted through the last layer of elzur defenses in the late afternoon. Hundreds of dark warriors spewed through the hole. Then, under the influence of Satan, they all uncharacteristically turned back to help the rest of their comrades break through. The freed demons fought and clawed and peeled back the elzurim from around the newly formed breach. More and more of the raging beaelzurim erupted through the fissure until an unrestrained stream of blackness exploded outward.

The dome around Zaben's stronghold created by the tight layers of elzurim looked like a glowing white mountain, and the demons shot out from the top of the dome like a volcanic eruption, creating an ever–widening hole. The eruption vomited black smoke and fire high into the atmosphere and ripped shards of the white mountain away from the rim of the hole. Within only a few minutes, all the vile contents of the stronghold escaped, and a massive black cloud of evil gathered and swirled above. The elzurim broke away from the dome and engaged the demons in the air, but with the unconstrained sky to maneuver through, they could not restrain the movements of the enemy.

The last of the evil horde gathered, and the entire mass boiled its way northward like a dark cloud.

# 20

## CROSSED PATHS

### Birth plus 16 months

It was almost evening at the far southern reaches of Israel below Beersheba, and the widow Hannah puttered about in her garden where ripe grapes hung from the arbor over the vegetable beds. The sun sank low in the west, and a strange dark storm approached from the south. The long black fingers of the boiling clouds moved fast, and the silent air around Hannah's house felt stagnant and eerie. Hannah didn't see any rain coming, but in the distance, flashes of lightning illuminated the clouds from within.

She glanced to the north and saw a couple of travelers kicking up a small cloud of dust on the southward trail. There appeared to be a donkey–drawn cart, a man pulling another small cart, and a woman walking beside. Hannah wondered where they might be headed and whether they had a place to shelter from the incoming weather.

She placed a cluster of grapes next to the black radishes in her basket.

* * *

Inside Hannah's house, the regional elzur captains and lieutenants gathered, reviewing the day's events and discussing strategies for the coming days. A quiet tension gripped the room. They all stared at the war map, transfixed by the huge black cloud of evil headed their direction from Egypt. Its final destination wasn't clear, and they hadn't received any information about what they were to do about it. For a long time they stood without saying a word and watched the ominous horde advancing northward.

Elric appeared through the back wall. All eyes turned toward him. He moved to the war map, rubbing his chin.

He muttered aloud, "They are nearer than I had hoped. This is going to be very close." He turned to the four captains. "I shall explain more in a moment. First, I must attend to something. If I don't get this done right now, we will have a difficult night."

Elric stepped out of the house and walked over to Hannah, who had pulled the last of a few weeds that had invaded her garden. He had no time for a dream—he would need to speak to her spirit while she was awake. He eyed the incoming storm, took a deep breath, turned, and spoke with a clear, strong voice.

"The travelers you see coming from the northern trail need your help. They are traveling with a young child. Invite them into your home. They must enter your house quickly and spend the night. They are weary from their travels and need at least a full day to rest."

Elric's words rolled up into a cloud of light and shot toward Hannah. The words hit her spirit, clad in a thick layer of light. Her armor soaked in his words like a thirsty sponge, and the message sank deep into her spirit. Elric smiled.

The stark contrast of the two of them standing together made Elric shake his head. Hannah looked small and frail. Her full height barely reached the middle of his huge solid torso. In the waning sunlight her slight frame cast a long shadow on the earth, while his enormous mass left no shadow at all. Elric crossed his arms and waited. The irony of this simple, single old woman, silhouetted against the red sky with the vast storm of evil bearing down them, struck Elric. His words reached her spirit, but did she hear with the ears of her heart? Would she choose to act? The course of all creation hinged on the actions of this one lady in this critical moment in time. Would she fulfill her role in history?

Hannah stopped, looked toward the travelers, set down her basket, and began walking toward the trail, several paces away.

Elric chuckled. *If only all humans responded like that. It would make my job so much easier.*

Hannah reached the trail before the travelers could make it that far south. She headed up the trail to meet them.

"Hello, welcome!" she called out from a distance, waving. They met on the trail, and she welcomed them again. "My name is Hannah. Welcome, welcome."

Joseph looked ragged but managed a tired smile.

"You look exhausted," Hannah continued. "How long have you been on the road?"

Joseph brought his small troop to a halt. "Three nights and three days."

"And with a baby. Good heavens, no wonder you're tired. What you need is a good hot meal and a bed to sleep in. Come. My house is right over here. I will take care of you."

Joseph's voice sounded tired and distant. "Thank you for your kindness," he said, "but we couldn't—"

"Oh, shush, shush." Hannah stepped up close to Joseph and turned toward the south. "See that storm? You don't want your pretty young wife and that baby out in the weather when that hits, do you?"

"Well . . . no."

"And do you have a place to stay tonight?"

"No."

"Then it is settled. I insist. You shall spend the night here."

Elric laughed. *She is good. I'm glad she is on our side.* And to Joseph he said aloud, "You should listen to her. It will do you good to get some rest."

Joseph looked toward the south. He gave an uneasy shudder. He looked to Mary, who gave a shy smile. He turned to Hannah and gave in with a grateful smile and nod.

They all walked back toward the house, but their pace was slow. Elric checked the progress of the dark clouds. *We're not moving fast enough. From the speed of the incoming horde, we won't get indoors before the enemy passes overhead.*

"Keep moving. Keep moving," Elric prodded. *This is going to be much too close.*

Hannah, Joseph, and Mary looked at the incoming clouds and quickened their pace. Joseph's cart bumped over a rock, and several tools spilled out of a pouch hanging on the side. They clattered to ground. All forward motion stopped. Joseph collected his dropped tools.

"Hurry, hurry," Elric urged.

A clap of thunder sent them scurrying. They reached Hannah's garden, and Hannah stopped and turned aside.

"One moment," Hannah called out. "I need to get my basket."

"No!" shouted Elric. "There's no time. We're not going to make it."

"Here it is," Hannah said.

"Go, go, go!" Elric lowered his voice, looking upward with a grimace.

Joseph shuffled the two women and the Baby through Hannah's front door and turned back. "I'm going to tie up the donkey and batten down the carts."

The door closed as the first edge of the dark cloud passed directly above the house. Elric looked up, let out a huge sigh, and stepped inside.

Elric entered the room and found the entire host of elzurim on their knees with heads bowed low. An awkward tension filled the air. The King hadn't told them to rise or even seemed to notice them. Elric broke the silence. "Arise, my friends. Behold the King in human flesh. He will not speak to you, for He is but a child of one year."

The room burst into excited chatter.

"Incredible!"

"How is it possible?"

"Does He need to eat like a normal human?"

"After all these centuries, it's even more amazing than I had imagined!"

"Quiet!" interrupted Elric. He motioned to the map and pointed his finger upward. "In case you have forgotten, we are not alone."

A deathly hush fell over the room. They all crowded around the map.

Elric spoke in a low whisper. "The Lord has promised He would overshadow this place with His protection and hide us, but we must be still and wait."

The weight of the danger passing close overhead felt heavy in the room as the elzurim watched the black cloud move over the map. Several of the warriors drew their swords and stared at the ceiling. This small group of angels was isolated and surrounded, and Elric could see in their eyes that they knew it. They remained still and waited. And waited.

For more than an hour the cloud of evil overshadowed their hideout. All the while the elzurim watched the map and waited. After the tension of the first half of an hour passed, the warriors couldn't help but steal glances at the young Child in the room with them. There He was. The promise of the ages. They were in awe. They were captivated.

They were surrounded by the enemy.

* * *

Molech's scouts in Bethlehem stood before Satan, who bristled with rage.

"Where is He? Where is the Child?" Satan roared.

"We do not know. Our lord, Molech, sent us here from Jerusalem two days ago to find another scouting detail he had sent to find the Child the day before. We have searched the entire city for two days, and we can find neither the Child nor the other scouts. We are afraid to return to Jerusalem without answers, so we have remained here and continued our search."

"This is the place." Satan seethed, glaring at Omer and Miriam's inn. "He was in this house. And He was surrounded by a small team led by a pathetic imp named Luchek. Have you seen him?"

"No, my lord."

"Then the King's warriors must have gotten the upper hand and stole the Child away to another hiding place."

Satan turned to Marr, "We will go to Jerusalem and see what Molech knows. Have your warriors conduct a more thorough search here in Bethlehem. Then spread out and scour all the surrounding regions. Begin here and go north, west, and east. Go as far as a three-days' walk for a human. We know He has to be within that radius."

"Shall I send any forces south?"

"No, fool. We came from the south. If He had been traveling south, I would have surely seen Him. Give orders that if anyone finds Him, he must report immediately to me. I will set up my throne in Herod's palace for now."

"Yes, my lord."

A loathsome black mist crept through Bethlehem that night, seeping through every crevice and leaving a sinister chill in the air.

Dogs barked, livestock rustled, and birds fluttered off. Babies all over town woke their parents with inconsolable cries and fussed all night long. It was a restless night, and all the people were glad to see the sunrise the next morning.

# 21

## MORNING

**Birth plus 16 months**

*E*lric looked over the three bundles on makeshift beds in Hannah's front room. They slept hard, even though the morning sun blazed through the windows. Timrok's five warriors were in the room with him. Some shuffled their feet. Most knelt. All stared at the sleeping Child.

"A different picture from what we faced last night," Prestus said.

"Mmm," replied Elric, nodding his head. "I wasn't sure we were going to make it in time. It was close."

Chase knelt closest to the Child. He stared without blinking. "I see Him," Chase said, "but I can't comprehend it."

Elric chuckled. "You should have seen the looks on the faces of the regional captains and lieutenants last night."

Elric listened to the deep breathing of the sleeping humans and folded his arms. "This is good. They needed this rest. We will stay here at least a day. It's a safe place for them to regain their strength for the rest of the journey. Now I have a new task for you five."

The warriors jumped into a smart line. They stood at attention, but their eyes kept glancing back toward Jesus. Elric smiled.

"Go find Zaben at the Egyptian palace. Gather him and his team. Then make a search for Timrok. It is my hope that he is only bound at the battle site and not carried off to captivity. If he is under guard, free him. Then bring them all back here."

"In His service," the team responded in unison. They turned and filed out of the house.

Elric took a deep breath and soaked in the peaceful quiet. They still had far to travel, but this was a welcome stop.

\* \* \*

In the field south of Nazareth, the morning came with peaceful stillness as Levi and Daniel watched the sun come up over the flock. It was one of those quiet, contemplative mornings—when the soul melds with the warming red glow and the mind searches for truth.

"Tell me more about the Messiah," Daniel said.

Levi leaned back on his elbows. "You are thinking of your vision again, aren't you? Very well. The Messiah—Moses tells us he will be a great prophet."

"What does a prophet do?"

"Tells about future things. But mostly, he hears directly from God and speaks His word to the people."

"Have you ever seen a prophet?"

"No. There has not been the voice of a true prophet in Israel for 400 years."

Daniel sat with his chin propped up in his hands and watched the orange horizon turn yellow.

"Hmm. What else?" Daniel asked, staring off into the sky.

"We know the Messiah will be a great healer. He will make blind eyes see, deaf ears hear, the lame will—"

"Could He heal my ear?" Daniel turned to see Levi's face.

Levi didn't flinch. "Of course. He's the Messiah."

"He sounds wonderful." Daniel leaned back on his elbows. "What else?"

"He will bring peace to Israel."

"How?"

"By defeating all our enemies."

"You mean the Romans?"

"All our enemies."

Daniel sat up. "Will He raise up an army?"

"I suppose He will have to."

"Will we be able to fight in His army?"

Levi smiled. "If your vision is true, and the Messiah was born a year and a half ago, I suppose we will both be able to."

Daniel jumped up and grabbed a stick. He slashed it through an imaginary battle. "Won't it be great—you and I, fighting side by side, behind the Messiah, crushing the Roman army?"

Levi smiled and nodded his head. "I will be there, right beside you."

\* \* \*

The morning in Herod's palace came with anything but peace. Satan set himself up in Herod's throne room, and a flurry of spiritual activity buzzed throughout the compound. The soaring ceiling and tall, majestic marble columns lining the vast room seemed more fitting for the regal black throne than the shambled ruins they had left in Egypt, and this new seat of power pulsed with energy. The commanders stationed throughout the room issued orders to their captains, and a never–ending swarm of messengers shuttled in and out. Molech stood to the left and behind the dark lord's throne, centered in the room and lifted high on a platform of billowing black smoke. Molech stood in silence after the berating barrage of rebuke he received during the night. He crossed his defiant arms and glared at the one who had trumped his place of power. Marr stood to the right of the throne and overcompensated for his failure in Egypt by barking an endless stream of orders to all his commanders. His words burned with anger, and he threw insults and blame at his officers like poisoned knives. The wounds deflected off of the commanders to the captains, who passed them on to their warriors. The upheaval in the throne room created a boiling torrent of malice that spewed out of the palace compound in every direction.

Into this seething darkness three unlikely forms in glowing white marched.

Jenli led the detail with his sword held at arm's length in front of him, the special blade formed by Timrok ablaze in scintillating blue flame. With his chiseled chin set with determination, his bright eyes darted about, pinpointing every potential threat. Behind him walked his prisoner, Luchek, whose arms and torso had been shackled with glowing white cords of pulsing energy. Luchek's head drooped low, and his eyes revealed the dread of his upcoming fate. Behind him walked Jessik and Kaylar, bright and shimmering. They, too, carried blazing swords held out for all to see. They prodded their prisoner along, eying their surroundings and turning around as they walked.

The brazenness of this march had exactly the effect Jenli wanted to see. The moment they entered the outer palace grounds, every demon along their path stopped and looked. With faces of gaping disbelief, each demon would reach for his sword—but then spot the flaming swords of vengeance and jump back out of reach. Jenli continued his march with purpose, never slowing or turning.

Jenli drove deeper into the enemy's stronghold, and the numbers of beaelzurim grew. Hundreds surrounded them on every side. In front of him, a group of dark warriors formed a wall, blocking his path. He pressed forward, and the masses gave way. They closed in around them, keeping a safe, but threatening, distance. Jenli approached the main palace. Hundreds of hulking demons lined the roof's edge like grotesque living gargoyles, and thousands more swarmed in and around the building. He clenched his jaw and held his sword up high.

After what seemed like an eternal march, Jenli and his team entered the main throne room of the palace. The room fell silent, and every sinister eye turned toward the trespassers. The commanders all held their palms upward, holding blistering red fireballs of energy that grew and pulsated while preparing to be unleashed. Every other beaelzurim in the room prepared their jagged blades for battle. The one on the throne sat—unmoved, unimpressed, and unthreatened. Without a word he waited for Jenli to approach his throne. Once Jenli reached the foot of the throne, he stopped and peered with an icy stare into the deep emptiness of the eyes of the dark traitorous cherub.

Satan broke the silence. "So, lieutenant, have you and your army come to send me to the abyss?" His words dripped with pompous deprecation.

Jenli stood firm. "May the Lord rebuke you." Stepping to the side, he said, "I have come to deliver a prisoner."

The two warriors pressed Luchek forward and his shackles disappeared with a silent flash. Without another word, Jenli turned and walked between Jessik and Kaylar toward the other side of the room where they had entered. He passed the two, and they did an about face and followed two steps behind. All three still held their blazing swords, but now they held them outward and pointed slightly down as if to say, "Our work here is done."

Every fiber of Jenli's being wanted to shoot straight up and disappear into the air, but he determined to walk out of this stronghold with all the dignity by which he had entered. So, he and his team marched out through the back wall without looking back and continued through the courtyards past the marble colonnades and thousands of enemy forces. Their pace remained slow and deliberate. Once they reached a place well outside the palace compound, they took to the wing and shot northward in case they might be followed.

As they flew, their swords flickered for several seconds, and then the brilliant blue flames went out. Jenli watched with disappointment as the power receded, and with reluctance he returned his cold steel to its scabbard. The other two followed suit with sad smiles.

Jenli pushed his sword into place and laughed. "Wouldn't you love to have been able to stay and watch Luchek get interrogated?"

"Not I," replied Kaylar. "It is not going to be pleasant."

\* \* \*

"You had Him! You had Him, and you let Him get away!" Satan suspended Luchek in mid-air with his massive hand wrapped around Luchek's throat. He shook Luchek like a limp rag doll and flung him across the room accompanied by a blast of fire from his fingertips. Luchek flailed out through the back wall. Satan snorted a puff of fire and smoke from his nostrils.

"Go get him and bring him back," he growled.

A moment later, two commanders carried Luchek into the throne room. Each had a hold of one arm, which left Luchek's feet dangling well above the floor. Satan regained his chokehold. Luchek dangled before him.

"How could you let Him get away?" This time he waited for an answer.

"They all were empowered by the flame of the vengeance on their swords. We had no chance against them."

"Of course your puny little team had no chance. And yet, you knew His location for over a year! You had plenty of chances to tell me! But instead, you squandered our best opportunity."

He shook Luchek again and gave him another fiery fling. The helpless form careened out the back wall again, and Satan gave another snort and rolled his eyes.

"Bring him back again," he muttered.

With Satan's grip around Luchek's throat again, the grilling continued.

"Tell me everything about the battle. Did you see Him? What did He do? Were there cherubim?"

Luchek scowled and gave a defiant sneer. "The battle was going very well, as a matter of fact. There were no cherubim. In fact, a captain was the strongest of their forces, and we had them on the defensive. Then, I personally fought my way into the house and saw the Child. He looked like any normal human child. He didn't seem to notice us. I don't know if He could even see us. Like I said, the battle was going very well for us. One of my team was able to fight his way past the defenses and reach the Child."

"He actually reached Him?"

"Yes, I saw the whole thing . . . all the way up until the moment his sword struck the Child."

The throne room became dead silent.

"What happened?"

"There was a blinding flash, and then my warrior was gone. Instantly to the abyss."

"An elzur struck him?"

"No. There were no elzurim even near him. It was the contact itself. The Son of Man cannot be touched. I think even the angelic captain was surprised. He shouted something to his team and disappeared. Seconds later every one of the elzurim had a flaming sword, and it was all over for us. As far as I know, I am the only one left. The captain spared me so I could come back here and relay the whole story to you. He wanted you to know that even though the King has human flesh, we are not able to directly strike Him."

Satan roared. Fire exploded from his mouth and hands. The fire filled the entire room. The larger, stronger spirits shielded their faces and eyes until the firestorm subsided, but the smaller spirits were blasted from the room with the flame's front wave. Luchek still hung suspended in the dark lord's left hand.

"Where did He go?" Satan demanded through clenched teeth.

"I . . . do not . . . know," Luchek gasped through his constricted throat.

The fire exploded again. Satan shook his ragdoll again and gave him another toss. This time, after the fire settled, he didn't send for Luchek to be retrieved.

# 22

## A CRY IN RAMAH

### Birth plus 16 months

*H*erod and several of his attendants and officials attended to the morning business of state in the throne room. Herod pounded his fist on the armrest of his throne as one of his officials received the brunt of his discontent. Herod had a sharp, angry headache, and the very air he breathed felt laden with vexation. He looked around the room, and it appeared everyone else also had edgy nerves. Every thought and action seemed to take extraordinary effort. He had already received several reports of bad news and was threatening his official with his life when a centurion entered the court and requested an immediate audience with the king.

"Your highness," the centurion said, "I bring news from the field."

Herod snapped back, "It had better be good news. I have had enough bad news already this morning."

"The detail of soldiers you sent to Bethlehem the day before yesterday did not find any signs of the magi from the east."

Herod gave a disgusted "Hmmph."

"However, I am glad to report that one of my scouts on the eastern border spotted them crossing it yesterday. It appears they headed south initially and then turned east. They have departed Israel and are headed back to their own country."

"Did they find what they were looking for?"

"I do not know, sir. We did not make any contact. Shall we pursue them?"

"No. There would be no value in that. Thank you. You are dismissed."

Herod tapped the armrest of his throne. *The magi must have given up on their quest and went on their way—which means the newborn King they thought had been born was nothing more than a delusion of their eccentric eastern mysticism. They were too ashamed to return and face me.*

He returned to railing his errant official.

* * *

Satan sat back on his throne and thought out loud. "It seems that even though the King has the mortal flesh of a man, we are not able to touch him directly." He tapped his talons on the high twisted armrest and continued his thought. "However, He is the Son of Man, and as such is subject to . . . " He paused and turned to Marr. "We have been misguided in our approach. Instead of trying to attack Him directly, we should be trying to reach Him through men." He shot a sinister glance toward Herod. "And I have the perfect man. With a single word from this mortal king, I can unleash a wave of destruction at the hands of *men* that will destroy the Son of the King of Heaven."

Every foul spirit in the room erupted in a frenzy of morbid approval.

"War?" asked Marr. "Shall I send word to Rome and partner with Herod to obliterate the nation of Israel once and for all?"

Satan raised his hand to quiet the roar of excitement in the room.

"No, that would take too much time. We need to act now before the elzurim can move Him out of reach. I prefer a more directed strike. The Son of Man is only a child."

The roar of approval at the thought of killing babies erupted even louder.

Molech stepped forward. "But, my lord, I'm not finished with Herod yet. A move like this would surely spell political disaster for him. I don't think he could recover from it."

"I care nothing about this man's political future," Satan said. "I need him now, and you have him prepared for my purposes."

"But he—"

A wall of flame from an upraised hand from the throne stopped him short.

Molech started again. "Then, could I—"

This time Satan's hand went up as a cautionary warning.

"Would you grant me permission to destroy Herod myself?"

Satan laughed. "After today, he is all yours. You have done well with this man. I commend you for your work, and I am happy to grant your request. Strike him with a consuming plague. Eat him alive from the inside. Make it as painful and horrible as you like, and extend his agony for as long as you can. After today, his services in my kingdom will be complete."

With a dramatic flair of regality, Satan stood up from his throne, spun around with a flourish and stepped down toward Herod, who sat on his own lesser mortal throne. Anticipation charged the air in the Middle Realm. Satan stood before Herod and swiveled around again. Then, without a word, Satan sat down and disappeared within the flesh of the man.

* * *

Herod continued castigating his failing official, when something occurred to him—a thought, strong and vivid, almost as though someone spoke directly to him.

*What if the magi did find what they were looking for?*

He stopped his verbal barrage and took up this new train of thought.

*Why else would they have left the country so soon? If they spent months traveling to Israel seeking some newborn King, they certainly would not have given up in one day's search after getting here. The only explanation is that they did find Him!*

Herod looked around at his subjects who stared at him with puzzled expressions. He announced, "Leave me. I need a few moments."

The king now sat alone with his thoughts.

*That has to be it. The magi actually found the newborn King. That means they intentionally avoided returning here to tell me. They tricked me! They have made me the fool! They have made a mockery of my throne.*

The rage exploded within him. The audacity of these men from the east made his head spin with uncontrollable hatred.

*I must pursue these insolent heathens and kill them for this injustice!*

*No. Wait. There is a larger issue. If they found what they were looking for, that means a new King is out there—one who will someday challenge me for my throne.*

On top of the hatred that already blazed within him, that old familiar paranoia about losing his power erupted like a pressurized volcano.

*I must kill this King before He can grow up and become a threat.*

*Yes, I must kill Him. But how will I find Him?*

*I know the magi were headed to Bethlehem. If I scour that city and all the surrounding areas, I should be able to find Him.*

*And how will I know who He is?*

*I know he is less than two years old based on the date that the magi said they saw the star. I should simply kill every Israelite male two years old and younger. I cannot afford to take any chances.*

*Kill babies? I can't do that. The people will be outraged. I would certainly lose favor.*

*Perhaps, but think of the favor this King will draw to Himself as he grows. Right now He is an unknown. If I do not eliminate this problem right now, He will surely bring down the entire kingdom.*

*I can't allow that. This must be done. What reason shall I give for such an order?*

*Ha! I am the king. I owe no reason to any man. I will simply accomplish the task and not offer any reason. I will strike quickly and silently, and the entire campaign will be complete before the people even know what happened.*

"Attendant," Herod called out. One of his attendants entered. "Send for the Primus pilus immediately."

The attendant nodded once and disappeared. The throne room remained quiet until the massive door to the court swung open again and the senior centurion of the Roman legion in Jerusalem, commander of the first cohort, entered with crisp, disciplined steps.

Herod's thoughts of late regarding this commander had been dark and treacherous. He suspected the chief soldier might be planning a coup, and this mission would be a perfect opportunity to test the centurion's loyalties. If he executed the king's orders without question, he would be allowed to live. If not . . .

* * *

The Primus pilus crossed the court toward the throne, and Marr moved to the place where he anticipated the centurion would stand. He stood there and looked into the eyes of his master—hidden behind the eyes of Herod—and smiled a wicked calculating smile. Within a few more steps the centurion reached the foot of the throne and stopped in the exact space Marr occupied. Marr smiled again, closed his eyes, and with an uplifted chin disappeared within the man.

* * *

The chief centurion felt a chill and became gripped with fear. He had heard rumblings about Herod's growing distrust of him, and it occurred to him as he looked around the empty room that a private meeting with the king might mean the worst. He knew the irrational ruthlessness of the king, and a mortal dread washed over him like none he had ever experienced, even in battle. He stood with all the stoic courage he could muster and awaited the words from the king.

"I have an urgent and vital mission for you," Herod said.

The centurion breathed an unnoticeable sigh of relief. "Yes, my lord."

"The nature of the mission requires utmost secrecy. You may select up to twenty of your most trusted soldiers, and you must tell no one of your business other than those on your squad. Can you do this?"

"My duty is to serve the king," the centurion answered without hesitation.

"I need you to go to Bethlehem, search every house, find every Hebrew male two years old and younger, and kill them. Then, expand your search into all the surrounding districts, destroying every Hebrew boy under two years of age."

Within only a few pounding heartbeats, a flood of thoughts and emotions crashed through the centurion's head.

*Kill young children? Why would he want to do that? This is even more irrational than usual. This is a test. He is testing my loyalty. I must obey the order. But babies? The role of a Roman soldier is to fight enemies of the state. And if I do not carry out the order?*

The fear for his own life gripped him again and bent his will until it snapped.

*If the king desires it, these young boys are enemies of the state. If I have to kill each of these enemies myself, I will see to it that every one is found and none is left alive.*

Without any emotion or hesitation, the centurion repeated his previous response: "My duty is to serve the king."

"Good," Herod said with a satisfied tone. "Select your men quickly and make haste to Bethlehem today. I have reason to believe He may already be . . . I mean, there may be some who may already be fleeing from your sword. Make a swift end to your business in Bethlehem and move into the surrounding areas. There is no time to spare."

"I will return by the end of this week with a thorough report of our success."

With a curt bow, the centurion marched across the court and left the king alone again with the low thud of the thick wooden door.

\* \* \*

Satan stepped out of Herod and gave orders to twenty of the surrounding beaelzur captains to move ahead and select twenty men whom they could indwell and to arrange for them to be ready for Marr to select through his human shell, the centurion. He turned to Molech and with an obliging wave of his hand indicated that Herod again belonged to him. Molech nodded once, stepped forward, and took his rightful place within Herod.

Herod's anger still boiled, and Molech reveled in the caustic energy. After several minutes of letting Herod simmer in his thoughts of paranoia and rage, Molech decided he wanted to demonstrate his control by pulling Herod away from the exalted throne of the dark lord.

Herod's jumbled thoughts came into focus. *I should go visit Mariamme. She always knows how to make me feel better. I know she will tell me I did the right thing.*

Herod rose from the empty expanse of the throne room and slipped out a back way to the secret inner room where he knew his love would be waiting.

# 23

## HIDING

**Birth plus 16 months, Day 1 of Herod's edict**

Elric stood with Grigor in the corner of the room at Hannah's house for a private conversation early the next morning. Grigor spoke with a low and solemn tone. "And you may divert a measure of your team to save as many as possible, but know that you cannot save them all."

"In His service," Elric said.

"By His word." Grigor disappeared through Hannah's ceiling.

The humans in Hannah's house started to stir for the day, but Elric's full attention turned to the war map and the activities unfolding there. A large black cloud rose out of Jerusalem and moved toward Bethlehem. Elric shook his head with one hand half-covering his eyes. Unthinkable horrors moved across the map. There would be no stopping the wave of destruction about to wash over the Judean countryside.

He looked over at the young Jesus who still slept, unaware of the importance of the escape they had made, and Elric couldn't help but let slip a small, bittersweet smile—and a large tear.

* * *

Joseph and Mary laughed as Hannah played with Jesus on the floor of Hannah's house. The midmorning sunshine filled the room with a warm glow, and Elric watched the energy of their laughter bounce off the earthen walls and dance about the cluttered room before floating upward toward heaven. He breathed it in and chuckled.

*If Lacidar was here, he would have a lively tune to play.*

He pictured the young Child fully grown, crowned with glory, vanquishing His enemies, and establishing His throne on the earth. He closed his eyes, raised his hand, and directed his own lively tune with a smile.

In the middle of Elric's second chorus, Zaben and Timrok stepped into the room through the front wall.

Elric turned with a hop and shouted, "Zaben! Timrok!"

Elric spoke the word "joy" into his hand, and a ball of energy formed. Timrok spoke "peace" into a ball of energy. The two smashed their orbs of light together with a blinding flash. They laughed as shards of peace and joy filled the air in the Middle Realm. Elric and Zaben exchanged joy and faithfulness.

Elric put his hand on Timrok's shoulder and said, "It is very good to see you." He turned to Zaben. "Both of you."

"Was there ever any doubt?" Timrok said. "I was . . . " His gaze bypassed Elric to Someone else.

Zaben already saw Him. Zaben and Timrok both stepped forward and dropped to their knees. Their eyes grew wide, and their mouths hung open. Timrok drew his two swords and laid them on the floor.

"I forgot," Elric said. "This is your first opportunity to see Him."

The two stared without responding.

"Zaben, your team has yet to see Him. Are they outside?"

Zaben nodded with his mouth still open.

"I'll bring them in," Elric said with a smile.

Elric returned with both Zaben and Timrok's teams. Each team formed a line along different walls. They knelt. And stared.

Elric let them soak it all in for several minutes. Then he said, "You have been wondering what the King would look like wrapped the body of a one–and–a–half–year–old human? Well, here He is."

All the angels stared at the humans in the room.

Jesus was hiding under a blanket.

"Where did He go?" Hannah called out in a singsong voice. "I can't find Him anywhere."

Giggling came out from under a wriggling blanket.

"I know He has to be around here somewhere."

More giggling.

"Peek-a-boo! There you are!" Hannah lifted the blanket and found Jesus bright-eyed and laughing. Jesus leapt from his "hiding spot" and bounded into Hannah's arms.

Mary laughed. "Now you have to give Him lots of kisses. It's part of the game."

More giggling, more laughing, more kisses, and some wrestling-kind of hugs.

"He wants to be found," Mary said as the young Boy squirmed in Hannah's arms. "It's His favorite thing of all."

Joseph nodded and said, "It's true . . . He will hide under that blanket and wait. Of course, He is hiding in plain sight, but sometimes it seems like He would wait all day. And His reaction is the same no matter how long it takes. More than anything, He wants us to find Him."

"He loves it," Mary said.

"It's almost as if that is what He lives for," Joseph said.

The weight of their words hit Elric like an unexpected avalanche. He slumped his back against the wall and sank to a sitting position on the floor.

"It's more than what He lives for," he breathed to his companions. "It's who He is."

All the angels continued staring in silence.

"I could stay and watch Him all day," Zaben said.

"All day!" Elric yelped. "Oh, no." Elric jumped up and moved to the center of the room. He motioned with his hand, and the war map appeared. "Gather around," he said. "Quickly."

Elric pointed toward the black cloud moving from Jerusalem. "The enemy is on the move. Herod has issued a decree to kill every Hebrew boy under two."

Timrok slid his swords back into their sheaths. "Then we will stop them," he said.

Elric shook his head. "No. Their numbers are too great. We cannot stand against this army, and that is not our primary mission. But we have the Word of the Lord to save individuals. Go to Bethlehem and the surrounding regions. Find the young boys. Rescue as many as you can from the hand of the enemy."

Timrok and his team shot straight up through the roof.

Elric caught Zaben by the arm. "Go first and tell Jenli. He should be in Bethlehem. His team should join the mission."

Zaben nodded.

"And leave two of your warriors here with me to serve as guards and messengers."

Zaben motioned for Emms and Lorr. They stepped forward with their hands on their hilts.

"Good," Elric said. "Now, go in the power of the Spirit."

"In His service," Zaben said.

Zaben disappeared through the roof, followed by his remaining three warriors.

Elric turned to Lorr. "Go to Judea and warn Lacidar. I don't know if the enemy will extend that far, but if they do—the prophet John is in danger."

Elric looked at Emms. "Stand watch in a concealed position outside. You will be my eyes while we remain here."

In a matter of seconds, Elric found himself alone again. He motioned with his hand, and the war map dissipated into a mist. He took a deep breath. He turned his attention again to activities of the humans.

Jesus was hiding under His blanket.

# 24

## SAVING SIMON

**Birth plus 16 months, Day 1 of Herod's edict**

Timrok stood outside the house of Jonah, a small earthen home in a tiny village a short walk northwest of Bethlehem. With arms crossed he lifted his eyes toward Jerusalem. The darkness churned and rose high into the sky above the horizon over Jerusalem and rolled southward toward Bethlehem. In the Middle Realm it looked like a slow—moving Saharan dust storm—an unstoppable wall of turbulent, gritty blackness with a hunger to choke the life out of everything in its path.

By the time the sun climbed to its noontime zenith, the cloud reached Bethlehem and began its siege. Timrok closed his eyes, and the battle played out in his mind—efficient Roman soldiers moving from house to house, driven by forces they didn't understand, or even knew existed, carrying out the will of the one on the dark throne. The valiant elzurim in the city, doing their best to stand against the beaelzurim, but unable to stave off the torrent.

He groaned and opened his eyes with a furrowed wince, knowing what he would see next. A shower of elzurim lights descended from heaven to escort the newly released innocent spirits of children into the presence of the King. For these young ones, their earthly pain was over; but for their parents, this was a pain that would cut them for the rest of their lives. The resulting bitterness would open new inroads for the enemy in their lives. He palmed his sword handles and gritted his teeth.

The sadness of the King fell down like a chilling mist, and Timrok found himself unable to hold back the tears. Streams of sorrow rolled down his hard face.

*Ten thousand battles, and the pain never gets easier. One day. One day the King will put an end to this pain.*

His mind drifted back to the Promised One back at Hannah's house.

*One day very soon.*

Through tear–stifled eyes he watched the distant battle for hours. He didn't count the escorts from heaven, but the number was far too high.

The cry of an infant from inside the house behind him brought him back to his task at hand. Timrok spun around and stepped into the house.

The cries came from Andrew, tiny, pink, and bundled. His mother, Joanna, held him close and nursed. Andrew settled down. His older brother, Simon, bounced around the room with a makeshift toy, lost in his own toddler world. Timrok smiled.

Timrok shot uneasy glances at his team. "They will be here soon," he said. "First the beaelzurim scouts. Then the men on foot."

All five of his warriors drew their weapons.

Timrok drew his swords. "But with the help of the King, they will not claim the sons of Jonah. Take up your stations."

The warriors spread around the perimeter of the room and disappeared within the walls. Timrok moved to the center of the room, crossed his swords in front of him, and took a deep breath.

Timrok stood like a silent stone statue. After a short time, a small, wiry demon darted into the room through the side wall. His hungry eyes trained in on the two boys. Like a flash of lightning, Timrok swatted the demon with a single stroke of his blade and sent the enemy crashing out through the front wall.

"The boys were seen," Timrok called out to his team. "But I think your positions were not compromised. We will do battle today."

Several tense minutes passed. The front door burst open. Timrok flinched. Jonah scuffled in with a small cloud of dust and a day's worth of weariness on his shoulders. Simon met Jonah with a squeal, bounded across the room, and vaulted as high as his tiny legs could spring. Jonah caught him in mid-flight, scooped him up to eye level, and buried his scruffy bearded face into Simon's neck amid more squeals. The young family enjoyed a light and cheerful moment, but Timrok stood on edge. Darkness approached.

After a short time, a loud, persistent, impatient rapping on the wooden front door interrupted the pleasant atmosphere. Timrok swallowed hard. Jonah barely had the latch released when two burly Roman soldiers pushed their way through the threshold into their small room. One of the soldiers carried a traditional Roman spear with its piercing wedge–shaped iron tip. The other had a broadsword— double-edged, simple, efficient. Both had leather footwear straps wound around their stout ankles and blood–stained leather bands around their wrists. In this domesticated family environment, the soldiers looked larger than life and fiercely intimidating.

Even in the face of all this muscle, Jonah shouted, "What are you doing? What is the meaning of this?"

The soldiers' eyes appeared dark and distant, empty and cold.

The one with the sword answered, "I need to see all your children."

"Why? What for?"

"I have special orders from the king. Are these two your only children?" he said, pointing the tip of his sword at the two young boys.

Timrok spoke to the two beaelzurim within the men, "You are not going to take these without a fight."

The two demons jumped out of the soldiers' bodies and landed in front of Timrok. They were both lieutenants, at least as powerful as Timrok.

One cackled and took a swing at Timrok. "Pitiful fool."

Timrok blocked the blow and shouted, "Now!"

Timrok's warriors stepped out of their hiding places brandishing their shining steel.

Prestus and Chase lunged toward the demon nearest them. Nalyd and Kylek pounced on the other. The demon tried to backflip away from Nalyd and Kylek, but Micah thrust his sword upward in mid-jump. His blade caught the front of the demon's shoulder and penetrated out the back with an explosion of yellow smoke. The demon screeched and fell to the floor. He clawed for his dropped sword, but Nalyd and Kylek bound him before he could regain his strength.

Timrok turned to see how the other battle progressed. Prestus had his foot on the back of that demon's neck, and Chase finished the bindings of light at the demon's feet.

"Very good," Timrok said. "Now we can deal with these soldiers without enemy interference."

He turned his attention back to the Physical Realm.

"Yes," Jonah said, "these are our only children. What is this about?"

The soldier with the sword stepped forward. "I need to know their ages and whether they are male or female."

Little Simon backed against the front of Jonah's legs. He wrapped one arm around his father's leg and buried his face in it.

Jonah answered with a low and guarded tone. "This is Simon. He is just over two years old." Then, pointing toward the tiny bundle in his wife's arms, "That is his new brother Andrew. He is almost three weeks old."

The soldier with the sword eyed Simon and without a word moved toward him. Timrok stepped in front of the soldier and stretched out his hand with a stiff arm. Within another step the soldier ran into Timrok's hand and came to an abrupt stop. The soldier cocked his head, as though trying to understand why he stopped. He stood for a moment, looking confused.

Timrok said, "This one is too old. You have no authority to take any over two years old. You should move on to another place."

Timrok's words rolled up into a ball of light and shot toward the soldier's chest. His spirit had a thick layer of black armor, and Timrok's words bounced off without penetrating his spirit.

"He is too old," Timrok repeated.

This time a splinter of light slipped between the cracks of the soldier's personal stronghold. The soldier rubbed his brows.

"You have no authority to take one this old," Timrok said.

Another splinter penetrated. The soldier stretched a crick out of his neck and bit his lip. He looked down at the young boy cowering between his father's legs. He took a step back. He lowered his sword. He stretched his neck again and glared over at Andrew.

He pointed his sword at Andrew and gave orders to the other soldier.

"Take him."

The other soldier leaned his spear against the wall and moved toward Andrew and Joanna. Jonah jumped across the room and flung himself onto the soldier's back, wrapping him up in his arms. The two struggled for a moment, but other soldier struck Jonah on the back of the head with his sword handle. Jonah crumpled into a pile on the floor. Joanna screamed. Simon cried. The soldier grabbed for Andrew, but Joanna held him with all her might. The soldier pulled hard. He couldn't pry the baby away. Timrok had his arms wrapped around both the mother and the baby. The soldier stepped back and rubbed his forehead.

"Come on," barked the other soldier. "What's the problem? Take the boy so we can finish here."

The soldier stepped back up and doubled his efforts. He pulled. Joanna wailed. Simon continued to cry. Timrok lifted his right leg and placed his foot against the soldier's chest. Right as the soldier heaved as hard as he could, Timrok pried his fingers away from the baby and gave the soldier a solid kick. The soldier flew backward out of control and smashed his head against the opposite wall and fell unconscious.

The other soldier roared. Leading with his sword he approached Andrew and his mother. "Have it your way. If you will not release him, I shall run you both through." He drew his sword back. Then with a battle yell, he thrust his blade forward.

Timrok stood between him and Andrew, and in a split second Timrok clapped his hands together, catching the advancing blade between his palms. For the second time in this house, the soldier found himself unable to complete his stroke. He pulled his sword back. He thrust it forward. Timrok caught the blade.

The soldier stepped back and let the tip of his sword swing down until it hit the floor. His face contorted with pained confusion.

Timrok spoke again. "This one is so young. He couldn't possibly pose any threat to the king. You would be justified to let this one go. Take your other man and move along."

The soldier looked down at the woman, sobbing uncontrollably.

"Mercy. Mercy. Mercy," Timrok repeated.

The balls of light from Timrok's words hit the soldier in rapid succession.

Prestus knelt beside Jonah. He extended his hand over Jonah's head. A layer of blue light glowed in his hand. He lowered his hand, and the light diffused into Jonah's spirit.

Jonah opened his eyes and rose to his knees. He swayed and reached for the wall. He used the wall to climb to his feet, and his hand brushed against the spear leaning there. He grabbed it and pointed the tip at the back of the soldier with the sword. Jonah's hair was matted with blood, and he looked awkward handling the weapon of war, but he stepped forward and pressed the tip against the soldier's back.

"Drop your sword," Jonah demanded. "Drop it now or I will kill you."

The soldier's head slumped forward. He let his sword fall to the ground.

"Now get your partner and leave my home."

Without another word and moving in slow, unthreatening motions, the soldier shuffled across the floor to where his partner still lay by the wall. He picked up a small pitcher of water on a nearby table and tossed its contents into the face of the unconscious soldier, who opened his groggy eyes.

"Come on," the leader of the detail said to his reviving partner. "There is nothing here for us. We should move on to another place."

The two soldiers made their way out the door, and Timrok addressed their demon escorts. "You have no place here. These boys will not be your prey today. And see for yourself—neither of them is the One you seek. Be gone from here."

Chase cut the bindings of the demons. They screeched and shot out through the front wall.

It took all evening for Jonah to calm his family down, even with the help of Timrok. Finally, after the children had gone to sleep, Jonah said, "This is the final stroke. We cannot continue living under the shadow of this madman, Herod. What reason would he have for wanting to kill our boys? We need to get away from here. We need to get far away from Jerusalem. Maybe his influence will not be as strong the farther away we get."

"But where?" Joanna said. "Where would we go?"

"To my brother's house in Bethsaida by Galilee. Maybe we could get a fresh start there. He is a fisherman. He could teach me the trade."

"We should do it," she said. "I am too afraid to stay here."

Timrok crossed his arms and smiled. "Simon and Andrew. I wonder if our paths will cross again someday."

\* \* \*

In Hannah's house, Jesus clutched His blanket and drifted off to sleep. Hannah moved the lamp to the other side of the room, and the late evening shadows settled in over Jesus. She came back and tucked the blanket around Him.

"He sure seems to like his blanket," she said.

"Yes," Mary answered, "it's a blanket we found in the stable the night He was born."

"A stable?"

"It's a long story. But He has had that blanket from the beginning, and He loves it. Not only does He like to play peek-a-boo with it, but

He carries it everywhere and likes to wrap Himself up in it, especially when we're outside."

Hannah fingered the edge of it. "The material is so smooth and soft, not coarse and scratchy like the linens I'm used to." She worked it in her hands. "And yet, it seems sturdy and durable." She paused. "You know, there is probably enough material here . . . " She stopped short.

"What?" Mary said.

"Oh, nothing. I'm sorry dear, I am always thinking practically. But it is not my place."

"No, please, go ahead. What were you thinking?"

"Well, it's no wonder He likes the blanket so much. The material is simply heavenly. I think it would make a marvelous outer garment. See, if you cut the material right about here, you would have enough to make Him a little tunic which he could wear all the time and still have a little left over for him to keep as a small blanket."

"Hmm," Mary said. "That's a good idea. I believe He would like that. He practically wears it now as it is. I will have to do that once we get settled someplace because right now I have nothing to work with."

"You know, dear, I would be happy to do it for you right now. I have everything we need, and I am experienced with a needle and thread."

"You have been so kind to us." Mary smiled with her head tilted to the side. "I couldn't ask you to . . . "

"Oh," Hannah said with a dismissing wave of her hand, "I love doing projects like this."

Mary snuck the blanket away from Jesus, and Hannah went to work, seated next to the lamp.

"This has been an excellent day," Joseph said. "We needed this rest. And your hospitality is greatly appreciated."

Hannah held her stitching up close to the lamp for inspection. "The pleasure is all mine. I enjoy the company. And I love having little ones in the house."

"It's so peaceful here," Joseph said. "I feel safe. It's hard to describe. And restful. If it's not too much of an imposition, might we stay another day? We still have a long journey, and another day of rest would—"

"Of course, of course, dear. Stay as long as you need."

Hannah finished the tunic, and Mary replaced the now–small remnant of the blanket back over Jesus and kissed Him on the forehead.

Mary whispered, "I'm excited about His new tunic, but I wonder if He will be upset about how small his favorite blanket has become."

Hannah rubbed Mary's back like a grandmother would and said, "Maybe he won't notice."

With the day well spent and all the work completed, the adults said goodnight and put out the lights.

Hannah lay awake half praying and half listening. An energy filled the air, and she could sense it. She heard no voices in her ears, but somewhere deep within her spirit she could "hear" very distinctive excitement, expectation, and reverence.

*There is something special about this family. In particular, this young boy is more than he appears to be.*

# 25

## SAVING JUDAS

### Birth plus 16 months, Day 2 of Herod's edict

Zaben watched the morning sun peek over the eastern horizon from the tiny settlement of Kerioth. Here in southern Judea at a distance just beyond the previous day's reach, one of the death squads would pass through his post first thing this morning. His team had spread out over the region to try to save as many as possible. He stood alone in Kerioth. The little village had dozens of children, but only one boy under two—Judas, the son of Simon. Zaben stood outside Simon's house and considered his plan. An operation of brute strength was out of the question. He smiled and bit his lower lip.

*Know your enemy. And know your charge. Victory does not always require strength of force.*

The soldiers would surely be working across a well–planned grid, and his plan hinged on the assumption that their grids would overlap to ensure no holes in the coverage.

*It is time to set up.*

He stepped into the house of Simon Iscariot. At eighteen months of age, his son Judas would be a prime target for Herod's men. Zaben took stock inside the house. The whole family still slept.

Zaben walked into the back room and found Judas sleeping next to his mother.

"Sleep," he spoke into the air. "Sleep."

His words spread out into a sheet of light from wall to wall and settled like a blanket over everyone in the house.

"Sleep," he repeated.

He moved over to Judas. "Good morning, young one," Zaben said. His hand glowed. With it he touched the back of Judas's head.

Judas's eyes popped open. He sat up, looked around, and patted his mother. She didn't respond. Judas bounced up and rummaged about the room. He found a toy and played with it on the floor.

"Out here," Zaben called from the other room.

Judas dropped his toy and ran out to the front room.

Zaben reached into the Physical Realm, lifted the door latch, and let the front door sneak open ever so slightly. The energetic light beaming through the open door caught Judas's attention and drew him toward the exciting world outside. In less than two snores from his father, Judas escaped outside and exercised his freedom as fast as his little legs would carry him. Zaben smiled, pushed the door shut without latching it, and flipped his wings once to take to the air and catch up with his young charge. As he reached Judas, Zaben translated in the Physical Realm as a large, brilliant butterfly, full of blazing red and bold yellow and orange colors.

He flittered in front of Judas and spoke into the spirit. "Catch me! Come, little one—try to catch me!"

The excited young boy squealed with glee and began the chase. Zaben bounced on the winds until he reached a low branch of a tree where he alighted, batted his enticing wings, and waited for his young hunter to catch up. When the tiny hands were within reach, Zaben hopped back into the air and weaved an erratic path out of Judas's reach while singing a lilting melody: "Fol–low me . . . catch me . . . looook at how pretty I am."

Zaben continued this dance all the way down the streets until he reached the village's well. There, he alighted atop the low stone wall around the well and waited again. Judas chased him all the way to the edge of the well's boundary. Zaben sat on top of the stone perimeter, just out of reach—right on the inside edge of the well opening. Judas reached, but the height of the wall touched below his armpits, which left his stubby arms stretched out on top of the wall inches too short. With a combination of hoisting with his arms and scrambling for niches in the stone wall with his feet, he crawled to the top of the edge. He laughed when he saw the butterfly there waiting for him. Judas perched in a precarious position on the wall and reached out to catch his prize. As he leaned forward, Zaben took off again and fluttered downward slightly into the dark hole. Off balance, Judas reached a little farther and fell headlong into the opening of the well.

He didn't fall far. Zaben met him there, not as a butterfly, but as a strong protective angel of heaven, and he supported Judas in his arms and descended to the bottom of the well. Zaben cradled him there above the surface of the water and sang a quiet song of peace and warmth in his own angelic tongue. Judas sat motionless with eyes wide. He patted Zaben's cheeks with his little hands and fingered Zaben's lips as he sang his soothing song.

\* \* \*

The village of Kerioth rested in quiet stillness but for a few birds welcoming the rising sun that morning. There was no one on the streets. No one to see a young boy disappear into the town well.

In the home of Simon Iscariot, Judas's mother woke up.

*Judas is already up. What mischief is he getting into?*

She hopped up and examined the room. She huffed once and moved to the main room. Nothing. She let out a tired, exasperated sigh, picked up her pace and stepped into the third room. Nothing. She raced back to the first room.

"Judas!" she called. "Judas, come out from your hiding place."

The rest of the family woke.

"Come on, Judas. Mama is not playing. Where are you?"

"What's the matter?" Simon asked, wiping the sleep from his eyes.

"I can't find Judas anywhere," she answered with a rising pitch.

"He has to be here somewhere. Judas?"

\* \* \*

A two–man team of Roman soldiers trudged up an old dirt path into the town of Kerioth. The grid plan called for Kerioth be to their first stop of the day, and the house of Simon Iscariot would be the first one they would check for any young Hebrew boys. Their chatter along the road had been light and almost jovial, but as they approached the town, they became serious, intense, and grim. Their duties required them to be razor sharp, and their attention heightened with every step.

* * *

Inside the house, Judas's mother screamed, "The door latch. Look! The door latch is undone!"

She pulled her frazzled hair back out of her eyes and cried.

"I know I latched the door last night before bed," she said. "And there is no way he could have opened it. He can't even reach it."

She went pale and cupped one hand over her mouth. Her eyes widened. She brought her other hand up, cradled her face, and said, "Somebody must have broken in during the night and taken him!"

"That's ridiculous. Why would anybody—"

"It's the only explanation. He isn't here, and he couldn't get out the door by himself!"

She threw the front door open and was about to scream Judas's name when she spotted two Roman soldiers coming from around the side of the house toward the front. With complete abandon she rushed the nearest soldier and screamed, beating on his chest plate with her bare hands. "Where have you taken him? What have you done with my son? You barbarian pigs! Where is he?"

The other soldier grabbed her arms from behind and threw her to the dirt at the feet of Simon. "You would do well to keep better control of your woman," he barked at Simon. He drew his sword.

She struggled back to her feet, but Simon held her beyond sword's reach. She continued her accusations and hysterics. People emerged from nearby homes and craned their necks toward the commotion. The two soldiers stepped back.

"It appears one of the other teams has already been through here," one soldier whispered to the other.

"I agree, and from the looks of things, this could get out of control for us quickly. I think we should move on to the next town."

"Agreed. We should go."

The two soldiers slipped off and disappeared over the hill.

Simon struggled with his panic–stricken wife as a small crowd of neighbors gathered.

"What is it? What's going on?"

"Judas is missing," Simon said.

"Those barbarians took him!" Judas's mother screamed.

"We don't know that," Simon said. "He has to be around here somewhere. We'll find him."

"They took my baby!"

"We'll help search for him," one of the neighbors said.

"We'll all look. We'll scour the entire village and the surrounding areas."

A search party formed. Judas's parents sobbed and clung to each other at the entry of their house, and a group of twenty searchers fanned out over the town. With the sun all the way up now, dozens of loud voices shattered the quiet of the morning, calling out the name of Judas.

* * *

Zaben heard voices approaching.

"Judas! Judas, where are you?"

Zaben smiled and looked into Judas's eyes. He stopped singing. He stopped glowing. Then, still supporting Judas, he descended into the water. For the first time since entering the well, the water reached as high as Judas's back. He let out a startled yelp. He thrashed and cried and struggled to stay out of the cold water. His cries became screams. His piercing wails echoed up the round stone walls of the well and blasted out into the morning air.

One of the searchers ran to the edge of the well.

"Judas?" he yelled down into the darkness. "Is that you?"

A frightened cry echoed up from below.

"I think I found him!" the man called out. "Over here at the well. He has fallen into the well!"

A crowd gathered around the well. Judas's parents came at a full run.

"How are we going to get him out of there?" one of the bystanders said. "He's not strong enough to hold on to a rope, and it's too tight for one of us to go in after him."

"Judas," the voice of Simon called from the top of the well, "Everything is going to be okay. I'm going to get you out of there. Just hang on."

Lowering a large wooden bucket used for drawing water up from the well, Simon called down again, "Judas, I need you to try to get inside this bucket. Can you do that for me? Here it comes."

Judas shivered and pushed the bucket away.

"Get into the bucket," the voice called down from above again.

Zaben put his hand on Judas's back. "Peace," he said. Zaben's hand glowed, and he touched Judas's back. "Peace." Zaben lifted Judas to waist level. "Little one, it's time to go home now. Let me help you up."

Zaben lifted Judas farther and helped his pedaling little feet into the bucket and guided his hands to the rope.

Simon inched the bucket upward, and his words echoed down the shaft. "I can't believe he was able to get into the bucket! And somehow I think he's hanging on."

Zaben steadied Judas until he ascended within arm's reach of the top. One of the helpers caught a hold of his little wrists and vaulted him up into the daylight and into his mother's arms. She cried even more.

Zaben stayed with the family the rest of the day, speaking words of peace and restoration and watching for any signs of the enemy. The enemy never reappeared.

The conversation between the adults that evening contained a mixture of grateful relief and sullen reflection.

"Why do awful things like this have to happen?" Judas's mother said. "Do you realize how close we were to losing our son? I thought we had lost him."

"I suppose we should be thankful it turned out like it did," Simon said.

"I know, but still . . . why did it have to happen at all? What possible purpose could something like this serve? If God truly cared for us, He would protect us."

Zaben could only smile and nod his head. How many times over the centuries had he listened to conversations like this?

Simon shrugged. "I don't know. Sometimes I think things happen for no reason. There is no 'why.' One thing I do know is that we need a better latch on that door."

"And," his wife said, "we need to watch more closely for those heathen Roman soldiers. I still say they had something to do with it. They had guilt written all over their faces. And did you notice the way they . . . "

Zaben spoke more words of peace and faith, but they couldn't penetrate through the wall of pain and bitterness. The conversation spiraled downward. He stepped outside and surveyed the surroundings. The black cloud had long passed beyond his post and now stretched out into the outer reach of Herod's edict. *I wonder if the enemy will press farther tomorrow or if they will start heading back to Jerusalem. I will need to keep a close watch to make sure Judas stays out of sight in case the enemy passes through on their way back.*

# 26

## MOVING ON

**Birth plus 16 months, Day 3 of Herod's edict**

Morning came early for Hannah, who had spent most of the night hours trying to understand the stirring she felt in her spirit. She rose before everyone, but soon the first rays of sun woke Jesus. He toddled around the room, touching this, investigating that, but then settled on a patch of sunlight on the floor and played with His blanket. Hannah smiled and took another sip of water from her cup.

Mary opened her eyes and sat up. She reached over and woke Joseph.

"Good morning," Hannah said.

"Good morning," Mary said, wiping the sleep from her eyes.

Mary let out an unexpected yelp and jumped to her feet.

"What's the matter?" Joseph asked.

Mary snatched Jesus' blanket and held it up above her head until the bottom of the blanket hung above the floor.

"Look at this!" she called out to Hannah and Joseph. "Look at how big the blanket is! Didn't we cut this down to almost nothing last night?"

Hannah and Joseph froze. Hannah looked toward the tunic she had made, and her mouth dropped open. She fetched the tunic and brought it over to the blanket that Mary inspected, flipping it front to back and top to bottom. They compared the material. Joseph joined the inspection.

"The fabrics are identical," Hannah said.

Mary nodded. "This is definitely the same blanket."

Joseph gasped and dropped into a chair. "It is a miracle!"

"It's as big as it was before we cut it, maybe bigger," Mary squeaked. She flipped it back and forth.

Hannah felt like she would explode. "What is going on here? Who *are* you? And Who is this little Boy? I get the feeling there is much you haven't told me. Where did you say you are going?"

Joseph fidgeted, his eyes darting around the room. "We didn't say . . . so you are sure that is the same blanket?"

"It's the same blanket!" Hannah squealed. "It is an honest–to–goodness miracle is what it is—like one out of the Scriptures! And it happened right here in my house!"

She pulled up a chair and parked it in front of Joseph. "My heart has been on fire since the moment you came into my house, and it has something to do with Him," she said, pointing toward Jesus. "What do you know about Him that you haven't told me?"

Joseph and Mary looked at each other with resigned eyes. Mary nodded to Joseph.

"I can't tell you where we are going," Joseph began. "For your own safety, it is best that you do not know."

"Why? are you in some kind of trouble?"

"No . . . I mean, yes . . . I mean, no, it's nothing like that."

"Maybe if you start from the beginning," Mary said.

Joseph took a deep breath and sat back in his chair. "We don't tell everyone about all this. We do not fully understand it ourselves. And not everyone would actually believe it."

"Try me," Hannah said.

So Joseph and Mary told about their journey from the very beginning—the initial messages from the angel, Elizabeth and John, the pregnancy, the birth, the shepherds, the prophets in the temple, and the magi. The whole tale took most of the morning and continued over the top of all the daily necessities. Meal preparation and eating and baby playtime and napping—all happened like blurred peripheral motion as the amazing story unfolded.

Hannah looked over at Jesus who napped on a pallet beside the wall. "The promised Messiah," she said. "I knew there was something about Him."

She sat on her hands and shook her head. "Yesterday I touched Him and played with Him like any other young toddler. How is it I am still alive? No one can see the Lord and survive."

"He has become like one of us," Joseph said. "There is much we do not understand."

"The Holy One of Israel. Here in my house."

"There is more," Joseph said. "After the magi visited, I had another vision of an angel who warned us that Herod was seeking to kill Him and that we needed to flee immediately. We left in the middle of the night and ran for three full days before reaching here, barely taking time to sleep. I don't know if Herod's soldiers will come down this far, but if they do, I still think it is best if you do not know where we are going."

Hannah pursed her lips and nodded in agreement.

"And we should leave first thing tomorrow morning. You have been very gracious to us, but for our safety—and yours—we need to continue our journey until we reach the place the angel instructed us."

\* \* \*

## Birth plus 16 months, Day 4 of Herod's edict

In the pre-dawn stillness, the vigilant sentinel Lacidar stood on the eastern side of Zacharias and Elizabeth's home. His eyes locked on the wall of darkness that had halted for the night beyond the horizon. The sun would be up soon, and with it would come renewed movement of the enemy. The big question—*which direction will the movement take?* Lacidar's team gathered—first Stephanus, then Kelsof and Ry, then BaeLee and Jaeden.

Without changing his gaze, Lacidar spoke in a low tone. "If they continue to expand outward, we will need to take action to protect the prophet John. Even though he is just over two years old, given the bloodlust of the enemy, we can't take any chances."

"What is your plan?" Stephanus asked.

"A simple Clarkan maneuver."

The team nodded.

"I will lead Elizabeth out with John on a picnic into the hillsides. If the enemy draws too close, one of you use a pack of wolves to drive the two into a cave. I will stand at the opening and provide both a hiding place and protection. Once the danger has passed, send the wolves away, and I will bring John and Elizabeth back home."

Lacidar focused again on the darkness to the east.

"Unfortunately, we do not know the intentions of the enemy. They have expanded to the full extent of Herod's orders, so they should turn back to report on their campaign."

"On the other hand," Jaeden said, "the one on the black throne in Jerusalem would have the men press to the ends of the earth."

Lacidar nodded.

Kelsof stepped forward. "Sir, shall I infiltrate the enemy's camp and ascertain their intentions?"

Lacidar smiled. "It is not necessary. I prefer patient vigilance. We will know soon enough."

\* \* \*

The orange glow of the sun sneaked over the horizon as Joseph finished hitching the cart to the donkey's harness. He hoisted an overstuffed pack of provisions from Hannah onto the back of the cart. He loaded the last of the full water skins to the cart. Hannah, Mary, and Jesus emerged from inside the house.

Mary lifted Jesus onto the cart. "He loves the new tunic," she said.

"It's big on Him now, but He'll grow into it," Hannah said with a smile.

"I'm sure He'll wear it all the time."

Joseph gave Hannah a hug and a kiss on each cheek. "Thank you again for your kindness."

"You thank me? You have given me the greatest blessing of my life. My eyes have seen the salvation of Israel."

"The blessing has been ours. Besides being a well-needed place to rest, your home has felt like an island of peace amid an ocean of danger and unknown."

Joseph looked off down the long path leading south.

"Being out in the open again," Joseph said, "I feel vulnerable."

Jesus bounded back and forth on the cart and hung His arms over the edge. He laughed and bounded back to the other side.

Hannah chuckled. "I believe the Lord will protect you."

Joseph hugged Hannah again. Then Mary hugged her.

"Blessings to you."

"And to you."

Then Joseph lifted the handles of his hand cart and headed toward the trail. Mary led the donkey. Jesus laughed and waved. They walked a brisk pace, but not as urgent as it had been at the beginning of the journey. They still had a very long way to go.

* * *

The light of daybreak spread over Lacidar and his team at Zacharias's home. Lacidar held his breath. The black cloud churned upward and turned east toward Jerusalem.

Lacidar exhaled a long sigh. "And the Roman death squads are returning home."

The rest of the team sighed with him. They smiled to each other and nodded.

Lacidar said, "Today, instead of trying to out-maneuver the enemy, I believe I shall enjoy a picnic in the hillsides with a mother and her son. You may return to your posts."

Lacidar watched the darkness recede. He reached for his resonar. He plucked a slow, sad melody. The resonar strings moaned. He hung his head and whispered a new song:

"The tide recedes

The tide recedes

Like an ocean wave spent on the helpless beach

The black tide recedes

Leaving behind

The hopeless foam

The cracked shells of lives

And the hungry scavengers

The tide recedes

The black tide recedes"

\* \* \*

On the evening of the fourth day of Herod's edict, Daniel reclined at the dinner table with his family. Jeremiah sat at his fatherly place of honor with his boys around him and Ruth serving. Levi and Daniel sat at Jeremiah's left, but Jesse's place to the right remained conspicuously empty. Daniel's eyes shifted back and forth from his father and mother, and he held his breath through the silence. As Levi passed Daniel the hot loaf of bread, Jesse bounded through the door and caused a stir. Daniel bit his lower lip and waited with a grimace.

"You are late," Jeremiah said. His voice rumbled low and gruff.

"Yes, Father. Please forgive me. I have come from town. A runner arrived with important news from Judea."

Jeremiah replied without looking up. "This news must be very great to keep you from your responsibility to your family."

"Yes, my father. I'm afraid it is most dire."

Jeremiah stopped chewing and looked up at Jesse.

"It is Herod," Jesse said. "He is killing all the male children under the age of two."

Jeremiah and Levi gasped. Ruth dropped a ladle.

Jesse continued. "The soldiers started in Bethlehem and are expanding out from there. At the time the messenger left, the soldiers had extended outward a two–days' reach. We don't know how far they will go."

Ruth suppressed a sob with her hand over her mouth. She shook her head muttered behind her hand, "He is a madman. Is there no end to his evil?"

"What do we do?" Levi asked.

"Our family is safe," Jeremiah said, "but we must warn everyone we know. There are many friends here in Nazareth with young children. They must go into hiding."

Jeremiah rose from his place and reached for his sandals.

"Why doesn't God do something?" Daniel said.

Jeremiah paused and looked at Daniel with a blank expression.

Daniel said, "If He truly cared about us, why does He let this happen?"

Jeremiah stared for another moment. Then he reached for his cloak and the lamp. "Jesse, you come with me. Levi, you come, too. Daniel, you stay here with your mother."

Ruth stood behind Daniel and ran her fingers through his hair as the others left.

"Either God isn't real, or He doesn't have the power, or He's mad at us," Daniel said.

"Shush, shush," Ruth said, patting Daniel's shoulders. "There is much we do not understand."

# 27

## SIFTING LIES

**Birth plus 16 months, Day 5 of Herod's edict**

Elric sat on the back of Joseph's cart with his feet dangling off. Timrok walked beside. Elric's keen eyes scanned the horizon toward the north.

"The afternoon grows late," Elric said. "Still no word from Jenli. Surely by now the soldier death squads should be getting close to Jerusalem. It is unclear what news the beaelzurim from the field will bring to their master. Will Satan think he has succeeded?"

"Captain, a warrior approaches from the south."

Elric turned. A light blazed toward them over the southern horizon mere feet above the ground.

"I think it's one of my team," Timrok said.

Prestus came to an instant stop next to Timrok and set his feet on the ground. His wings folded away. Elric jumped to meet him, and the three warriors walked behind the cart.

"Captain," Prestus said, "there is a caravan ahead that you will overtake before nightfall. There are two beaelzurim traveling with them and a small troop of Roman soldiers."

Elric rubbed his chin. "These soldiers . . . do they know anything of Herod's edict?"

"No sir. I do not believe so. They are traveling with merchants and a cash box. It appears to be strictly commercial."

"I don't like it," Elric said. "Is there another route we can take? Or could we divert the caravan?"

"Not through this region. The nearest alternate route we could use is at least another twenty miles away."

"I don't want to slow Joseph down," Elric said. "However, I also do not want any unnecessary entanglements with the enemy."

They continued walking without talking. Elric looked toward the heavens. *Perhaps Grigor will come with directions from the Throne.* They walked farther. No word came.

"The Lord did say we would be operating with little direction," Timrok said.

"Mmm," Elric said. They walked farther.

Elric lifted his chin and furrowed his brows. "Then we shall overtake the caravan and pass by. As long as the enemy does not recognize the King, we should be safe. Timrok, send word to the others along the route to be prepared to intervene if events turn bad. Keep a low profile—we don't want to attract any attention."

"In His service."

* * *

With smart determination and sharp disciplined steps, the Primus pilus marched into Herod's throne room. Herod dismissed everyone else from the hall.

Alone with Herod, the chief centurion announced with a commanding voice, "Your highness, the task delivered to me has been accomplished according to your orders."

"Very good," Herod said without smiling. "You are sure that you reached every target within a sufficient distance of Bethlehem?"

The centurion approached the throne and unrolled a scroll containing a map. The map had a blood–red circle scribed around the extended region of Bethlehem. A meticulous grid overlaid the circle with Bethlehem at the center.

The scroll crinkled as the centurion pressed his finger across it. "Each of my teams was assigned sectors on this grid. And notice how there are overlapping regions along the sector edges. This entire area was fully covered. Their search was methodical and exhaustive, and I am confident that every potential target was found."

His words marched forward with sterile, businesslike calculation.

He continued, "Each of the teams has reported in with a detailed accounting, and every one reports complete success. Would you like to see the overall numbers?"

"No, that will not be necessary."

The centurion bowed his head.

"In fact," said Herod, "I would like for you to destroy your report and any other materials related to this mission. Neither you nor your men—nor I—shall speak of this matter again."

"Yes, sir."

"You have done well, and I commend you for your expeditious and thorough handling of a . . . delicate . . . situation. We can all rest easier knowing the kingdom is secure."

"Thank you, sir. By your leave . . . "

Herod gave a rolling gesture with his right hand, and the Primus pilus executed an about face and marched out of the court.

Herod remained pensive for several minutes before returning to the day's schedule. Had they found—and destroyed—the promised Messiah King? He had no way to know for certain. His head told him it would have been impossible for the Child to have slipped through his net. Something deep inside, though, couldn't be sure.

\* \* \*

Satan sat on his twisted throne lifted high upon the billowing smoke in Herod's palace, and he crossed his arms. Marr stood to his right and snapped a whip of fire over the heads of his underlings.

"Silence!" Marr shouted. "Silence."

The entire entourage of warriors from the mission clamored toward the throne, each one shouting about his individual success on the mission. The Middle Realm in Herod's court filled with a writhing mass of pushing and clawing and elbows and shouts.

"Silence!" Marr roared again with a crack of the whip.

The frenzy continued.

Marr shouted above the din, "Captains, remove all these warriors from the court. We will hear their reports one by one."

The captains cleared the room of all but the senior beaelzur officers—local commanders and generals from other regions and their staffs. A captain ushered in the first warrior from the field. He stood before the throne like a triumphant drunkard, giddy with the blood of the innocents.

"I am happy to report, my lord, that the Child King has been destroyed," the warrior said. "I personally found Him and led my men to His location. Then by my own hand, I used the men to strike the Son of Man."

"How do you know it was Him?"

"First of all, I could clearly discern His Divine nature within the flesh. So, I knew immediately that it was Him."

Marr held up his hand to stop the rapid–fire report. "How is it that, in the initial sighting of Him by Luchek, His glory was not visible?"

The warrior snarled and puffed yellow smoke from his nostrils. "*I* saw it."

"And then?" Satan said.

"Then, when the soldier's sword struck the Child, there was a huge explosion of light."

The warrior looked around as if expecting exalting approval of his great victory. Instead, every eye remained incredulous, every face unmoved.

Satan blinked once and asked in a monotone voice, "Where is the body?"

The warrior's gaze shifted to the ground, and he shuffled his feet. "The body . . . vaporized in the flash of light."

Satan looked over to Marr.

"Next," Marr announced. "Bring in the next one."

The second warrior from the field sauntered in with cool composure. Confident and strong, he stepped into position before the throne and gave a curt bow of his head.

"If the previous warrior told you he destroyed the Son of Man, it is a lie. For I alone have accomplished this."

"Carry on," Marr said.

"It was the sixth house I visited in Bethlehem. A young couple of the correct age and lineage with a single son of the correct age."

"Did you see the Spirit of God within him?"

"Not until I struck him."

Satan and Marr shot glances at each other and nodded.

"When my human soldier ran him through with his sword, his sword exploded. The blood itself became light and everything else turned dark. I presume you saw the darkness fall?"

"We did not," Marr said.

"What happened to the body?" Satan asked.

"I watched the body slowly fade into nothingness while the mother held Him in her arms. She screamed in ultimate soul anguish and physical pain because, as His blood on her hands disappeared, it scorched her skin, leaving her with permanent scars. It was the King. I am sure of it."

Marr nodded. "And after you killed the King, you continued on to the next house?"

The warrior smiled, revealing his stained crooked fangs.

"Of course," said Marr. "Bring in the next."

* * *

Marr had a tired, discouraged countenance after hearing so many unverifiable reports. He took a deep breath and droned another question. "And after you killed the King in a blinding flash of light," Marr said, "what happened to the body?"

"My team of man-soldiers was transporting Him back here for my lord, when a beam of light shone down from heaven onto the body and whisked it away. There was nothing I could do."

"That will do," Marr said. "You are dismissed."

Turning to the one on the throne, Marr said, "That was the last report from the field, my lord."

Satan tapped his talon on the armrest of the throne. "Every one claims to have killed the King. None can produce a body. Only one of these accounts can be true, if any. These are all most likely fabrications of glory-hungry deceivers."

He chuckled to himself.

"I am surrounded by a host of self-serving liars. Truth is obscured by a veil of pride."

He took his scepter in his right hand, stood up, and paced in front of his throne.

The scepter served as an awesome and overt symbol of power, and Marr eyed it with both fear and disdain. Its length spanned three quarters of the height of the dark cherub in his current form—black, crooked, and pulsing with malevolent energy. Its tip came to a razor–

sharp point with the shape of a single dragon's claw. The crown of the staff formed the shape of a large macabre human skull with grotesque ram horns that protruded downward and twisted together with the hundreds of tangled serpent shapes that formed the tapered staff. The skull looked like translucent black onyx with a perpetual fire burning deep within, and the eyes glowed with living hatred. Every time the staff lifted and touched down on the smoke–covered floor, it produced a low–pitched thud like the rumble of distant thunder. The room became silent but for the thudding of the staff.

"I do not believe the Son of Man has been destroyed," he said. "I would have expected to have seen a disturbance in the heavens, an earthquake, darkness, something. I have observed nothing at all. Furthermore, there is no body. With a body, I could wrap Him in death and keep Him there while I ascend to the High Throne. As it is, even if He was killed, we have lost the leverage we needed by not having the body. Therefore, we have no choice but to proceed under the assumption that He is still alive."

"What is our next move, lord?" Marr asked. "Shall we intensify our search for the Child?"

"Your search will be fruitless," Satan growled. "The King has hidden the Son of Man from us, and He will not reappear until His time. Everyone should continue to watch for Him and for any signs that might point to His location or time of His revelation; however, I believe our best chance to destroy Him as a baby is passed. Continue to be vigilant. Perhaps through a misstep of his human parents or the elzurim, another opportunity may present itself. We still want to find and destroy Him before He reveals Himself to mankind."

Satan spun with a flourish at the end of one of his pacing paths and raised the point of his scepter over the small crowd of generals and continued with his orders, directing the clawed end of his staff individually at each in passing.

"We know we must reach Him through the hands of men. Begin raising up powers and individuals to oppose Him. Weaken the faithful in Israel and strengthen the divisive religious. I want unprecedented sickness and oppression. If the Son of Man plans to raise up an army to try to strip my kingdom from me, I want Him to find nothing but shambles of broken men and a wall of well–prepared opposition."

Pointing to a half dozen generals in particular, he said, "Bring in your forces from the other regions of the earth. This is a critical time, and your operations elsewhere are secondary. Other than the diversion in Egypt, it appears the King has chosen to hold the level of elzur forces in this region constant, so with our increased numbers, we should be able to have our way."

One of the generals shouted from the back of the assembly, "And who is to be prince over this region? After what happened in Egypt, surely you do not intend on letting Marr . . . "

Marr formed enormous fireballs of plasma in each hand and shot them at the general. The general deflected both with the palms of his hands, sending the shards of energy and fire into the smoky atmosphere. Satan laughed and raised his hand to Marr.

"And who should take his place?" Satan said. "You?"

Marr laughed a mocking laugh. The rest of the room remained stone silent.

Satan raised his hand up to Marr again and warned him with his eyes. "No, Marr shall continue to maintain his authority here.

He is most familiar with the human powers in play, and I need that knowledge during this time."

Marr's smug demeanor standing next to the throne drew the hisses of the other generals. Satan turned and stepped toward Marr, his eyes burning like red–hot coals.

"Actually, Marr's miscalculation in Egypt is precisely why I want to keep him in place. The disgrace of his failure shifts the leverage of power back to its rightful place. He now has much to prove."

He paused and spoke so only Marr could hear. "And little room for error."

Satan spun back around. "The Son of Man will not begin His campaign before He reaches an appointed age. Twelve years is the soonest He can be revealed. Thirty is the traditional age for a prophet to be revealed. Forty is the King's typical period of testing. We already have a good power base developed here in the kingdoms of men, and our armies are strong; but it is going to take a concentrated effort to prepare for His campaign in this short amount of time. You generals shall continue to focus on leaders, governments, and systems; but the rest of your forces must concentrate on individuals. The Son of Man will need to muster an army from the faithful in Israel. Therefore, your job is to promote those who belong to us and decimate and oppress those who do not."

Satan turned and sat down on his throne with his hand still perched atop the scepter in its vertical position of power. He gazed over his subjects with a burning stare. He snorted a blast of fire from his flared nostrils. "If anyone learns of the Son of Man's actual location," he said, shooting a sarcastic sneer toward Marr, "I must be notified immediately. I will tolerate no more blunders like the one that took place in Bethlehem."

After asserting one more glare of superiority over his inferiors, he lifted his staff straight up and brought the clawed tip crashing down onto the smoke–covered floor. An explosion of fire and smoke rocked the throne room and blasted through every exterior opening. All the lesser spirits eavesdropping on the proceedings while stacked up on the outside of the arched portals received a blast of fire in their faces that sent them flailing in all directions like gnats caught in a summer storm. Inside the room the flash lasted only a moment, followed by a rush of blazing wind, followed by a deathly silence. The generals lay strewn about like discarded rubbish, and Satan and his throne and the billows of black smoke had vanished. A wistful layer of smoke swirled across the stone tile.

Marr jumped up off the floor and barked to the rest of the generals, "You heard the lord, get to work!"

\* \* \*

A sudden gust of desert wind blasted through Herod's arched windows and billowed the bottoms of the heavy curtains. A weighty, ornate lampstand crashed onto the tile floor with a metallic clatter. Herod and everyone in the room gasped from the unexpected startle. After an awkward moment of silence, Herod motioned with his hand and an attendant picked up the lampstand. Herod continued with his daily business.

# 28

## A NEW PLAN

**Birth plus 16 months**

Elric crested a small hill on the trail and spotted the caravan traveling ahead of them. Joseph led with his hand cart. Mary walked behind Joseph's cart, the donkey's rope slack in her hand. Elric walked beside the cart where the Child slept.

"Hey, look at that," Joseph called back to Mary.

"Keep up your pace and pass them by," Elric spoke into the air. "Pass them quickly."

Elric's words spun up like a tiny tornado and whirled into Joseph and Mary's spirits.

"It's a caravan," Joseph said. "I wonder if they are bound for Egypt. If they are, perhaps we could join their company."

Mary shook her head and said, "Something inside tells me we should pass by and continue on our own."

"Pass them by," Elric said again.

"We should at least see where they are going," Joseph said.

Mary shook her head again but pursed her lips tight.

"Pass them quickly." Elric said. "There are enemies amongst them."

Elric's words swirled through the rising dust, and soon the sounds of Joseph and Mary's carts on the uneven gravel became lost in the larger din of many hooves and scuffling feet and multiple wheeled equipment and snorts of beasts and livestock.

Joseph approached a pair of men on camels, bringing up the rear. "Good afternoon," Joseph shouted over the clamor. "What is your destination?"

"Egypt, most of us," answered the nearest merchant who swayed with the rhythm of his beast.

Joseph turned back toward Mary and echoed, "Egypt." He lifted his eyebrows and motioned toward the men as if to say, "Should I ask them?"

Mary began by shaking her head again, but then shrugged her shoulders.

"Kind sir," Joseph said in his raised voice, "would it be possible for us to join up with your caravan? We are also going to Egypt."

The second merchant, a kindly man with a sun–baked complexion and a scruffy, dirty beard answered, "It is not a matter for us. You need to get permission from him." He pointed toward the daunting Roman soldier who approached from the front on a powerful steed with a bright red crest above its head.

"A Roman soldier!" Mary stopped and scurried to the back of the donkey cart. She climbed onto the cart and held Jesus close. She fumbled with His blanket and covered Him as much as possible while mouthing silent prayers.

Elric continued walking with his chin up and eyes fixed on the soldier. *Here we go. I wonder if they know of Herod's edict.*

The soldier pulled his horse up short of Joseph and announced in a commanding voice as his steed pranced in place, "Who are you, and what is your business?"

A low-ranking demon alighted beside the horse and expanded to the full extent of his power. He had the typical hollow pits of evil for eyes, and his teeth formed rows of stained conical spikes. He had a notably flat nose, but his bony eyebrows and chin protruded with grotesque prominence.

"A captain of the host," the demon said, squaring up against Elric with a drawn sword. "Are you here to do battle? I have over a dozen swords under my command, so you will be no match for us."

Elric drew his sword and tightened his jaw. *He lies, of course, about the strength of his numbers. I would run these two beaelzurim off, but I am constrained by my current mission. And it appears this demon has spent all his time traveling with these soldiers—which means he probably does not have up-to-date information of all the recent happenings in Jerusalem and Bethlehem.*

Joseph swallowed hard and bowed before the soldier. "I am Joseph of Nazareth," Joseph said. He cleared his throat and motioned toward Mary with a trembling hand. "And this is my wife, Mary. We are traveling to . . . to the south. I was talking with these kind men who tell me you are on your way to Egypt. I was asking them if we could join your caravan for as long as our paths overlap."

Elric answered the demon with a cool, even tone. "I am merely escorting my charges to their destination."

"I see," the demon said. He examined the three travelers over Elric's shoulder.

Elric tightened his grip on his sword.

The soldier eyed the young couple and the bundle in Mary's arms. Jesus tried to peek out from behind the blanket, but Mary pulled the blanket back over His head.

"And what manner of charge would require the services of a captain, I wonder?" the demon said.

"We all have our assignments," Elric answered without changing his tone.

"Yes. We do. See to it that you do not disturb mine," the demon grunted. "You have no authority here. Keep your distance. We shall *all* be watching you."

"Very well," announced the Roman soldier. With a prancing jump of his horse, the soldier trotted back up to the front of the column.

Joseph turned to Mary. "See, everything is going to be fine. We will be much better off traveling with a group."

Mary answered with a strained smile.

Elric's eyes fixed on the two beaelzurim. They conferred together and shot uneasy glances toward him as the shadows of the caravan drew long in the late afternoon sun.

\* \* \*

That night, Elric stood beside Joseph at the edge of the campfire. The warm orange glow lit the faces of the merchants around the campfire perimeter.

"Do the soldiers always keep their distance like that?" Joseph asked.

Elric turned his eyes toward the Roman soldier's campfire, set off by itself. The soldiers' bronze and iron glimmered in the firelight. No beaelzurim amongst them. *Where are they?* Elric scanned the other three campfires in the midst of the camp. Not there, either. *Where are . . .* an extra set of eyes appeared on the other side of his own campfire circle. The enemy's form stayed hidden in the shadows, but his glowing red eyes made his unwelcome presence known. Elric's hand found its hilt and gripped hard.

"Of course," answered one of the merchants. "They like us less than we like them."

All the men in the circle laughed. The laughter echoed through the stillness of the clear night air.

"But I do prefer traveling with them," another merchant said. "Sometimes these trails can be treacherous, especially when you are carrying money. I always try to travel with one of these armed tax–transport caravans. Much safer."

"The soldiers will actually protect you?" Joseph asked.

"Well, more specifically, our coinage."

"For a price!" one of the others said.

"Yes, for a price, of course. But I think—and I'm sure the rest of my friends here would agree—that it is worth it."

The rest nodded. The fire crackled and danced.

"It's all very legitimate," he said. "They take a careful inventory of your cash box, record it, and then take possession of it for the duration of the trip. At the end, they re-count the money, take their percentage and you are on your way."

"And we always pack extra provisions for them for the trip," someone said.

"They especially like it when we pack plenty of wine."

Light–hearted laughter echoed again.

The two beady red eyes hovered near the ear of one of the merchants. It looked like the shadow spoke to the man. Elric turned his ear toward the shadow but couldn't make out the words.

"So," blurted out the man to Joseph, "are you traveling with any money?"

"Don't answer him," Elric prompted. "He does not need to know."

Joseph paused and shuffled his feet in the dirt.

In that same instant, Elric caught some motion out of the corner of his eye back where Mary and Jesus lay by their carts. The second demon warrior. The demon didn't go near Jesus and didn't seem at all interested in Him. Instead, the demon poked his head into all their belongings. In particular, he investigated the chest filled with gold from the magi. In a single powerful wingbeat Elric pounced on the enemy with his sword flashing. The blade sizzled and cracked as it slashed through the night air. It caught the intruder mid-torso and sent him spiraling off into the darkness amid a cloud of yellow smoke. Moments later, the intruder reappeared on the other side of the campfire, and now four sinister red orbs peered back across the flames.

The demons spoke aloud. "You should put your treasure into the soldier's box." Their voices sounded smooth, and the words bounced across the air like tiny tongues of fire until they shot into the spirits of everyone there, including Joseph.

One of the merchants broke the uncomfortable silence with an understanding, helpful tone. "You need not answer about the money you have. It's none of our business. However, by your hesitation, I sense that perhaps you are carrying more than you care to reveal."

"If I were you," another merchant said, "I would definitely think about taking whatever you have and checking it in with the soldiers."

"Oh, I agree," several others said.

Joseph nodded and rubbed his chin.

Elric countered, "You do not need their protection. The Lord is your shield. Trust Him."

The enemy voices didn't let up. "Listen to reason. Rely on the soldiers. It is the safest option. Trust us. Trust these men."

Elric gritted his teeth and shot across the top of the campfire flames with his sword bearing down on the two enemy warriors. They split and flittered off in opposite directions. Elric couldn't chase them down without leaving Jesus, so he returned to his post near Joseph and continued countering the suggestions of the enemy.

*What is their objective?* He watched the two beaelzurim conferencing at the other end of the camp. *Why would they care about this gold? What would—where are they going?* Both of the demons flew off to the west and disappeared over a distant hill. *Oh. Now it all becomes clear. I need to act fast.* He flashed a signal to one of Timrok's hidden warriors. In an instant, Chase appeared at Elric's side with his sword drawn. He turned with his sword each direction, ready for battle, but lowered it with a puzzled expression.

Elric said, "Go immediately to Egypt and fetch Zaben. We have a change in plans."

\* \* \*

Elric and Zaben crouched low in the dirt behind Joseph's cart. They spoke in hushed tones.

"Things have not progressed as planned," Elric said. "Joseph has joined up with this caravan, and with their pace, our entire timetable will be off. To make matters worse, I believe the enemy is planning an ambush."

Zaben didn't look worried or surprised. "An ambush? For the money?"

Elric nodded.

"Have we received authority to protect these other travelers?"

"No. Our charge is the King."

Zaben bit his lip and smiled. "I have an idea how we can use this turn of events to our benefit."

The two went to work. For lack of time, they laid out a new plan in rough. It would be up to Zaben to work through all the details, prepare things in Egypt, and pass along the plan to Timrok's team.

Elric returned to his post, seemingly unmoved, just before the two beaelzurim reappeared from their mysterious errand. They eyed him and ducked into the night shadows. Elric returned an icy stare and crossed his arms.

# 29

## AMBUSHED

**Birth plus 16 months**

The following morning, Joseph opened his trunk for the Roman detail commander.

The commander gasped. "By the gods!"

"It won't be a problem, will it?" Joseph asked.

"No, no. But how is it a young couple of your apparent means should have a treasure of this size?"

Joseph closed the chest lid. "It was a gift."

"Yes, of course." The soldier stepped back and raised his chin. "At your request, I will put this in the official stores and assume responsibility for its safe passage. You agree to the fees for this service?"

"Yes."

"Brutus, bring the ledger. Joseph, you stand here and witness the counting."

The two beaelzurim cackled and rubbed their hands together with glee during the counting. Elric stood back and pretended not to notice.

The remainder of the day plodded by with dry and dusty monotony. They traveled with few breaks and stopped at early dusk to set up camp for the night. The evening campfires hosted pleasant and lighthearted conversations, and the soldiers kept to themselves a stone's throw away from the others. By the time the last of the campfire embers flickered out, the night settled into a cool stillness, and everyone slept hard from the long day's effort—everyone except three rival spirits.

Elric kept a careful distance from the two beaelzurim. He watched their activities but never moved from his station beside Joseph and Mary.

The two demons worked on the soldiers. They ambled from one soldier to the next speaking words of sleep and exhaustion into the air. Their words settled like clouds over the soldiers and hung in the Middle Realm air like a thick fog. They came to the two night watchmen who sat at their posts on opposite ends of the cache wagon.

The demons stood face to face with the watchmen and breathed puffs of reddish–orange smoke into their faces.

"Sleep," the spirits said. "Sleep."

The words formed into layers of fog that settled over the watchmen. The men shifted in their seats and rubbed their eyes. They blinked with heavy eyelids. Their heads nodded. They stretched. They blinked some more. Their limbs went limp, and their chins sank into their chests.

The two dark shadows wisped throughout the remainder of the camp, burying everyone else in a fog of slumber. Even the beasts and livestock became groggy and lethargic. The shadows shot cautious glances Elric's way, and his muscles grew more tense with each grave moment. One of the demons approached too close to Elric's position, and Elric flashed his sword, pulling it part way out of its scabbard. The demon withdrew and slinked among the soldiers. The other demon flew off over the hill to the west.

Elric pushed his sword back into its place and waited. *It won't be long now.*

* * *

Silent and motionless, Elric stood over Joseph, Mary, and the Baby. Their heavy breathing, with the snores of the rest of the travelers, mixed with the crickets' song like a peaceful lullaby over the camp. But there was no peace in the Middle Realm. A noxious mist of stupor hung over every living thing. Lethargy. Darkness. Death. Elric brushed away a floating tuft of mist with his hand.

*Any moment now. They must be close. They should be . . . yes. There it is.* The unmistakable, erratic beating of beaelzurim wings echoing over the hill. *And next . . .* The muffled hooves of a dozen horses stepping softly through the western darkness. *If the Roman watchmen were awake, they would surely hear the incoming band of bandits. But they are buried so deep that it would take a trumpet blast to rouse them.*

The one demon who had left earlier returned, leading a band of men and another four demons with them. *Six enemy spirits now.* Elric drew his sword for all to see and stood still. He glanced around the outer perimeter without moving his head. He motioned with his hand for Timrok's concealed team to stay down. *This is not going to be easy for Timrok and his team to watch.*

The bandits stopped well outside the camp and grouped together. The demons flapped like bats over the heads of the troop of horsemen and shouted inciting war chants. Their words formed tornados of fire that swirled through the air in the Middle Realm. The waves of energy pulsed outward until the horsemen became engulfed and controlled by it. The men's eyes blazed with fervor.

Elric jutted his jaw outward with clenched teeth and breathed hard through his flared nostrils.

The physical world lay under a blanket of stillness. Quiet, peaceful, still.

The mounting pressure of evil reached an exploding point, and the horsemen surged into the sleeping camp. They targeted the unsuspecting Roman soldiers, and the sleeping watchmen on the perimeters fell first. Before they could open their eyes, the watchmen were overrun.

The raiders liberated the watchmen's spirits from their mortal bodies, and the beaelzurim slung their pulsing black cords of energy like a whip, wrapping around the dazed and confused spirits. It all happened in a blink, and the demons went on to help lead the battle. They didn't indwell the horsemen, but they did use the human hands to wield the physical steel. They burst from one human attacker to the other, seizing the hilt like a glove over the human hand and guiding its course.

The remainder of the Roman soldiers woke from the sounds of the attack, but two of the demons flapped their wings, raising a dense cloud of spiritual dust. The trained, disciplined fighters floundered about, stumbling over their sandals, clamoring for their weapons, and bumping into each other. They failed to put together a cohesive defense and became easy prey for the fast–moving attackers. Severed arms and heads littered the blood–soaked dirt only moments into the fight, and soul after soul entered eternity met by the bindings and jeers of spiritual beings the dying men didn't even believe existed.

Half a dozen soldiers made it to their feet and took a stand. They swung their swords at the fast–moving horsemen. One of the horsemen fell. A soldier ran him through in a vicious thrust. In a rage, the soldier continued slashing and stabbing the dead body and failed to see another attacker coming from behind. With a single strike of a horseman, the soldier fell in a heap beside the man he had just killed. In that instant, the two slain men stood face to face, their spirits each bound by unbreakable chains.

Elric shook his head and brushed a tear from his eye. *Just a moment ago, they were mortal enemies, filled with hatred toward each other. Only now do they realize they were mutual victims of a different enemy, an enemy they didn't know existed and had no power to fight. Now their eyes are open, but it's too late.*

The physical realm, quiet and peaceful only moments before, rocked with the pounding of horses' hooves, clanging metal, and men's cries. *And here I stand, constrained to let this evil run its course.* In the center of the battle, a soldier's sword met the sword of an attacker with a crash. *The steel—it doesn't ring out as crisply as it does in the Middle Realm, and the collisions don't throw as many sparks. And the pace of combat is much slower.* The soldier screamed and fell to the ground. *But the cries of pain from the men are more desperate. More permanent.*

In the midst of the mayhem, the attackers hitched two spare horses to the wagon that held all the guarded treasure. The wagon leapt forward through the battle and charged toward the western shadows.

The other men in the camp awoke and rushed toward the fight with swords and long knives in hand. Too late. The cache wagon reached the edge of the camp, and the horsemen withdrew and raced after it. The pack of marauders disappeared behind a noisy cloud of dust.

\* \* \*

The camp became quiet again, but now the silence dripped with death and despair. The only sounds in the Physical Realm were the groans of the wounded. In the Middle Realm, all six of the beaelzurim rummaged through the carnage, laughing and taunting the fallen, whose spirits now stood bound, awaiting their eternal fate.

Only four soldiers remained functional, including the team commander, and they had each received minor wounds. With slow and solemn movements, they checked the conditions of each of their fallen comrades. Most had already gone, but some had suffered mortal wounds and still grasped for life as they awaited imminent death. With reluctance, the ones left standing took their own weapons and used them to end their fallen comrades' suffering. With each mercy killing, at least one of the demons helped drive the final thrust.

With each death, Elric flinched and gritted his teeth. *Your day is coming. You will answer for all this death. The day of the King's vengeance is nearer than you know.*

He looked back at his charges. Mary held Jesus as He slept. Joseph crouched low beside them. Joseph had no weapon and shook with fear. Elric spoke peace and comfort. Kneeling beside them He rested his hands on their backs.

Something stirred in the Middle Realm all over the battle site. Mighty demons—one for each of the fallen men—appeared and ushered the spirits of the fallen men away. The enemy paraded their spoils before Elric and reveled in their triumphs. He gritted his teeth and remained still and stone-faced. A few somber moments passed, and they had all departed—the souls of the fallen along with their escorts. The other four demons flew several swooping victory laps over the battlefield and left.

Now the silence carried a hollow emptiness.

Across the camp, the remaining two demons surrounded the Roman detail commander. Elric shook his head—he had seen this situation thousands of times before. The commander sat, defeated, with his head between his knees, and the two demons stood on either side of him, speaking to him. *If they are successful, there might be another one lost tonight.*

"What am I going to do?" one demon said. "I am a complete failure. I have lost all these men—and the cache wagon. It's all my fault. It's all my fault."

The demon's words pummeled the commander's spirit with a nonstop stream of poison.

The other demon spoke. "What will happen when we get to Egypt? My career is over—my life is over! I will probably be executed for this failure. Look at all this blood. It's my fault. What good is a soldier who cannot even protect a fortified position? I am a . . . "

The crowd of men from the camp pressed in around the commander. They pelted him with questions in rapid fire from all directions, and he couldn't begin answer them all.

"What happened?"

"Why did your men not put up a fight?"

"Did you not have night watchmen on duty?"

"Why don't you pursue them?"

The soldier lifted his head and blurted out, "There are too many, and I don't have enough men left."

The grilling continued. "Who were they?"

"Where did they come from?

"Should we send someone to track them so we can mount a counterattack later?"

"What do we do now? Our entire livelihood was on that wagon."

This question brought all the others to a halt. The group became quiet.

The commander struggled to his feet. "I don't know what to do," he said in a low, defeated voice. "I have never had a loss like this. I suppose the only course of action is finish our trip and see what the officials in Egyptus have to say."

One of the merchants asked, "Will Rome cover our losses since they were officially under your charge?"

"They should, by statute. But it will depend on the proconsul."

"Typical Roman bureaucracy," muttered several of the men. The men shook their heads, threw up their arms, and turned back toward their tents.

"Wait," called the commander. "I'm very sorry we lost all the money. But look around. I also lost these good men. Could some of you help with the fallen? I need to get them wrapped up and placed on wagons. I can't leave them out here on the trail."

"Look at the way they are all staring at me," said one of the demons to the soldier. "They hate me. They all hate me. They all think it's my fault. I'm all alone. There is no one who cares about what I'm going through. I am completely alone. They are all against me. The whole world is against me. I'm alone."

A handful of men turned back. "We will help. We can't leave the dead lying here in the open. They deserve to be brought home."

# 30

## DARK THOUGHTS

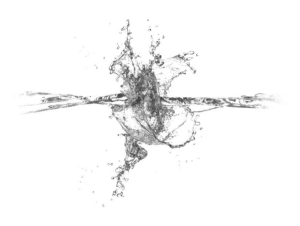

**Birth plus 16 months**

The next morning, Elric stood in the middle of the camp with the rising sun to his back. The lines of merchants with their carts and animals plodded by on each side. It felt somehow wrong to just walk away from this place. The blood of so many innocent men called out from the ground. The spiritual energy of their cries for justice rose and coalesced in the air of the Middle Realm. They swirled together and became large spiritual stones and fell back to the ground. As the physical world passed by, Elric gathered the stones and built a pile—a small monument to the lives stolen by the enemy. He knelt in front of the pile with his hand on top of the final stone.

"One day," he said. "The King will establish justice on the earth." He looked toward Jesus in the back of Joseph's cart. "One day, very soon. The enemy will be put beneath His feet."

He stood and turned south. The caravan had already traveled well down the trail. With five strokes of his wings he caught up and alighted next to Joseph's cart. His wings folded into his back, and he walked alongside. The men in the caravan were solemn. There were no conversations, no laughter. Only the sounds of the carts and hooves.

From this position, Elric checked the lead Roman soldier in front. The soldier swayed to the cadence of his mighty warhorse with his back as straight as he could marshal. The two demons walked alongside and fed his dark thoughts with even darker thoughts. Elric strained to hear their words over the caravan noise.

"I can feel the stares of all the men in the caravan," one demon said. "I know they are looking at me. They hate me. They think I'm worthless. My last three soldiers don't think any better of me, either. I am all alone. All alone. A failure."

Elric clenched his fists.

The demons cackled to each other and continued their attack.

"It is hopeless," called out one.

"Completely hopeless," echoed the other.

Elric tightened his jaw and breathed through his nose.

"It's hopeless," the soldier muttered.

"Aargh! Enough!" Elric shouted. He leapt with a roar and led with his blade toward the enemy. Just before he made impact, the two darted out of reach.

Elric turned to the soldier and spoke in a loud voice. "It's not hopeless! You still have much to live for. Turn to the King for strength—He can give you life and a future."

Elric's words formed into small darts of light and shot toward the soldier's spirit. The man's black spiritual armor blocked most of the words. Elric spoke them again.

Words from the King rained from the throne room, trying to penetrate the soldier's shell.

"The King is already speaking to you. Of course He is. I just need to keep the poison of the enemy out of your spirit so you can hear the King." Elric touched the soldier's leg. "Listen to me. You are not alone. The King loves you. He is with you now and He . . . "

Elric glanced back. The two demons approached Joseph and Mary from behind. *They are baiting me to draw me away from the soldier. But I have no choice.* With a flash of his wings, he returned to his position beside Joseph—and the demons scurried off. Moments later they came back to work on the soldier, dragging him deeper into the depths of despair. Their words formed giant meat hooks that clawed at his shoulders and pulled him down.

Elric ground his teeth. *Grrr! I can't let them . . .* He charged toward the soldier. The demons scattered. Elric spoke a few words of light into the air to strengthen the soldier. One demon circled around behind Joseph and Mary. Elric raced back to his post. This time, though, one of the demons stayed behind Elric's position while the other worked on the soldier.

*I am constrained again.* All he could do was watch from a distance as the soldier's thoughts turned darker and darker.

* * *

For the lead Roman soldier, the dreary day turned into a despondent night. The rest of the travelers huddled around their campfires scattered about the nighttime campsite, but he withdrew from everyone and stared into the flames of his own campfire. The hushed voices from all around the camp sounded distant and detached. He could only hear the crackling of his fire—and the thoughts that wouldn't go away. He didn't hear voices in his head, but something within him formed thoughts that stampeded through his consciousness.

*I will never recover from this. There is no hope. I am all alone.*

One of the men's voices from across the camp caught his attention—just the voice, no discernable words.

*Just listen to everyone out there talking. I know they are all talking about me. Blaming me. Cursing me. They hate me, I know it. I don't care. I hate them, too. This whole thing is their fault. If I didn't have to travel so slowly so they could all keep up, I could have been to Egyptus by now.*

He glanced over at his three men. Two poked at their fire with sticks while the third redressed a bandage on his arm.

*Worthless, undisciplined cowards. I hate them, too. They are as much to blame for this as those miserable merchants. Why can't I get a squad of skillful soldiers? I always get the rejects. I hate them. They have all ruined my life.*

An ember snapped and pulled his gaze back to the flickering glow of his own fire.

*My life is ruined. This is it—there is nothing left. There is nothing left in life worth living for.*

He pulled his dagger from its sheath and fingered its tip and razor edges. Its lethal steel glowed in the light of the campfire.

*It would be much easier if I didn't have to face tomorrow.*

The reality of where his thoughts were taking him registered with his body, and his hands instinctively dropped the dagger into the dirt. Everything within his physical being strived for self-preservation, and these thoughts sent a convulsive shudder through his bones.

He sat motionless for a long time and watched the flames of his campfire retreat into the orange core of the embers. All the while, he couldn't shake the hopelessness of it all. He picked up the dagger and brushed off the dirt.

\* \* \*

Elric took a deep breath and shook his head. *This is a critical moment. I don't think he can stand the attack much longer.* One of the beaelzurim continued his barrage upon the soldier, dancing around him, clawing at him, speaking to him, breathing sulfurous smoke into his eyes. Elric clenched his sword handle and pulled the sword part way out of its sheath. He looked back into the nearby shadows. The two glowing red eyes of the second demon peered back at him. He pushed his sword back into place and gritted his teeth.

The frenzied chanting of the attacking demon rose higher and higher. Elric squeezed his eyes shut tight.

"Do it! Do it! Do it! Do it!" the demon shouted.

Elric heard a gasp. He opened his eyes. The soldier slumped over. Both the demons erupted in triumphant laughter. One of them bound the spirit of the confused dead soldier, and the other jeered and mocked him to his face. A few moments later another mighty demon appeared and took the man's spirit away.

The quiet camp slept, unaware of the battle that had just been fought. Elric wiped his eyes with the sleeve of his tunic. He sat down on Joseph's cart and gazed up into the stars.

* * *

Days later, Elric looked up at the high outer walls of the Egyptian palace from his seat on the back of Joseph's cart. The air in the Middle Realm felt calm, quiet.

He shook his head and crossed his arms. *Only weeks ago, this place was the center of the most concentrated demonic siege since the Rebellion. And Zaben and his team, along with four legions of elzurim, held the enemy off for over a year and then held them in place long enough for the King to escape from Bethlehem.*

Now it appeared to be devoid of beaelzurim presence. Abandoned.

The caravan of battle–shocked and road–weary travelers rumbled past the thick walls of the northern entrance. Elric spotted Zaben atop the battlement wall and let a small sad smile slip from his lips when their eyes met.

Zaben gave a single nod of his head.

# 31

## DARK BEGINNINGS

### Birth plus 16 months

The lazy summer afternoon heat rested like a blanket over the flock of sheep in the fields outside Nazareth, and Levi and Daniel did their best to stay cool under the shade of some palm trees. Daniel was ten years old—awkward and curious, and Levi was seventeen—wise and energetic.

"I'm confused," Daniel said.

"About what?" Levi said.

"Oh, you know, God, spiritual things."

"What's the problem?"

Daniel tossed a small stone and shrugged. "I guess it's because of Father. Ever since he started following the teachings of the Sadducees, he believes there are no such things as spiritual beings. But I saw something that night. If there aren't any angels, they must have been something else. But I know I saw something. It makes me wonder if . . ."

"Anything he's ever taught us is true?"

"See? You understand. You're the only one I can talk to."

"You're my little brother."

"I'm Jesse's little brother, too. And I can't talk to him at all. He treats me like Father. He is always correcting me and making me feel stupid."

"They don't mean any harm."

"But what if God doesn't even exist? What if all the stories about our heritage are made up?"

"I will agree that some of the teachings of the Sadducees don't seem right, but I still think God is the Lord and we are His chosen people. And I believe the Messiah will come and save us—maybe very soon."

"I don't know."

"Besides, how else would you explain the angels you saw?"

Daniel remained quiet for a minute. "Maybe they're ghosts. Spirits of dead people. Maybe they're all around us all the time, and we can't see them."

"Ghosts?" Levi scrunched up his face.

"Yes, think about it. If there truly are angels, and if God is truly up there looking out for His chosen people, wouldn't He have done something about all those babies Herod killed? Wouldn't the angels have stopped it?"

"Well—"

"But if they're just spirits, they can't actually stop bad things from happening."

"I suppose I don't know enough about all this kind of thing."

Daniel scratched patterns in the dirt with a stick. "Do you think we can talk to them?" he asked. "Do you think the spirits can hear us?"

"I don't know," Levi said. "I do think God hears us, and He is a spirit."

"I wonder if they can talk to *us*." Daniel tilted his good ear upward.

"Well, *you* heard something once, didn't you?"

"Yes, but that was just one time, and there were a lot of them. And I don't think they were talking directly to me. Have you ever heard anything?"

"No. I must not be as perceptive as you are."

Daniel smiled.

Levi leaned back on his elbows. "You know, God talked to Moses and Samuel and all the prophets, so I do think it is possible for people to hear *His* voice sometimes."

"I wonder why we don't see and hear from spirits all the time?"

"I don't know for sure." Levi paused. "Maybe it's because God wants us to live our lives by simple faith in *Him*. If we were constantly listening to spirits, we would not be relying on Him. Not only that . . . "

Levi stopped talking and sprang to his feet.

"What?" Daniel asked. "What is it?"

"I don't like the looks of this," Levi said, pointing down the gently sloping hill. A wide foot path ran along the base of it, and two Roman soldiers in full gear had left the path and marched toward them.

"This cannot be good. Daniel, I need you to step back and stay behind me. Go on! Do as I say." He pushed Daniel back with his arm.

"Oh, Lord, help us," Levi whispered under his breath.

The two soldiers clanged to a stop in front of him.

* * *

Four humans faced off in the hot afternoon sun on a hillside outside Nazareth—two muscled, well-armed soldiers and two young shepherds with wooden staffs and dusty sandals. Another presence who cast no shadow stood beside the soldiers—a beaelzur lieutenant named Vorsogh. His craggy face looked almost reptilian. Instead of a nose, he had an inset cleft bordered by two spiny ridges. His cheekbones were high and sharp. His eye sockets were deep, bony, and black; and his eyes were burning red. His arm was as big around as a man's chest, and in his twisted hand he held a rugged blade, gray-black and well-used.

The instant Levi's prayer left his lips, a warrior in white alighted next to Levi. The angel's wings disappeared into his back, and his sword swung into a defensive position.

Vorsogh smiled with an unsurprised sneer.

Levi spoke first. "If you are here for directions, just keep following that path. Nazareth is up the road about three miles."

The angel stepped in front of Levi and squared up with Vorsogh. "Take your men and leave this place."

Vorsogh huffed a dismissive snort. "Step aside, puny puppet of the King. I will take what I want here, and there is nothing you can do to stop me."

One the Roman soldiers answered Levi, laughing, "We are not here for directions. We are in charge of bringing back supper for the whole company. We require two of the sheep from your flock."

"In that case, let me take you to our father," Levi said. "I'm sure he will be happy to sell you the sheep for a fair price."

The other soldier stepped forward. "I think you do not understand. We intend to take what we want, and you are going to step aside."

Vorsogh huffed again, hearing his words being echoed by the soldier.

"You can't do that," Levi said. "You have no right to come and take whatever you want. There are laws."

The soldier grabbed Levi's outer garment in his fist and shoved it up into Levi's chin.

"I am the law, and you had best do as I say."

He gave Levi a backward shove, and the angel took a swing at Vorsogh, shouting, "Enough! Call your men off!"

The two spirits became locked in a fierce battle. In the Middle Realm, flames, flashes, and sparks filled the air accompanied by loud crashes, clangs, and shouts. The two combatants spun, dodged, and flew in high–speed arcs.

Daniel hid behind a palm tree, but when the soldier manhandled Levi, Daniel rushed out shouting, "Leave my brother alone!"

"No!" shouted the angel to Daniel between a thrust and a parry. "Get back!"

Daniel pounded with both fists on the chest of one soldier, but his adolescent hands bouncing off the bronze chest plate only made the two soldiers laugh. The one soldier put his hand on Daniel's head and held him back beyond the short reach of the boy's arms. Then he placed his foot against Daniel's hip and gave a solid kick, sending Daniel flopping backward out of control.

"Leave him alone," Levi shouted. He jumped back to his feet, grabbed his staff, and raised it toward the soldier.

"Don't do it!" the angel yelled to Levi. "Get back! You cannot win."

The other soldier pulled his sword.

"Kill him!" screeched Vorsogh to the soldier. "Kill him!"

Time seemed to screech to stop. Each frame of action clicked forward in a slow blur.

Levi advanced toward the soldier.

Daniel jumped back to his feet.

Vorsogh clipped the angel's knee with his blade, sending the angel falling backward.

The soldier swung his sword in a horizontal arc toward Levi.

Vorsogh pounced toward the soldier and wrapped his hands around the soldier's swinging hilt.

Daniel leapt in front of Levi, reaching for the arms of the soldier with the advancing sword.

The angel leapt toward Daniel and pushed him downward from above.

Daniel fell face first toward the ground.

The soldier's steel whistled a hair's length over Daniel's head.

The soldier's steel caught Levi mid-torso and nearly cut him in half.

Levi screamed in pain.

Vorsogh screamed in victory.

The angel screamed in defeat.

Daniel screamed in horror.

The whole event played out in an instant, and time resumed its regular course.

Levi struggled frantically to find his breath, but his life pooled beneath him and flooded down the hill, and he slipped away quickly. Daniel knelt beside Levi and fumbled to push organs back into his ruined body. The soldiers scrambled into the flock and retrieved the spoils of their conquest. Covered in shiny red blood up to his elbows and all over the front of his tunic, Daniel kept screaming for help and screaming in anger and screaming in helpless anguish.

Vorsogh flew off with a triumphant shout as soon as he felt the soldier's blade do its work. Another human life cut short, dozens of other human lives scarred beyond repair—this had been a wonderful victory for him indeed. He circled back and found a hiding spot to watch the aftermath.

The angel warrior in white knelt beside Daniel and tried to comfort him and calm his shattered mind, but he could not break through the hysterics of the moment. Then, another angel showed up and greeted Levi's liberated spirit.

"Come," the angel said to Levi. "I am here to take you to your rest."

"What about Daniel?" Levi asked. "I am the one who takes care of him."

"The *Lord* is the one who takes of him," the angel said. "You have been the Lord's instrument until now. Now your work is finished."

"Will he be all right?"

The angel paused for a moment. He put his hand on Levi's shoulder. "Daniel will face some difficult choices in the near future. If he makes the wrong choices, I am afraid the enemy will have free rein over him."

"But he will be delivered, right?"

"With God, all things are possible. Come, it is time for you to meet the King. In His presence is fullness of joy, and He has been longing to speak with you face to face."

The two spirits disappeared.

Vorsogh watched the words of peace and comfort from the remaining warrior and the Spirit of the King rain down on Daniel. None of the light penetrated into Daniel's spirit. A thick veil of darkness blocked every word. Vorsogh smiled. This could be a unique opportunity to move in and take advantage of a weak mind in a vulnerable state. Silently he watched—and waited.

# 32

## PROVISION

**Birth plus 16 months**

oseph gawked at the expansive ceilings and the magnificent court room of the Roman proconsul in Egypt with his mouth half open. Besides the temple in Jerusalem, he had never seen such grandeur. He felt small and out of place, and he tried to take in all the details of the architecture, the artwork, the . . .

"Technically," one of the merchants next to him whispered, "some percentage of our losses should be restored; however, the outcome of matters like this depend on the disposition of the Roman governor deciding the case."

Joseph nodded.

"And from what I hear, this proconsul is a hard man. I will be surprised if we receive anything."

The large group of dusty travelers standing at the back of the court turned their ears toward the front, bit their fingernails, fidgeted their feet. Joseph stretched to see past the men in front of him. At the front of court, the three soldier escorts from the caravan, flanked by the palace centurion, stood at attention and spoke with the governor. Joseph couldn't make out the words of their muffled voices. *From the expression on the governor's face, they must be recounting the horrors of the nighttime raid.* Four merchants stood with the soldiers as representatives for the others. The governor also spoke with them.

The talking finished. The governor sat back in his tall wooden chair.

"And now we shall know," the merchant next to Joseph whispered, still biting his nails.

The proconsul sat forward on the edge of his seat. He lifted his voice for everyone in the court. "You men have suffered much." His voice echoed off the stone floor and walls. "In the wake of such villainy, there is no reimbursement I can offer you to reestablish your faith in the common decency of your fellow man. Seeing death the way you have steals a part of your soul that can never be replaced."

The merchant next to Joseph stopped biting his nails and let his hand drop to his side. He turned to Joseph and let out a long sigh.

The governor continued, "However, since your treasures were under the guardianship of the Roman Empire, it is my judgment that your financial losses should be restored in full."

The merchant's eyes and mouth opened wide. Joseph grabbed him by the arms and they both laughed. For just an instant, the other merchants did the same. Then, the proper decorum of the court gripped the entire group. They turned toward the governor and bowed.

To the centurion, the governor said, "Take these men to the treasury and see to it they are reimbursed according to the records."

"Yes sir."

"And then, see to the fallen. Their families need to know that they served and died with honor."

* * *

As he'd done in the proconsul's courtroom, Joseph took in the grandeur and size of the room of the main treasury. While not as big and ornate as the proconsul's court, it still made him feel small. He took another step forward in the line.

"They brought in the head treasurer to administer the reimbursements," the merchant in front of him said.

The man at the table had a pile of parchments strewn in front of him. He double checked one record, made markings on others. Then he spoke to an attendant who retreated to the vault and returned with four large canvas bags. The treasurer counted out coins, refilled the bags, handed them to the merchant at the front of the line, and made more entries on a ledger. The operation proceeded in a professional manner, and the treasurer didn't appear to begrudge a single transaction.

"I almost feel guilty," Joseph said to the merchant behind him. "It isn't anyone's fault that those bandits stole everyone's money. It certainly isn't the fault of that poor man doing all the work and pulling from his accounts."

"Don't feel guilty," the merchant said. "This is why we travel under Roman guard. We are only being reimbursed for what is rightfully ours. This is their lawful duty."

"Yes, I know," Joseph said. "Here, you go ahead of me."

"Are you sure?"

"Yes. Please."

Joseph continued looking around the room. *The columns are so magnificent. The craftsmanship of the stonework is exquisite. Each pillar must have taken years to—*

"Excuse me," the man behind him said. "Are you going to . . . " He motioned forward with his hand.

"Oh, I'm sorry. Please go ahead."

Soon Joseph found himself at the very end of the line. *It doesn't feel right. It's so much. What will the treasurer say when he sees my entry in the ledger? It was a gift. I didn't work for any of . . .*

"Next."

Joseph took a deep breath and stepped up to the man at the table.

Without looking up from the ledger, the man said, "Name please."

"Joseph. Joseph of Nazareth."

"Joseph of . . . " The man looked up. His eyes brightened, and he repeated, "Joseph?"

*Does he know me? How could someone in Egypt . . .* He squinted and examined the man's face. "Benjamin? Is that you?"

Benjamin leapt up, wrapped Joseph in a hug, and exchanged excited back slaps. They stared at each other with beaming smiles.

"What are you doing here?" Joseph asked.

"It's a long story. What are you doing here?"

"It's a long story."

They both laughed and slapped each other's shoulders.

"Well," Joseph said, "I see my cousin who set off to make his fortunes in exotic places has done very well for himself!"

"Oh, this?" Benjamin shrugged and waved his hand toward the magnificent room. "This is just . . . well, yes, the Lord has truly blessed me. But more than that, I am married now. And we have a little boy."

"You do? Me too!"

"That's great! It's so good to see you. How long has it been? It has to be at least ten years. You weren't old enough to even grow whiskers, and now look at you."

They laughed again.

"I must have you over for supper tonight. Do you have a place to stay while you are here?"

"No."

"Then you must stay with us. I insist. This is amazing. What a coincidence to meet you here like this!"

"Yes, what a coincidence."

They both stood, grinning at each other.

"Good heavens," Benjamin said, returning to his seat. "There are still accounts to settle. Let me see how much this ledger says is owed to Joseph of Nazareth."

"Oh, my," Benjamin choked out with a shocked expression. "Apparently, my cousin has done well for himself, too."

Heat rushed to Joseph's flushed cheeks, and he swallowed hard. "Yes, well, the Lord has blessed us. I will tell you all about it later."

\* \* \*

Elric, Zaben, and Timrok formed a line along the side wall of Benjamin and Rachael's palace residence and watched the humans on the evening of the caravan's arrival to Egypt.

"This is Jesus' first chance to play with someone His own age, isn't it?" Zaben said.

Elric laughed. "Yes. Isn't this wonderful?"

Timrok spun and dodged the two toddler boys in raucous play. "It makes me want to dance!"

The four adults carried on their conversation over the noise, and Elric only half-listened. The wives were introduced, and Benjamin said that maybe he remembered a little girl named Mary from Nazareth and concluded this Mary must be the same one. They reminisced about childhood days and laughed.

"And how is your mother?" Benjamin asked.

"I'm afraid she passed almost two years ago," Joseph said.

"Oh, I'm sorry."

"Thank you. She was very sick, but she died peacefully, and I was able to be with her until the end."

"She was a good woman," Benjamin said. "I always loved her."

"Yes, I miss her."

"Look!" Rachael said, "Jesus is trying to play peek-a-boo with little James, but James doesn't know what to do."

"Oh, that is His favorite game," Mary said. She got down on the floor and "found" Jesus under His blanket. Jesus squealed and giggled and ran around the room. Then He flopped onto the floor and hid under His blanket again. All the adults laughed. So did Elric, Zaben, and Timrok.

"Come here, James," Mary said. She put James's hands down near the edge of the blanket. She helped him grasp the blanket and whispered, "Jesus is hiding. We're going to find Him. Do you want to help me?"

James grinned and nodded.

"Get ready. One . . . two . . . three!" Mary helped James yank the blanket off with a dramatic whoosh. "There you are!"

Jesus laughed, jumped up, and ran around the room. James screamed and chased Him for five laps. Timrok stood in the center of the laps with his arms up and spun around with each lap.

"James," Mary said, returning to her seat. "I love that name. If I have another son, maybe I will—"

"Hold on there," said Joseph. "We have enough to worry about already. Let's not start thinking about . . . "

All the adults laughed.

Benjamin and Rachael told their story of how they met, how Benjamin had gotten promoted to his position, how Rachael had lost her family and home, and how they had ended up in this beautiful house inside the palace grounds. Joseph and Mary both remarked how much they liked it.

"Now," Benjamin said, "let's hear your story. What circumstances bring you to Egypt?"

Joseph looked at Mary. Mary gave a little shrug and nodded her head.

"It's complicated. And a little hard to believe, even for us," Joseph said. "Maybe we should eat supper and put these two to bed so we can talk without any interruptions."

"Yes," Rachael said. "Good idea. You two take the boys outside and let them run around while Mary and I prepare the meal."

Elric, Zaben, and Timrok stepped outside with Benjamin, Joseph, and the two boys. Timrok watched the boys play for a few moments but kept scanning the street and rooftops.

"I need a better vantage," Timrok said. "Captain, by your leave."

Elric nodded once.

Timrok flew to a nearby rooftop and disappeared from view.

Elric and Zaben watched the boys run for some time without saying anything. They both basked in the pure joy of children at play.

Elric finally broke the silence. "Nice work preparing the heart of the proconsul."

Zaben bit his lip. "I had little to do with it. The Lord had already done the work."

"Nevertheless, your plan unfolded exactly as you foresaw. You have a keen eye for strategy."

They watched the boys a while longer.

"Was it hard?" Zaben asked. "In the desert, having to stand by while the enemy claimed their victory?"

Elric's head drooped low. "All those men. My heart aches. The Lord's heart aches. And if not for this mission, I know I could have—"

"We do what must be done," Zaben said. "We cannot control the enemy. We cannot control the men."

"The Lord's day is coming soon," Elric said. "I long for the day when the King finally restores all things."

Rachael opened the front door. "Supper is ready," she called out. "Come in and eat."

Mealtime conversation centered around life within the palace compound and the strange year they just had. But something seemed to have changed a couple of weeks ago, and life appeared to be getting back to normal.

Elric, Zaben, and Timrok smiled at each other.

With the meal done and the two boys nestled into bed, the adults settled in for the first quiet moments of the evening. Joseph and Mary began their story with Zacharias and Elizabeth. Benjamin and Rachael hung on every word with wide eyes. Then Mary shared her experience with the angel and her pregnancy.

"Do you mean to say," Benjamin stuttered, "that Jesus is—"

"I told you it's a little hard to believe," Joseph said. "There is a lot more."

Zaben chuckled. "It's not every day that a long–lost cousin mysteriously shows up and has a Son who is the promised Messiah. These kinds of things don't happen to ordinary people."

"They will believe," Elric said. "Look at how the King is speaking to them. His words are reaching their spirits."

Every detail seemed to leave Benjamin and Rachael more and more stunned. And yet, with every step of the journey, Benjamin and Rachael gasped less and nodded more.

"And now that you have made it to Egypt, what are you supposed to do? Where are you supposed to live?" asked Benjamin.

"We don't know. The angel didn't tell us that."

Elric smiled at Zaben and Timrok. He crossed his arms and stepped forward.

"You have property that is available. You could offer it to Joseph." Elric spoke to Benjamin. "Offer him Rachael's family property."

Benjamin sat back in his chair and said, "Hmm." He turned and whispered in Rachael's ear. "You know your father's property? With the burned-out house? What would you think if we . . . "

Rachael nodded without hesitation.

"I have an idea," Benjamin announced. "Remember the house that we told you about that Rachael left after it burned down? That property still belongs to her family. The house is mostly a loss, but there is a good amount of land there and it has a well. We have no need for the place as long as we are here in the palace. I have been wanting to restore the house, but I don't have the time to get out there and get the work done. Here is what I propose—if the house was made ready, you and Mary could live there. And we will charge no rent."

"Oh, no, we could never—"

"For the rent, I will barter your services as a carpenter. I shall provide the materials. You provide the building skills. You can rebuild the house. What do you think?"

Joseph's eyes filled with tears. "I think . . . " He paused and looked to Mary. She nodded and wiped her eyes. "I think that sounds wonderful!"

"Yes!" Benjamin shouted. He slapped Joseph's knee. "This *is* wonderful! You and I can ride out there first thing tomorrow, and I will show you the place. Mary and Jesus can stay here with Rachael. We will survey the house and make plans for rebuilding it. Then, we will work on getting the materials, and you can get started. Until you get the place into a livable condition, you will stay here with us."

"But, if there is much to be done, it could be months before we—"

"You stay here as long as you need. I'm excited to have family close, and the boys will have fun together."

Zaben crossed his arms and smiled. "First, they run for their lives. Then all their gold is stolen, and they are in a strange country with no place to stay and no money and no job. Now, in a single day, their money is restored, they are reunited with distant family, and they have a place to live."

Elric nodded and put his hand on Zaben's shoulder. "A job well done."

Timrok grunted. "Well, we didn't exactly plan on losing the gold."

Elric put his other hand on Timrok's shoulder. He smiled and gave Timrok a playful shove.

* * *

## Birth plus 18 months

Everything that could burn in Rachael's old family home had been destroyed in the fire, but much of the mud brick and mortar walls remained intact. Joseph began by cleaning out all the charred remains. After patching parts of the walls in disrepair and applying a fresh coat of plaster on all the walls to cover the scorch marks, he set the main timbers for the roof structure. After two months of hard work, Joseph completed the straw and mud roof, and he felt the time had come to make the move. Much work remained to complete the house, but he wanted to let Benjamin and Rachael get their normal lives back.

At the palace home, Benjamin and Joseph loaded Joseph's donkey cart. "Do you know how long you will be here in Egypt?" Benjamin asked.

"No," Joseph said. "The angel only said that he would tell us when it's time to return."

"For our sake, I hope it is a long time. Stay in the house as long as you need. And please come back to the palace often to visit."

"We will. Thank you again for all your generosity."

They all exchanged hugs and happy waves. Joseph and Mary left with Jesus to start a new adventure.

* * *

The King on Joseph's donkey cart passed by the ten–mile perimeter about Rachael's land, and the senturim at the border averted their eyes. They followed Elric's strict instructions not to acknowledge the King when He crossed their borders, but Elric could sense them struggling not to bow down. The muscles in their necks twitched, and they stood rigid as stone. Elric suppressed a grin. After the carts passed, Elric caught them stealing a glance at the Son of Man, and he laughed out loud.

"Remember," he called out to the nearest senturi, "no beaelzurim cross this border. You have the authority to exercise the sword of vengeance."

The senturi replied with a stoic nod.

Joseph and Mary unpacked and hauled things into the house. Elric stood by the skeleton of the old burned-out stable and stared out over the horizon. Moments later, Zaben arrived. Then Timrok. Then Jenli and Lacidar. Each approached like a silent comet, performed a graceful flare maneuver, touched down, and tucked their wings away.

"Things will be quiet now," Elric said. "In this remote place with the senturim in position, we can stay hidden for as long as necessary."

"How long will the King stay here in Egypt?" Jenli asked.

"I have received no word. Again, we will trust and wait."

Zaben bit his lower lip and furrowed his brows. "This is a most peculiar mission. We all know there is a never-ending stream of direction and revelation coming from the Throne, but we receive none of it. The silence is unnerving."

Elric pursed his lips. The lieutenants all gazed off into nothingness.

Zaben said, "We need insight into the enemy's movements if we are to prepare for our next phase. Our position here is not favorable for this."

"Agreed," Elric said. "It would be useful to see within Herod's camp. The war map will help, but—"

"Send us in," Timrok said.

"Into the center of the enemy's stronghold?" Zaben said.

Timrok smiled a sly grin. "Why not?"

Jenli laughed. "It's easy if you carry a flaming blue sword."

"Nothing so overt," Elric said. "But it is a good idea. We need eyes on the inside."

Timrok nodded. Zaben raised his eyebrows.

"Our presence must be completely unknown. You can translate into the Physical Realm in the form of small animals. Others from your team can do the same or occasionally openly accompany a human into the stronghold. If the enemy thinks they're on routine escort assignment, they should not suspect our objectives."

Jenli and Zaben gave pensive nods. Timrok gave enthusiastic nods.

"Lacidar," Elric said, "you and your team will continue to stay with the prophet, John."

Lacidar said, "In His service."

"We will all meet here each week to hear reports. Sunrise on first day of the week. And Timrok." Elric put his hand on Timrok's shoulder. "No fights. Engage none."

"But what if someone needs—"

"Engage none. Remember, you're not even there."

# 33

## DECLINE OF A KING

**Birth plus 18 months**

A small gray lizard crept through the open window casement of Herod's palace and into the shadows of a corner in the throne room. From its hiding spot, it watched everything in the king's court with knowing eyes.

Herod sat on his throne, conducting important matters of state.

"Look at him," Molech said to his beaelzurim officers from his own spiritual throne. "Herod thinks he is in control of his entire world. He has no idea he is nothing more than a puppet in my hands. Now, our master is done with him. I almost regret having to destroy him. This man's ruthless heart and seared conscience has served us well for many years."

"What is your plan for the man?" one of the demon officers asked.

Molech snorted a puff of yellow smoke from his nostrils and tapped his talons on his armrest. "I will destroy him from the inside out. I will squeeze every drop of pain from him I can. I will start slowly, perhaps a stomach ailment. Then, I will continuously increase his maladies and prolong his agony for as long as the man's mortal flesh can endure."

Molech's officers laughed, licked their lips, and rubbed their hands together.

Molech coughed an unintelligible word into his right hand, and a small plasma ball formed in his palm. He held it up between his fingers and chuckled.

"Men have no concept of how their spirit, mind, and body are interconnected. I have full access to this man's soul. And with this single word in the spirit, I can cause enzymes and chemicals and neural pathways to shut down, open up, turn sideways."

He gave the fireball a flick. It whistled across the room, hit Herod, and disappeared within his flesh. All the demons watched with wild eyes. Several minutes passed.

Beads of sweat formed on Herod's brow. His face flushed. He held his forearm up to his forehead, then dabbed it with a cloth. Without a word, Herod jumped up from his throne, raced down the platform, and wheeled around the thick floor-to-ceiling curtains hanging behind the throne. All his attendants and officials looked at each other with mouths open. They shrugged their shoulders.

Then the unmistakable sound of retching echoed through the silent court.

Molech sat back on his throne and sneered. "As natural as carving meat with a knife."

* * *

## Birth plus 19 months

Timrok's sword crashed down on Lacidar's sword, sending sparks across the back yard of Rachael's rebuilt house in Egypt. The force of the impact made Lacidar stumble backward. Timrok leapt and landed both feet on Lacidar's chest. In an instant, Lacidar lay flat on his back, the edge of Timrok's blade hovered close against Lacidar's stretched neck, and Timrok's knee pressed his full weight on Lacidar's chest.

Timrok pulled his sword back with a flourish and jumped back to his feet. He extended his hand and hoisted Lacidar up.

"You're still being too mechanical," Timrok said. "You need to *feel* the motion of the fight as it unfolds."

"Over four thousand years—you would think I could master this. I'm a musician, not a warrior."

Timrok looked at the sword in his own hand and shook his head. "I never thought I would have to use one of these, either."

Elric stepped around the corner of the house. "None of us did," he said. "But be of good cheer. The Day of the Lord is finally within sight. Very soon, the King will set everything aright."

"I am ready," Lacidar said.

Timrok made a sudden joust. Lacidar blocked it with a sideways parry.

"Until then," Timrok said, "let's sharpen your skills. I have an idea for you. It is a technique I use often, and since you are a musician, I think it might work for you."

Lacidar took one step back and raised his sword.

Timrok said, "Sing for me one of your favorite songs. Something upbeat with high energy."

Lacidar cocked his head.

"Just do it."

Lacidar paused for a moment. "Great is the Lord. Mighty are His deeds," he sang.

"Good! Good," Timrok said. "I love that one. Now start again and follow me."

"Great is the Lord . . . "

*Tink, tink.* Timrok's sword struck Lacidar's, and the steel rang out like a bell.

"Mighty . . . " *Tink.* "Are His . . . " *Tink, tink, tink, clang.*

Timrok stepped back and smiled. "Do you hear it? Your sword is your musical instrument. Instead of fighting me, sing your song and play your instrument."

A twinkle formed in Lacidar's eyes. He lifted his sword and launched into the full first verse. Each stroke of his sword punctuated his song with perfect precision.

Timrok blocked each blow and shouted, "Excellent! Excellent! Now, add your dance to the Lord."

Lacidar leapt into the air with a spin and almost caught Timrok with two of his well-timed thrusts. Lacidar's feet sprang back off the ground. He flipped backward in a tight somersault, landed, and spun with a low pirouette in time with "establish justice and righteousness forever." His blade sliced a horizontal disc through space as he spun, and it clipped Timrok just behind his knee.

Beams of light blasted out of the gash. Timrok dropped to one knee with a surprised yelp.

Elric laughed and shouted, "Yes!"

Timrok's wound sealed, and he stood.

"I am so sorry," Lacidar said.

Timrok laughed, still trying to regain his strength. "I think this technique might be helpful for you."

"Why has no one shared this with me until now?"

The first rays of sunlight broke over the edge of the horizon. All three turned toward the east. Out in the field to the east, Jenli sat cross-legged, facing the sunrise with his dagger in his hand. As soon as the sunrise appeared, he scraped the edge of the dagger across his cheek and chin. He repeated on the other side. Then he shaved all the stubble on the top of his head.

"When I first met him," Elric said, "he had long, flowing, black hair."

"Why does he do that?" Timrok asked.

"It is his reason. And it is for him to tell."

Jenli hopped to his feet and walked toward the house. Just before he reached the house, a single point of light streaked in from the north, low and fast. It was Zaben, and he alighted in front of Elric just as Jenli arrived.

"We are gathered," Elric said. "Let's go inside."

Once inside, Elric said, "Herod's condition?"

"He continues to suffer severe stomach and colon pains," Timrok said. "He vomits almost everything he eats."

Jenli said, "And Molech has struck him with something new. He now has a skin condition all over his body. The itching is intolerable. He tries hot baths and warm oil baths, but nothing helps."

"The enemy is torturing the man," Elric said. "These diseases are not yet unto death. How is Herod responding? Is he able to hear the calling of the Lord?"

Jenli shook his head. "No, sir. His personal strongholds are too strong. None of the King's words are penetrating. In fact, he curses the Lord for his pain."

Elric sighed. The four lieutenants' gazes dropped to the floor.

"My heart aches for him. So blind. So imprisoned." Elric sighed again and lifted his chin. "Is the enemy raising up a successor?"

Zaben said, "The power struggle within the enemy ranks has been building for some time. Again, the beaelzurim commanders Molech, Asherah, and Yarikh maneuver for position."

"Always these three. Who are each trying to promote?"

"Molech is in the best position right now because he owns Herod, and he intends to install Herod's son Antipater. Antipater is still away at Rome, but he is the current heir according to Herod's written will. Asherah is trying to promote Archelaus. Yarikh is directing the ascent of Philip. Other lesser powers are trying to promote some of Herod's other sons—Herod Antipas, Olympias, Herod, and Phasael—but it appears one of the top three will emerge as the new prince over this region."

"I agree," Jenli said. "And with Antipater away, Asherah and Yarikh are working hard to discredit him before Herod. Herod can sense the tensions, and the paranoia of losing his throne is driving him mad."

Elric shook his head and groaned. He looked over at Jesus playing on the floor. A slight smile pulled up one corner of Elric's lips. "The day we await is in sight. All this pain and strife . . . " He drew in a deep breath and let it out. "Good work. Continue your operations. Watch particularly for signs that will tell us timing."

"In His service," they replied in unison.

\* \* \*

## Birth plus 20 months

A month later, Elric and Lacidar stood behind Rachael's house and watched Mary and Jesus in the backyard garden.

"These four months have been very good for Joseph and Mary," Elric said to Lacidar. "Here there are no pursuers, no pressures, no expectations. It's just the two of them and their young toddler. He learns new words every day and is discovering all the wonders of life. He seems like any other little boy His age."

"Joseph, you need to come here and see this," Mary called out. Her knees sank into a furrow of rich brown soil, and dirt covered her hands.

Joseph circled around the back of the house, past the reconstructed stable, and out to the plot of land he had prepared for a garden. By the time he got there, Jenli, Zaben, and Timrok arrived.

Timrok stepped forward and said, "What are we—"

Elric held up his hand. Timrok stopped. The five angels watched with twinkling eyes and silly grins. Mary knelt in the soil while Jesus stood several steps in front of her in the middle of the trough.

"Watch this," Mary said to Joseph.

She handed Jesus some seeds. He snatched them with His chubby little hand and spun around with a squeal. He bounded down the row, hardly able to contain His excitement, pulled a divot of dirt aside with His empty hand, and placed the seeds into the hole. Then with both hands, He covered the seeds with soil, stood straight upright, and clapped. Joseph and Mary both clapped along.

"Isn't it the cutest thing?" Mary said.

"It's amazing," Joseph said. "It is almost as though He understands what that seed is to become."

"He certainly loves planting seeds. And He doesn't seem to get tired of it. We are going to be out here all day."

She handed Jesus some more seeds.

"You do know you could get the job done yourself in a tenth of the time," Joseph said.

"But He loves it so much."

They both clapped again at another successful planting.

Joseph laughed and kissed her on the forehead. "Have fun, dear," he said. He turned and went back to his work.

Elric put his hands on his hips. "He may look like any other little boy, but He is who He is."

The others nodded.

"Come inside," Elric said. "Let's hear your reports."

They all stepped through the back wall and into the quiet house.

"Herod's abdomen is completely inflamed," Timrok said. "Now his feet and ankles are swollen and have broken out with lesions. And Molech has struck him with gangrene of the genitals . . . with worms." Timrok paused and handled his swords. "Are you sure I can't pull my team together and . . . "

Elric shook his head. "We have no authority in his life."

"He has consulted every doctor," Jenli said, "but there is no remedy, no relief."

"And is there anything new in the struggle for power?"

"Molech's position weakens," Zaben said. "Yarikh and Asherah are reaching Herod through his other sons and attendants. The dark secrets the enemy whispers in private are told to the king. He now knows it was Antipater's lies that drove Herod to kill two of his other sons for treason. He also knows Antipater is trying to build support for a coup and actually tried to poison him."

"It will not go well for Antipater when he returns from Rome," Elric said.

# 34

## POWERS

**Birth plus 20 months**

Asmall gray lizard crept up the wall behind the heavy curtains in Herod's throne room. It poked its head out, just enough to see into the court. Molech stood in front of his throne, facing away from the court with his massive arms crossed.

"Send in Asherah and Yarikh," Molech announced with a commanding rumble.

Two hulking beaelzur commanders sauntered into the room. Their statures matched Molech's, and their crusty hands gripped their sword handles. Their faces contorted with disdain.

Molech continued facing away and waited for Asherah and Yarikh to reach their place. He lifted his chin. "Herod has discovered the secret doings of Antipater," Molech said. He exhaled a thin line of sulfurous smoke through his turned-up nostrils. "And now Antipater is on his way back from Rome to answer for crimes against the throne." He turned, glared at Asherah and Yarikh, and sat with pompous deliberation. "I don't suppose either of you know how word of Antipater's actions would have reached Herod?"

Without hesitation, Yarikh said, "I did it."

"It was me," said Asherah.

Molech gave an indifferent flip of his wrist. "It doesn't matter. I will put Antipater on the throne, and none of your feeble tactics will stop me. Even if I have to kill Herod now before he changes his will, I will do what is necessary. Know this, neither of you will prevail."

Yarikh and Asherah each grunted and walked out of the throne room.

The small gray lizard blinked and continued watching.

\* \* \*

## Birth plus 23 months

Elric and Zaben pored over the war map in Hannah's house. The ever-changing landscape of politics, natural events, and enemy activities swirled through the colors of the map.

"Look," Zaben said, "Herod is moving to his palace in Jericho tomorrow."

"M-hmm," Elric replied, distracted by another area of the map—out around the edges where things weren't as clear. "Every day

I search for answers. Slowly, things are coming into focus, and the pieces of our timetable are starting to fall into place."

Zaben joined Elric at the edge of the map.

"We will not have as much time in Egypt as I had hoped," Elric said. "It appears Herod only has about six months left."

"And his successor?"

"It appears his kingdom will be divided into three."

"Molech, Yarikh, and Asherah."

"Yes, the power will be divided between them. None of the three will be the sole prince."

Zaben bit his lip and nodded his head. "This is excellent. This will work to our advantage. When Jesus begins His campaign, we will be able to concentrate on taking one part of the kingdom at a time."

"Indeed. And there is a more immediate benefit. Look over here. The struggle to establish their power bases after Herod's death will create great disarray. All the subordinate forces will be distracted by realigning allegiances."

"That will be our opportunity to slip back into Israel."

Elric waved his hand over the map. It disappeared like a mist.

"We will not move until the King gives His word, but yes, I believe it will be in this time."

* * *

## Birth plus 27 months

A plain gray dove alighted on the stone banister of Herod's third palace in Jericho in the afternoon sun. It cocked its head to one side and watched.

Herod's attendants carried him in his chair from his bedchambers to the balcony overlooking the enclosed courtyard. Three sides of the courtyard were lined with majestic columns with red and black painted bottoms, grooved plaster tops, and Ionic capitals. The fourth end of the courtyard had a semicircular plaza where forty prisoners huddled together at spear-point of two dozen Roman soldiers. The ragged group of dissidents below on the cobblestone courtyard looked insignificant and pathetic in their chains. The demons who had stirred the uprising for which the men stood accused snaked around the men, sneering and launching accusations at them.

Molech stood at the edge of balcony and called down to the demons in the courtyard, "This is a most excellent gift you bring. Your dedication to my regime will be rewarded once I reassert my throne after Herod's passing."

Molech stepped backward and sat down within Herod.

Herod coughed, sat up straight, and drew in a shallow wheezing breath.

Herod's court official stepped forward and unrolled a scroll. He spoke. "Primus pilus, Chief Centurion, Commander of the First Cohort, Roman Legion, Jerusalem. To his royal highness, the most excellent King Herod, King of Israel, to whom my most humble allegiance remains, greetings." The court official paused and cleared his throat. "Whereas the Jewish teachers Matthias and Judas have conspired to incite rebellion amongst the people, and inasmuch as this group of zealous students have followed Matthias and Judas in the treachery of pulling down, defacing, and burning the royal eagle ordained by the honorable King of Israel to adorn the outside of the main temple gate, I deemed it expedient to seize the dissidents

POWERS                                                          287

to prevent further uprisings and to detain them until appropriate judgment could be made. By reason of the capital nature of this offense, I send the accused under armed guard to the royal palace at Jericho to stand before the king for final adjudication. May the king rule in justice. May the king live forever." The official rolled the scroll and stepped back.

Herod pulled his shoulders up and back and took in a strained breath. He winced and fought back a convulsion in his arm.

"Burned my eagle?" he shouted loud enough for the men in the courtyard to hear. "Burned my eagle? You had the audacity to deface my—your own—temple? Do you have any defense against these accusations?"

Matthias stepped forward. The chains around his ankles jingled across the ground.

"Hear, o king, the words of righteous men, accused of a righteous act. Since the days of the holy man of God, Moses, the law of God strictly forbids the worship of any graven image. This eagle, which you have affixed to the house of God, is an abomination. It defiles the temple. It defiles the people. The leaders in the Sanhedrin have made petition to you, but you would not hear. It was therefore our righteous duty—"

"Treason!" Herod shouted. His words echoed off the walls of the courtyard. "I find you all guilty of nothing less than treason!"

"What shall the punishment be, your highness?" the official asked.

"Burn them," Molech said from within Herod.

The gray dove on the banister ruffled its feathers and stepped side to side along the banister rail.

"Burn them alive," Herod said through strained breath. "They burned my eagle. They shall suffer the same fate. Do it right here in this court before me. I want to see their flesh consumed by the flames."

The condemned prisoners stood by, and the Roman soldiers brought wood into the courtyard, building up the mound for the fire. The soldiers raised thick, tall logs upright and lashed them together into a cylindrical bundle at the center of the mound. They heaped up stacks of timber around the center until the mound stood several feet high. They saturated the entire pile with oil. The preparation took hours to complete, and the prisoners grew faint from the onslaught of the demons tearing at their minds.

The soldiers forced the condemned to climb the pile. One of the students resisted, but a guard ran him through with his sword and tossed his lifeless body onto the kindling. The other men clambered up the mound, stepping over and around him. The soldiers lashed them all to the center bundle of logs with thick chains around their chests and ankles.

With all the preparations complete, an attendant summoned Herod from his chambers. Once positioned on the balcony of power, Herod raised his right hand, and a deathly silence fell over the entire place. He waited several moments, glaring down at the men. The demons in the courtyard danced around the mound in a frenzy.

Herod spoke. His voice sounded low and guttural and didn't even sound human, "Light the fire."

The gray dove jumped from the banister and swooped downward into the courtyard. It leveled off, circled twice, and flew back to its place on the rail.

The flames shot high into the air, and the screams of forty men in writhing agony filled the courtyard. The demons danced among the flames and frolicked all about the bonfire. They started at the base of the mound and streaked upward with the flames while swooping their wings up the front of the men's burning flesh—as though licking up the pain as the flames tore at the men's skin. The screams lasted several minutes, but then, one by one they became replaced by the crackling sounds of the well-fueled fire. When the screams ceased and the smoldering figures stopped moving, Herod gestured with his shaking hand, and his attendants carried him back to his chambers.

Molech stepped out of his host and stood at the edge of the balcony. He closed his eyes and breathed in the smell of burning flesh.

One of Molech's captains said, "Almost like the days of old, master?"

Molech smiled. "It is not as satisfying as infant sacrifices offered in my name." He took in another deep breath. "But it is very good."

The gray dove on the banister left its perch and fluttered off toward the south.

* * *

### Birth plus 27 months

Elric and Jenli stood inside the house of Joseph and Mary in Egypt, where Jenli had just given his report.

Elric covered his mouth with his hand and shook his head. "Molech has always had a taste for fire."

"I think he does it because he knows his ultimate destiny," Jenli said.

"Possibly. Although we know they are all blinded by jealousy over the special place that man holds in the heart of the King. All they *want* to see is the pain they are causing Him."

Lacidar appeared in the room through the back wall.

"You two should come out and see this," Lacidar said.

"What is it?" Elric asked.

"Come see."

Elric, Jenli, and Lacidar stepped out back into the morning sunshine. Timrok and Zaben stood shoulder to shoulder facing the backyard garden where Mary and Jesus worked in the dirt.

"He *will* do it," Zaben said.

"*No*, He won't," Timrok said.

Elric wedged between them and turned his head left, then right. "What is the great debate?"

"Jesus is helping Mary pull weeds," Zaben said. "Even at this age, He seems to understand the difference between a weed and the crop."

Jesus ran down His row, stopped at a weed, gave a vigorous yank, shouted "Aha" at the upturned roots in his hand, and laughed all the way to Mary, where he laid the weed in a neat little pile.

Elric laughed. "I see. What, then, is the controversy?"

"See this weed on the end of His row?" Zaben said. "It's partially wrapped around the good plant's stalk. If He pulls it, it might damage the good plant. But the weed needs to come out. I say He will do what needs to be done."

"No, He won't," Timrok said.

Elric laughed and put a hand on each of their shoulders.

"Which will it be, captain?" Zaben said. "Will He pull it? I would pull it. It is best to eliminate all the weeds. The garden will be a better place. Sometimes sacrifices need to be made to achieve the end goal."

Timrok and Elric looked at each other and shook their heads.

"No, He won't do it," Elric said. "He will not take the chance of harming the good plant. He may only be a boy, but He is still who He is."

Jesus came upon the weed in question and stopped cold. He paused. He reached down and fingered the weed.

"See? See? He is going to do it," Zaben whispered.

Jesus stood back up. He paused again. Then, He bounded off to another weed.

"Ha!" Timrok shouted. He reached across Elric and smacked Zaben's shoulder. "I knew He wouldn't do it!"

Zaben grumbled under his breath. "I would have at least cut it out." He took a swing with his sword.

They all laughed.

Elric said, "Our easy days in Egypt are almost over. Herod's time is nearly done, and soon we will need to move Jesus back into the open."

The laughter stopped, and they all turned and watched Jesus. They smiled when Jesus ran across the field, yelling and chasing the birds away from the garden.

# 35

## DEATH OF A KING

**Birth plus 28 months**

Antipater strode into the throne room of Herod's Jericho palace with a bold face and arms raised and outstretched. He passed a small gray lizard that hid in the inconspicuous shadows of the corner. The lizard cocked its head so one beady eye could watch the room. Antipater reached out toward his father, but Herod stopped him.

"Even this is an indication of your murderous intents. Would you kill me once you had me in your arms? You are a vile wretch under heinous accusations. Do not touch me until you clear yourself of the crimes that are charged upon you."

Antipater stumbled backward, and horror washed over his face.

"What charges, my lord?"

"You lied about your half-brothers, Alexander and Aristobulus, resulting in their executions by my hand. Their blood is on your head. And in your treachery to steal my throne, I have learned that you tried to poison me."

"No, Father. I am innocent of these accusations. These are all lies fabricated by those who wish to see me brought down."

Yarikh and Asherah bounded in through the front wall of the court, flanked by their loyal captains. Molech looked up but turned his attention back to Herod.

"You should listen to your son," Molech spoke to Herod. "These accusations are unfounded. Lies of your enemies. Antipater is your eldest son—you should trust him."

Molech's words shot into Herod's spirit like arrows into warm butter. Herod sat back in his throne and rubbed his eyes with his shaking hands. He propped himself up so he could breathe.

Yarikh and Asherah shouted accusations into the air of the Middle Realm.

"He tried to kill you!"

"All he wants is your throne!"

"He's a liar and traitor!"

Their words pounded Herod's spirit.

"Enough!" roared Molech. "Remove these antagonists from my throne room."

Two dozen demon captains drew their swords and converged on Yarikh and Asherah.

Antipater took a step toward Herod with pleading eyes and his hands open. "Please, my father, you have to believe me. My love and allegiance is ever before your eyes. I am . . . "

Before Molech's troops could engage, Yarikh formed a plasma ball with the word "treason," and Asherah formed one with the word "liar." They shot their fireballs at Herod, turned, and flew out of the room. Both of their fiery darts blasted into Herod's spirit.

"Enough!" shouted Herod. "You are a liar and a traitor to the throne. I appoint you to court where you are to be judged. Prepare your defense against tomorrow, for I give you so much time to prepare suitable excuses for yourself. Remove him to prison."

Roman guards seized his arms and dragged him out of the court. All the way, Antipater screamed, "This is a mistake. I'm innocent. There is no proof. Listen to—"

The thick arched-top wooden doors slammed shut, and all turned quiet.

An attendant approached the throne. "My lord, with the weight of evidence against him, he is sure to be found guilty. When shall the execution be completed?"

Molech buried his face in his hands. The yellow smoke from his breath seeped around his fingers. "Not now," he said. "I need time."

Herod sat up and struggled for a breath. "Not now," he said. "Later, when I am stronger. Right now, I must have rest."

Molech ground his teeth. He turned to his captains. "We are out of time. I must finish Herod quickly before he can change his written will."

* * *

A large gray moth fluttered across Herod's lamp-lit bedchamber and alighted on a marble pillar. As still as stone, it disappeared against the gray streaks of the marble.

"It is working, my lord," the beaelzurim captain said to Molech. "By your word, Herod grows sicker and weaker every day. He is far too weak to make changes to his will."

"Yes, but even more, his thoughts grow darker and more hopeless. I believe I finally have him ready. It is time."

Molech disappeared within Herod.

Herod called out with an inhuman sound, a gasping crackle. "Attendant."

The door opened.

"Bring me an apple. I should like to try to eat something. And bring me a knife that I might pare the apple."

The attendant bowed and left the room. He returned with an entire basket of apples and a paring knife and left the king alone.

"Now, do it! End this misery," Molech commanded Herod.

Herod picked up the knife with his right hand and looked around the room. He raised the knife.

"Do it!" repeated Molech.

Yarikh emerged through the bedchamber door. He kept whispering behind him, "Hurry, hurry, hurry." Yarikh whisked across the room and hid behind a marble column. The gray moth crept to the other side of the column.

The bedroom door cracked open, and an attendant announced quietly, "Master, your cousin, Achiabus, is here to see to the King's welfare."

"Quickly, quickly," Yarikh shouted.

Achiabus shouted, "No!" He pushed past the attendant, rushed in, grabbed the king's arm, and peeled the knife out of his trembling hand.

Molech roared and leapt out of Herod. He charged Yarikh with his sword. Their swords crashed just once.

Yarikh shouted, "Ha ha!" and disappeared through the wall.

Molech turned back toward Herod and let his sword drop. It hung down, limp.

"And see to it that the King is never left alone," Achiabus said to the attendant. "Or his blood will be on your head."

\* \* \*

## Birth plus 29 months

Timrok's report at the weekly meeting came in rapid fire. He barely took time to breathe. "Then Asherah created sounds of crying and wailing in the ears of Antipater and his cell guard. Antipater presumed they were sounds of mourning for the death of Herod and tried to bribe the guard into setting him free with promises of amnesty and rewards once he was on the throne. But when the chief jailer heard of it, he went with the news directly to Herod, who naturally had a fit of rage and ordered an immediate execution, right in his jail cell, so the executioner—"

"Antipater is dead," Zaben said.

Timrok's animated arms fell to his sides, and he looked at Zaben with his mouth still open.

Elric nodded with a smirk and asked, "What of Molech?"

"He has disappeared," Jenli said. "We presume he is working to gain the promotion of one of Herod's other sons, but we do not know who."

"Yes," Elric said, "he will not give up so easily."

"Neither will Yarikh and Asherah," Zaben said. "All three are battling for the mind of Herod. This is a crucial time."

\* \* \*

The next day the gray moth took its position on the marble column in Herod's personal chambers. The room was well-lit and filled with courtiers and officials. Herod sat, propped up in a tall–backed chair, shaking and fighting a convulsive cough. Asherah, Yarikh, and Molech stood across from Herod, silent and anxious. Herod made his announcement, interrupted by his frequent coughing.

"Due . . . to the traitorous . . . actions of Antipater, I . . . am forced to revise . . . my will and to bequeath my kingdom to . . . a more worthy son . . . before there is . . . murderous anarchy among my heirs. Let it be known before these . . . witnesses that it is my wish . . . that the entirety of the kingdom . . . be given to . . . upon my passing, and not before . . . to . . . my son Herod Antipas."

In the human world, all the attendants gasped and whispered among themselves.

In the Middle Realm, Asherah and Yarikh exploded upon Molech. Before their swords could reach him, Molech shouted, "Ha ha!" and shot up through the roof.

One of Herod's most trusted advisors stepped forward and whispered to the king. "Your highness, Archelaus is the older brother. We naturally assumed you would—"

"Cunning . . . he is," Herod said. "He has an eye toward . . . my throne. I am . . . tired of treacherous . . . sons. Antipas is . . . the more faithful. He . . . is my choice."

Herod dismissed his court, rose out of the chair, and struggled back to his bed.

* * *

Three days later, Herod's room filled again with advisors, legal officials, and attendants. The silent gray moth hid on the gray veins of the marble. A gray mouse huddled in a corner. A small snake with a black forked tongue slithered behind the curtains.

Asherah, Yarikh, and Molech all stood motionless, waiting to hear Herod's words.

"I have been . . . deliberating over three of my . . . sons, Antipas, Archelaus . . . and Philip, as to which one is worthy . . . to rule over my kingdom . . . after my passing."

The three demons glared at one another.

"I have decided that . . . none . . . of these has the stature to . . . maintain so large a kingdom with the . . . skill that I have demonstrated over many . . . years. I have therefore decided . . . to divide the kingdom up . . . among the three."

"Archelaus shall be named . . . king over most of my kingdom . . . Idumaea, Judea, and Samaria."

"Philip . . . shall be named tetrarch over . . . Ituraea and Trachonitis in the northeast."

"And Antipas shall be . . . named tetrarch over Galilee and . . . the east bank of the Jordan."

"I have made my wishes known . . . in the presence of all these witnesses. Prepare the legal documents . . . and ready them for my . . . certification. Upon my death, you . . . must send these documents to . . . Rome to be confirmed by the emperor."

Without a word, Molech, Asherah and Yarikh walked out of the room in three different directions.

\* \* \*

The next day, at a special meeting of Elric's team, the four lieutenants stood around him in the center of Joseph and Mary's room at Rachel's family home in Egypt. Timrok bounced from foot to foot; Jenli scrawled something on a ledger; Zaben bit his lip; and Lacidar waited with his chin up and arms crossed.

Elric broke the tension. "Report?"

Timrok's pent up energy gushed out. "There is so much to tell you today."

"Only one thing that matters," Zaben said under his breath.

Timrok stopped bouncing and motioned with his hand to Zaben.

"Herod the Great is dead," Zaben said.

\* \* \*

With supper finished, Daniel's family congregated in the main living area of their home in Nazareth. Daniel occupied his regular spot, isolated in the corner. His vacant eyes stared into nothingness. Vorsogh crouched low where he whispered poison into Daniel's spirit. Vorsogh paused his dark works when there came an insistent rapping at the front door. Jeremiah rose and answered it. He greeted the man at the door with a warm hug and a kiss on each cheek.

"Yadid, my friend, what brings you out this pleasant evening?" Jeremiah said.

"Have you heard the news?" Yadid asked.

"No, I have heard no news. Come in, come in."

Jeremiah closed the door and motioned for Yadid to sit.

"Can I get you a cup of water? Here, have some dates."

"No, thank you," Yadid said. "I am here only long enough to share the good news."

"Good news? How blessed are the feet of those who bring good news. Let us have this news."

"King Herod is dead," Yadid said.

"What?" Jeremiah covered his open mouth with his hand and looked at Yadid with unbelieving eyes.

"It is true. Confirmed by the mouths of multiple witnesses."

Everyone in the room, except Daniel, leapt to their feet with a shout. Jeremiah grabbed Ruth and danced her across the room. They all laughed and hugged.

Vorsogh touched Daniel on the back of his head with two fingers. Daniel still had a thin layer of light as a breastplate from the innocence of his youth, but Daniel's thoughts of late had formed a very nice helmet of darkness. Vorsogh avoided the breastplate and only touched the stronghold of darkness.

"A shallow celebration," Vorsogh whispered to Daniel. His words formed numbing needles that pierced into Daniel's spirit. "There is no true justice in this. Herod never paid for the slaughter of those innocent children."

Daniel scowled and pursed his lips.

"Never mind the cup of water," Jeremiah shouted. "This calls for wine!"

Jeremiah poured a cup of wine and said, "Sit, Yadid, sit. You must tell us everything you have heard."

Yadid sat and took a sip of wine. "As I understand it, the whole country is celebrating. Not openly, of course. But the people are glad."

"Praise be to God," Jeremiah said, lifting his cup of wine.

Vorsogh sneered. "There is no praise due any god. If there was a God, He would have destroyed Herod before he killed all those babies—before his soldiers killed Levi." His words sank deep into Daniel's spirit.

Yadid took another drink. "I heard Herod was afraid no one would mourn at his death. I heard he was holding all the prominent men in Israel at his palace in Jericho with orders to have them all executed upon his death. That way, every family in Israel would have reason to mourn."

Ruth gasped. "He was an evil monster."

"What has become of the men?" Jeremiah asked.

"Herod's sister was the one charged by Herod to carry out his order. She did not do it, though. She released them all."

"Thank God," Ruth said.

Yadid glanced toward Daniel and leaned in close to Jeremiah. "What is the matter with your boy?" Yadid whispered. "I think he has not blinked once since I've been here."

Jeremiah leaned into Yadid and turned his head away from Daniel. "He has been like this since Levi was killed. It has been very difficult for all of us, but Daniel has taken it the worst. He has become very distant. He rarely speaks. He is not well. We keep hoping he will get better."

Vorsogh whispered to Daniel. "They are talking about you. They think they are so superior to you. They don't understand your pain."

Daniel blinked once and continued staring into nothingness.

# 36

## OUT OF EGYPT

**Birth plus 30 months**

*E*lric stepped back from the war map and crossed his arms. Zaben, Lacidar, Timrok, and Jenli stood on the opposite side along the wall of Hannah's house.

"Most of the turmoil among the human powers will be settled once Caesar confirms Herod's final will," Elric said. "And it appears he will. What do your teams see within the enemy camps?"

"The darkness in Judea under Asherah is strong," Lacidar said. "Asherah used Archelaus to murder three thousand Pharisees who opposed him and has imprisoned hundreds of political rivals. The army that backed Herod now stands behind Archelaus. He is at least as ruthless as his father. And Asherah has much to prove to secure his position."

"Molech is still staggering from his losses," Timrok said. "He continues to try to promote Antipas, but he seems to recognize his sphere of power is lost. And so do his followers. Many of the beaelzurim who served under him for the last half century are not interested in the region of Galilee. They are trying to align themselves with Asherah."

Zaben said, "And the forces already loyal to Asherah do not welcome those who will dilute their own spheres of power. There are many clashes."

Elric nodded and rubbed his chin. "Securing the loyalties of officers is a thorny proposition when self-serving ambitions are the rule."

"Yarikh faces similar problems to Molech's," Jenli said. "Few of the beaelzur captains are willing to limit their activity to the northeastern region, and they are challenging the regional powers throughout Judea for authority within Asherah's regime."

"This is exactly the disorder we expected," Elric said. He stepped forward into the map and bent his neck to see into the swirling layers of color. "All the churning of the power struggles leaves the enemy preoccupied and in disarray."

He stepped back and motioned with his hand. The map disappeared.

"They do not seek the Son of Man," he said.

"There is still no word from the Throne?" Zaben asked.

"No, but I expect we will—"

An explosion of light flashed. Without a sound Grigor appeared before Elric. The sweet fragrance of Holy Spirit filled the air.

"A word of the Lord," Grigor said.

Elric bowed his head once.

"Out of Egypt I now call my Son. Bring Him up into the land of Israel. There I will train Him up and prepare Him for the work He must do. The Passover is seven days hence. You shall begin the journey on the morning after Passover."

"In His service," Elric said.

Grigor's eyes darted around at the lieutenants, and he flashed a quick smile. "By His word." He unfurled his wings and disappeared.

*  *  *

The moon was nearly full, and as it made its course across the cloudless sky, it gave a gentle blue luster to the Egyptian landscape. Joseph and Mary's bedroom was dark. Crickets sang their lullaby. Jesus slept. Quiet stillness nestled over all.

Joseph had slipped into the hazy space between conscious thought and dreamless slumber when he noticed a tiny light in the distance. The light emerged from the backdrop of his mind and became a small translucent white bird. It made a graceful flight toward him, and Joseph extended his hand—an invitation, a landing place for the bird. It drew near. *That's not a bird*—but a man with agile, flowing wings.

*I feel like I'm awake. I'm standing. And my eyes are wide open.*

Joseph lowered his hand and took a step back. The figure alighted in front of Joseph and smiled. The two stood face to face, enveloped in a misty white cloud.

The peaceful warmth of the mist wrapped around Joseph like a blanket. He looked into the eyes of the visitor.

*This man looks familiar. He reminds me of the angel who delivered the message to flee to Egypt.*

The angel spoke. "Get up, take the Child and His mother, and go to the land of Israel; for those who sought the Child's life are dead."

Joseph breathed a long sigh. The nagging fear of someone showing up unexpectedly to do Jesus harm floated away into the mist. This last year in Egypt had been so restful—but he knew this day would come eventually.

"Yes, my lord," Joseph said. "When shall we depart, and how quickly do we need to travel?"

"Haste on the journey is not required. However, you are to depart on the morning of Passover next week."

"Travel on a high holy Sabbath? Should we not wait until after the Feast of Unleavened Bread is complete?"

"This is the word of the Lord to you. Make your preparations for Passover. Prepare enough matzo for your journey. You may celebrate the Passover seder with your relatives Benjamin and Rachael, but you must depart on the following morning."

"Yes, my lord."

The angel turned and flew away just as he had entered. He became smaller in the distance, like a small bird, and all the light drew toward him like a pinpoint magnet. As the light receded, it pulled the very breath from Joseph's lungs.

Joseph sat bolt upright. He gasped.

His bedroom sat dark and still. He strained his eyes for the spiritual presence he knew was there. Nothing. He and Mary and Jesus were alone. He nudged Mary.

"Mary, I just had another vision from Lord. It's time to return to Israel."

\* \* \*

Elric, Zaben, Lacidar, Jenli, and Timrok stood like timeless statues around the Passover table at Benjamin and Rachael's house within the palace grounds. The table had been prepared according to Jewish custom, with the roasted Passover lamb, unleavened bread, and bitter herbs. Elric stood behind the empty seat reserved for the Messiah with his arms crossed. The ceremony began.

After Benjamin performed the Yachatz, Joseph turned to Jesus and whispered, "Now is the time. Just like we practiced. Ask your question—good and loud."

Jesus sat up tall and said with a squeaky little voice, "Why is this night different from all other nights?"

Joseph and Mary smiled at Him and nodded their approval.

"This is a very good question, young man," Benjamin said. "I am glad you have asked it. Let me tell you the story of Moses and the miraculous deliverance of Israel from bondage in Egypt."

The angels nodded with wise, ancient smiles as Benjamin recounted the story of Moses. Elric closed his eyes. For the humans retelling this narrative—which they had only heard through generations of oral tradition—this ceremony served as a way to connect with their heritage and remember how God had intervened once upon a time.

But not for Elric. He was there. He battled hard against an enemy entrenched behind an unbreakable stronghold—the great demon prince, Ra, and his commanders, Hathor, Horus, Isis, Sobek, and the others who held that land back then. Elric gritted his teeth.

"Then, Moses said to Pharaoh," Benjamin continued, "'The LORD, the God of the Hebrews, sent me to you, saying, "Let My people go, that they may serve Me in the wilderness. But behold, you have not listened until now." Thus says the LORD, "By this you shall know that I am the LORD: behold, I am going to strike the water that is in the Nile with the staff that is in my hand, and it will be turned into blood."'"

*I can still see it—the banks of the Nile when Moses struck the waters with his staff.* Ra and his minions lined the opposite bank and defied the army of the Lord and the Lord's servant Moses. The Lord turned the water into blood, and Ra snorted with spite. He used Pharaoh's magicians. They poured large clay pitchers of water onto the ground before Pharaoh, and Ra turned that water into blood and laughed. *The hardest part to watch wasn't the haughty rebellion of the enemy. It wasn't even the death of everything in the river. It was the hardness of Pharaoh himself.* He wore his stronghold of darkness like a stone wall. When Moses spoke the words of the King, the words wrapped around Pharaoh, pressing to get in. But Pharaoh's armor was too strong. And then, the saddest part—the light from the Lord's rejected words faded, turned to darkness, and clung to the outside of Pharaoh's spiritual armor, making it even harder than before.

Benjamin told the story of each of the ten plagues the Lord used to break Pharaoh, and Elric replayed in his mind his own role during each one. Benjamin reached the final plaque. Elric's eyes welled up. *I can still feel the tension of that night as the Hebrews applied the blood of lambs to their doorposts and hid behind those doors.* And the sorrow of watching the death of every firstborn male in every house that didn't have the lamb's blood on their door, including Pharaoh's. And the anticipation of the battle to be fought the next morning.

But then the glorious victory when, after 400 years of bondage, the entire nation of Israelites left Egypt. Elric laughed aloud through his tears. By the King's hand and the unseen army of elzurim, the King extracted the Israelites right out from under the beaelzurim's grip. Elric led Company 12 of Legion 5 on the left flank of the Pillar of Fire until the nation of Israel had crossed the Red Sea.

Elric wiped his eyes and looked around the room. Jenli and Lacidar wiped their eyes. Zaben bit his lip. Timrok had both hands on his swords and a big, stupid grin on his face.

Elric cleared his throat. "That story never gets old," he said.

The lieutenants nodded.

Zaben stopped biting his lip and crossed his arms. "Do you realize what tomorrow is?"

Everyone shook their heads.

"It's day 400! Jesus has been in Egypt 400 days! And we are leading Him out on the morning of Passover. It has to mean something." He looked toward Elric. "Has the Lord given you anything about this?"

"No. It is interesting." Elric paused for a few seconds. "But I would not read too much into it. Jesus was not in bondage here. We are not bound for the Red Sea, and we are certainly not going to

Mount Sinai. We will never be east of the Jordan, so we will have no need to cross it, and I do not anticipate even getting close to Jericho. No, I think He has called His Son out of Egypt just like He did the nation of Israel, but I do not see that parallel affecting our plans for the journey."

Zaben forced a slow nod. "We may not be at the Red Sea seven days from now, but I think we should be on our guard. These days do not line up by accident."

"Mmm," Elric said, rubbing his chin.

The humans prepared for bed.

"Status of your teams," Elric said. "Lacidar?"

"In Judea with Zacharias, Elizabeth, and John. We are ready."

"Jenli?"

"Preparations in Nazareth are complete."

"Zaben?"

"Already in strategic positions along the route. All is quiet."

"Timrok?"

"We are ready for escort. We will not be seen, but we will be all around you."

"Very good. Tomorrow we move."

* * *

Joseph cinched a rope holding down a large coarse linen–wrapped bundle on the back of the donkey cart. Benjamin watered the donkey. Sunrise drew near.

"It's strange leaving Egypt on the morning of Passover," Joseph said. "It almost feels . . . somehow . . . historic. Do you suppose it means anything?"

"I don't know," Benjamin said. "Are you sure you are to be traveling at all? This is supposed to be a holy day."

"I have specific orders from the Lord. If He says to travel, who am I to question?"

"At least you're not leading an entire nation out of Egypt."

"This is a good thing. I am no Moses."

Benjamin laughed. "And you do not have Pharaoh chasing you."

"That is a good thing, too."

"Of course, if you want people to write books about you and talk about you throughout the generations, you have to do something truly remarkable."

"I have no need for the remarkable. Here, pull down on this rope on the other side there. Good. Now tie that one off. I think we are ready."

"Are you sure you will not wait for a few days?" Benjamin said. "There is a caravan headed north that you could join."

"No, the last time we joined up with a caravan, it did not go well. Besides, we were specifically told to—"

"I know, I know. You are supposed to leave this morning. Look, here comes Mary and Rachael and the boys."

"We are so sad to see you leave," Rachael said.

"Thank you," Mary said. "Your gracious kindness toward us will remain in our hearts forever."

"It has been a very good year," Joseph said. He grabbed Benjamin's shoulders. "Thank you. Thank you." They hugged.

"The blessing has been ours," Benjamin said.

Rachael and Mary hugged. Joseph hugged Rachael and Benjamin hugged Mary.

The two boys watched all the hugging. They hugged each other. The adults all laughed. Rachael and Mary dabbed their eyes.

"Come now," Joseph said, lifting Jesus to his hip. "It's time to go."

Rachael stepped forward and put her hand around the back of Jesus' neck and head. She looked into His eyes and smiled. She kissed his forehead.

Joseph walked to the donkey cart and hoisted Jesus onto the back of it.

The journey began. Joseph led with his handcart; Mary walked beside the donkey; and Jesus bounced around in the donkey cart wearing His favorite tunic and waving to everyone they passed. He acted like every person He saw was some long–lost best friend, and He waved and waved to get their attention. Some smiled and waved back, which made Him laugh. Others were too busy or too sophisticated to be bothered by Him and passed by—working hard not to make eye contact. He didn't seem to notice. He just waved to the next person.

Six days of a dusty trail passed. Eating the matzo for every meal became monotonous, but it turned out to be good for travel. As the sun set, beginning the seventh day of the Feast of Unleavened Bread, Joseph set up their makeshift camp beneath a stand of palms and "enjoyed" some more matzo bread in celebration of the feast.

"I think we are not far from Gaza," Joseph said. "But we should rest here the entire day tomorrow to observe the holy day."

Mary nodded.

It was a starry night, skirted with palm silhouettes, and accompanied by a stout southward breeze.

Joseph lay on his back gazing at the stars. "This is the night when the Lord parted the Red Sea. Out here in the wilderness, you can almost imagine what it must have been like—the Red Sea on one side and Pharaoh's army on the other."

\* \* \*

While Joseph, Mary, and Jesus slept, Elric, Timrok, and Zaben stood guard on high alert. Thoughts of the Red Sea deliverance filled Elric's imagination. He scanned the horizon in every direction for any signs of pursuers. Nothing. The night appeared quiet.

# 37

## THE RED SEA

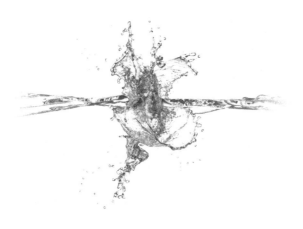

**Birth plus 30 months**

A full midnight moon glowed over the temple ruins in the ancient city of Babylon. Marr headquartered there amid the old stone pillars of the main temple court. Molech, Asherah, and Yarikh stood just beyond the reach of Marr's sword but several steps in from the ring of fire that surrounded the entire throne room with them in the middle. The flames burned bright red and orange at the base, while blue tips shot thirty feet in the air, blocking out all onlookers and locking in the three commanders. Marr's voice rumbled across the stone floor as he roared, "I don't care about your petty squabbles and maneuvering for power. None of that matters compared to our primary goal—to find and kill the Son of Man. Have you forgotten our mandate?"

The three commanders glowered at each other and shot angry, spiteful glares toward Marr.

"My troops have scoured all of Israel and have found nothing," Molech said with defiance.

Marr growled and sat forward on his throne. "Fools! Could it be that He is not in Israel?"

The three commanders continued to glare at Marr with their chins up and teeth clenched. None answered the question. He led them with another. "He disappeared just as we converged on His location in Bethlehem, right? And you cannot find Him anywhere in Israel, right?" Marr paused and tapped his talon on the throne armrest. He shook his head. "And there are prophecies that say He will come up out of Egypt."

The lights went on the commanders' eyes. Simultaneously they muttered, "He must be in Egypt!"

Marr sneered. "While you three were so consumed with carving out positions within *my* realm, you let the Son of Man slip down to Egypt and hide there for over a year!"

Asherah forced a sharp puff of hot smoke out of his nostrils. Yarikh curled his upper lip and showed one of his filthy fangs. Molech crossed his massive arms.

Marr clenched the armrests of his throne. Flames shot out from between his strained fingers. "Here is what you are going to do," he said. "Choose ten worthy beaelzur captains under your commands.

Each of them will muster 100 beaelzur warriors. Then, they are all to go to Egypt and find the Son of Man. And they shall not return until He is found."

The three commanders glanced at each other with contempt and looked away.

"I don't care where the forces come from." Marr said. "They all belong to me. If the three of you cannot accomplish this order together, I can find more capable commanders."

"It shall be done," Molech said with a raspy tone.

"I thought so. Move quickly—I want the entire army mobilized by dawn."

Marr raised his right hand and slowly brought it back down. The ringed wall of fire dropped, responding to his arm's position until the fire smothered out at the same time his hand returned to its resting place on the throne.

The three commanders turned and flew off.

\* \* \*

Just before dawn, one of Zaben's forward scouts came blazing into camp.

"The enemy is coming! A whole legion is headed this way!"

Seconds later, one of Timrok's team arrived with the same news. One by one within the next two minutes, all of Zaben and Timrok's teams appeared with frantic reports of an incoming horde.

Elric looked down at the three humans—sleeping, unaware of the dangerous evil about to wash over them. He had tried to develop a plan for this eventuality all night, but he never came up with a suitable way out. They had no cover within miles. No place to hide. No place to run.

He took stock of his team—twelve warriors, plus himself, and all had already taken defensive battle-stances around Jesus with their resolute faces turned toward the north. Timrok stood in front. *They are ready to fight to protect the King, but we don't have the numbers to wage a successful battle.*

Elric slid his sword into its sheath and got down on one knee. "Lord, we need your help," he said.

The memory of an ancient defeat sent a spark of pain through his head, and his left eyebrow and upper cheek muscles squeezed two involuntary blinks. He instinctively hid his secret pain behind his hand. He looked up to see if a legion of the King's warriors would descend to join the battle. He remained down on one knee for a full minute, waiting for reinforcements.

Without a sound, Grigor shot down into the camp and landed in front of him. The two talked privately, and then Grigor disappeared as quickly as he had arrived. Elric turned to address the team.

"Put your weapons away," he said. "We will not need to fight today. Today, the Lord Himself will deliver us from our enemy."

They all sheathed their swords without hesitation and turned back to the north. Timrok complied too, but his face gave away his disappointment.

As the rising sun lit the eastern horizon and set it ablaze in red, the fast–moving clouds from the north became visible to the elzur forces surrounding the little human camp. The black clouds boiled and rolled forward like a wave just above the terrain, swallowing the red glow of the sunrise and spewing back out fire and smoke. The wave drew nearer. Elric winced. *It's like standing before an entire ocean of evil—a tidal wave of malevolence about to crush us. What is the King going to do? How is He going to deliver us from that?* He braced his feet, gritted his teeth, and lifted his chin toward the high wall of blackness approaching.

The wave reached the outer edge of the camp. The roar of thousands of demon wings rose like the crashing of a mighty ocean wave. The front of the wave began to split.

Timrok called out, "What's that? What's happening?"

The wall separated as though a giant invisible wedge split the flood just before it reached the camp. The sides passed around the camp, and the wave wrapped back together again, closing them in from the back side. Elric stared at the panorama surrounding them with his mouth wide open. On every side flew hundreds of demons with twisted faces and raging eyes, caught up in the furious momentum southward. Their bat-like wings beat the air of the Middle Realm, and they jostled for flying space. *They don't see us . . . or the camp.* They didn't even seem to notice that they had diverted around it. Elric glanced straight up—clear blue sky. The wave glowed red on the inside from the crimson lightning, and boiling fire flashed between the beaelzurim. High walls of smoldering redness engulfed the camp all around.

Zaben said, "The Lord is parting this . . . this . . . Red Sea."

Elric never took his eyes off the wall of evil streaming by them. "Yes. Yes, He is."

The camp remained in the midst of the sea of demon warriors— untouched, unmoved, and unnoticed—for several long minutes. Finally, the last of the wave closed around the back side of the camp and faded away over the southern horizon. The sky became quiet. The entire troop of elzurim sighed and looked around at each other with nervous smiles. Timrok and Zaben nodded to their teams without a word, and the warriors dispersed and disappeared to their posts.

"That was amazing," Zaben said. "Why can't it always be that easy?"

"What would be the challenge of that?" Timrok said.

The three laughed.

"It does make our work more interesting," Elric said. He checked the humans. *Still sleeping. They will never know what had just happened.*

Zaben nodded. "The Lord likes variety. Every adventure is a new one. Every mystery unfolds in a new way."

"I like it," Elric said.

"As do I," said Timrok.

"You were right about the significance of this day," Elric said. He paused. "However, even knowing that something might be coming—I don't think we were supposed to be prepared for what just happened."

"This whole mission is shrouded in mystery," Zaben said.

# 38

## HOME GROUND

**Birth plus 30 months**

*M*ary walked two full wagon lengths ahead, leading the donkey with the reins in one hand.

Joseph called forward to Mary, "Are you sure that's it?"

Mary turned her head back toward Joseph without missing a stride. "Yes, that's definitely the place."

"I can't believe you were able to find it."

"I told you I would be able to recognize it if we passed close enough." Mary stopped and waited for Joseph to catch up. "You were the one who brought us to the right region in Judea. How did you know how to get here?"

Joseph shrugged. They continued walking.

"You must have been led by the Lord," she said.

"I suppose. I never heard any leading. I just followed the trail and went in the direction that felt right."

"Here we are," Mary said.

"You get Jesus," Joseph said, "and I'll tie up the donkey."

They stepped up to the weathered wooden door of the small house and paused long enough to look at each other with anxious smiles. Joseph knocked. The door cracked open and a pair of eyes peered out. The eyes stopped on Mary. Then the door flung open.

"Mary! What a surprise!" There stood Zacharias with a huge, stunned smile erupting through his gray beard.

"And this must be Joseph. It is so good to meet you. And this," he said, lingering for a second on Jesus, "must be . . . " He lingered another second. "Oh, good heavens, come in! Come in! Elizabeth—look who's here!"

* * *

Tumur watched the surprise visitors disappear inside Zacharias's house. The elzur captain who arrived with them remained outside and scanned the area. Tumur ducked low and couldn't make out the face of the captain. After a short delay, the captain went inside, and Tumur breathed out a long stream of smoke.

*Very interesting. That was Mary from Nazareth—with a husband and child.*

He searched the local horizon for his old partner, Luchek. Nothing. Wisping like silent fog, Tumur moved around to all his normal hiding spots. He didn't find Luchek anywhere.

*How long ago did Luchek leave with Mary? Three years? He must have discovered that Mary—and her child—are not the ones we seek. It is the only explanation.*

He dragged his upper lip back and forth across his stray, upward–pointing fang.

*The boy looked very ordinary. There was no sign of divinity there. Still, why would they require a captain as an escort?*

He peered at the outside of the house.

*I shall have to watch these visitors closely.*

* * *

Inside Zacharias's house, Elric and Lacidar stood just inside the door.

"I have been interested to see John's reaction to Jesus," Elric said to Lacidar. "What will the anointing of the Holy Spirit on a three–year–old look like when he sees the King?"

Lacidar laughed. "There's your answer."

John's eyes stayed fixed on Jesus. The adults talked, and John hid behind Elizabeth—without ever breaking his gaze.

"He knows something is different about Jesus," Elric said, "but he's too young to understand."

Jesus bounded around the room until He found some of John's toys on the floor. John peeked from behind Elizabeth. Jesus flopped down onto the floor and grabbed a toy. John ran over and held out his hand for his toy without saying a word. Jesus laughed and handed it to him. Jesus played with another toy, and John held out his hand for that one. Jesus laughed and handed it to John as though it was a game. Jesus jumped up and ran to Mary, who held His blanket. Snatching the blanket, He giggled all the way to the corner of the room where He squatted down and hid under the blanket.

The adult conversation stopped.

"Watch this," Mary whispered to Zacharias and Elizabeth. "This is His favorite game." She raised her voice. "Where did Jesus go? I'm looking everywhere. I know He has to be—"

"Over here!" John shouted. He rushed across the room and flung the blanket off Jesus. "Here He is!"

Jesus sprang from His spot and ran as fast as His little legs could go. John stayed right behind Him, squealing and laughing. They completed three laps around the room. Jesus plopped down and covered Himself with the blanket. Before anyone could wonder where Jesus had gone, John hopped up and down and ran circles around Jesus. "Here He is! Here He is!" John ripped the blanket off Jesus again, pointed, hopped, and laughed.

"I don't think John understands the game," Elizabeth said.

Everyone laughed.

Elric and Lacidar smiled at each other and nodded.

After they finished supper and got the boys to sleep, the parents gathered in the quiet of the lamplight.

"Where to from here?" Zacharias asked.

"We don't know," Joseph said. "We will probably try Bethlehem or Jerusalem. I feel like we should be in Jerusalem near the temple. But the last time we tried to settle in Jerusalem, it seemed like all the doors kept closing for us and we ended up back in Bethlehem. I think we will probably start with Jerusalem again and see what happens."

Elizabeth shot Zacharias a concerned look.

"What? What is it?" Mary asked.

"Remember how ruthless Herod was?" Zacharias said. "His son Archelaus is ruling over Judea now, and it looks like he is going to be as bad, or worse, than Herod. He has killed thousands already."

"Tell them about Simon," Elizabeth said.

"There was a man named Simon, of Peraea, who once was a slave of King Herod. While everything was in disorder, he claimed himself king."

"He had many supporters," Elizabeth said.

"He actually claimed he would be Israel's messiah. He burned down Herod's palace at Jericho and plundered it. He also destroyed many other of the king's houses with fire and plundered them. Eventually, Gratus, the commander of Herod's infantry—"

"The army that used to support Herod now supports Archelaus," Elizabeth said.

Zacharias nodded. "Gratus and the Roman army completely destroyed all of Simon's fighters. Simon escaped at first, but Gratus caught him and cut off his head. This was a significant uprising, but anyone who even speaks out against Archelaus has seen a similar fate."

"He is an evil tyrant," Elizabeth said. "I fear for our own safety even out here. If I were you, I would try to stay as far away from him as possible."

"But where can we go?" Joseph asked. "How much of the region is under his control?" His eyes filled with dread.

Zacharias scrunched up his old wrinkled face, "He only has Judea and Samaria."

"Only?"

"It could be worse. Fortunately, Archelaus does not have control over all of Israel as Herod did. Antipas is tetrarch over Galilee and the east bank of the Jordan, and Philip is tetrarch over Ituraea and Trachonitis. They both seem to be better than Archelaus. Perhaps you could return to Galilee? That was your old home before all this started."

Joseph shrugged his shoulders. "Yes, but I have no family left there and Mary's family is a little distant ever since the pregnancy. And it's too far from the temple in Jerusalem. Should we not be close to the temple so He can be trained by the best teachers in the land?"

Zacharias tucked his chin down into his beard and looked up at Joseph through his bushy eyebrows. "Don't make too many assumptions about the spiritual leaders in the temple."

"Even so, it just makes the most sense. And, if that is where the Lord wants us, should we not trust Him to protect us from Archelaus—or whoever is in power?"

The debate over where to go continued for a while longer before everybody became too sleepy to continue. They prepared for bed, and Zacharias led them in a prayer for guidance and clear direction from the Lord.

Before Zacharias finished his prayer, Grigor slipped through the ceiling and alighted in front of Elric. His wings folded into his back without a sound.

"A word of the Lord," Grigor said.

"Yes?" Elric replied.

"The Lord has heard the prayer of Zacharias and wants you to deliver His answer to Joseph tonight. Speak to him in a dream and tell him not to go up to Jerusalem. He is to settle in Nazareth, his hometown."

"In His service," Elric said.

Grigor paused a moment and looked Elric and Lacidar in the eyes. His eyes had a twinkle that seemed to say, "I know things from the throne, and I know what you are going through." He shared a look of common purpose, common brotherhood.

"By His word," Grigor said. He unfurled his silent wings and with a single burst disappeared.

Elric's attention returned to the humans in the room.

"Fear not," Zacharias said. "The Lord will make His will known to you somehow. Simply trust and do not be anxious. Get a good night's sleep. We shall talk more tomorrow."

* * *

Joseph walked through a dense green garden along a quaint path under a happy springtime sun. Scores of wildflowers bloomed red, yellow, and purple. Birds twittered. Spotted butterflies danced on a cool breeze. Everything brimmed with life and hope and expectation. Ahead in the distance, Jerusalem stood high on a hill, shining like polished gold in the sun. Surrounded by so much life and beauty, he skipped down the path toward the glowing city on the hill. His movements flowed like an effortless song, and he almost felt as though he floated along with the butterflies.

As his journey continued, the lushness of the garden drew thin. Flowers and trees became fewer and fewer until all the plants were simple shrubs. The butterflies disappeared, and the birds became scarce. He still pressed forward, but his steps became labored, and he had to fight for his breath. Farther down the trail brought even less vegetation. He trudged onward and soon found himself in a desolate wasteland. Visible waves of heat rose from the lifeless sand, and a single vulture circled overhead. *I have to get to Jerusalem. But it's getting so hard.* He looked up to the hill for inspiration. The appearance of the city had changed. Now it looked pale and dark gray, hiding under the shadow of gloomy black clouds.

Joseph stopped and looked around. Nothing but flat, lifeless desert in every direction. Fear and despair wrapped themselves around Joseph like a snake and stole his breath. *What's that up ahead?* Just before the edge of the horizon, a large boulder jutted out of the sand. *Is that a man sitting on top of the boulder?* He scanned the endless desert. *There's nothing here but that. I suppose I should go investigate.* He drudged through the sand for a long time, every laborious step taxing his strength and will. He drew nearer to the boulder, and it became clearer that a man did indeed sit atop it. Joseph approached the man. *I've seen this man before.*

"Hello, Joseph," the man said with a pleasant smile.

"I know you," Joseph said with panting breath. "You're the angel who appeared to me before."

The angel smiled.

"What is going on?" Joseph asked. "Where am I?"

"The more important question is 'where are you going?'"

"I am going to Jerusalem."

"Why?"

"I . . . I don't know."

"Do not go up to Jerusalem. There is nothing but death awaiting you there. Return to your home country of Galilee. Go to Nazareth. This is the word of the Lord for you."

Joseph turned and looked up at the hill toward Jerusalem. Nothing but a black cloud remained. He turned back, and the angel had disappeared. Joseph felt very alone, surrounded by endless desert everywhere. The sand spun around him in a whirlwind. He closed his eyes, and panic swirled through his mind.

Joseph woke up. He strained his eyes into the darkness. Mary and Jesus slept. Joseph gave Mary a nudge.

"Mary, wake up. I had another dream."

* * *

Two weeks later, Zacharias tore a bite–sized piece of bread, dabbed it into the olive oil, and popped it into his mouth. Between chews he said, "This has been the most excellent two weeks of my life. Are you sure you must leave now?"

Joseph nodded. "It is time. You have been more than gracious to let us stay with you, but we have clear direction from the Lord."

"Yes, I know." Zacharias rubbed his forehead. "It is for selfish reasons, I'm sure, that I desire you to stay. This last year has been . . . difficult. I have been facing mounting friction from the other priests ever since the birth of John. I admit, I may have been overly enthusiastic retelling John's miraculous birth. But it seems like there is something deeper feeding their hostility toward me. And lately, it's difficult to execute my normal duties without strong resistance and animosity. But this time with you, with Jesus, has helped me see again what I know in my heart to be true—that our son, John, is the prophet who will go before the Messiah. And the Messiah, the Promised One, is here."

Zacharias watched Jesus playing on the floor. He shook his head.

"This little one will someday conquer Rome and establish His kingdom forever. What I would give to be a part of His army that finally vanquishes Israel's enemies and ushers in a new era of peace and joy on the earth." Zacharias sighed. "Do you think we will see you again?"

"I don't know," Joseph said. "Perhaps during a Passover festival in Jerusalem?"

"Perhaps."

# 39

## NAZARETH

### Birth plus 30 months

The morning sun crept up behind low puffy clouds and gave the Nazarene marketplace a warm orange glow. Elric stood beside a busy produce stand with rows of wooden boxes holding mounds of colorful fruits and vegetables. His hand rested on Joseph's shoulder as Joseph looked over the produce. Elric scanned across the street over the heads of a dozen milling patrons. Jenli emerged from around the corner. *There he is.* Their eyes met, and Elric nodded once. Jenli smiled, bent down, and spoke something to the man walking beside him. The man paused a moment, then turned left toward the produce stand where Elric stood.

Joseph placed a handful of figs into his small basket.

"Joseph! Joseph, is that you?" the approaching man called out.

Joseph turned his head. It was the man who had bought his family house and property after the man's horse died while under his care. Joseph swallowed hard and gave an awkward smile.

"Right on time," Elric said to Jenli.

Jenli smiled and rubbed the stubble on the back of his head.

"It's great to see you," the man said to Joseph. "You are the last person I would have expected to happen upon today."

"Yes, it is quite a coincidence," Joseph answered, shuffling his feet.

"How are you? Is Mary well?"

"Yes, we are doing very well. Mary is back at the inn with our three–year–old boy. I just came to the market to pick up a few things." Joseph kept looking down at his basket and avoiding eye contact.

"Oh, yes," the man said, "I remember—her days were almost complete when you left here. That was a most unfortunate situation for you, wasn't it? I have labored under deep regret every day since you left."

"Be at peace. It was difficult time, but things have worked out for the best."

"What brings you back to Nazareth? Are you moving back or just passing through?"

"We're not sure. I need to stay in Galilee, probably Nazareth. We will need to find work and place to live."

"That's wonderful!" The man pulled Joseph aside out of the jostling of the produce stand customers.

"This is an amazing coincidence," the man said in a more close–up voice. "I have been trying to sell your old place for almost a year now. How would you like to buy it back? I will make you a good deal."

Joseph's eyebrows raised.

The man continued. "Ever since you left, I have tried to figure out what to do with the place. I don't need the house myself, but I can't let it sit empty. I rented it out a few times, but each time the tenants had to leave for one reason or another. I couldn't keep it rented. Eventually, I decided I needed to sell it. Unfortunately, every buyer has backed out at the final moment. I have lowered the price three times, and still it has not sold."

"Interesting," Joseph said.

Elric smirked and glanced over at Jenli, who pursed his lips and raised his eyebrows.

The man said to Joseph, "I would be willing to sell it to you today for half the current value of the property."

"Half?" Joseph's voice cracked.

"This was your family's property. My soul could have peace again if you took it back."

"This is an amazing offer."

Elric and Jenli watched the men work out the details. "Very nice work," Elric said to Jenli. "All the pieces came together today exactly as planned."

"Thank you, captain. Does Joseph have enough money to purchase the house?"

"Oh, yes. He still has most of the gold left. He can easily pay the entire amount and have a sizable reserve. Is there work for him here in Nazareth?"

"We have four jobs already arranged. He has enough work to keep him busy for at least year—and there are more being prepared."

"Excellent. We will be able to settle here for a long time."

* * *

## Baptism minus 27 years

Mary waved to Joseph from the front door of his old family house as he wheeled his handcart full of tools down the path. He squinted against the rising sun on his face and pushed the cart past their garden. The young garden stalks stood full and green, and the vines spread thick and deep. They had planted late, but Mary remained hopeful they would still see a fall harvest. She watched Joseph another minute more and turned back into the house with a satisfied smile.

After only three months back in Nazareth, life had already taken on a comfortable rhythm. She pictured Joseph returning home tonight, sweaty and tired from a hard day's work. She thought about supper, but a fleeting image of her father and mother interrupted her and tied her stomach in a knot. Her family had been accommodating about their return, but they obviously still carried the family shame of her situation. She wondered how long they would remain distant. She took a deep breath and tried to remember all they had been through so far. It amazed her how easily all the details of the move back to Nazareth fell into place. She closed her eyes and wondered what would come next.

Just then, a noise from the other room caught her attention. She knew what that meant. The first part of their daily routine consisted of morning prayer time, and once again, Jesus must have woken up and started without her. She turned the corner and found Him already on His knees. A rambunctious three-year-old, eager to spend time in prayer—Mary shook her head and smiled. She knelt down beside her young Son and joined the conversation already in progress.

* * *

Elric watched from the corner of the room as Mary and Jesus prayed. *I love watching words spoken in the flesh enter the Middle Realm to do their work.* Some words turned to light and rested back on their spirits and their house. Some shot outward like arrows toward faraway marks. Some rose like fragrant incense upward through the spiritual air, through the roof, spiraling heavenward. Every word full of energy, full of purpose.

At the same time, warm shafts of light rode back down the waves of energy toward Mary and Jesus. The King was speaking. He was always speaking. The words hit Mary—like water on dark, well-waxed glass. A tiny shadow of the rays penetrated the surface of her spirit, but most of it beaded up and rolled off. Elric shook his head.

*She can't hear. None can. Ever since the Fall. If only there was a way to make a man's spirit alive again . . .*

The words also hit Jesus. Every word from the Throne penetrated the Son and didn't escape. His spirit was alive, and other than the lack of visible face-to-face contact, no barrier existed between Him and the Father. He only had the understanding of a human three-year-old, so the conversation with the Father sounded simple, but it was very real.

*This is how it is supposed to be.*

* * *

Prayer time finished. Still on their knees, Mary put her arm around Jesus' shoulders.

"You know, God likes it when we talk to Him. He always hears our prayers," Mary said.

"Mm-hm, I know," Jesus replied in His childish little voice.

The matter–of–fact tone in His reply struck Mary off guard. She believed it, but in reality most of time she felt like her prayers just bounced off the ceiling. Sometimes she thought she could sense the Lord's presence, but usually she even wondered about that. She sat up and stroked Jesus' back.

"So, does He answer you?" Mary asked.

"Oh, yes, He talks to me all the time."

"You hear His voice?"

"Not in my ears. I just know what He says in here," He said, rubbing His chest with His little hands.

"What does He say?"

"He says He loves me."

"That is right, honey. The Lord does love you. He loves all of us. What else does he tell you?"

"He says He is my abba. Isn't Abba my abba?"

Mary cleared her throat and rubbed her forehead.

"Well, dear . . . the Lord is the Father of everything because He created everything. He is our Father in heaven."

Jesus smiled and nodded.

Mary looked around the room and pulled a stray strand of hair back behind her ear.

"Does He . . . tell you anything else?"

Jesus paused and fidgeted. "He told me you have a baby in your tummy. Where is the baby, Ima? I don't see him."

Mary went flush.

She was a few weeks late and had been feeling a little off, so she suspected she might be pregnant. But there was no way Jesus could have known anything. She hadn't told Joseph yet. She wasn't even sure about it herself—until now. The unexpected confirmation washed over her like a flood. She laughed, and a stream of tears overflowed her eyes and ran down her cheeks.

She wiped her eyes and answered, "Well, you can't see him yet, honey. But I guess he is in there." Her voice cracked. "He will grow and grow, and Ima's tummy will get very big, and eventually he will come out. Then we will get to hold him—or her. It could be a boy or a girl."

"I think it's a boy," Jesus said.

"Oh, you do?" Mary laughed. "Then I guess you are going to have a little brother!" She couldn't stop the tears.

Jesus looked confused by Mary's flood of emotions, and He got up and wrapped His little arms as far around Mary as He could reach and patted her on the back.

"It's all right, Ima. It will be all right."

Mary laughed and cried even harder. "I know. Ima is very happy and very excited."

She hugged Him back, and they got up and danced around the room.

# 40

## A BROTHER FOUND

**Baptism minus 26 years**

A late autumn breeze carried a crisp chill across Nazareth. Behind the warmth of the walls of their home, Daniel poked at the wood in the fireplace while Ruth pulled coins from a small wooden box. Vorsogh stood beside Daniel, whispering toxic drops of despair into his spirit.

"Daniel," Ruth said. "Daniel, look at me."

Daniel turned his head and gazed in the direction of Ruth with vacant, glassy eyes.

"I need you to go to town and buy some fresh fruit. Can you do that for me? Daniel?"

Daniel got up and reached for his cloak.

"Good," Ruth said. She dropped the coins into a small leather pouch and held it out for Daniel. "Go straight to the marketplace and come right back home. Do you understand?"

Daniel took the money pouch, turned, and walked out the door with one slow, miserable motion. Vorsogh walked along.

Just outside of town, a lone tent sat beside the trail. In the Middle Realm, it stood like a mighty stone fortress—dark, cold, and sinister. Vorsogh snorted a puff of yellow smoke. *Excellent.* He chuckled and flew ahead to the tent. A woman, full of a beaelzur spirit, stood outside the tent, calling to people passing by.

Vorsogh alighted in front of her and said to the demon within, "I have a charge that is ready. I will bring him to you if you will open him up to me."

A small ashen spirit, half the size of Vorsogh, stepped out of the woman. He had smooth skin and a hairless, round head. "Step inside," the spirit said with a soft and airy voice.

Inside the tent, no less than twenty demons filled the space. Some stood along the walls. Some swirled through the murky smoke in mid-air. Some clung to the ceiling and watched from above with menacing red eyes.

"Tell me about him," the spirit said.

"The boy's name is Daniel. He is twelve. I killed his brother two years ago, and I now have this young one lost in despair. We could 'reunite' him with his brother."

"His brother's name?"

"Levi."

"Bring him in."

\* \* \*

Near the edge of town Daniel came across a large tent beside the road. It looked to be the tent of some nomad or group of nomads, and a woman stood in front of the open flap of the tent. The woman called out to all the passersby.

"Fortunes told! Come in and let me tell you your future."

Daniel passed close enough to see the woman's face. She looked dirty and trail-worn, and her eyes unnerved him; but her voice sounded smooth and compelling. Daniel gave a *humph*. *I have no future*. He passed by without giving her any more notice.

He walked a stone's–throw distance and heard over his shoulder, "So much sadness for one so young."

Daniel kept walking.

"Daniel! Do you miss your brother?" The woman's voice sounded compassionate but mysterious.

Daniel stopped cold. Chills shot up and down his spine, and the hair on the back of his neck stood up straight. He turned around and eyed the woman. "How do you know my name? And how do you know about my brother?"

"I know . . . many things," the woman said.

Daniel approached with small cautious steps. Something deep in the pit of his being told him this woman was dangerous, but his head spun with wild thoughts, excitement, and emotions that he hadn't experienced in a very long time.

Daniel continued forward. "Do you know my brother?"

The woman replied with a soft and mysterious voice, "Not in life."

"Who are you?" Daniel asked.

"I am . . . an intermediary. A bridge between this world and the next."

"You talk to spirits?"

"Yes," she replied with a teasing smile.

"And do they talk to you?"

"Yes." Her eyebrows raised high, and her eyes looked like pools of deep wisdom.

"So, it is possible," Daniel said. He paused. The woman's gaze felt like it could see right into his soul. "Would it be possible to talk with my brother? I mean, for me? Can you help me talk with my brother?"

"Perhaps." She turned her chin and looked away with a coy coolness. "There is a price. Do you have any money?"

Daniel pulled out the leather pouch. The coins clinked into his hand out of the pouch.

The woman smiled. "That will do," she said, holding out her hand.

Daniel turned his hand over and let the coins drop into the woman's open palm. She smiled again and took him by the hand.

"Come inside."

The inside of the tent had a dark and secretive atmosphere. A single table sat poised in the center of the room with several chairs stationed around it. Three drippy candles atop human skulls on the weathered wooden table provided the only light and cast eerie dancing shadows on the walls and cluttered shelves. The shelves were filled with many small beakers and bottles of mysterious powders and liquids. A heavy layer of smoke from incense hung low from the murky ceiling. The air felt thick and difficult to breathe, and Daniel had to fight back the oppressive fear crushing him. His skin turned cold and clammy. *This place hides a dangerous unseen presence. I should go. This is too scary. No! I've always wondered about talking with spirits. Now I might actually have a chance to talk with my brother.*

"What do we do now?" he asked.

The woman closed the flap of the tent. "Just relax," she answered with a cool and controlled tone. "Please, have a seat." She pulled out a chair for him. "Very good." She sat down across from him and reached across the table. "Now, take my hands."

Her cold, dry hands gave Daniel a sharp chill. She closed her eyes, raised her chin, and cocked her head as though listening to some voice that only she could hear.

"Your brother's name was Levi. Am I right?"

"Yes! Yes! That's right! Can you—"

"Shhh. We need to be very still and quiet. Close your eyes and clear your mind. The spirits cannot be rushed or coerced. Open yourself up to them and they will speak. Relax. Relax. Very good."

For several minutes they sat with their eyes closed in the flickering candlelight. In the deathly quiet, Daniel's heart pounded all the way up in his throat. He kept repeating in his mind, *Come in, come in, please come in.*

Finally, the woman breathed an ominous whisper, "He is here."

Daniel squeezed her hands and waited.

"Daniel, Levi is here, and he wants me to give you a message."

"Yes, what is it?"

"He says he misses being with you."

"I miss him, too! Can you tell him I miss him?"

"He says he knows you do."

"Can you ask him if he will talk to me directly?"

The woman opened her eyes with a wild intensity. Daniel's stomach leapt into his throat. He swallowed and shifted in his seat.

"Be careful of what you ask. Are you sure that is what you want?"

Daniel hesitated for just a second, swallowed again and answered, "Yes, yes, I am sure."

The woman closed her eyes and became still. She twitched. The twitch turned into mild trembling . . . restrained shuddering . . . violent shaking . . . horrifying convulsions. Daniel pressed hard against the back of his chair, his eyes wide and his jaw slack.

She stopped. Her head slumped down. She looked dead.

Daniel took a deep breath. The air filled his lungs with a blistering fire—and an unmistakable sense that he was not alone, like the hollow shell of his meaningless existence had somehow been filled. He grabbed his chest and fought for another breath.

"Daniel," a voice said.

He glanced at the woman across the table. Still no signs of life.

"Daniel."

Daniel rubbed his deaf ear. Was that his brother's voice . . . in his deaf ear?

"Levi? Is that you?" Daniel said, turning his ear upward.

"Yes, Daniel, it is me, Levi."

"I can hear you! I can hear you! I *knew* it was true. And you can hear me?"

"Yes. Why have you called me?"

"I missed you and wanted to talk with you again. Can you see me?"

"Yes, of course."

"But I can't see you. Why can't I see you?"

"It is a difficult thing for the living to see into my world. Very few are able."

"But it is possible, isn't it? I have seen spirits before. Can you make yourself visible to *me?*"

"I will try," the voice said, "but remember, most people are not able to see into the spiritual realm."

"I will be able. I'm ready. I want to see you!"

He waited. Nothing. He squinted into the darkness. Still nothing. He strained against hope, against fear, against his feeble flesh, against . . . *There!* The faint outline of a person appeared in front of him in the shadows. Gradually, the outline filled in until the full figure of a young man became clear. It looked like Levi with the same clothes he wore when he was killed. Not actual flesh and bone—but transparent with the color of a ghostly gray mist.

"I can see you! I truly can!"

"That is very good, little brother. Tell me, what is it you would like to know?"

*It's a dream come true! Quick . . . a question worthy of this special moment.* "What is it like? Are there spirits everywhere around us like I thought?"

"Yes, just like you thought. And it is very peaceful here."

"So, have you seen God?"

The spirit smiled a knowing, concerned smile and answered, "Daniel, there is no God. After you die, your spirit just stays here on earth and joins all the others."

"What do you and all the spirits do?"

"We help people and guide them and bring them comfort in times of need."

"What about angels? Have you seen any angels?"

"No, of course not, they are nothing more than the souls of men who have gone on before."

"I miss you," Daniel said. "I miss these talks. Is there any way you can stay with me all the time and be *my* guide?"

"Yes, I will stay with you. I promise. You will not always be able to see me, but I will speak to you. You can always believe in me."

The image faded away into the shadows.

"Wait!" Daniel called out. "Don't go!"

"I am still here."

Daniel tapped his deaf ear. Still dead except for the sound of Levi's voice.

The voice said, "I told you I would always be with you."

Without warning, the woman's head sprang back upright. She looked stunned and disoriented. She stared at Daniel for several moments and scanned the room.

"You heard from your brother?" she asked.

"Better than that—I actually saw him!"

"That is good. That is very good." She stood up and shuffled over behind Daniel's chair. She pulled the chair backward and said, "Thank you for coming in today. I am always happy to reunite family with their beloved. I trust your experience was rich and fulfilling."

Without another word, she ushered him out of the tent and bid him farewell.

* * *

Vorsogh stepped from the tent into the sunlight, looking at the world through Daniel's eyes. *Ahhh, yes. It feels so good to be wrapped in human skin.* The coolness of the autumn breeze prickled against Daniel's face.

His face. His body. His direct connection with the Physical Realm.

The power he now commanded over this pathetic human made Vorsogh feel heady and godlike.

"Come, little brother," Vorsogh said, "let's go to the market for some fruit."

"But I just spent all the money Mother gave me."

"Worry not. Just trust me."

# 41

## A BROTHER GAINED

### Baptism minus 25.5 years

*A*festive ceremony filled Joseph and Mary's home with many people and many smiles on the eighth day after the birth of Jesus' brother. Elric stood with Zaben, Timrok, and Jenli against the wall and watched the ceremony while their teams kept a safe perimeter outside. The crowd became quiet. The honored Mohel, Raziel, recited the Brit Milah blessing.

"Our God and God of our fathers, preserve this child for his father and mother, and his name in Israel shall be called *James*, the son of . . . " Raziel stopped and smiled at Joseph.

The memory of this very moment during Jesus' Brit Milah welled up within Elric. During that ceremony, Raziel acknowledged Jesus' true father. *No other person in the room besides Raziel, Joseph, and Mary, knows the significance of this particular moment.* Elric suppressed a laugh and dabbed the corner of one eye with his finger. Jenli smirked at Elric with raised eyebrows. Elric tightened his lower lip, raised his chin, and stared at Raziel.

Looking Joseph right in the eyes, Raziel continued. "*Joseph.* May the father rejoice in his offspring, and his mother be glad with the fruit of her womb, as it is written: 'May your father and mother rejoice, and she who bore you be glad.'"

After the official ceremony completed, the real festivities began. People laughed and ate and milled about. The children all ran out of the house for the freedom of outdoor play. Jesus ran right in the middle of the small pack.

Elric and the three lieutenants stepped outside with the children. Elric made a quick scan. *Two of Timrok's team are within close striking distance. The other three are concealed and close. In the mid-range distance—there, there, and there—Zaben and Jenli's teams are in place. The perimeter around the King looks secure.*

"I do enjoy watching the children play," Timrok said.

"Mmm," Elric replied, still scanning the area.

"I see Jesus is wearing a new tunic cut from your cloak material," Jenli said. "Was Mary surprised when the Lord restored the material to its original size again?"

"I don't think so," Elric said. "She appears to recognize the importance of this covering, even though she does not know its true purpose. And she has the faith to believe this provision will continue."

The girls played in the shade of the house and took turns decorating each other's hair with fresh–picked flowers. The boys chased each other with sticks and fought epic sword battles amid a cloud of dust.

Elric watched a stick–sword fight and smiled. "Jesus looks like every other young boy in the street—with no indicators of who He is. Joseph has a very normal looking family, especially now that there is an additional sibling."

"For two years we have remained hidden in Nazareth," Timrok said, "with not a single unsafe encounter with the enemy. Do they no longer seek Him?"

Elric stared across the horizon. "They still seek."

Zaben bit his lip and joined Elric's gaze across the horizon. "Their strategy has changed. They know the King cannot be touched, except through the hands of man. I perceive a three–layered plan in action." He paused. Jenli and Timrok turned and waited. "First, they raise up false messiahs to lead armed revolts."

Elric nodded. "Simon of Peraea."

"War causes much destruction," Zaben continued. "The enemy knows it is possible the King could be swept away in the heat of an insurrection. Unrest is high across the nation. The people are looking for a messiah. The enemy is raising up leaders."

"Are there any of note right now?" Elric asked.

Jenli pulled his ledger from inside his tunic and flipped through it. "There is a shepherd named Athronges and his four brothers. Athronges has already declared himself messiah and makes war against Archelaus. His brothers each command sizeable armies. They are brutal, murderous men."

"If we are not careful, the King could be caught in the middle of someone else's battle," Elric said.

"Eventually each of the false messiahs will be destroyed," Zaben said. "The enemy will raise them up, then crush them at the hands of the Romans. This leads to the second layer of their plan. After years of devastating losses, the people will lose heart."

Elric crossed his arms and nodded. "So, by the time the King is ready to begin His campaign, the people will not have courage left to support Him." He raised his chin. "And the third layer of their strategy?"

"Physical oppression," Zaben said. "Sickness, disease, leprosy, demon possession. All these are increasing in the land. Those that the King would call upon for His armies will be too weak and lame to serve."

"There was another possession right here in Nazareth a few months ago," Jenli said. "A young boy. The son of a shepherd."

Timrok put his hands on the handles of his swords. "The enemy can cripple the entire nation. All we need is the King and ten good men. We have seen deliverance with less."

"Timrok is right," Elric said. "But, still, we must be mindful of the enemy's tactics."

Around the side of the house, Jesus had been cornered by three other boys—sticks drawn and ready to strike. Just as they moved in, Jesus swatted two of their sticks aside with His stick and ducked out through the middle of them, laughing as He ran.

"How long?" Zaben said. "How long until the King begins His campaign? Have you received any word yet?"

Elric looked upward into a blank sky. "Nothing."

They all watched the boys play for several minutes without a sound.

"We should be doing something," Zaben said.

"What?" asked Timrok. "We proceed only at the word of the King."

Zaben chewed on his lip and scowled. "Preparing. The King expects us to prepare."

Timrok crossed his arms. "Preparing what?"

Zaben paused and looked down at his feet.

"Jesus," Jenli said. "We help prepare Jesus. He is only four and a half, but I think he is ready for formal education at the hand of a human mentor."

"Yes," Zaben said.

"Do we have such a mentor?" Timrok asked.

Elric nodded. "Raziel. He is our man."

All three lieutenants nodded.

"I agree," Elric said. "Jesus is receiving great wisdom from the Holy Spirit, but He still needs the training of men. The sooner we begin, the better. Zaben, begin speaking to Raziel."

Zaben smiled. "In His service."

# 42

## AT THE HANDS OF MEN

### Baptism minus 25 years

*J*oseph led his donkey cart up to the crowd gathered at the edge of Nazareth. Mary swayed with the rhythm of the rocky trail in the back of the cart with James in her arms. Five–year–old Jesus hung His arms over the side rails and laughed and waved at everyone. Two weeks' worth of provisions were stacked high in the cart, including a large tent, wrapped in a tight bundle.

Elric walked beside Joseph with Timrok at the rear. They stopped, and Zaben and Jenli approached from out of the crowd.

Elric glanced at the sliver of sun just peeking over the horizon. "Is the caravan ready?"

"Almost," Jenli said. "There are three more families to come. Then the full group will be assembled."

"Very good," Elric said. "You two keep your teams hidden. Zaben, your team will guard the front and rear. Jenli, your team will cover our side flanks. Timrok."

Timrok stepped up from behind, scanning left, then right.

"Disperse your team among the caravan, but you stay close to me. Remember, there will be enemy warriors traveling with us." He looked Timrok in the eyes. "Keep your distance, and do not engage unless the King is threatened."

Timrok nodded.

"This trip is an important test for us," Elric said. "We will have to make this pilgrimage to Jerusalem for the Passover Feast every year. I don't have to tell you that our risk of exposure is extreme. Be on your highest guard."

Jenli said, "Our last time in the temple courts with the King for His dedication nearly ended in ruin. How do we prevent the same this time?"

Elric's left eye twitched twice. "The King's tunic serves well as a veil against the enemy," he said. "And your teams are skilled at deflecting beaelzur warriors away. Our problem is hiding Him from people who can perceive with their spirit."

"Prophets," Zaben said.

"Mainly, yes. They will speak out if they perceive Him. So, we must deflect them away from the King so they do not see Him."

"There are so many people in the courts, and our numbers are few," Jenli said.

"If a prophet sees the King, speak to him to remain silent."

"And if he does not hear?" Timrok asked.

"A touch of dumbness should help him understand."

The three lieutenants nodded.

A stir arose amongst the crowd of people. Wagon wheels turned, beasts of burden snorted and neighed, and feet and hooves thumped on the ground.

"It appears we are underway," Elric said. "Deploy your teams."

\* \* \*

The caravan from Nazareth rumbled down the trail after the completion of the Passover.

"This has been an excellent trip," Elric said to Timrok, walking alongside Joseph's cart. "The journey to Jerusalem was easy. The week of Passover was quiet. One full day of travel behind us. Another three and a half days, and we will be back in Nazareth."

Timrok glanced over at Mary, who walked beside Joseph with James in her arms. Jesus walked just behind, His little legs taking four steps for every one of theirs. "Joseph's family looks just like all the rest of the travelers," he said.

Elric smiled and nodded. "Anonymity is a welcome traveling companion."

Xarjim, one of Zaben's warriors, shot in from behind and landed next to Elric. His wings folded into his back, and he leaned in close to Elric. He said with a low voice, "Captain, a group of fifty rebels under Athronges is fleeing this direction. They are pursued closely by a full Roman cavalry unit."

"This is the last surviving band of Athronges's rebellion," Timrok said. "These are desperate men."

Elric took a deep breath. "If they reach the caravan, they may try to mix in with the travelers and hide from the Romans."

"And the soldiers will have no mercy on any they believe are harboring fugitives," Timrok said.

Christov, another one of Zaben's warriors, streaked in from behind.

"Captain," Christov said.

"We already know," Elric said. "Xarjim, you contact Zaben in front of the caravan. Tell him to take his team and intercept Athronges's men. Divert them away from the caravan. Christov, find Jenli at our left flank. His team is to intercept the Roman cavalry. Divert them also."

"In His service," the two warriors said. They disappeared in a flash.

Elric turned to Timrok. "Form a battle line with your team at our rear. Divert the soldiers if you can. Engage all beaelzurim with them. I will stay with the King."

"In His service." Timrok sped away into the mass of travelers and disappeared.

Elric looked behind. In the distance, a cloud of dust approached. Several miles behind that, another cloud of dust closed the distance fast. Elric jumped up onto the back of the cart, crossed his arms, and watched the approaching clouds. Every minute brought the clouds closer. He looked out across the caravan, plodding along, with no idea of the mortal danger that rushed toward them. He looked back at the incoming band, close enough now that he could almost make out the forms of the horses and riders.

Without warning, the front line of horses in the first group reared up and came to a halt. The riders behind piled up into a bunch. Then, with a burst of speed, the troop turned hard to the right and raced on.

The dust cloud of the Roman army stopped. It, too, turned right, following the rebel troop. Elric took in a deep breath, held it, and let it out. He looked back at the caravan, still plodding along. He smiled and shook his head. *All quiet here. They'll never even know the danger that . . .*

*Crash!* The clanging of steel blades pierced the spiritual air at the rear of the caravan. Elric spun around. Sparks shot into the air of the Middle Realm and enemy war shouts rang out, but the skirmish remained obscured by the human travelers. Timrok leapt into the air high enough to be seen over the crowd and somersaulted downward with both blades flashing. All became quiet.

A moment later, Timrok stood before Elric. "Captain, a small contingent of beaelzurim has been subdued, but two Roman soldiers made it through and are searching the people."

Elric paused a moment and rubbed his chin. "Let them complete their search. There is nothing here to find. They will be satisfied and not return."

The two Roman horsemen weaved their way through the moving caravan. They paused here, doubled around there, paused at another traveler. They approached Joseph's location from behind. The two riders sat high and powerful on haughty war horses which pranced and snorted. The shine of the armor on their helmets and breastplates had a stark contrast to the sea of earthy linen on the pilgrims. One horseman trotted up beside Joseph and used the tip of his blade to pull back Joseph's tunic hood, exposing Joseph's face.

Elric pushed the blade away and commanded, "Move along."

The soldier eyed Joseph. He eyed Mary and the two boys. He gave his horse a kick and trotted up to the next family.

Ten minutes later, the two horsemen galloped off in the direction of the receding dust clouds.

Elric and Timrok walked along in silence.

Several minutes later, Raziel, the priest from Nazareth, called out to Joseph from their left. He traveled on foot and waved his arm at Joseph.

"Joseph, Joseph," Raziel shouted above the noise of the hooves and wheels. "I've been looking for you."

Joseph slowed the cart and waited for Raziel to make his way over.

"Romans," Raziel said, joining up with Joseph.

"Yes, they are a force to be feared," Joseph said.

"Someday. Someday the Lord will deliver us from their tyranny." Raziel looked back at Jesus, riding on the cart again.

"Yes," Joseph said. "Someday."

They walked for a while without talking.

Raziel blurted out, "You know, Jesus is a very smart little boy."

"Yes, he seems to learn things quickly."

"It's more than that, He has remarkable focus, and He truly seems to understand things."

"M-hm," Joseph said.

"And did you see Him in the temple? He was completely enamored with it. It was almost like it felt like home to Him."

"Yes, it was very cute."

"Joseph, I have been thinking." Raziel paused.

"Yes, what?"

"Well, would you be willing to let me tutor Him privately?"

"Oh, no, we could never afford that."

"No, no, I would not ask for money." Raziel stopped walking and pulled Joseph aside. The rest of the troop plodded by. He spoke low. "The more I see of Him, the more I think He might truly be the Messiah. He is going to need a solid education, and I fear for what might happen if He is put in with everyone else. I believe He is going to start asking deep questions and may attract the wrong kind of attention. He is different, and He knows it. But if I were to teach Him privately, not only would it be safer, but I could tailor the lessons to His ability. I think He will progress much faster than others. I will teach Him all the Scriptures. I will teach Him Hebrew, Greek, and Latin."

"Our own private rabbi . . . do you not have other responsibilities in the synagogue?"

"Yes, of course, but I know I could set aside time each day for this. I have been praying about this for some time, and I truly believe the Lord wants me to do this. What do you think?"

"I think it sounds . . . amazing. Are you sure?"

"Yes, yes! I am very excited about it."

"When should we start?" Joseph asked.

Raziel put his arm around Joseph's shoulder and began walking again. "Let's start right away. I think He is ready for it. I shall begin coming to your house as soon as we get back."

"To our house? You mean you're not going to tutor Him in the synagogue?"

"I think it will be safest in your home. I want Him to have a chance to develop without attracting too much attention from either His peers or the religious leaders. I believe He will reveal Himself when He is ready, and until then it is our job not only to train Him up, but to protect Him from potential outside threats while He is young and vulnerable."

Elric turned and smiled at Timrok. They both nodded their heads and laughed.

Something in the distance caught Elric's eye.

"Look," Elric said. In the distance one large dust cloud rose into the air. "The Romans have caught the rebels."

"That will mark the end of the Athronges rebellion," Timrok said. "Death surrounds us round about."

Elric nodded. "The sooner the King begins His campaign, the better."

# 43

# PATHS OF DARKNESS

**Baptism minus 24 years**

Marr sat upon his regal black throne in Babylon, waiting for his three commanders to arrive and make their report. He tapped a talon on the armrest and snorted out a puff of yellow smoke. It had been a month since the last worthless report from Molech, Asherah, and Yarikh, and Marr didn't expect today's report to be any better. Marr's continuous tapping echoed across the empty court. Minutes ticked by. He blew another puff of smoke, stopped tapping, and turned his right hand over, palm up. A pulsing red plasma ball of fire formed and suspended between his fingertips. He stared deep into the flames.

Finally, the three commanders arrived and stood before the throne. Marr moved his hand to the side, revealing the three commanders from behind the ball of fire. Deep black smoke rolled from the throne, swirled along the floor, and billowed up to their waists.

Asherah took a step forward. "I am pleased to report that our forces gain ground daily," he said. "There is dissension and political unrest in every region. Herod Archelaus is a dutiful puppet. By his hand, we have massacred thousands. We have false messiahs gaining followers."

Molech interjected, "Our latest messiah, Theudas, convinced four hundred people to follow him to the Jordan River where he claimed he would divide the waters and lead them into a new Promised Land. The Roman army killed many of the followers and cut off Theudas's head."

Marr looked at the three without blinking.

"Sickness is on the rise, and new people are being possessed every day," Yarikh said. "The religious leaders' hearts are growing harder and more legalistic."

Marr squeezed his hand into a fist, crushing the fireball and sending the energy blasting through his clenched fingers in shards of flame and crimson lightning.

"Fools!" he roared. "Where is the Child King? How hard can it be to find One so conspicuous?" He paused, but not long enough for them to answer. "Do you have any news from the legion in Egypt?"

"No news worthy to report," Asherah answered.

A new fireball formed in Marr's hand, and he stared into it without looking up. "Continue the search. The King has to be there because He will be called up out of Egypt before He begins His campaign. I want Him found! Every day He grows stronger. We must find Him and destroy Him before He comes of age."

"Shall we send *more* forces to Egypt?" Yarikh asked.

"No," Marr said with a grumble. "Continue your work in Israel. I have no confidence your legions will be able to find Him, and we must continue to weaken the King's people in preparation for His coming campaign as our lord has commanded."

The three commanders gave a slight head bow, turned, and left.

\* \* \*

Daniel wandered through the streets of Nazareth with no particular purpose or direction. His parents had gone to some Brit Milah ceremony, but he had no interest. He was glad to be fourteen and old enough to make his own choices. He drifted through the town and side streets as though all the buildings and people were mere shadows in another world. He had a real world elsewhere.

"Levi," he whispered under his breath. "Are you there? Why don't you talk with me? I haven't seen you since two years ago, and you haven't said anything all day. I can tell you're there. I can feel your presence."

He shuffled down another side street, lost in thought. While glad to have his brother with him, he noticed that Levi had become more aggressive. The destructive suggestions Levi made sometimes surprised him. It didn't matter, though.

"Just don't leave me alone again," he said.

"I am always here," the voice said in his right ear.

Daniel touched his otherwise deaf ear and smiled.

"I have kept our secret for a long time," Daniel said. "When can I tell somebody about you?"

"Not ever," Vorsogh said. "No one can ever know."

"But I—"

"They won't understand. None are enlightened as you. They don't even deserve to know the truth about the spirit world."

"I suppose."

Daniel came around the corner of a building and saw Joseph and Mary's house, a beehive of activity. Daniel stopped and watched around the corner from a distance. This is where his parents had gone—somewhere in the middle of this big party. Joseph and Mary had had another son. They named him Joseph, but Daniel didn't care. He just watched and sneered at all the silly, superficial happiness.

"None of these people understand true pain and loneliness," he said.

The usual pack of young kids ran around and played games. The six–and–a–half–year–old Jesus spent most of His time keeping his two–year–old brother James corralled. Daniel watched it all with disdain.

"I can't even remember what it was like to have that much ridiculous energy. They're so naïve."

Vorsogh spoke into Daniel's right ear. "If one of the little kids comes close enough, we should punish him for being so young and blind."

\* \* \*

While standing guard at Joseph and Mary's house during baby Joseph's Brit Milah ceremony, Timrok spotted a teenaged boy with an evil spirit who had wandered within the inner radius. The boy watched the King from around the corner. Timrok sent flashes of light to signal the imminent danger to his team. *The boy with the demon lingers too long. Something has to be done.*

Timrok pulled one sword partially from its sheath, and two sparks of light flashed from its steel. Like a bolt of lightning, Prestus shot down from above and took a stand in front of the demon. Prestus's wings folded away, and he drew his sword. He spoke to the demon within the boy.

"What is your business here, foul spirit?"

"No business at all, puny puppet. We are just passing through."

"Then you should continue on. I will not permit any of your evil deeds here at this celebration today."

"Suppose I do make this gathering my business—what are you going to do to stop me?"

From around another corner, Timrok stepped into the street, flanked by Kylek and Micah. Without drawing their weapons, Kylek and Micah put their clenched fists on their hips. Timrok crossed his arms. Silence filled the air of the Middle Realm. The four angelic warriors waited for the demon's next move. A full minute passed. Muscles drew tight. Eyes stayed fixed.

"Come, little brother," the demon spoke to the boy. "I am bored with this stupid party. Let's go someplace more interesting."

Timrok and his three warriors watched the enemy and his flesh-host skulk away. They passed beyond Timrok's outer perimeter.

Without a word Prestus, Kylek, and Micah disappeared to their posts. Timrok turned and marched back to the house.

The children ran and played with wild abandon. Standing near the outside wall of the house, Joseph and Raziel huddled close for a private conversation. Elric stood close.

Timrok approached. "Captain," Timrok said, "an enemy warrior wandered within our inner perimeter, but we have—"

Elric held up his hand and waved Timrok closer. "Come listen," he said.

Raziel continued, "It is truly remarkable!" The volume of Raziel's voice stayed low, but his enthusiasm bubbled high.

Joseph asked, "The tutoring is going well, then? You don't think Jesus is too young?"

"On the contrary. He is more advanced at six years old than most teenagers I have taught. He is focused; he learns quickly; he seems to remember everything after being taught just once. And it's more than that." Raziel stopped and looked around. "His ability to learn and assimilate Scriptures is almost scary. When I read Scriptures with Him, it's almost like—like it is not the first time He has heard it. It is as though all I am doing is reminding Him of something He already knew. And then, once He has heard it, He practically has it memorized! It's amazing! I have never seen anything like it."

"Then, you are still happy to continue the tutoring?"

"Happy? You could not keep me from it. There is definitely something about this boy, and I want to be a part of whatever is going on."

"Is He asking difficult questions?"

"No. He seems to be completely in a receiving position. He is like a thirsty sponge just waiting to be—"

A makeshift ball bounced up and stopped in front of the two men's feet. The kids all stopped and looked at the two adults. Joseph reached down and tossed it back to Jesus, who caught it and ran off amid the shouts and laughter of the energetic pack.

The two men laughed.

"Come," Raziel said, "I keep you from your party."

The two went back inside the house.

Elric turned to Timrok and asked, "I'm sorry, you have a report?"

Timrok smiled. "Perimeter is secure, captain."

Elric put his hand on Timrok's shoulder and grinned. He turned and stepped through the side wall and disappeared into the house.

# 44

## CONTROL

**Baptism minus 23 years**

In the early fall, not long after Daniel's fifteenth birthday, a sudden chill woke him from a restless sleep. He blinked and rubbed his eyes. Sunlight filled the room.

*Morning already.*

He reached for his blanket to cover himself from the chill but stopped and stared at his bare arms with a confused scowl. *What are all these scrapes and scratches? And why am I wearing my tunic and sandals?* He sat up and looked at his feet. Mud covered his feet and sandals. He checked his arms again.

"Levi," Daniel whispered, "what's going on?"

"What do you mean?" Daniel heard in his right ear.

"I put my night clothes on when I went to bed last night, and I know there were no scratches on my arms. And this morning . . . " He looked again at his shoes and arms.

"Surely you do not think I did this to you."

"Well, no, but . . . "

Daniel jumped up and ran out of the house. He wandered out behind the big olive tree in the back yard, whose gnarled trunk and limbs had seen the stories of generations.

"I was obviously outside doing something last night," Daniel said.

"You must have been sleepwalking. Do you remember anything?"

"No." Daniel smacked his forehead with the palm of his hand and waded through the mud of missing memories and muddled thoughts. "I don't remember."

*I don't even know my own thoughts anymore. I'm so angry, and lonely, and confused. Sometimes I just want to hurt . . .*

He stopped mid-thought and rubbed his forehead.

"Levi," he said, "is it possible for me to hear *your* thoughts?"

No response.

"Levi?"

"Of course not. Why would you ask this?"

"I don't know. Sometimes my thoughts seem like . . . "

He couldn't bring himself to say, or even think, *an untapped fountain of malice and evil just waiting to be unleashed,* but that's what he felt.

Instead he paused and said, "Not my own. Dark, scary thoughts."

"These are your own thoughts. We all have a darkness within."

"But not like this," Daniel said. "This is—"

"Guilt."

"What?"

"Deep inside you know that if you hadn't slipped and fallen that day, you could have stopped the Roman soldier, and I would still be alive."

"Aughh!"

He looked around for somewhere to run away. *There's no place to go. Nowhere to get away from Levi.* He paced in circles, pulling his hair, and hitting his forehead with his palms.

He walked circles around the old tree and muttered, "I hate myself. I hate my life. I hate everyone."

\* \* \*

Two weeks later, Daniel awoke in the pre-dawn light after a nightmare. He yawned and reached up to wipe the sleep from his eyes.

He stopped short.

Dried blood covered his hand. Blood stains went all the way up to his elbow.

He suppressed a scream and held up his other hand. More dried blood. He leapt out of bed and shuffled to the front door, being careful not to wake anyone. He grabbed the pitcher full of water and ran behind the old olive tree out back. With frantic motions he scrubbed the blood off his hands and arms. *I don't see any cuts anywhere.* The blood couldn't be his.

"Oh, no, oh, no, oh, no," he muttered as he washed.

*Ughh—blood on my sandals, too.* He had almost enough water left to wash those. He did the best he could and covered the wet leather with dirt and rubbed the dirt over the bloody spots. He checked the fabric of his outer garment. Blood splatters. He pulled the tunic off, wadded it into a ball, and slumped down on the ground with his back against the tree.

"What is happening to me?" He buried his face into his tunic. "Levi? Levi, are you there? You're supposed to be my spiritual guide. Tell me what's going on."

"You are powerful," the voice said in his ear.

"What? I'm losing control!"

"Fear not. I am in control."

Three weeks later, the same experience happened again.

Another two weeks later, it happened again.

A week after that, Daniel was tending the sheep alone in the field, wide awake. The next thing he knew, he found himself in town with wet hair. Half the afternoon had passed, and he had no idea where he had been or what he had done during that time. A dog in an alley barked and barked, backing away from him. Daniel slinked away toward home, his eyes darting about for signs of any remnants of mischief he might have done.

\* \* \*

## Baptism minus 22 years

Elric stood like a statue in the corner of Joseph and Mary's house, his arms crossed, watching the midday mayhem fill the house. Mary bounced a three–month–old Elizabeth on her shoulder.

Elizabeth suffered bad colic today and, at the moment, she could not be consoled. At the table over in the other corner, Raziel introduced the syntactic behaviors of Greek lexical items to the eight–year–old Jesus, but every time Elizabeth cried out, Jesus turned toward her. Four–year–old James chased two–year–old Joseph around the room, who laughed and squealed at full volume. On one pass, little Joseph's elbow knocked an empty cooking pot to the floor. It made a loud clatter.

"James! Joseph! Settle down!" Mary shouted.

Elric smiled. *How many times over the ages have I watched this scene?*

His mind drifted back to another family back in the days when Israel still lived in the wilderness under Moses. Back when Elric had the charge of Kenaz, the younger brother of Caleb, son of Jephunneh of the tribe of Judah.

Elric stood like a statue in the corner of Kenaz's tent, his arms crossed, watching the midday mayhem fill the tent. Kenaz's wife bounced a three–month–old baby girl on her shoulder. She suffered bad colic today and, at the moment, could not be consoled. Four–year–old Othniel chased two–year–old Seraiah around the room, who laughed and squealed at full volume. On one pass, Seraiah's elbow knocked a platter of manna to the floor. It made a loud clatter.

"Othniel! Seraiah! Settle down!" the mother shouted.

Elric smiled and stepped outside.

Rubbing his arms, he closed his eyes and tilted his nose upward. *The tension is building. Strife fills the air.* On the other side of camp, a dark cloud rose in the Middle Realm from among the tents. *Korah. He is stirring up dissension among the Levites against Moses and Aaron.*

The words of rebellion spoken by the men rose into the air of the Middle Realm and coalesced into a cloud, blocking out all light from the Throne. *These men—they have no idea they are giving legal right for the enemy to invade the camp. They are inviting it.*

A full battalion of beaelzurim appeared and swirled above the cloud.

*Here it comes.*

The demons dove downward through the cloud. Crashing and clanging steel rang out in the Middle Realm. Out at the edge of the camp, more battle cries sounded.

Elric's hand went for his sword, and he unfurled his wings. He stopped. He looked back at the tent with Kenaz's family inside. He let out a long exhale, folded his wings, and pushed his sword back into place. He looked toward the tent of meeting, where the pillar of fire spiraled upward for all to see—the very presence of the spirit of the King in the center of the camp. *The King's presence is physically visible, and still, men choose to rebel.* He shook his head.

He closed his eyes and longed for the days before all this strife and rebellion. He raised his hands and counted off the tempo for a new song of worship. He brought his hands down to start the song, but there was no music. He opened his eyes. He had no choir—only the rising smoke of strife and the sounds of war. Tears welled up in his eyes. His heart felt like it would burst.

"Someday," he said aloud. "Someday, the King will restore all things."

He stared at the dark cloud rising on the other side of camp, and a hollow ache gripped his heart. *And it's going to be a long, long time before that day.*

Jesus jumped up from the table and shook Elric's attention back into the present.

Jesus ran over to his crying sister in Mary's arms. He rubbed her little head and whispered, "It's all right, it's all right."

She settled down, and Jesus went back to the table with Raziel.

"Tell me, why do you jump up to check on little Elizabeth when she cries?" Raziel asked.

Elric smiled. *I know why. And I suspect you do, too.*

"Her tummy hurts, and she needs me," Jesus said.

Elric rubbed his chin and waited to hear how Raziel would handle this moment. He was a skilled teacher, wise in the Scriptures and Jewish traditions. And, he was a worthy mentor, wise in the ways of life and more interested in pleasing God than pleasing men.

"I see," Raziel said. "So tell me, whose job is it to care for the little babies?"

"The Lord, our Father, of course. He takes care of everyone."

"Yes, very good. I agree. But how does He do that—most of the time?"

"What do you mean?"

"I mean, who actually prepares your food, cleans up all the messes, and tucks you and your brothers in at night?"

"Ima does that."

"That's right. The Lord is taking care of you, but He is using your ima to do it. You see, God likes order. He sets up authorities over us to take care of us and help us keep His laws. So, while it is very good that you care about your little sister, at the same time you need to trust that God is going to take care of her through your parents. We all have our own responsibilities. Your parents take care of you and your brothers and sister. I teach you Scriptures and how to read and write. Your job for now is to learn—and to play with your friends, of course."

They both laughed.

"I can do that."

"I knew you could," Raziel said. "Now, we only have a little more to do. Then we will be done for today."

Elric closed his eyes and took a deep breath. His heart felt like it would burst again, but not with a longing for a distant future. *The time is close. The King is finally here, and the time is close.*

\* \* \*

## Baptism minus 21 years

Dawn had just broke, and Jeremiah and Daniel stood outside their house. Jeremiah thundered, "It's one thing when you disappear and neglect your duties at home and in the field, but then there was the incident with the men in town, and now this?"

Daniel "awoke" to find himself in the middle of his father's tirade. He had no idea how he had gotten there or what his father had said before that last sentence. He looked around to see what "this" thing he had done might be. He checked himself. Bloodstains covered his hands, his arms, the whole front of his tunic.

"These are our neighbors, our friends," his father continued. "How could you do such a thing to their dog? They say they saw you torture and mutilate it last night. And when they tried to stop you, you threatened to do the same to them! What do you say to this?"

Daniel looked down at his blood–stained hands. He didn't have anything to say. He kept looking at his hands, first the palms, then the backs, then the palms again. He could not deny he had done the deed, but he found it interesting he had no remorse. Just emptiness. And power.

"I don't even know you anymore," Jeremiah said with a defeated, disappointed tone. "I know the loss of Levi was hard for you. It was hard for all of us. But over the last five years, you have become a completely different person. We have been putting up with your attitude and have been lax about your responsibilities—hoping that eventually you would . . . would . . . be normal. But this is too much. You bring dishonor and shame to our family. And more than this, I fear you may do something worse."

Daniel stared at his bloody hands with a blank expression.

"You leave me no choice," Jeremiah said. He turned his back on Daniel and took a single step toward the house. "From this day forward, you are no longer my son. You are dead to me." Bitter tears carved a path down his cheeks and disappeared into his beard. "Go—you are a stranger and are not welcome in my house."

Without looking back, Jeremiah walked to the door, pulled it open, stepped inside, and pulled it shut. The lock bolt clanged into place, and then—silence. Oppressive silence. It smothered Daniel and choked out his breath.

*My whole life just disappeared behind that door.* Anger percolated up from his gut, pressurized his brain, and shot back down his whole body. He shuddered.

"Let's teach them a lesson, little brother," the voice said in his ear. "He can't do this to us."

Daniel reached for the bloody knife he had hidden in his cloak, pulled it out, and took a step toward the door. Everything else in the world blurred away, awash in blood–red rage. Only that closed door remained. The door that just shut him out. The man behind that door that would feel the sting of his . . .

"Daniel," a cheerful voice called out from his left side. "You are up early. What are you doing?"

Daniel's intense focus shattered like glass. He froze. He jerked his head toward the voice. *It's Jesse!* His eldest brother approached from over the nearby hill to the south.

*Run!*

Like a panicked wild animal, Daniel broke into an all–out run to the north. He ran and ran and ran, too afraid to look back. His legs started screaming. His heart pounded in his ears. Finally, he stopped and bent over, his burning, heaving lungs unable to continue. He straightened up and looked behind. No one chasing him. Still panting hard for air, he lumbered forward.

He passed through Nazareth just long enough to steal a skin flask and fill it with water. Pressing hard down a trail, he shot desperate glances over his shoulder every dozen steps. An hour passed, and nobody seemed to be following. He settled into a slower pace.

*Where am I going to go? Everyone around here knows me. I need to get to some place new. Someplace completely different. The Sea of Galilee. I loved it there. That's it, I'll start a new life by the water.*

# 45

## SPECULATIONS

### Baptism minus 20 years

*E*lric and his lieutenants assembled in the widow Hannah's house around the war map. The map swirled with dizzying lights, colors, shimmering clouds, and interlacing ribbons of time. The pace and density of all the components was higher than normal, and the team intensified their focus to pull all the pieces together.

"What do you see?" Elric asked.

Zaben stepped forward and motioned with his hand. "Political winds are blowing. Key human players are moving into position on both sides. The enemy extends its tentacles into every area and is gaining ground on every front. Sickness, demon possession, leprosy, corruption, strife—the advances of the enemy are accelerating."

"The King's honor is being openly challenged," Timrok said. "Just look at this. And yet we do not fight. Instead, we are hiding."

"Waiting," Lacidar said.

"I see pain," Jenli said. "Every one of these is a wound to the heart of the King. I sense great pain from the Throne."

"What do you see, captain?" Zaben asked.

Elric rubbed his chin and shook his head. "It's what I do not see. Everything here seems to point to the imminent Day of the Lord, but the day remains hidden."

"Why does He continue to withhold information we need?" Zaben said.

Elric clenched his teeth and raised his eyebrows high. His left eye twitched twice.

Lacidar stepped up. "We have all we need for our present station. Everything about this mission is a mystery hidden in Him from the beginning of time. We knew this when we started. We continue our assigned tasks. And we wait."

Elric nodded. "Yes, well said. And this we shall do." He paused and stared deep into the map. "But we are close. I can sense the nearness of the day."

After a lingering final survey of the map, Elric stepped back and crossed his arms. "Lacidar," he said, "do you have a report from Judea?"

"Despite our best efforts," Lacidar said, "the enemy has infiltrated the religious leaders in Zacharias's synagogue. They are all against

Zacharias, and there is talk amongst them of cutting Zacharias off, banning him from the synagogue."

Elric nodded without flinching. "And how about John?"

"John progresses well. He is almost eleven. Zacharias tutors the boy and has built a significant collection of scrolls of Moses and the prophets at home, so John has ample access to the Scriptures. Zacharias seems to sense his time is limited, so he is pouring everything he can into John while there is yet time. John has personally accepted his Nazirite vow and is strong in the spirit."

"This is good news. Has the word of the Lord come to him yet?"

"No."

Elric took a deep breath and gazed back at the map.

"Sir?" Lacidar said. "What about Jesus? How are things going in Nazareth?"

Elric laughed. "Yes, I forget you do not get to see Him as we do. Everything is quiet there. Jenli and Zaben provide an excellent, invisible–yet–strong outer perimeter. Timrok's inner perimeter is impenetrable."

Timrok crossed his burly arms and nodded.

"Of course," Elric said, "I can tell the King is hiding us under His shadow, so the enemy has not been able to draw near."

Jenli slapped Timrok's shoulder, and all the lieutenants laughed.

"But," Elric interrupted with an upraised hand, "but . . . all those who have gotten close have been diverted with the utmost skill, valor, and discretion."

Timrok nodded again and said with his arms still crossed, "With valor."

The lieutenants laughed. Elric smiled.

Elric continued. "Mary has had another son. They have named him Simon. It is perfect—they look like a very normal family in every way. There is nothing remarkable at all to draw the attention of the enemy."

"Except the King Himself!" Timrok said.

"Yes, of course," Elric said, "but even He appears normal. The Father is hiding the light of Jesus' spirit from the enemy, and in His flesh, He appears like any other ten–year–old boy."

"What is He like now?" Lacidar asked. "Does He understand who He is?"

"I think so," Elric said. "The Father speaks to Him constantly. The rabbi Raziel is an excellent human mentor, but I can tell that Jesus' wisdom is growing through revelation in His spirit."

"Does He see you?" Lacidar asked.

"No—at least I don't think so. Sometimes I think He can sense our presence, but His focus is always on the Father—or the people around Him."

"Does He know what His mission here is yet?"

"It is hard to tell. I don't think He does. In almost every respect, He is just another young boy. Right now, His world is all about playing and learning and being part of a family. Joseph has begun teaching Him some basic carpentry skills, and everyone assumes Jesus will follow in Joseph's footsteps."

"It is just amazing," Lacidar said.

Elric noticed Zaben examining a portion of the map, absorbed in his own thoughts.

"What is it, Zaben?" Elric said.

"I was just looking at King David."

A thin blue string of light originating from Judah, son of Jacob, wove through the map to David, where it became flat, wide, and bright for a time. Then, after Solomon, it dimmed and spiraled off into a tiny filament that threaded through clouds and vortices of blackness. Here in Nazareth on the map, the string became flat again and straight—and brilliant. Elric moved down by the map where Zaben stood.

"What do you see?" Elric asked.

"David was more than just the line through whom the King would come. He was a shadow of the Messiah."

"Yes."

"David was first anointed king by Samuel as a boy of twelve," Zaben said.

"Jesus is already ten," Timrok said.

Zaben nodded and pointed to a spot on the map. "And David slayed Goliath when he was fifteen."

"And conquered many Philistines," Timrok said.

Zaben continued. "What if we are only two years away from—"

"The prophet John has not even begun his ministry yet," Lacidar said. "The word of the Lord has not even come to him."

"I know," Zaben said, "but what if the word comes to him sometime within the next two years, and he anoints Jesus as King when He is twelve. Then John spends the next three years preparing the way, helping raise an army. Then, at fifteen the Lord's campaign begins. He slays the Goliath of Rome and destroys His enemies."

Everyone stood in silence, looking at the map.

Jenli shook his head. "But David didn't sit on the throne over all Israel until he was thirty. And most of those years, he spent running for his life, hiding in caves."

Zaben nodded. "This is what I have been searching out. I thought the Lord would defeat His enemies in a single day. This does not fit."

Everyone stood in silence.

"David defeated Goliath in a single day," Lacidar said. "But it took years to subdue the Philistines. Perhaps, the King's campaign will take time, too."

"Captain?" Zaben said. "You have been silent."

Elric first rubbed his chin, then crossed his arms. "This is all interesting. And I want to hasten that day as much as any. However, the shadows of the fathers do not provide true light. Only a word from the throne." He paused. "One thing I do believe—when that word does come, the very nature of our mission will change."

"We stop hiding," Timrok said, "and fight for the King."

* * *

## Baptism minus 19 years

Molech, Asherah, and Yarikh stood before Marr, knee deep in black smoke emanating from Marr's throne. The great prince on the throne had a fireball suspended between his fingertips and an embittered scowl on his face.

"Is this all your report?" Marr asked.

"Yes, my lord," the three commanders muttered in nervous unison.

Marr gazed into the fireball. "I have decided," he spoke to the flames, "it is time for new leadership in Jerusalem. It is my understanding that people are being stirred up in every province against Archelaus, to the point of sending numerous calls for Caesar Augustus in Rome to remove Archelaus from power."

Asherah shot hateful glances toward Molech and Yarikh. The two smirked without taking their eyes off Marr.

Marr continued. "Augustus has had enough—enough uprisings, enough complaints about Archelaus, enough troubles with the Herodian regime. I have, therefore, decided to cut off the rule of Herod's house over Judea and Samaria and place it directly under the authority of Rome. I have a man ready—a Roman cavalry officer currently under Quirinius in Syria. Asherah's region will become a Roman province, and this man, Coponius, will be its first governor."

"But, my lord," Asherah said.

"You will retain authority over the region."

Asherah crossed his gigantic arms across his chest and lifted his chin. Molech and Yarikh sneered.

"What is the value of this move?" Molech asked through gritted teeth.

Marr looked at the fireball pulsing in the air above his fingertips. He gave it a spin with a flick of his fingers, and it whirred in place with a low hum while sparks and bits of flame flung outward.

"None of you will be able to find the Child. Of this I am sure. He will raise an army and launch His campaign. But, with the region of Judea under direct Roman control, I will have the full force of the Roman Empire at my disposal without this layer of Herodian politics." Marr sat back on his throne and gave the fireball another spin. "Roman control also changes the role of the chief priest in Israel—who will have to be the liaison between the Jewish people and Rome. His role will become more political, and since he controls the temple treasury, we shall create a corrupt alliance between him and the Roman governor. Once we own the chief priest, we will be able to bring not only the military might of Rome against the King's forces, but to control the masses through the religious leaders."

Marr slowly squeezed the fireball between his finger and thumb, and it shrank amid crackling sparks and sizzling smoke. He squashed the energy to nothing and blew the small cloud of black smoke away with a single puff.

He continued. "Begin preparing for a succession of chief priests. Once we find our man and establish his position, we will keep him in place as long as needed."

"What of Archelaus?" Asherah asked.

"He will be ordered to Rome where he is to be stripped of his title and banished to Vienne in Gaul."

\* \* \*

## Baptism minus 18.5 years

Asherah sat on his throne in the palace in Jerusalem and oversaw the arrival of Coponius. Asherah's captains stood by in his court.

"This is Molech and Yarikh's fault," Asherah said. "They are always trying to undermine my authority." He held his palm upward. "I hate them." A small plasma ball formed in his hand. He gave it a flick, and it sizzled across the court and shot through the wall into the air of the Middle Realm.

"And the elzurim of the King," he said. "They resist me at every turn. Where have they hidden the Son of Man?" He held his hand out, and another fireball formed. He flicked it across the court without aim.

"And Marr." Asherah ground his teeth and clenched his fists. "Over the last ten years, I have accomplished much with Archelaus. So many deaths, so much rebellion, so much chaos and dissension. Marr should be rewarding me for my masterful leadership. Instead, he extends his own reach into my dominion and installs his own man."

Asherah formed a dozen fireballs and fired them off in rapid succession. He sat back on his throne and took a deep breath. He watched with disinterest as Coponius's men moved furniture around in the palace headquarters and hung Roman shields and accouterments on the walls.

"At least my throne is still in its proper place," he mumbled. "These men will always come and go, but my throne spans the generations."

Aside from the background noise of men working, the air in the Middle Realm became pregnant with silence. Asherah could feel the stares of his captains. He shifted on his throne and sat up. He positioned his arms on the armrests and cleared his throat.

"The first order of business will be to confiscate all Herod's estates held by Archelaus for the possession of Rome. Next, we will institute a rigorous tax plan. Most importantly, though, we are going to take control of the functions of the office of the Jewish high priest and place a man of our choosing into that position. See to it that everything is prepared to accomplish these goals quickly. I will begin speaking to Coponius as soon as he is in place."

Asherah called one of his captains up for a private conference. The remaining beaelzur officers left with their orders.

"I have a special mission for you," Asherah whispered to the captain. "If this is going to be a Roman province, then I want our man to have the local authority to execute capital punishment. I will make sure Coponius makes this request. I want you to go to Rome and make sure the request is granted. Maybe eventually we will be able to use this power against the Son of Man when we find Him."

# 46

## ANTICIPATION

**Baptism minus 18.5 years**

*J*enli alighted in front of Joseph and Mary's house just long enough to get Elric's attention. "Captain, come quickly!" he said.

The two raised their wings and shot into the air. Within seconds, they stood at the brow of the cliffs at Nazareth overlooking the plain. Zaben joined a moment later. Below, amid a sea of dust, a large army approached, several thousand strong.

"Who are they?" Elric asked.

Jenli answered, "Judas the Galilean, from Gamala, and his army of Zealots."

"This is the Judas who began the sect of Zealots?" Elric asked.

"Yes," Zaben said. "He is calling the whole nation to assert their liberty and stand against the Romans. He has been active for years."

Jenli said, "The new taxes levied by Coponius have stirred him and the priest Zadok to lead a revolt. He calls the taxation no better than an introduction of slavery. Many supporters are joining him."

"Why does he come to Nazareth?" Elric asked.

"He is going town to town," Jenli said, "driving Roman occupation forces out and building more support."

"This is an enemy ploy," Zaben said. "An attempt to sweep away innocent people—and possibly the King—in open warfare."

"I agree," Elric said. "We must prevent them from entering Nazareth. Where can we divert them?"

"Sepphoris is just four miles from here," Jenli said.

"Yes," Elric said. "That is good. There is a Roman armory there. Go down and convince Judas that Nazareth is not worthy of their effort. There is little Roman presence here, and Sepphoris is a better prize."

"In His service," Jenli and Zaben said in unison. They opened their wings and disappeared in a single stroke.

Elric remained on the brow of the hill and watched. Minutes later a large dust storm rose in front of the advancing army and washed over it. The entire troop came to a halt. For an extended time, the army stayed swallowed in blinding dust and wind. Eventually, the wind died down, but the army remained motionless for another extended time. When it started moving again, the army veered off in the direction of Sepphoris.

Moments later, Jenli appeared next to Elric.

"Good work," Elric said.

"It was difficult to reach Judas." Jenli said. "There are many beaelzurim in their camp. Zaben is staying near them for now. The plan is to remain in Sepphoris for a week. Then our objective is to get them to move on farther south and bypass Nazareth altogether."

"Very good. Inform your team and Zaben's. We need extra vigilance for this next week. The Zealot army is not in Nazareth, but the danger to the King is still very grave. I will tell Timrok."

* * *

Joseph and Jesus worked at a construction site in Nazareth, building up a good sweat. Along with a crew of half a dozen men, they sorted through piles of large building stones. It had been five days since Judas the Galilean took Sepphoris, and Elric and Timrok stood guard at the worksite with swords drawn. The two angels faced in opposite directions. Their eyes caught every movement of everything in the Physical and Middle Realms. They held tight grips and tense muscles.

"I prefer wood projects," Joseph said to Jesus as he hoisted a large stone off a pile. "Tables, wagons, animal pens, out-shacks." He moved another stone with a strained groan. "But in our trade, we take any work that comes along. And it's time you learned to work with stone."

Joseph moved another stone aside. "What we are looking for is a stone we will use as the cornerstone for the building. It is the most important stone we will set today because it will become the foundation off which everything else will be built. It has to be perfectly square, level, and true."

Jesus struggled with a stone less than half the size of the one Joseph had just moved.

He finally conquered it, and one of the other workmen beside Him said, "You have a strong boy here, Joseph."

Stepping up next to Jesus, the man said, "Let me see those muscles."

Jesus flexed His muscles and showed off His biceps, which the man felt with exaggerated amazement.

"Yes, you are a strong one. How old are you, son?"

"Almost twelve."

"Well, I'm glad to have you on the crew today. You listen to your father—he is a good man. He will teach you everything you need to know."

"Yes, sir."

"You know," Elric said to Timrok over his shoulder, "the irony of everything He does is overwhelming. Here He is, the very cornerstone of all creation, being taught the importance of a cornerstone by a man."

Timrok laughed. "And a man pretending that the King is strong by squeezing His little biceps."

"Every day He amazes me," Elric said.

"Did you hear about what happened in Sepphoris yesterday?" Joseph said, loud enough for the whole crew.

One of the men answered. "I heard that Judas the Zealot routed the Roman detachment there and looted their armory earlier this week."

"Ha!" another worker said. He lifted a stone and tossed it onto a pile. "Kill them all, I say."

"I heard several men from Nazareth went over to join the cause," another worker said.

"You haven't heard, then, have you?" Joseph said.

The workers all stopped and looked at Joseph.

Joseph's voice became low and solemn. "The Roman army attacked Judas and crushed his army."

"All of them?"

"Two thousand survived, but they were captured and are all to be crucified."

All the workers' jaws dropped. No one moved. No one blinked. Jesus watched all their reactions. He looked up at Joseph.

"And Judas?" one asked.

"He is to be executed, too," Joseph said.

A squad of eight Roman soldiers appeared on the trail and marched by the worksite. A beaelzur warrior walked alongside. The soldiers marched past, eying the work crew: seven sweaty men and a boy, standing defenseless amid piles of building stones. The demon eyed Elric and Timrok. Elric prepared his sword.

"Keep moving," the demon said to the Roman squad leader.

The squad passed out of sight, and Elric and Timrok resumed their vigilant watch. The men relaxed and went back to work.

One worker put his hand on Jesus' shoulder. "You keep working on those muscles, son. Someday . . . someday a leader will rise out of Israel, and he will save us from all this. Maybe, if you're strong enough, you'll be able to fight with him."

\* \* \*

## Baptism minus 18 years

Daniel awoke with blood on his hands.

"Not again! Levi?"

Daniel stumbled down to the edge of the Sea of Galilee and leaned forward to scrub his hands and arms in the water. His skin bristled each time he submerged his arms, and he sucked air with each chilling splash. He looked at his tunic.

"Ughh," he sighed.

He pulled the tunic off and threw it in the water, not gently, and scrubbed the new blood stains against the rocks. After getting the tunic as clean as he could, he plodded back to his campsite and stretched the tunic out on a tree limb. He sat with his head between his knees and fought through the fog in his head. The anger and hatred simmering just below the surface rose to a full boil. He pictured all the fights he'd had with people in the towns. He thought about all the food and supplies he'd stolen to survive. He thought about the loneliness of his worthless existence. He imagined having to face people in town, not knowing what, or who, he had killed during the night.

"Levi," he said, "now we have to move again. This is the third time we have had to move in the last three years. First Tiberias, then Magdala, and now Gennesaret. I was afraid we were going to go to jail after Magdala. I still don't know how we escaped that. We don't dare take a chance of staying here now. What's the next lake town to the north, Capernaum?"

"Actually," Daniel heard in his ear, "I was thinking we should go down to Jerusalem for the festival. It starts in about two weeks."

"Passover? I don't care about that. I hate everything about the religion of my father. Why would we go there?"

"Perhaps the King will be there. Perhaps we could see Him."

"What?" Daniel said.

"I mean, think of all the opportunities to find new supplies. Thousands of people staying in tents all around the city. Everything out in the open. And not just that—think about the money. All the moneychangers and merchants in the outer temple court. All the people pressing in and all the chaos."

"I could make a fortune," Daniel said. "It would be easy."

"Especially with your skills."

Daniel paused, only briefly. "Let's do it. This could be a new start for me. I could steal enough money to be comfortable for a long time. I could even move back up here to Capernaum and maybe get a real job. Maybe be a fisherman. I've always wanted to do that."

"Good choice," the voice said in his ear. "I have a feeling there are great possibilities waiting for us in Jerusalem."

\* \* \*

Elric and the lieutenants huddled around the war map. Faces looked solemn, but eyes sparkled with anticipation.

"Tomorrow the caravan from Nazareth leaves for Jerusalem," Elric said. "This Passover pilgrimage is no different from any other we've taken over the last ten years."

The lieutenants' heads nodded, but their eyes told a different story.

Elric cleared his throat. He turned to Lacidar. "Zacharias and Elizabeth will be coming up for the festival?"

"Yes, captain. And the prophet John."

"Right. Very good."

Elric gazed off into the map with his arms crossed and jaw tight.

"Captain," Lacidar said, "shall I arrange a meeting between Jesus and John?"

Elric paused, still searching the map, and said, "No. Without word from the Throne, I think it best to avoid forcing anything. Don't prevent it, but don't initiate it."

"Yes, sir,"

Everyone stood in silence, staring into the map. It became so quiet in the Middle Realm that Elric noticed Hannah on the other side of the room. She hummed a psalm and lit an oil lamp. Elric smiled.

"Captain?" a voice said from behind.

Elric and the lieutenants turned toward the voice. Grigor stood behind them, sleek and silent.

"Grigor!" Elric said. "We didn't hear you come in."

"A word of the Lord for Captain Elric," Grigor said.

Elric waved his hand over the map, which disappeared, and he moved to the corner of the room with Grigor. The conference didn't last long. Elric nodded his head several times and received a parchment from Grigor.

"In His service," Elric said.

"By His word," Grigor replied. He opened his wings and shot through the roof with a flash.

Elric stepped back to the lieutenants, trying hard to hold back a smile.

"What is it?" Timrok asked.

"Do we have new direction?" Jenli asked.

"Not exactly," Elric said. He took a deep breath, and then couldn't contain it anymore. His whole face erupted in a smile. "This trip is going to be a pivotal one."

"I knew it!" Zaben shouted.

Elric held up his hand. "Grigor did *not* say the King would start His campaign now. He only said that the Son would be tested by the Father."

"He will pass the test. He will pass the test," Zaben said, bouncing on his toes.

"And," Elric said, "I have received a list of the Son's inner circle. Twelve names."

"The King's generals," Timrok said. "Excellent."

"May we see the list?" Jenli asked.

Elric handed him the scroll. Jenli held the parchment out, and the others crowded around.

"I have been away from my regular duties for too long," Jenli said. "I do not recognize any of these men."

"I saved a pair of brothers, Simon and Andrew, during Herod's time," Timrok said, looking at the list. "But they would be too young to be generals, and they lived by Bethlehem."

"There was a Judas in Kerioth that I rescued," said Zaben. "But he would be too young, too."

"We do not have time to muster the generals now," Elric said. "We need to focus on our current mission. Our primary goal is still to keep the King hidden. After this trip, we will search out these other men."

"And start raising the King's army!" Timrok said.

"Where is Lacidar?" Elric asked.

Everyone looked around the room.

"Where did he go? I didn't see him leave," Elric said.

Lacidar descended through the ceiling and alighted in front of the group.

Elric shook his head. "What are you doing?"

Lacidar pulled his Lacidian resonar from behind his back. "I couldn't help it. This calls for a celebration!"

Lacidar strummed the resonar once and closed his eyes. Then his fingers let loose, and a fast tune charged the room with jubilant energy.

"Ha ha!" shouted Timrok. He spun twice in the air and came down with his feet bouncing. He locked arms with Jenli, and the two danced like wild children. Zaben joined the dance—twirling, jumping, shouting.

"The King is here!" Lacidar sang.

"The King is here!

Victory, victory, the King is here!

His enemies are scattered, the evil days are shattered,

Victory, victory, the King is here!"

Elric stood back against the wall, smiled, and closed his eyes. He raised his right hand, found the beat with his finger, and directed the song as though he had a full choir.

On the other side of the room, Hannah hummed to herself. "The King is here, the King is here."

# 47

## PASSOVER BEGINS

### Baptism minus 18 years, Day 1 of Passover

On the first day of Passover, Elric stationed himself in the Court of the Gentiles before Solomon's Portico. Jesus sat behind him, under the shade of the portico with a class of other young students. A prominent–looking rabbi in a distinguished robe led the class, but Elric couldn't hear any of their discussions. *As long as I can't hear them, none of the enemy outside this radius can, either.* Timrok and his team kept the same radius, the last buffer before the King.

Thousands of people scurried and milled about, while Elric stood like a statue, six full feet taller than any man and larger than most of the beaelzurim there. From where he stood, he tracked the movement of every enemy in the court. Zaben and Jenli's team had melted into the crowd, but occasionally Elric spotted one of them working.

Amongst the teeming crowd in the courtyard, one man, accompanied by a beaelzurim, walked in a direction that would bring them within earshot of the little class in the shade. At the prompting of Kaylar, a friend of the man called his name, diverting him in a different direction. Another man with a demon escort was turned away by the prompting of the demon himself, who preferred to avoid contact with Prestus, approaching on an intercept course. Elric stood motionless with his arms crossed in the middle of all the chaotic motion and turned back beaelzurim with nothing more than a commanding stare. One demon didn't get the message and continued forward. He met the horizontal barricade of Elric's sword at chest level. After a brief moment of a defiant gaze, the demon turned and snaked off. One by one, individual by individual, Elric's warriors gave the King the space He needed without being detected or overheard.

\* \* \*

In the shade of Solomon's Portico, surrounded by towering thick white columns, a gray-bearded sage shared his ancient wisdom with two dozen wide-eyed teenaged boys seated at his feet. Jesus positioned Himself near the front, taking in and weighing every word. Raziel stood behind the class and grasped the lapels of his robe with satisfaction as he watched his apprentice interact with the senior rabbi.

One of the younger students dared to ask a challenging question, although his bravery was belied by his thin, crackling voice. "I always feel bad for the animals," the boy said. "Why do we have to kill so many? I mean, it's not like God does anything with them. We just slaughter them, and it seems like such a waste."

The rabbi stroked his beard and raised his bushy eyebrows. "This is an excellent question—one that reaches to the very heart of our religion." He paused. "I would like to turn this question back to the class. Does anyone here know the answer to this very important question?"

For a moment all the boys looked around at each other, no one knowing what to say. Jesus popped His hand straight up in the air.

"Yes, young man?"

"It is because it satisfies the Holiness of God."

"Yes, yes, very good. Let us explore that thought. What does it mean to 'satisfy' His holiness? Here is the real issue: *He* is perfectly holy, but *we* . . . we are not. Remember the words of King David, 'For no person living is righteous in Your sight.' So, if He is absolutely holy and we are unrighteous, how can we ever hope to stand before His throne? Let me try to create a picture in your mind of His holiness. Listen to the words of the prophet Isaiah."

His voice became low and theatrical, and he stretched out his arm like a great orator. He started softly. "'In the year of King Uzziah's death, I saw the Lord sitting on a throne, lofty and exalted, with the train of His robe filling the temple. Seraphim stood above Him, each having six wings; with two he covered his face, and with two he covered his feet, and with two he flew. And one called out to another and said, "Holy, Holy, Holy, is the Lord of hosts, the whole earth is full of His glory." And the foundations of the thresholds trembled at the voice of him who called out, while the temple was filling with smoke. Then I (Isaiah) said, "Woe is me, for I am ruined! Because I am a man of unclean lips; and I live among a people of unclean lips; for my eyes have seen the King, the Lord of hosts.'"'" By the time he reached the end, his voice boomed across the stone alcove.

The rabbi stopped speaking and lowered his hand. Every eye fixed on the great sage, and while the rest of the world buzzed all around them, their little corner froze with anticipation.

His voice became low and controlled, and he began again. "So, I ask you, how can we stand before such a throne? What are we to do?"

Without hesitation Jesus popped His hand up again.

"Yes?" said the rabbi.

"He covers the sin with blood. According to Moses, 'the life of the flesh is in the blood, and I have given it to you on the altar to make atonement for your souls; for it is the blood by reason of the life that makes atonement.'"

"Excellent," the rabbi shouted. "This is exactly right!"

Raziel tightened the grip on his lapels, smiled, and looked around.

The rabbi continued. "Atonement, Kippur . . . it is by the blood of an innocent sacrifice that God has promised to forgive us for our sins. Today I am going to teach you a new word, one which most of you have probably never heard before. But it is an important word and a key concept for you to understand. The word is 'propitiation.' It is a legal term that means 'an act which appeases the wrath of an offended party and reconciles the offender to the offended.' As the great Judge, God has agreed to accept the death of a substitute as a 'propitiation' for our offenses. This is what the blood of the sacrifices does for us, both as a nation and as individuals. Does everyone understand? Good, good. Very good question. Let's take another question."

Jesus raised an eager hand. The rabbi nodded.

"What if a *person* became the sacrifice?"

The students in the class gasped and looked at Jesus. They sat with mouths open in the silence. They turned back to the rabbi.

"Well, now," the rabbi said, stroking his beard, "let us think about this. As you all may know, this is a practice that has been observed by heathen peoples, but we would never consider offering a human sacrifice. First of all, remember that humans are made in the likeness of God, so to kill a human is an offense to God and His greatest creation. Every human life is too valuable, and God would never ask any person to forfeit his own life in this manner. Second, that sacrifice could only be applied to one other person, so practically speaking we would lose half the population on every Day of Atonement." In a playful sinister tone he added, "A very gruesome prospect indeed."

The class chuckled. The rabbi smiled at their crinkled-up noses.

"But most importantly—and this is the main issue—the sacrifice needs to be innocent, and as we have already discussed, no man is sinless before God. Therefore, there is no person who would be qualified to be the sacrifice."

All the boys nodded.

Jesus had another question and an upraised hand. "God is perfect and without sin. What if He became the sacrifice?"

The class gasped.

"You are an astute young man with very profound ideas," the rabbi said. "Yes, very profound indeed."

He paused for a moment and rubbed his hand over his mouth with a slow, deliberate gesture.

"To begin with, this, of course, is a hypothetical question only because we all know it is impossible for God to die. He is the eternal self-existent one Who knows no beginning or end. It is by His hand that everything exists, so if He were to die, everything else would also cease to exist, and the whole question is for naught. However, hypothetically . . . what would happen? God would have to take on a human form in order to die a sacrificial death. Because God, in that case, is in a human form, and He is sinless and innocent, He would certainly qualify to serve as the sacrifice. Also, because He is infinite, I suppose His death could serve as a propitiation for all men, not just one. And, since He is ageless, for all men for all time, past, present, and future."

The old rabbi stopped speaking. He smiled and raised his big bushy eyebrows. "Yes, that would certainly be the perfect sacrifice," he said with a wistful tone. He laughed and pointed toward the boy who had asked the original question. "And it would save many bulls and goats."

The rest of the class laughed along.

The remainder of the afternoon went by like a blur. Deep thoughts, Scripture lessons, intriguing questions—impressionable boys on the brink of manhood became caught up in the enchantment of sitting at the feet of a wise old rabbi and surrounded by the majesty of the great temple.

The last session finished, and Raziel brought Jesus back to the camp where the whole troop from Nazareth stayed. A hundred Nazarenes milled about rows of tents, mingling and celebrating the first day of the Passover week. Groups of men talked and laughed around campfires. Children darted around the tents from one end of the camp to the other. The festival was underway.

# 48

## A WEEK OF WAITING

### Baptism minus 18 years, Day 2 of Passover

On the morning of the second day of Passover, the marketplace in Jerusalem teemed with people. Thousands of pilgrims jostled through the streets, pushing from one vendor to the next. Daniel weaved his way through the masses. In front of one vendor, he bumped shoulders with a man on the street, fell backward, and knocked a basket of matzo bread from the vendor's stand to the ground.

"I'm so sorry," Daniel said to the vendor, reaching for the fallen bread.

The two scrambled and scooped the bread back into the basket. With the vendor distracted, Daniel slipped two full handfuls under his tunic. They finished picking up the bread, and Daniel hurried down the street.

Daniel ducked into an alley and sat on an empty wooden crate. He lifted his tunic and pulled out the bread, a handful of dates, and a small wineskin. He leaned back against the building and popped a date into his mouth.

"This was an excellent idea, Levi," he said. "You were certainly right about our opportunities here. Yesterday I got new sandals, a blanket, a new knife, and enough food to last a week."

He took a bite of bread and washed it down with a mouthful of wine.

"And I do enjoy the wine."

He ate some more bread.

"Today, I think I will find some new clothes. Maybe even a small cart to haul all my belongings. And I need to find some money."

"We need to go into the temple grounds," Daniel heard in his ear.

"No," Daniel said. "I don't want to go there. There is plenty for us here on the streets."

"The moneychangers are there. That is where we need to go."

"But the vendors on the streets have money, and so do all the people. Why go up to the temple?"

The voice became stern. "We go to the temple. Tomorrow."

"Fine," Daniel said. He tilted the wineskin back and finished every last drop.

\* \* \*

Elric stood in position in front of Solomon's Portico. Zaben moved in close. He looked up at the waning sun, then back at Jesus who sat with the class.

"The afternoon grows long," Zaben said. "Day two, and still no pronouncement from the King?"

Elric's gaze remained on the activities in the court. He answered without moving his head. "There are seven days of the festival."

"Is the prophet John here? Have you even seen him?"

"Zacharias brought him into the Court of Women, where he is sitting under the tutelage of the rabbis there. Lacidar's team is with him."

"Why does Jesus remain out here? He should be in an inner court. Shall we move Him?"

Elric looked down at Zaben. He returned his attention back to the outer court. "*We* do not move *Him*."

"Yes, captain. Of course."

"Jesus and John will meet when the Lord chooses. I would not expect anything this early in the week."

\* \* \*

## Baptism minus 18 years, Day 3 of Passover

Daniel stepped through the gate into the outer temple court on the morning of the third day of the festival. Every fiber of his being cringed, and he struggled to catch his breath. His eyes scanned the expansive courtyard with all its columns and majestic architecture. *It is all I remembered it to be.* He steadied himself against a wall. He couldn't move. Fear locked up every joint. Even though he didn't want to, he let his gaze drift up to the main temple structure, stark white and imposing. His whole body shuddered.

"Don't look at the temple," Daniel heard in his ear.

"I don't remember it being so scary before," Daniel said.

"Don't look at it. Keep your focus down here in the outer court."

A choir of Levites began to sing under the colonnade to their left.

Daniel shuddered and covered his good ear.

"Quickly," the voice said. "We should move away to the other side."

Daniel forced his legs to move. He meandered through the crowd, and he couldn't help but scan everywhere, examining every person.

"Why do I feel like I'm looking for something—or someone?" Daniel asked.

He heard no answer.

"Levi?"

"Money, of course. We're looking for opportunities to steal money."

"Right. Let's get to work so we can get out of here."

* * *

## Baptism minus 18 years, Day 4 of Passover

As the sun set on the fourth day of Passover, Daniel started a campfire at his hideout just outside the city. The wood crackled, and sparks floated upward. Daniel pulled out his leather pouch and dropped coins into it one at a time. With each clink of metal, he smiled and nodded his head.

"This was a very good day, Levi," he said. "Between yesterday and today, I have enough money to live on for months. As much as I don't want to go back to the temple grounds, I think we should go there again tomorrow."

"Tomorrow," the voice in his ear said, "we go into the Court of Women."

"An inner court? What for? There are no moneychangers there."

No answer.

"You are looking for something, aren't you?" Daniel said. "What are you looking for?"

No answer.

"Well, I'm not going," Daniel said. "I'll go as far as the outer court, but I refuse to go in any farther."

"We will see."

* * *

## Baptism minus 18 years, Day 5 of Passover

On the fifth day of Passover, Vorsogh used Daniel's body to climb the fourteen steps to the Beautiful Gate. He had already helped Daniel appropriate a sizable pocket of coins for the day, and he saw no sign of the Child King anywhere in the outer court. *Now I will take my turn.* With Daniel's consciousness pushed aside, Vorsogh had full control of Daniel's flesh. He stepped into the Court of Women. A choir on his right drove him to the far left. Even though concealed in flesh, Vorsogh could feel the penetrating eyes of the senturim from each corner, and he pressed as far under the colonnade as he could. He scanned the court, being careful not to look upward toward the temple.

*Hmm, over there*—a small group of young students sitting at the feet of a rabbi. From here, they looked to be about the right age. He moved over for a closer look.

*There! What is that? I don't think that is the King Himself, but His spirit is very strong on this boy. I wonder . . .*

\* \* \*

## Baptism minus 18 years, Day 6 of Passover

John, the son of Zacharias, took his regular seat with the other students in the Court of Women and waited for the day's rabbi to come out for this, the sixth day of Passover. These last five days of the festival had been intoxicating. There seemed to be something special about being this close to the temple—the buildings, the priests, the smell of the sacrifices on the altar. He wanted more.

Out of the corner of his eye, he noticed a young man, maybe twenty years old, off to the side, watching. The man looked unkempt and out of place. And there was something very unsettling about his eyes—wild, unnatural. *Why does it feel like he's watching me?* He rubbed the bristled hair on his arms. *And I'm not sure, but I think I saw him yesterday, too.* John looked back to where his mother, Elizabeth, sat with the other women. She smiled and gave him a little wave. He waved back.

The rabbi appeared, flanked by his apprentices with dozens of scrolls tucked under their arms. The rabbi shuffled up to the front of the group of students and sat down.

"Good morning, students," the rabbi said with a cheerful voice. "It is another beautiful day in the Lord's house. Let's get right into our lesson for today."

John sat with wide eyes for at least an hour. The lesson finished. The rabbi rolled up a scroll, handed it back to an assistant, and said, "We have time for questions. What is on your mind today?"

At first no one raised a hand. John slid his hand into the air.

"Yes, young man. What is your question?"

"Before the Messiah comes, the Scriptures say that Elijah is to prepare His way. Is this Elijah himself, or just his prophetic anointing?"

"Well, now," the rabbi said. "You want to dig into the deep mysteries first thing in the morning? Very good."

The rabbi pulled the sleeves back on his robe and crossed his arms. "Prophecy is not an easy subject. We often can only surmise its meaning from other contexts. But, from my understanding, I believe it will be Elijah himself."

John nodded.

"Is there more?" the rabbi asked. "I have a feeling I didn't completely answer your question."

"Will the prophet know? Will he know he is Elijah?"

"Oh, yes, I most certainly think so. If he is Elijah, he will know it."

John nodded again.

"Good question," the teacher said. "Is there another question? Yes, over here."

* * *

## Baptism minus 18 years, Day 7 of Passover

Elric and his lieutenants gathered outside Joseph and Mary's tent on the night after the seventh day of Passover. Jesus and the rest of the family slept inside, and the remainder of the tent village rested in the quiet of the night. Smoldering embers of old campfires died out and became still.

"I don't understand it," Zaben said. "I was so sure we would see Him anointed King this week."

"And I thought the Son was to be tested," Jenli said. "I did not see any test. Did anyone else?"

Everyone shook their heads. They all stood with arms limp and nothing to say.

Elric lifted his chin and rested his hand on his sword hilt. "Well, tomorrow we return to Nazareth. It will be good to have the King back in a more secure environment." He turned to Lacidar. "Is John returning home tomorrow, too?"

"No," Lacidar said. "Zacharias was asked to stay another week and help with some temple duties. Elizabeth and John will stay here with him."

"Very good," Elric said.

Elric looked into the faces of his lieutenants and smiled. "This changes nothing. Our mission continues as planned. If we were to be fighting for the King today, He would have told us."

The lieutenants nodded.

"Return to your posts. Stay vigilant. We are still very exposed."

Mostly in unison, they answered, "Yes, captain. In His service."

# 49

## THE TEST

**Baptism minus 18 years, Day 1 after Passover**

*E*lric stood guard outside Joseph and Mary's tent in the late–night calm on the day after the Passover festival. He thought about the past week and couldn't help but wish that things had gone differently. *If the King had begun His campaign, our duties would have been very different tonight.* He surveyed the sleepy camp and sighed. *Morning will start a busy day for these pilgrims. All the tents need be torn down, packed, and loaded for the trip back home.* He sighed again. *I will be glad to return to the safety of Nazareth.*

Two hours before sunrise, Jesus awoke and slipped out of the tent. Elric raised his eyebrows and scanned left and right. Jesus started walking. *What is He doing?* Jesus continued walking, heading out of the camp. *We have a problem!*

Elric flashed his blade. Timrok and two of his warriors appeared.

"It looks like He is headed into town," Elric said.

"Where to? What for?" Timrok asked.

"I don't know. I have received nothing from the Lord about this. My guess is He is headed to the temple. He loves it there. Rally the troops."

In an instant, Zaben and Jenli's teams maneuvered through town, establishing safe corridors, and being inconspicuous. Timrok's team stayed close and hidden. Elric smiled to himself at the prowess of his team. So quiet, so invisible, so effective.

Elric followed Jesus to the temple. By the time He got there, Zaben and Jenli's teams had established posts and tucked away out of sight. The grounds felt peaceful and still, especially compared to the bustle of the last week. Even the birds hadn't begun singing yet. An occasional priest crossed the courtyard, getting ready for the day. Several vendors set up carts. A few crickets chirped. Jesus found an out–of–the–way corner, settled in, and began praying.

Sunrise—activity picked up all around the grounds, the daily temple routines began, and Jesus hadn't moved from His prayer corner.

Zaben walked over to Elric, who stood beside Jesus.

"I love the smell of the presence of His spirit," Elric said with his nose tilted upward.

"Yes. Yes, of course. But—"

"What is it?" Elric asked.

"The time is late. By now the caravan will already be loading and getting ready to leave."

Elric chuckled. "Yes, but . . . " he looked over at Jesus deep in prayer, "I am not going to interrupt that."

"Perhaps a little whisper to Him that it is time to go?"

"If the Father wants Him to move, He will tell Him. We will deal with the consequences as they develop."

"You know the caravan will not wait."

"You are right. You and Jenli go back to camp. Stall them if you can, and get Mary and Joseph's attention. Maybe Jesus will finish here, and we will make it back in time."

* * *

Back at the camp of the Nazarene pilgrims, the beasts of burden had become restless and edgy. The men at the front of the caravan struggled to get everything loaded for the trek and couldn't understand why everything seemed to be taking so long.

Joseph wrestled a large bag filled with food onto a camel near the front of the caravan. He stopped. He cocked his head. "Has anyone seen Jesus?"

A man nearby tried for the fourth time to get a large tent roll secured to the back of a camel and answered, "No, I haven't seen him all morning."

Another man with arms laden with water skins answered, "Neither have I. I wonder if he is back with the women helping with the rest of the children."

"That must be it," Joseph said.

Something in his gut kept nagging at him. He scanned for Jesus through all the chaos. *Ughh, there's still so much work to get done.* And they were already behind schedule. *Jesus is always so responsible. Surely, He must be with Mary.*

\* \* \*

At the rear of the caravan, the women struggled with delays of their own. Between crying babies and missing bits of this and that, it seemed clear the troop wouldn't be on the trail any time soon. In the midst of the mayhem of loading the family donkey cart, Mary realized she hadn't seen Jesus all morning. She asked around, and none of the kids knew where He was. None of the other women had seen Him. Mary, being pregnant again—four months along—didn't have the energy to search all the way up to the front of the caravan. Jesus had traveled with the men on the trip down to Jerusalem.

*He is twelve now, after all. Surely He must be up front with Joseph.*

\* \* \*

After a frustrating half-morning delay, the caravan to Nazareth finally began its amorphous plod outward. Hundreds of feet, tromping beasts, and rattling wheels of carts kicked up a thick cloud of dust and noise. With the company underway, Joseph fell back and joined Mary with the cart and the children.

"That was painful," Joseph hollered over the noise to Mary. He took the reins of the donkey. "I don't understand why that took so long."

Mary walked alongside Joseph. "Is Jesus up front with the other men?"

"No. I haven't seen Him all morning. I thought He was back here helping you."

"He's not with me. I haven't seen Him, either."

Joseph looked at Mary. He looked back at the cart. James, little Joseph, Elizabeth, and Simon all bounced around in the cart. Elizabeth waved. Joseph waved back.

"You know Jesus," Joseph said. "He's always trying to help everyone. He probably saw some work to be done and went to help. I'm sure He's with some of our relatives or another family who was struggling to get loaded. He'll show up once things settle down."

"I don't know," Mary said. "I have a strong feeling that He's not here."

"Where else would He be? He wouldn't wander off into Jerusalem by Himself."

"Don't you think we should look for Him?"

"We're already moving. We can't stop the whole caravan now. He has to be with the caravan somewhere. Don't worry. Have faith. Why don't you go ride with the children? You shouldn't overexert yourself."

"I just—"

"Don't worry. We'll find Him."

* * *

Jesus had a peaceful morning in the temple, praying by Himself in a secluded spot. Elric basked in the sweet aroma of the Spirit that he always enjoyed when in the inner court of the King's Realm. *I wonder if Jesus can smell it.* Most humans couldn't. *I wonder if any enemy forces can smell it.* He scanned the outer courtyard. None seemed to notice.

Jenli alighted next to Elric and reported, "Captain, the caravan has left. Neither Joseph nor Mary responds to our leading. Initially, they were separated and thought Jesus was with the other. But we were able to bring them together. They realized too late that Jesus is not with either of them, but now they are trusting He is among their relatives. They will likely not know He has been left behind until they make camp tonight."

"This is an interesting turn of events. We certainly did not foresee this." Elric rubbed his chin. "I suppose He just needed more time here at the temple."

Elric looked up and waited. He closed his eyes and waited. Opening his eyes, he said, "Here is the plan. You and Zaben stay with the caravan and keep trying to reach Joseph and Mary. In the best case, you could have them break away from the caravan and be back here in an hour. In the worst case, they will realize He isn't with the caravan tonight when they make camp. They will have a full day of travel back, but they could be here tomorrow night. Send the rest of your teams back here to provide cover in the temple. Perhaps, Jesus will just stay there. If He strikes out toward camp and realizes He has been left behind, we will deal with that if the time comes."

* * *

By midmorning on the day after the Passover festival, the regular routine of temple activities marched on, although with a less hectic pace with all the Passover pilgrims on their way home. An aged rabbi with a long wiry white beard and high cheekbones set up for the morning lesson under the shade of Solomon's Portico. Years of wisdom carved age lines into his face, but his eyes still sparkled with the energy of a young man. Word had gotten around among the priests about a young boy who had been asking many deep questions and displaying unusual knowledge of Scriptures. This elder rabbi volunteered to take the day's lesson in hopes of seeing what everyone had been talking about. Several other rabbis stood by with hopes of the same.

By the time Jesus left His solitary corner and joined the class, the lesson had already begun. He approached the gathering, and the rabbis in the wings whispered and pointed to each other. Jesus sat in the middle of eight boys, a much smaller class than it had been all week. The day's lesson centered on the promised Messiah, and the teacher had already established from Scriptures that the Messiah would come from the line of King David and would sit on the throne over all Israel. Jesus entered the lesson while the rabbi showed that the Messiah would conquer all of Israel's foes and sit as the great Judge by reading from the book of Isaiah.

"'And behold, the day of the Lord is coming, cruel, with fury and burning anger, to make the land a desolation; and He will exterminate its sinners from it. For the stars of heaven and their constellations will not flash forth their light; the sun will be dark when it rises, and the moon will not shed its light. Thus I will punish the world for its evil and the wicked for their iniquity. I will also put an end to the arrogance of the proud and abase the haughtiness of the ruthless. I will make mortal man scarcer than pure gold and mankind than the gold of Ophir. Therefore I will make the heavens tremble, and the earth will be shaken from its place at the fury of the Lord of hosts in the day of His burning anger.'"

Jesus shot up His hand. The rabbis off to the side whispered to themselves. The teacher handed the book to an attendant, looked up, and noticed Jesus for the first time. He glanced over to his companions, who gave him an affirmative head nod.

"Yes, young man, you have a question?"

Jesus sat up straight and spoke clear and loud. "How do you explain the apparent inconsistencies in the role of the coming Messiah? In Isaiah it also says, 'The Spirit of the Lord God is upon me, because the Lord has anointed me to bring good news to the afflicted; He has sent me to bind up the brokenhearted, to proclaim release to captives and freedom to prisoners; to proclaim the favorable year of the Lord.' These two passages seem to describe the Messiah very differently."

The rabbis on the side elbowed each other.

"You are insightful for a boy your age," said the teacher, shooting a glance at the other rabbis.

He turned back to the class and raised his chin. "That is the thing about prophecy, isn't it? We do our best to understand it, but we often do not fully comprehend it all until we look back on the events and examine it in retrospect. This is one of those difficult cases, and there are at least two interpretations. One possible explanation is that there are actually *two* Messiahs. One will be the conquering savior and judge, while the other one will be the kind and compassionate shepherd of Israel who will lead us into peace and joy. There are many respected rabbis who hold to this view. Another explanation is that one Messiah will accomplish both. First, He will vanquish our foes and punish the wicked. Then He will heal His people and 'bind up the brokenhearted.' Personally, I think there is only one Messiah. The passage you quoted from Isaiah even illustrates this because right after it says, 'to proclaim the favorable year of the Lord,' it continues by saying, 'And to proclaim the day of vengeance of our God.' Since it is clearly the same Messiah in a single passage, I believe this means that a single Messiah will accomplish both. So, tell me young man, what do you think?"

Jesus paused for a moment, then replied, "I think there is more about this that needs to be understood."

"Well said," the rabbi said, nodding. "Very well said."

* * *

From his regular position in front of Solomon's Portico, Elric looked up at the sun, which stood high overhead. He looked back at Jesus, engrossed in some discussion with the rabbis. He caught Timrok's attention and motioned for him. Timrok made his way over.

"We need to feed Him," Elric said.

"Yes, captain. I will see to it."

Timrok weaved through the bustling crowd and evaluated different vendors as though trying to pick someone on which to bestow some great honor. He stopped at one, bent over, and spoke to him. With one wing he covered their two heads. Timrok straightened and waited. He bent over and spoke to the man again. He waited some more. Timrok moved on. He tried another man. No response. He tried another. Again, no response. He spoke to a fourth vendor. The vendor collected up some things into baskets and covered his stand with a blanket. Timrok looked over at Elric from across the courtyard, smiled, and gave a head nod.

The rabbi finished some important point in his lesson and reached for another scroll.

The vendor approached the class, his arms full of two woven baskets, a square one filled with fresh matzo bread and a large round one filled with dates and figs. "Excuse me, rabbi," he said. "I am sorry to interrupt."

"Yes, what it is it?"

"I was just sitting at my table when it occurred to me that these fine boys have been sitting here studying with you all morning, and they must be getting hungry."

"This is not the time or place for that," the rabbi gruffed. "Go sell your wares in the courtyard like everyone else."

The other rabbis moved toward the vendor.

"No, no, no, no," the man said. "These are a gift. I thought about all the other boys who are out running in the streets and playing while these young men have chosen a more noble way to spend their day. I want them to have this. It is a gift."

The rabbi smiled and bowed his head. "In that case, thank you very much for your kindness. May the Lord bless you."

"Thank you, sir. And may the Lord bless you," the man said. He backed away with a bowed head.

"Well, boys," the rabbi said, "it appears that it is time to break for lunch. Pass these baskets around and help yourself."

\* \* \*

That night, Elric and his lieutenants gathered around Jesus, who had curled up against the wall in the outer court of the temple. Sparse torches on sconces cast a warm glow on the main court areas, but most of the court lay buried in night shadows.

"Is He just going to sleep there?" Jenli asked.

"He came here to pray," Elric said, "and sleep overtook Him. I don't think He intended to stay."

"Now what do we do?" Timrok said.

"We watch over Him tonight, and we watch over Him tomorrow," Elric said. "Do Joseph and Mary know He is missing yet?"

"Yes," Jenli said. "They begin the trip back here tomorrow morning. They are very upset."

Zaben knelt down next to Jesus and watched Him breathing. Zaben looked up at Lacidar and asked, "The prophet John is still in Jerusalem?"

"Yes," Lacidar said, "he spent the day in the Court of Women like he has all week. He will be there again tomorrow."

Zaben stood up and smiled at Elric.

"What are you thinking?" Elric asked.

"This is His test. Did you hear anything the Father said to the Son today?"

"No."

Zaben bit his lip and paced tiny steps. "I believe He knows the course the Father has set before Him. The question is, will He step into that course?"

Elric paused for a moment. He said, "No, I do not agree—not completely. I agree that He must know His course by now. However, I believe there is no question as to whether He will follow it. The real question is, what is that course? This we still do not know."

"Don't forget," Zaben said, "He has the flesh of man. There is a choice He must make."

Elric put his hand on Zaben's shoulder. "Yes, you are right about that." Elric looked down at Jesus and smiled. "The good news is, we will know this matter tomorrow—or possibly the day after. The time is close."

# 50

## SUBMISSION

**Baptism minus 18 years, Day 2 after Passover**

On the second day after Passover, Vorsogh positioned Daniel's body—without Daniel's conscious will—in the Court of Women, where he had observed a most interesting boy for the last four days. He stayed in the shadows, but he drew close enough to hear the discussions of the class.

*What is it about this boy?*

He had learned that the boy's name was John, but he still knew too little about him.

*I am convinced he is not the King. But I think he may be the prophet who precedes the King.*

He paced like a hungry wolf, looking back over his shoulder at John each time he turned away.

*I need proof. Give me something.*

\* \* \*

The second night after Passover, four elzur lieutenants and a captain gathered beside the twelve–year–old Jesus, who had fallen asleep while praying in a secluded spot in the outer court of the temple grounds.

"What is the status of Joseph and Mary?" Elric asked.

"They are back in Jerusalem," Zaben answered.

Jenli said, "We tried to bring them directly back here to the temple, but they would not hear us. They are too upset. They went immediately to the local authorities, convinced He would be there. Then they just started searching the streets."

"Tomorrow morning they plan to search the marketplace," Zaben said.

"Get them here as quickly as you can," Elric said.

Zaben and Jenli nodded.

"What happened here in the temple today?" Zaben asked Elric.

"It was a very interesting day, indeed." Elric knelt down on one knee as though he wanted to share a secret. The others knelt down with him.

"Today, I stayed with the class and listened to Jesus interact with the rabbis. I wish I had been doing that all week."

"Why? What did He say?" All four lieutenants' eyes glimmered.

"He spent most of the day challenging all the extra rabbinical laws, traditions, and rituals that have been added since Moses."

"He challenged the elder rabbis?"

"He did not challenge them directly, but He did make them try to explain why all the extra laws were necessary and if they truly served any spiritual purpose."

Timrok stood up and put his hand on his sword. "That sounds to me like a King about to set His house in order."

"It does," said Jenli.

Zaben bit his lower lip and smiled.

Elric stood up. "Tomorrow we shall see."

\* \* \*

## Baptism minus 18 years, Day 3 after Passover

Almost midday, on the third day after Passover, Zaben and Jenli entered the outer temple court and marched directly up to Elric and Timrok, who stood guard under the portico near a class already in session. Jesus sat in the middle of the class. An elder rabbi led the discussion with a dozen other teachers standing by.

"Captain," Zaben said to Elric, "it took us all morning, but Joseph and Mary are finally here."

Joseph and Mary came through the gate looking frazzled and tired.

"Very good," Elric said. "Now we shall see what the King will do."

All the angelic team shared excited smiles and rested their hands on their sword hilts.

Joseph spotted Jesus. "There he is!" he said, pointing to the small group gathered beneath Solomon's Portico.

"Jesus!" Mary squealed. She ran toward him and screamed, "Jesus!"

Joseph followed a step behind. Mary reached the edge of the class with her arm outstretched to Jesus.

Joseph approached the rabbi, bowed his head low, and said, "Master rabbi, I am sorry. Please pardon the interruption."

The rabbi nodded once. Mary grabbed Jesus' hand, and Joseph backed away with his head still bowed. Off to the side, away from the class, Mary clung to Jesus with both arms and sobbed uncontrollably. She sobbed for a long time, holding Him tight. Joseph stood behind her with his hand on her shoulder. Finally, she regained her composure. She loosened her grip enough to look into His face, but kept her hands locked on His shoulders.

Through broken sobs she said, "Son, why have you treated us this way? Your father and I have been anxiously looking for you."

Jesus looked almost confused by all the dramatics. With a calm voice He answered, "Why is it that you were looking for Me? Did you not know that I had to be in My Father's house?"

"Why were we looking for . . . " Mary took an exasperated breath. "We left for home three days ago! We thought you were lost. Or taken. Or who knows what? I don't understand what you were thinking."

"Come," said Joseph. His voice sounded calm and practical. "There is still time to eat, refresh our provisions, and get in a half a day of travel. We will never catch the caravan, but our relatives are watching after your brothers and sister, and we need to get back to them as quickly as we can."

"Here it is," Elric said with a tight throat. "What is He going to do?"

* * *

In the inner Women's Court, Vorsogh peered through Daniel's eyes at the boy named John, sitting in the middle of the late–morning lesson. The boy's father, Zacharias, stood next to another priest behind Elizabeth's seat, and Vorsogh pressed against the wall in the shadows behind them. Elizabeth and Zacharias smiled at the interaction between the rabbi and the young students. The priest beside Zacharias remained stoic and pious. Vorsogh, using Daniel's body, put on a look of disinterest and turned away with short jerky movements whenever someone looked his direction.

John answered a question from the rabbi leader, and Zacharias beamed. Zacharias crossed his hands behind his back and leaned sideways. He whispered to the other priest, "That's my boy."

"Mmm," said the priest. "Smart boy. You must be very proud." He eyed Zacharias and Elizabeth and raised his eyebrows. "*That's* your boy? A man your age with a son in his youth?"

Zacharias puffed out his chest. "He is our miracle child. My wife was barren, but the Lord opened her womb in our old age. Everything happened exactly as the angel told us it would."

"An *angel* told you that you would have a child?"

Vorsogh's ears perked up. *An angel?*

"Oh, yes," Zacharias said, "while I was serving in the temple, an angel named Gabriel told me we would have a son."

Vorsogh twitched. *Gabriel!*

"You saw the angel?" the priest asked.

"Yes, yes, of course."

"Did the angel tell you anything else?"

Zacharias lowered his voice. "I don't like to tell many people this." Zacharias looked around.

Vorsogh turned his head away.

"The angel said his name was to be John, and that he would be the prophet that goes before the coming Messiah."

"Is that so?" the priest said with an incredulous tone.

"I knew it!" Vorsogh shouted with Daniel's voice.

Vorsogh, still inside Daniel's body, jumped out of the shadows and made a move toward John. In an instant, another demon jumped from the shadows onto Vorsogh's back. The attacking demon had a small, gaunt stature, bulging eyes, and one stray fang that wouldn't stay behind his lip.

"What are you doing?" Vorsogh screeched.

"Leave the boy alone!" the small demon said, clawing at Vorsogh within Daniel's body.

Vorsogh reeled around, but he couldn't free himself. *This human flesh—too constraining—I can't . . .*

Vorsogh leapt out of Daniel's body, grabbed his attacker by the neck, and smashed him to the ground.

In the Physical Realm, the class came to a halt when a strange young man jumped from the shadows and started flailing his arms and spinning around. Then he fell unconscious, face first on the ground. Nearby priests rushed over and knelt over him.

Vorsogh growled and said, "Who are you?"

"I am Tumur, and you can't have this boy," Tumur said with a voice low and defiant.

Vorsogh picked Tumur up over his head and threw him across the court. Tumur tumbled to a stop, got up, and melted away into the crowd. Vorsogh spun around. *Grr. Now I've lost the advantage of surprise.*

An elzur lieutenant stood between him and John. Two more elzur warriors approached fast.

*Outnumbered and out of time.*

In rapid succession he shouted words into his hands. "Blindness! Leprosy! Lesions! Cancer! Heart disease! Sickness! Epilepsy! Sickness!"

With each word, a small fireball formed, and he hurled them toward John with both hands. Two dozen flaming missiles blasted through the spiritual air in a relentless stream. The angel lieutenant braced and held up a round shield with the figure of an ox in front of the fiery barrage. Most of the plasma balls bounced off in all directions. Some of them were absorbed by the shield. None of them appeared to hit John.

Vorsogh glanced left and then right. The two warriors in white approached fast, almost a blade's distance away. He reached for his own sword. "You insignificant slaves are no match for me. I'll crush you beneath my—"

Sizzling heat split through the top of his skull. The front end of a blade sliced downward between his eyes, and paralyzing pain shot down through his whole body. Everything went black.

He opened his eyes. An elzur lieutenant stood over him with his foot on his chest. Vorsogh wrenched upward, but he couldn't move. White cords of energy bound him head to foot.

"Remove him from here," the lieutenant said. The lieutenant called up to the senturim standing guard at the corner of the temple, "This one shall not enter here again."

Vorsogh thrashed against the bindings, but they held strong. He gave up and let his head fall limp. The angels hoisted him up by the bindings and lifted off.

\* \* \*

Elric held his breath, waiting for Jesus' next move. *Will He go with Joseph and Mary? Will He stay in the temple? Will He announce the beginning of His campaign? Will John come over and anoint Him King?*

Lacidar alighted next to Elric. Lacidar still held his weapon out, and his shield glowed from some residual heat.

"Captain," Lacidar said. "There has been an attack on John. It was a single attacker, and he has been subdued."

"How is John?" Elric asked.

"He is unharmed. But . . . " Lacidar's arm with his shield fell down to his side.

"What?"

"Many fiery darts hit others."

"Zacharias and Elizabeth?"

"They were both hit. We do not know if anything reached their spirits."

"Their spiritual armor is strong. I trust they will be—wait. Jesus is about to answer His test."

Jesus looked around at the temple. His eyes passed by all the majestic columns. He gazed past the tall wall of the inner court and fixated on the sacred inner temple edifice that housed the Holy of Holies. Elric could see it in His eyes—the yearning to be reunited with His Father, while the walls of stone, flesh, and time stood between.

Jesus hesitated for another moment. He looked back at Joseph. "Yes, sir," He said. He picked up Mary's traveling sack.

"That's it?" Zaben said.

Elric laughed. "It is not His time. This was His test—would He submit to His human parents and wait for His appointed time? He has to go with them to fulfill the law to honor His father and mother."

"No, this has to be His time," Zaben said. "Go get John. Hurry, it's not too late."

Elric put his hand on Zaben's shoulder. "We need to move. Now." To Lacidar he said, "See to John." To the other lieutenants he said, "Deploy your teams for travel."

"In His service."

"We will regroup after we get Him back to Nazareth."

Something across the far side of the outer court caught Elric's attention—two priests carrying an unconscious young man on a cot from the Court of Women.

* * *

## Baptism minus 18 years, Day 4 after Passover

Daniel awoke with the morning sun blazing in his eyes through a window casement. He blinked and squinted and sat up. He checked his hands. No blood. He looked around. The room had several beds.

Shelves along all the walls held vials and clay pitchers and small wooden boxes. A man sat at a table reading parchments.

"Where am I?" Daniel asked.

"Oh, you're awake," the man said. "We were very concerned."

"What is this place?"

"This is the temple infirmary."

"How did I get here?"

"You passed out in the inner temple court."

"How long have I been—"

"Since yesterday afternoon."

"I have to go," Daniel said. He jumped to his feet and moved toward the door.

The man stood up from his chair. "Wait! You can't just—"

Before the man could stop him, Daniel escaped through the door and ran. He passed through the temple gate without looking back and ran all the way down the steps from the temple mount. He darted around people in the street and didn't stop until he reached the city gate. He paused and turned back to make sure no one followed. Then he stepped outside the city wall and started toward his hideout.

"Levi? Are you there?" he said, still panting from his run. "I don't sense you at all. Where are you?"

He reached his camp, and he rooted through all his piles to make sure everything was still there. Then he sat with his head between his knees and rocked back and forth for a long time.

"Levi, where are you? I'm so scared. What am I supposed to do?"

He curled up in a ball and fell asleep.

The next morning, he awoke with a start—like all the air had just been sucked out of his body. Terror flashed into his empty soul. He jerked upright to a sitting position and screamed.

"Daniel," he heard in his deaf ear.

"Levi! Levi, is that you?"

"Yes."

"Where have you been? I thought you left me."

"I would not leave you. You belong to me."

"What are we going to do now?"

"I am through with Jerusalem. Let's go back to Galilee."

* * *

## Baptism minus 18 years, Day 8 after Passover

Elric, Timrok, Lacidar, and Zaben gathered around the war map at Hannah's house on the night after returning Jesus to Nazareth. Everyone stood in silence, peering off into the map—or through it. Elric crossed his arms and took a deep breath. He held it, then slowly released it with a tight jaw. His left eye twitched twice—the involuntary tick from a distant, secret pain. He glanced around at the lieutenants. They didn't seem to notice.

Jenli popped in through the ceiling, and everyone's attention turned to him. His wings folded away as his feet touched the ground. He held a parchment in his hand.

"What did you find?" Elric asked.

Jenli unrolled the scroll for everyone to see. "Every one of these twelve are too young to be generals today. A few of them are yet to be born. Timrok, these are the same Simon and Andrew you rescued during the days of Herod. Their family moved to Galilee, and their father is now a fisherman. Zaben, this is the Judas you rescued during the days of Herod. Every one of them, if they are born, are but children."

"This means we still have years to wait," Zaben said. "Probably until He is thirty."

Elric turned back to the map, crossed his arms again, and took another breath.

"A mere blink in the face of eternity," Lacidar said.

Elric nodded. Again, silence overtook the group.

Without taking his eyes off the map, Elric said, "The King gave us these twelve names for a reason. They are not ready to be generals in the King's army today, so we must help prepare them. It appears we have time."

He turned toward the lieutenants.

"Zaben and Jenli, with you and your two teams, we have twelve warriors. Each of you twelve will take as a charge one of these men. If they are not born yet, watch over their family until they are. I leave it to you to make the individual assignments."

"Sir," Zaben said, "What of the defenses in Nazareth?"

"Timrok's team will maintain our inner line of defense. For our outer perimeter, we shall reduce our number to five. Establish a rotation of your two teams—part time with the twelve, part time in Nazareth. When we travel to Jerusalem for the Passover feasts each year, we will all go."

Jenli pulled a ledger from his cloak and started writing on it. "Yes, sir," he said.

Elric turned back toward the war map. Zaben held the scroll with the twelve names out at arm's length next to Jenli, and the two made assignments.

Several moments later, Grigor flashed through the roof like a whisper and landed in the middle of the map.

"The word of the Lord," he said.

Elric made the map disappear with a wave of his hand.

"The Son has committed Himself to His earthly family," Grigor said, "and the Father is well pleased. The Son will complete His full days there to honor His mother and support His family. It is almost time to prepare John to receive the word of the Lord. The enemy has dealt a fatal blow to Zacharias and Elizabeth in the temple. Soon their flesh will manifest the wounds received through their spirit. After their passing, you must move John to the wilderness, where he will remain until his days of preparation are complete. After this, the prophet's voice will be heard throughout the land. The Son will come to the prophet to fulfill all righteousness. And then . . . " Grigor paused and held back a smile, "Then the King will be revealed."

Elric bowed his head once and said, "In His service."

"By His word," Grigor replied. In a flash, the messenger disappeared.

Elric turned around to the lieutenants and said, "There is the word we were waiting for. We have our assignment and . . . where is Lacidar?"

Lacidar appeared through the roof behind them and said, "I am here." He pulled his resonar out from behind his back and strummed a chord.

"I don't care if we have to wait a hundred more years before the King is revealed. He is going to be revealed, and we are partakers of His great plan. Patient endurance honors the King. And I, for one, am excited to bring Him this honor."

He strummed his instrument again. Then his fingers went wild over the strings. Timrok leapt into the air, spun three tight circles, and came down dancing, drawing Jenli and Zaben in with him. Lacidar sang his song again while Elric directed.

"The King is here! The King is here!

Victory, victory, the King is here!

His enemies are scattered, the evil days are shattered,

Victory, victory, the King is here!"

# 51

## LIFE MOVES ON

### Baptism minus 17 years

The following year, on the trip home from the Passover festival, Raziel traveled with Joseph near the middle of the caravan. Jesus led the donkey cart, and His younger brothers James and Joseph bounced around in the cart and climbed all over the packs and boxes. Joseph and Raziel plodded behind the cart.

"How old are you now, James?" Raziel called out above the noise of the wheels.

"Eight and a half," James said, draping his arms over the rail.

"I'm seven," little Joseph shouted, jumping up and down. His eyes barely cleared the rail with each jump.

"You boys are getting big," Raziel said. "You did a good job this week. I'm sure your father is proud. Do you miss your ima?"

"Yes, I suppose so," James said. The two boys spun around and climbed up a pile of packs.

Raziel turned to Joseph walking beside him. "I know it had to be hard for Mary to miss the trip this year."

"It was," Joseph said, "but it was too much with little Jude. Traveling with a three-month-old."

Raziel laughed. "Say no more."

"Elizabeth is only five," Joseph said, "but she's a big help with Simon and Jude. So, Mary wasn't completely alone."

"They are beautiful children, all six. You have quite a family."

"Thank you. Tell me, how did Jesus do in the temple this year?"

"Well, He decided to travel home with the caravan this year."

"Uhhgh, don't remind me of that."

Raziel laughed and slapped Joseph on the back. A cloud of dust rose from his tunic.

"He was different this year," Raziel said.

"How so?"

"Last year, He seemed like He was ready to take on the world. And I thought He just might. He challenged the leaders with very provocative questions. He displayed wisdom far beyond that which He has learned from me. There were times when I wondered . . . "

"What?"

"Nothing. I just get excited sometimes. But this year—this year He spoke up very little. And He wanted to spend most of His time in the inner courts, praying and listening to the singing."

They walked without talking. Both watched Jesus in front of the cart, leading the donkey.

"It's different for Him," Raziel said, "The temple. For me, I always feel like a visitor there. For Him it's like—"

"Home," Joseph said.

"Yes, like home."

\* \* \*

Daniel watched some men coming in off the Sea of Galilee just south of Capernaum. They unloaded their catch of fish into large baskets and hoisted them onto carts. Daniel stayed hidden at a safe distance.

"It would be easier to just steal what we need," said the voice in Daniel's ear.

"I know," Daniel said, "but our money is gone, and I'm tired of stealing and running from town to town."

"Better still, we could kill these men and take their whole load to market and sell it ourselves."

Daniel pulled his knife from his belt and fingered its sharp edge. He stared at the men. He gazed out across the lake.

"No," he said. "It's not just about the money. I want out on the water. We will do it my way."

He put the knife away and walked toward the fishermen. Hatred rose from within him with each step, but he did his best to hide it and put on a pleasant face.

"Good morning," Daniel called out to the fishermen.

"Morning," and "Shalom," came the polite but short replies of the men. They continued their work.

"Just kill them," the voice in Daniel's ear said.

Daniel scowled and shook his head. He put his innocent face back on and said, "Do you have any need for an extra hand? I am new in town and looking for work."

"Sorry," replied the most senior of the three.

His skin looked weathered and leathery, and Daniel could tell this man had layers of wisdom from the sea. Daniel couldn't help but respect the man. He envied him. He hated him.

"We are a small operation," the man said, "and I have all the help I can use." He lifted a full basket of fish onto a cart with the other full baskets of fish. "You might want to check with a man named Zebedee a little farther up the lake. I don't know if he is hiring right now, but I do know he has paid crew members."

"Thank you," Daniel said. He passed by the men and continued along the shoreline.

A mile later, Daniel came upon a cluster of several boats with at least a dozen men loading fish, hauling nets, and tending sails. Seagulls squawked and filled the shoreline air with motion. Daniel approached this work crew like he had the last, with a cheerful and innocent look.

"Good morning, I am looking for a man named Zebedee. Are these his boats?"

One of the men stopped and pointed toward a man who stood on the back of a cart receiving a basket of fish from one of the crewmembers. "Yes, that is Zebedee on the cart."

"Thank you."

"Sir," Daniel said, approaching the cart. "I am new in town and looking for work. Could you use an extra hand?"

"Well, I don't know—possibly," Zebedee replied. "Where are you from, son?"

"Just outside of Nazareth," Daniel said.

"I am from Nazareth originally. Do I know you?"

"I don't think so."

Zebedee looked down from the back of the cart, and Daniel could feel his gaze burn straight through him.

*Does he know me? Has he heard about me? Does he know my family?*

Daniel looked down at his feet and fought back the urge to run.

"Tell me, what brings you all the way up here to Capernaum?" Zebedee asked.

"I have always wanted to be a fisherman. I love the sea. Capernaum seems like a good place."

Zebedee continued to eye him without saying anything. Daniel shuffled his feet and fidgeted with his hair.

"I have had a rough year, sir," Daniel said. "I am hungry, and I could use a job. Please, I will work hard for you, and I want to learn."

Zebedee raised his hand. "Very well, son, I will give you a chance. You can start right now. We have to get this fish to market while it's fresh. What did you say your name was?"

*I can't tell him my real name. If he does know my family, he'll . . .*

"Levi," Daniel blurted out. His voice had a deeper and raspier tone than normal, and the sound of it startled himself. He reached his hand up to his throat, but just scratched an imaginary itch. Zebedee didn't seem to notice.

"Well, then, Levi, you can start by hauling those baskets of fish from the boats over there to the cart here."

"Yes, sir."

Daniel ran across the shore toward the boats.

"You told him my name was Levi," Daniel whispered as he ran.

"You had to answer something," the voice said.

"Now I am you, and you're me?"

"We have always been one."

Daniel strained to lift a full basket of fish. Through gritted teeth Daniel said, "Just don't ruin this for us. I have a job now. Maybe now we can live without stealing. Maybe now we can stay in one place."

\* \* \*

## Baptism minus 16.5 years

Daniel collapsed onto his makeshift bed mat at the end of a dark alley in Capernaum.

"That was a hard shift last night," he said to Levi. "I'm exhausted."

"Six months of this. I don't know why we do it," the voice in his ear said. "It was easier when we just stole what we needed."

"Because I love it. I love being out on the water. I always wanted to be a fisherman. And now I have some real skills. And now I don't go to sleep hungry. And I have some change in my pouch."

"I hate the crew."

"Me too."

"We should kill them and take over the boats."

"No! Why do you always want to kill everyone? I need them. I need this job."

"You know you want to hurt them. You like the power. Every time we fight with someone, and I help you—you feel the power. You like it. You want more."

"Stop it! Just stop it!" Daniel shouted.

He reached for a full skin of wine, pulled its stopper, sat up, and swallowed several large gulps.

"A girl then," the voice said. "We could go find a young girl and—"

Daniel jumped to his feet and pounded on his forehead with his fist. "Stop it, Levi! I just want to sleep." He drank some more wine. "I just need quiet."

He ran out of the alley and turned down another, smashing his shoulder against the building to redirect his momentum. Stumbling forward, he turned again. He stopped long enough to guzzle some more wine. He ran again with aimless abandon.

"I just need quiet," he muttered. "I just need quiet."

He turned another corner, and there down the street stood the town synagogue. He shuddered. He took another drink, wiped his mouth with his sleeve, and stared at it.

Tall and impressive, its white limestone walls stood out in stark contrast with the gray basalt buildings of the town. The foundation of massive limestone blocks rose the full height of a man, and the front porch on the south side had smooth limestone steps leading up on each side. The inane emblems of the misguided religious—menorahs, ram's horns, incense shovels, palm fronds, clusters of grapes and pomegranates, and geometric shapes—adorned the limestone reliefs on the capitols.

For no rational reason at all, he staggered forward until he reached the synagogue. He leaned one hand against the side wall and slid along it until he reached rear of the building. He leaned his back against the wall and sank down to the ground. He took another drink.

"Levi? Are you there?" he said.

He heard no reply. He took another drink.

"Levi?"

His brain became numb from the wine, and Levi had become quiet. It felt like a dark curtain had been lowered between him and his darkness.

He closed his eyes and went to sleep.

\* \* \*

## Baptism minus 16 years

Five grim elzur faces surveyed the war map at Hannah's house.

"It is clear we are on the brink," Elric said.

Elric crossed his arms and looked into the faces of his lieutenants. Zaben had a distant gaze and bit his lip. Lacidar's eyes welled up with tears. Timrok looked stern and never took his hands off his sword handles. Jenli wept silently with his eyes closed.

"I expect John's trials will begin within the year," Elric said.

"It grieves the King," Jenli said without opening his eyes. "I sense John's pain in the King's heart. There is joy—and passion—beyond the pain. But right now, there is pain." Jenli wiped his eyes.

Elric grimaced. "The enemy is ruthless. There are so many casualties. There is so much pain in the walk through the battlefield."

"But the wilderness . . . at his age," Lacidar said.

"It is best," Zaben said. "We will be better able to protect him from the enemy."

Elric's left eye twitched twice. "True. The encounter in the temple two years ago was . . . unfortunate. As always, we will turn what the enemy intended for harm into something good." He put his hand on Lacidar's shoulder and gave it a squeeze.

Lacidar lifted his head and blinked the tears out onto his cheek. "There is joy beyond the wilderness." He took a deep breath and let it out. "If it takes a hundred years, it is worth it to receive the word of the Lord."

"A voice of one calling in the wilderness," Zaben said.

"And then," Timrok said, "the revelation of the King."

Elric squeezed Lacidar's shoulder again and smiled. "You will be happy to know that Mary just had her baby. They named her Rachael, after their relative in Egypt. She is beautiful."

Lacidar smiled. "Seven children. Your house is noisier than mine."

Elric laughed. "And I love every moment."

# 52

## INTO THE WILDERNESS

### Baptism minus 15 years

In the bedroom of Zacharias, John peeled a damp towel off Elizabeth's forehead. He felt her forehead with his hand, shook his head, and folded a new cool towel over it. Her body had been failing for a year now, but over the last month, she had taken a dramatic turn for the worse. She suffered constant pain, and the doctors didn't know what to do for her. She had been bed-ridden for over a week, and today her condition grew even worse. Her shallow, inconsistent breaths brought her in and out of consciousness. Once in a while, she became lucid enough to give John a weak smile and squeeze his hand.

John looked around the empty room and glanced toward the front door.

"Come on, Father," he mumbled. "Why aren't you home yet?"

*I can't do this alone. I don't know what to do.*

He dabbed Elizabeth's forehead again. "Hang on, Ima. Father will be home soon."

The morning dragged by. Cool towel after towel couldn't bring the fever down. Finally, Zacharias came through the front door just after midday. John let out an audible sigh of relief.

Zacharias held his hand over a basin and poured water over it with a pitcher. "How is she doing?" Zacharias asked. He washed his other hand.

"Not good at all. She's not even conscious most of the time."

"That is probably for the best."

"And her fever has gotten worse. She isn't going to make it, is she?"

His own words echoed off the walls and pierced his heart. He dropped down into the chair next to the bed. He broke down. All the tension and grief erupted in a flood of tears, and he fought for air between deep, uncontrollable sobs.

Zacharias shuffled over to John and stroked his long hair—the hair that had never been cut, the hair of the promised prophet. "John, don't be sad. Your mother and I . . . we are old and spent. But we have had a full and blessed life. The Lord has given us so much. He gave us you. And we have seen the Messiah. And that is more than we could have ever dreamed of."

John looked up at Zacharias through his tears.

Zacharias's eyes welled up. He sat down beside John, and the two cried together.

After a long time, when he had no more tears left, John wiped his face with a towel, sat up straight, and took a deep breath. "What was the big meeting about at the synagogue?" John asked.

"Oh, nothing that is worth talking about right now," Zacharias said. He reached over, changed Elizabeth's towel, and stroked the brittle skin on her gaunt arm.

"What? What is it?" John said.

"Now is not the time."

"Father, you have to tell me. Is something wrong?"

"Well, they decided . . . " Zacharias buried his face in his hands.

"What? They decided what?"

"I have been cut off from the priesthood. I am no longer—"

"What? Why?"

Zacharias shrugged.

"So, what does this mean?"

"Well, for one thing, they will be coming to take our house soon."

John stood up. "They can do that?"

"I am afraid so. Remember, we are Levites and we do not own this property."

"But aren't these supposed to be men of God?"

"Beware, John. Beware of the hard–hearted religious. Do not look at the outward appearances of men. It is what is in the heart that matters."

Elizabeth coughed—one weak, shallow cough. She coughed again. She coughed three times. She started a nonstop string of coughs that convulsed her whole body. Zacharias dabbed her forehead and face with the towel. She stopped for a moment. She coughed twice more, spraying a fine mist of blood. She became quiet. John held his breath. She didn't move. Her chest didn't rise and fall.

"No!" John shouted, moving toward her. "Mother! Mother!"

"John, no," Zacharias said. "You can't touch her. Remember your Nazirite vow."

John backed away and shoved his hands under his armpits.

"Oh, Elizabeth," Zacharias moaned, dabbing the blood off her face with a towel and a trembling hand. "My bride. The love of my life."

He wiped his stream of tears on his shoulder and went back to dabbing Elizabeth's face.

"I love you so much."

The old man grabbed his chest. He jerked and slumped over where he sat.

"Father, what is it? What's the matter?" John said.

"I don't . . . know. Can't . . . breathe. My heart . . . "

"It's okay. It's okay, just breathe. It will be okay."

"John?"

"I am here, Father."

"John, you . . . are . . . the prophet. John?"

"Father."

"You . . . are . . . "

Zacharias drooped over sideways and landed half-curled-up next to Elizabeth.

John moved toward his father but pulled up short and wedged his hands under his armpits. A shockwave shot through his brain and left him motionless and numb.

Both parents—lifeless and empty.

John stared at them. His mouth hung open. *I can't believe this . . .*

A pot of anger boiled up within his belly. It rose into his chest, and the heat burned inside his cheeks. His throbbing pulse pounded in his temples. He ran circles around the small house, knocking things off the table and screaming.

"No! No! Why?"

He threw over the chairs.

"Why are you doing this to me, God?"

He pulled at his hair.

He looked at the lifeless body of Zacharias. "It was all too much for him," he shouted. "It's their fault!"

He crashed out of the house and lumbered toward town, fighting through the steady river of tears. He reached town and went straight to the synagogue. He burst through the heavy ornate wooden doors.

Inside, the atmosphere felt slow and reverent with quiet incense hanging below the tranquil rafters. Five priests in elaborate robes stood together near the front sipping from silver goblets.

"You killed him!" John's booming words echoed through the cavernous quiet.

"Is that Zacharias's boy?" one of the priests said to the others.

"What is the matter, son?"

"I am not your son, you brood of vipers."

"Calm down, young man, and tell us what is troubling you."

"My mother is dead, and now, because of you, my father is gone, too."

"I assure you, we have no idea what you are—"

"You killed him! It's your fault. His blood is on your hands."

John turned, bolted out the door, and ran all the way home.

Back at home, John circled around the room like a cornered wild animal.

*What am I going to do now? I can't bury them. I can't even touch them.*

He looked at them with his hands under his armpits. After several more minutes of staring at them through a wall of tears, he took a blanket and covered them, being careful not to touch them or the bed.

Something deep within his spirit stirred. The men from the synagogue would be showing up any minute to see about his tirade in the synagogue. He had to get out before they got there. They would be taking the house. Who knows, maybe they would take him. He needed to get away.

*Where will I go? How will I live?*

He must leave before the men got there. Time was short.

He gathered everything he could think of that he might need. He grabbed a large sack and threw in some food. A knife. A small blanket. A cup. A skin of water. He made his way around the room, deciding what he needed to carry with him. He came upon the shelf containing all the Scripture scrolls his father had collected for their studies. He paused and caressed the length of one of the scrolls, remembering the many hours his father had spent with him in the lamplight. His eyes welled up again, and he sank against the wall, staring at the scrolls.

He had to get out. The men would be here soon.

His eyes darted back around the room again, double-checking for anything that would be useful. *At the moment, nothing seems useful.*

*Nothing seems necessary.* He eyed the scrolls again. In one continuous motion, he scooped up every one of the scrolls under one arm, grabbed the sack with the other, and flung open the door. Men in the distance were heading his way. He took one last moment, looked back at his parents, clenched his teeth, and ran toward the hills.

* * *

## Baptism minus 15 years

Lacidar knelt next to John as the darkness settled in over John's first night in the wilderness. John lay flat on his back, and Lacidar rested his hand on John's chest. Jaeden and Ry stood near John's feet. The makeshift camp under a tree glowed a warm orange from the waning campfire, but the darkness outside the ring of light grew deeper now that the sun had gone down. Every unknown sound from the vast dark wilderness made John twitch and turn. He pulled the blanket up tight around his neck.

"How am I going to survive?" John muttered toward the emerging stars. "I have no trade skills. I don't know how to hunt or fish. I have no money."

He smacked his forehead.

"Why didn't I grab the small stash of money Father had at the house?"

He flopped his arm over his eyes.

"I have enough food to last for a week, maybe. Enough water for a couple of days. The first thing I need to do is find a steady source of water. I can't very well take water from other people's wells, and I don't know of any springs or streams in the nearby hills."

Lacidar straightened his back and said, "Go to the Jordan. The Lord will provide for you there."

Lacidar's words spread out like a warm sheet and sank into John's chest.

Something in the darkness snapped a twig. John jumped and turned his head in that direction. After watching for a minute, he pulled the blanket up around his neck again.

"Maybe I should just go to the Jordan," John said. "At least there's plenty of water there."

He fidgeted from his side to his back and back to his side again. Another sound startled him. He rolled on to his back again.

"Of course, I have no idea what I'll do when I get there," John muttered.

"He is never going to be able to sleep tonight," Jaeden said.

"Yes, he will," Lacidar said. "He needs the rest. The journey ahead is hard."

Lacidar placed both hands over John's eyes, and spoke, "Peace. Rest. Sleep."

His words rolled down to his fingers where they floated like soft blue clouds and sank through his hands into John's spirit.

"Peace," Lacidar repeated.

After several seconds, John became still. A minute later, he fell asleep.

Lacidar stood up. "He will sleep now. That was a hard day."

"Even harder than I expected," Ry said.

"It is a heavy load for a boy not yet sixteen," Lacidar said.

Jaeden pointed toward the pile of scrolls under the tree. "We did get him to bring his Scriptures with him."

"Yes," said Lacidar. "That was good work. He was such a mess I wasn't sure he would be able to hear you. He doesn't know it now, but those scrolls are his life."

Lacidar peered out into the darkness. "BaeLee, Stephanus, and Kelsof will continue to keep watch at our outer perimeter. I am going on to the cave we have prepared for John in the wilderness by the Jordan. I will scout the route and clear out any of the enemy. Then I will stand guard at the cave and make sure everything is ready there. Your task is to get John there—John *and* the scrolls. He will be weak and disoriented, so you will probably have to prop him up the whole way. Continue speaking peace and strength into him. He has a long, hard road ahead."

"In His service."

"I will see you in two days."

* * *

Two days later, John crested a rocky butte and caught his first glimpse of the Jordan river. Its calm blue–green waters stretched out left to right before him.

*I can't believe it. I was beginning to think I was going in the wrong direction.*

He sat on a large rock and reached for his water skin. He lifted it high over his parched open mouth and squeezed out the last two drops.

*It feels like I've been walking for weeks. Another day without water and I'd have been dead.*

He closed his eyes and sighed.

"Maybe that would have been better," he said out loud. "I'm probably just going to die out here, anyway."

Something within him stirred. *The river is right there. Go get water. Tomorrow is another day.*

"I don't think I can make it," he mumbled.

He breathed in a long stream of air. His chest filled with a tiny spark of hope. *You can make it.*

He opened his eyes and sighed again. He looked down at the river.

*I can make it.*

He stood. He forced his weak legs to take a step. Strength seeped into his legs from an unknown reservoir. *I can make it.* He took another step. More energy strengthened his depleted legs. *One step at a time. Just keep going.* With each step, he found just enough power to take another.

Finally, he reached the bank of the river near a sandy stretch of beach. He dropped everything, fell to his knees, and collapsed face first into the water. The refreshing, cleansing water enveloped him. He came up out of the water for air, and it felt like an entire desert full of dust and grime had been washed away. For a long time, he lay in the water letting the current carry away the dirt. He drank it in. He let the waters flow through his matted hair. He felt almost human for the first time in days.

*I need to find a place to camp for the night.* He filled his water skin and looked up and down the banks of the river. No good campsites at the riverside. *I don't know why, but I feel like I should try to find a secluded spot back in the desert a little way.* He walked along the bank. *That's interesting over there*—a rocky ravine leading up into some hills.

He turned into the ravine. A mile up the canyon he stopped and sat on a large rock. He took a drink of water. *I don't even know what I'm looking for. What am I doing out here? There's nothing out here but . . . what's that?* There, on the opposite side, was a good–sized cave twenty feet above the canyon floor. It looked like it would be inaccessible to any wild animals from below or above. And it looked high enough to avoid floodwaters. *I think I can get up there.* He scrambled up the rocky cliff side and made his way to the cave entrance.

The low entrance forced him to stoop down to get through, but once inside, the smooth rock ceiling opened high enough that he could stand upright. *This space is too small.* It would not be easy to spread out a bed in this space. A small passageway jutted off hard to the right. *I wonder where this goes.* He ventured around the corner and pressed his way back into what appeared to be another cavern. His eyes adjusted to the shadows, and he found himself inside an enormous room—much bigger than any room in any house he had ever seen. The ceiling reached at least the height of four men put together, and the walls felt solid and dry to the touch. The level floor had patches of soft sand. Although stale and musty, the air felt cool; and although dim and indirect, the light from the entry provided sufficient illumination to see around the entire room. The elbow hallway from the entrance gave protection from the wind and rain.

"This is perfect," he muttered. "Finally, some good luck."

He dropped his carrying bag, stood all his scrolls up against a wall, and examined the room in more detail. He found a nice soft bed of sand where he could sleep.

"This is good. I'll camp here until I can find a permanent place to live."

# 53

## ALONE IN THE WILDERNESS

### Baptism minus 15 years

The next morning, John woke to gentle light seeping into the cave. *Now what? I have nowhere to go. Nothing to do. Nobody to look for. Nobody looking for me. Nobody . . . nobody.*

Still exhausted from the trip, he went back to sleep. He slept all day.

The next morning, he got up, drank most of the water in the skin, and ate. He stood at the entrance of the cave and peered out across the rocky wilderness. Everywhere he looked, he saw only loneliness, hopelessness, and lack of purpose. He turned back into the cave and went back to sleep.

On the third morning, he tipped the water skin up and took the last swallow of water. He replaced the cap, slapped the skin against his leg, and sighed. Taking a forced breath, he stood up and hiked back down to the Jordan. He refilled the water skin and trudged back to the cave to hide. He didn't have a conscious thought the whole trip. Thinking required too much effort. He had too much pain to care. He went back to sleep.

On the fifth day, he ate the last three dates and the last piece of stale bread. *I don't know what's around here. I have no idea where I'm going to find food. It doesn't matter. If I starve to death, the pain will be gone.*

On the seventh day, the hunger pains spoke louder than the mental pain. *I have to find something to eat. I'll look around while I refill my water.* He sat by the bank and stared at the water passing by. *There are probably fish in there, but I have no way to get them.*

The final words of his father echoed in the back of his brain, "John, you are the prophet."

John laughed out loud. "Some prophet. Here I am in the wilderness with nowhere to go and no food. Where is God when I truly need Him?"

A large locust hopped from the riverbank up onto his leg.

John laughed again. "Thanks, God. Maybe I'll just eat this bug."

He snatched it up by its tail and hind legs and looked at it with a crooked smile.

*Maybe it won't be so bad.*

He laughed again. "That's right," he said to the locust, "maybe I'll just eat you."

*Go ahead. Just do it.*

He watched the locust a while longer. Its little antennae jerked this way and that. It tried to kick with its imprisoned legs. John's stomach growled.

*Eat it already.*

"All right!" he shouted.

He closed his eyes and took a chomp. The creature crunched between his teeth and filled his mouth with locust guts. The thought of it, the sound of it, the taste of it, was too much. He spat it out and retched. Even with nothing in his stomach to come up, he retched all the way from his toes.

He rinsed his mouth, staggered back to the cave, and went to sleep.

\* \* \*

Up the ravine, not far from John's cave, a hive of honeybees wedged between a crook in the branches of a tree. Lacidar translated the edge of his sword into the Physical Realm and cut off a small layer of the hive. A section of honeycomb brimming with fresh honey chunked to the ground. The bees swarmed around the broken piece of honeycomb, but then abandoned it and returned to the main hive.

\* \* \*

The next morning, John's hunger commanded even more attention than the day before.

*I have to find something to eat. Maybe I'll head up the canyon instead of down. Maybe I'll find some kind of fruit tree, or figs, or dates, or something.*

A little way up the canyon, not far from his cave, John came across a tree with a beehive in it. A nice piece of honeycomb lay on the ground below.

His heart leapt, and he let out a little laugh.

*I wonder if I could be so lucky.*

He retrieved the honeycomb without disturbing the bees—honeycomb filled with wild honey.

"Yes! Yes!"

With his treasure in hand, he rushed back to his cave.

Inside the cave, he extracted some of the honey into his cup and devoured the sticky golden nectar with his fingers. The sweetness filled his starving frame with a warm, intoxicating glow. But, after downing a whole cup full, he realized he couldn't get full on honey.

*I need something with more substance. Something I can chew. Hmm. I have an idea.*

Back by the river again, this time with a cup full of honey, John looked for another locust. There were plenty of them around, and within a minute he caught one by its hind legs.

"Let's try this again," he said, dipping the wiggling bug into the honey.

He swirled it around in the cup for a long time, just to make sure he had it well-coated. He pulled it out and watched the honey drip off it. He dunked it back into the cup and swirled some more.

*Now you're stalling.*

He held it up to mouth level with the honey dripping off of it, closed his eyes, and did it. He winced at the crunch, but the wonderful sweetness of the honey masked the rest of it. *Don't think about it. Don't think about it. Just get it down.* He swallowed. He waited a minute to make sure it would stay down. *It seems to be okay.* He tried another. And then another. Soon, he had eaten ten.

*It's nothing like real food, but at least it's something. Maybe I won't starve to death. Still, I don't know how this might settle. I think that's enough for today.*

The next day he filled up, and the day after that.

And the day after that.

\* \* \*

After a month of living in the cave, John set out one cool morning for his usual walk. He picked a handful of figs in the canyon he had named "Lonely Canyon," and, turning his back to the rising sun, walked up a new ravine he had yet to explore. A short distance up the ravine, he came across a wild olive tree. He inspected the fruit— too early to pick. He fingered the olives and tried to remember the times he picked this fruit with his mother. Even now, a month after his parents' deaths, all his memories remained shrouded in a cloud of pain. He stared at the olives with a blank expression. He couldn't picture his mother. His mind saw nothing.

He blinked hard, but the numbness wouldn't lift. He looked up and down the ravine.

*I'll name this Abandoned Olive Gulch. I need to remember how to get back to this olive tree.* He stared down the ravine, forming a mental picture. He turned and continued up to the top where the gulch began. Standing on the high ground, he surveyed the wilderness in all directions. A gust of wind blustered across the rocks and flapped his tunic. He pulled it tight around his body and shivered.

*Another month or two, and I'm going to freeze to death.*

Off to his left stretched the Jordan river. Behind him, nothing but wilderness. To his right . . .

*What's that?*

John hiked toward something on the ground that looked out of place. The air became foul. He covered his nose with his hand and grimaced. Right there, in the middle of his wilderness, a dead camel lay rotting on the ground. Flies filled the air with the incessant drone of their buzzing. The putrid odor made John's eyes water. Scavenger birds had turned the mound of flesh into a gruesome sight. But in the midst of this macabre scene, John saw one thing—the warmth of an animal pelt.

He sat down and stared.

*It would be easy to skin the beast and get a covering for winter. I do have a knife. But there's that rule in the Nazirite vow about touching a carcass.*

He put his hands under his armpits.

*But what does that vow mean now that I'm out here in the wilderness? Still, the vow was an important commitment to Father. But none of it means anything if I die this winter from exposure.*

For the first time since he left home, John spoke a prayer. "God, I need your help. I need this animal skin for a coat and a blanket. But You know the vow I have taken. Show me how to do this without breaking my vow."

He sat for a minute looking at the camel. Nothing happened. Only the sound of buzzing flies. He shook his head and laughed at himself.

*What was I expecting? It's not like God is going to speak and give me instructions. Maybe He will write a note and have a bird bring it. Maybe the camel itself will start speaking and tell me what to do. It was a silly prayer.*

He sat there, listening to the flies buzz. After a long time, John got up, circled around the camel several times, and turned to leave.

*Maybe I'll come back tomorrow. Maybe by then I'll know what to do.*

He took a step toward his cave, but his eye caught some motion off to the left. He turned his head, and there, just beyond the next ridge, the top of a man's head bobbed up and down below the ridge line. John ducked. His heart raced. *That's the first person I've seen out here! Who could it be?*

He forced himself to breathe slower.

*Maybe he could help me. I have to take the chance.*

He jumped up and ran toward the man. "Excuse me, sir," John called out. "Sir, can you hear me?"

John crested the ridge. *There are two men, not one.* The men talked with each other on their casual hike through the canyon.

"Excuse me, sirs," John called out again.

The men stopped and turned toward John.

"Well, hello, young man," one of the men called back.

The other man put his hand over his eyebrows and looked toward John, "We are trying to find our way to the Jordan. Do you know the way?"

"Yes, I can show you the way. It's not far from here."

The men sauntered up toward John. They appeared older, although John couldn't precisely judge their age. They had swarthy tan skin, dark hair, and piercing eyes. *They seem to be safe enough, but why would a couple of travelers have no traveling packs?*

The first man said, "What a surprise to find another living soul out in the middle of this wasteland. What in the world are you doing way out here, son?"

"Well . . . I . . . live out here," John said.

"No, that is awful. Why?"

"I am . . . I don't know. Don't worry about me. I'm doing fine. But I have a problem I wonder if you could help me with."

John explained his predicament with the camel and asked if the men would be willing to skin the animal and clean the hide for him.

"We would be happy to help. My name is Ry, and this is my good friend Jaeden," the first man said. "What is your name?"

"My name is John. The camel is over here."

Hiking back toward the camel carcass, John said, "Those are interesting names."

"We're not from around here," Jaeden said with a smile.

After several hours of work, the two men had the skin prepared. They washed it in the Jordan and stretched it out on some rocks near John's cave.

"Now, you need to let this set for several weeks," Ry said. "We left the hair-side down so the skin side can tan."

He pulled a large skin flask full of some kind of oil out from under his tunic. John remained too intent on their instructions to wonder what this man would be doing with a large container of oil.

"You need to rub this into the skin so it will not get dry and hard. After a few weeks of doing this, you will be able to cut the hide into a blanket, an overcoat, or whatever you need."

"Any questions?"

"No, sir. Thank you both very much for your help. I can't tell you how much I appreciate everything you have done."

"You seem like a very strong young man. I think you are going to be just fine. May the Lord bless you."

"And you." John bowed, and the men walked off.

# 54

## NEW OPPORTUNITIES

**Baptism minus 14.5 years**

The black of midnight filled John's cave, and the snoring of the young prophet, who nestled under a camel–skin blanket, provided the only sound in the Physical Realm. Jaeden and Ry stood guard just inside the cave entrance. Elric and Lacidar stood near John.

"Thank you for the update," Elric said to Lacidar. "I will be back next week."

Elric turned to leave but stopped when a bright light descended through the high stone ceiling of the cave. Elric peered into the light, his hand on the hilt of his sword.

Commander Kai appeared. His huge frame dwarfed the room, and the glow he carried lit the spiritual air like the afternoon sun.

Elric snapped to attention. "Good evening, commander."

"Elric. Lacidar. It is good to see you, my friends. Please be at ease."

Standing next to Kai, Elric felt small. Power and authority radiated from the great commander, and Elric could muster only so much "at ease" in his presence.

"I bring news," Kai said. "The widow Hannah has passed."

"Bless the Lord," Elric said. "She was a valiant warrior for the Kingdom. Finally, she can rest in the joy of the King. I am very pleased for her. I am curious though, was it a hard transition? Was she sick?"

"No, she was healthy and full of life. She went to sleep last night, and the King called her home."

"Excellent." Elric beamed with genuine gladness. Lacidar smiled and nodded his head.

"It has left us with a small situation, though," Kai said. "And actually, that is why I am here."

"Yes, commander. What is it?"

"With her gone from the battlefield, we need to move our situation room to another location. The umbrella of grace that covered that place is now removed. I would like to make this cave our new center of operations for this region."

"You know, of course, sir, that John is nowhere near the level Hannah was."

"Not yet. But he will be. And much more. Over the coming years, he is going to become the front line of our operations. Strategically, placing the war room here is the right move."

Lacidar grinned and bounced on his heels. Elric remained stoic but nodded his head, "By your word."

Kai smiled and pulled out his giant broadsword. He held it out horizontally and spoke a word. The sword began a low hum. It started to glow—red, orange, yellow, a brilliant blue. The frequency and volume of the humming increased with the changing colors until they all reached a fierce and breathtaking climax. The commander lowered the tip of his blade. It touched the ground, and an explosion of light and intense blue fire erupted. Every surface of the cave—the walls, the ceiling, the floor—caught fire and burned with searing blue flames. After several minutes, the flames subsided, and the walls remained a translucent glowing white, so pure they had sparkles that twinkled like starlight. In the center of the room, a blue cloud rose from the floor. It swirled and pulsed and organized into a transparent form. After another minute of humming and sizzling, the war map appeared.

Kai slid his sword back into place and smiled. "I will notify the regional captains. Operations will begin here tomorrow." He waved his hand over the map, and it disappeared.

"It is a good work that you do," Kai said. "The King is pleased." He unfurled his giant wings, and with a single flap he disappeared.

Elric glanced over at John. He lay, unmoved, under his camel-skin blanket. Again, his snoring made the only sound.

* * *

The next day regional captains filled John's cave. As each entered, his giant frame shrank to a size small enough for the room. Elric and

Lacidar stood against a cave wall and watched the ten warriors with two golden braids on their sleeves gather around the war map. The captains went straight to work, not paying any notice to their new surroundings. They pointed at spots on the map and made animated gestures as they planned timelines and strategies. They discussed how Rome had just replaced Coponius with Marcus Ambivulus as procurator of Judea. But most of their discussion centered on the new appointment of Annas as the High Priest and how the Roman procurator now controlled the activities of that office.

The lieutenants filed in and gave their reports. The provincial power struggles between Molech, Asherah, and Yarikh continued to smolder. They continued to have outbursts and flare-ups, but no shifts in the seats of power appeared likely. Rebellions and discontent festered throughout the entire region. The tentacles of darkness stretched out from the highest seats of power down into every person's house. The darkness grew, and pressure built throughout the region.

The logirhim arrived with words from the Throne. The messengers came and went. Lieutenants shot in and out. Captains directed operations on a hundred fronts.

Elric leaned in toward Lacidar and whispered, "It has been a while since I've seen the larger picture. Our mission is so focused, it's easy to forget all the parts that have to come together."

"Do you miss the regional work?" Lacidar asked. "The complexity, the pace?"

Elric's eyes sparkled, and a slight grin curled his lips. "No. What I miss is from long ago—perfection, peace, holiness . . . music."

They watched the controlled mayhem in the middle of the room for another minute.

Elric crossed his arms and said, "Every day we get closer. Even as we wait, I feel like time is speeding up. The revelation of the King is so close—it feels like a mere breath away."

\* \* \*

Tumur spied the new developments around the cave where his young charge, John the prophet, had settled.

*What is all this? I drive John into the wilderness where I can keep him bound up in loneliness and despair, and now this? Months of nothing, and now John's cave becomes a headquarters for the enemy?*

He watched ten more logirhim arrive and a dozen elzur lieutenants depart.

*How can I reach the prophet now?*

He snorted a puff of yellow smoke from his nostrils and sank back into his hiding spot.

*Wait, this could be the break I've been waiting for. If John is at the heart of the King's plan, surely one or more of these angels might have a direct connection to the Son of Man. Maybe one of them could lead me to the prize I truly seek. All I have to do is follow each of these unsuspecting lieutenants to their assignments and, eventually, one of them will lead me to Him. Finally, after all the years of waiting, maybe now my persistence will pay off.*

# 55

## FOUND

**Baptism minus 14 years**

Tumur peeked out from his hiding place near John's cave. His small, gaunt frame tucked easily into the cleft of a rock with only his bulging round eyes peering from within the shadows. Across the valley, a steady stream of elzur lieutenants filed out of John's cave with their assignments.

One emerged and flew south. *No.* Another came out and flew west. *No. Already followed him. Six months of this, and I've found nothing. Nothing!* Another emerged, looked left and right, and flew north. *Well, here's one I haven't followed yet. Let's see where he leads.*

Tumur took off, flying low and ducking in and out of concealments along the way. He tailed the lieutenant all the way to the region of Galilee.

*A fast one, this. Almost as though he doesn't want to be followed. Looks like he is headed to Nazareth. Good. I haven't searched there yet.*

Tumur stopped on a hill just outside of town and tracked the angelic lieutenant with his eyes to one of the houses in town.

*Let's see who lives here.*

He flew into town just above the rooftops and alighted on one several blocks away from the house. The moment his feet touched down, a warrior in white appeared from out of nowhere with his sword drawn. He carried a round shield with a lion embossing.

"You are out of your domain," the angel said. "Be gone."

Tumur reached toward his sword, but the angel raised his blade and stepped forward. Tumur turned and flittered off without a word.

He flew far around the outskirts of town. He snorted a puff of yellow smoke and looked back. *Let's try this again.* He approached from the opposite direction at rooftop level and landed on a nearby house.

A warrior in white met him with a drawn sword.

Tumur retreated to a hill outside of town. He spotted a pair of Roman soldiers on the road leading to town. He flew down and alighted behind them. Scanning left and right, he started walking with them. They passed through the city gates and down a main street. They turned left down a smaller street. As soon as they made the turn, a huge elzur lieutenant with two swords and no shield stepped out from behind a building. He took a stance in the middle of the street, blocking their path. Tumur stopped. The two Roman soldiers continued walking and passed through the angel. Tumur hesitated, then took one step forward. The angelic lieutenant reached for his swords. Tumur stopped. He turned and flew back to the hill outside of town.

*This is very interesting, indeed. This is the most promising prospect I've found yet. I need a way to learn more.*

He sat on the hill and looked down over the town. He picked at his stray fang with a filthy fingernail.

*Hmm. Passover is approaching. Perhaps the pilgrimage to Jerusalem will provide an opportunity to get a closer look.*

He found a place to hide and waited.

Two weeks later, the caravan bound for the Passover festival in Jerusalem formed just outside the city gates. *Let's see if the mysterious family takes the trip.* From the house of interest emerged a large family—a man, his wife, five boys, and two girls. With a donkey cart full of provisions, the family merged into the caravan.

*Excellent.*

He spotted the warriors in white. An elzur captain walked with the family.

*I've seen this captain before. I think he might be the one I used to see come to Zacharias and Elizabeth's house.*

A burly lieutenant with two swords followed behind.

*Hello.*

Five more warriors formed a perimeter around the family. Flashes of light in the distance along the horizon caught his eye.

*Interesting. There are even more enemy forces out there that I don't see.*

The caravan rumbled southward, and Tumur followed at a safe distance. Night fell, the troop made camp, and the captain and lieutenant stood watch over the one family. The other warriors kept an outer perimeter.

*There is definitely something special about this family.*

Four days later, the caravan plodded into Jerusalem and made camp. Tumur waited under the cloud of settling dust for the next day when the suspicious family would visit the temple. The next morning, without a word, every one of the elzurim around the camp made toward town at different times along different routes and melted into the bustle. Then, the captain led the way for the family. The youngest in the family, a girl, looked no more than two and rode straddled on the mother's hip. The oldest, a boy, appeared to be about sixteen.

*Exactly the age for the Son of Man. The mother seems vaguely familiar, as though I've spied her before. Could she be the one that Luchek followed all those years ago? With the covering on her head, I can't be sure.*

He slinked in to get a closer look at the boy.

*There is nothing about Him that looks extraordinary. I need to get closer.*

An elzur warrior appeared from out of nowhere and diverted him away. He didn't resist. *That's fine. I know their destination.* He took to the air and headed straight for the temple. He alighted on top of the broad outer wall and perched like a sinister invisible gargoyle and waited.

The family arrived and weaved their way through the outer court. *This is a perfect spot to watch from. I don't know what to look for, but I'm sure I'll see something if I stay persistent.* The father and the boy left the rest of the family and headed toward the Court of the Israelites. *That's strange . . . it's subtle . . . but I definitely think I see . . .*

Everywhere the boy moved, a region devoid of beaelzur presence seemed to develop around Him. It looked like an invisible bubble that insulated Him from the forces of darkness. With all the motion and jostling and mixing, it would be impossible to notice it from ground level. But with his perspective and attentive eye . . . *I need to test it—to see just how close I can get.*

With a few erratic flaps of his leathery wings, he landed just outside the no–enter radius. Without a break in his motion, he proceeded inward toward the boy. In an instant, an elzur warrior, much bigger than he, appeared from the right and pressed his formidable forearm into Tumur's chest.

"Take it somewhere else," the angel commanded, low and firm.

"I was just going over—"

"Somewhere . . . else," the angel said.

"You have no right to restrict me from—"

The angel reached for his sword.

"Fine, fine," Tumur grunted. He smiled, flapped his wings, and took off.

Back on the top of the wall, he resumed his gargoyle stance and watched for more signs. A moment later, without warning, a broadsword almost as wide as his whole body appeared in front of him in a huge sweeping arc. The sword flat-bladed him across the chest and launched him with more force than he'd ever known. A maniacal laugh squeaked out. *Senturim!* He tumbled through the sky at least a mile before he could regain control of his flailing body. This provided the final confirmation. *I have seen enough. There is no need to continue the search.*

He had found the Son of Man and decided to return to Nazareth to formulate a plan for conquest and glory.

\* \* \*

Tumur perched on the brow of the cliff at Nazareth and gazed down at the distant road leading to Jerusalem. With the sun disappearing behind the horizon on his right, his foot tapped an anxious cadence. *Another week and a half before the festival is over and the Son of Man is back at home.*

A thin trail of yellow smoke seeped out his nostrils.

*Then what? I* should *report this to Marr—or Molech, Yarikh, or Asherah.*

He sneered and grunted.

*Glory–hungry power mongers. I hate them all. Every one would steal my prize. I owe no allegiance to them.*

He brooded as the silent nightfall crept across the landscape.

*But if the dark lord finds out I withheld information about the King . . .*

He stretched his neck, stroked it with his hand, and swallowed hard.

*But if I destroy the flesh of the Son of Man myself . . .*

His bulging eyes widened, and he cackled.

*Power, glory, my rightful place on the mountain of the King.*

He cackled again.

*Yes—I will claim the prize for myself. But how? How can I reach Him? This captain and his team have the King hemmed in. I'll never get close enough.*

His eyes wandered across the panorama below. His mind wandered through strategic options. Several minutes passed. Something on the distant trail caught his eye—a troop of eight Roman soldiers on a brisk march. Their long spears rested against their shoulders, and the iron tips bobbed up and down with each deliberate step. Tumur smiled.

*That's it.*

\* \* \*

**Baptism minus 13.5 years**

From his perch on the cliff at the edge of Nazareth, Tumur's gargoyle frame cast no shadow in the early–morning sunlight. He sulked with his chin in his hands and waited. Hours passed, and he sat still as a stone statue. He spotted something on the trail below. He squinted and waited another minute to be sure. Two Roman soldiers trudged up the trail toward Nazareth.

"Yes!" he shouted.

He jumped to his feet and wrung his hands.

*For this I have waited weeks. The Boy and His father are working outside by their house, and I finally have vessels to work with. This is it! My time has finally come.*

He stepped off the edge of the cliff and plummeted downward. He opened his wings and swooped down toward the sloping plain. He alighted just behind the marching soldiers. He tucked his wings away and joined the march. With one hand on each of the Roman soldiers' shoulders, he walked between them and spoke into their spirits. For half an hour Tumur walked with the men. Just before they reached the city gates, he flew off to a rooftop—just outside the elzur perimeter, but still within eyeshot of the Son of Man's house. He ducked down and waited.

# 56

## MAN OF SORROWS

### Baptism minus 13.5 years

Elric looked up toward the sun, just past its zenith, and squinted. Another quiet day in Nazareth. He scanned all around Joseph and Mary's home—nearby houses, rooftops, trails, and streets. Quiet. None of Timrok's team were visible. He glanced back at Joseph and Jesus, working on a project at the side of their house. Joseph knelt on a half-finished wagon bed.

"That one's secure," Joseph said to Jesus. "Hand me another plank."

Jesus grabbed one from a freshly cut pile and passed it up to Joseph.

Elric's attention returned to the surroundings. *Our world here in Nazareth is so small. No one has any idea that the King is here. They all go on about their lives—never knowing that, day by day, we draw closer to the moment when He is revealed. The time is so close. The day we have longed for since—*

A flash of light from the right. A signal from Timrok. Elric's jaw tightened, and he focused down the street. Timrok appeared from around the corner, on the street walking fast. He motioned with his hands. Elric unsheathed his sword.

Two Roman soldiers turned the corner and marched up the dirt road that passed by Joseph and Mary's house. They carried traveling packs on their backs and conspicuous broadswords at their sides. One soldier—probably the ranking one—had a smaller pack, but the other had an enormous one. They kept a brisk pace, but they looked weary from a long trek. Elric studied them for any signs of enemy spirits. They appeared to be alone. Timrok drew up beside them and spoke to them as they walked, but his words bounced off their darkened spiritual shells like water. The soldiers would pass by Joseph and Jesus on the road within seconds, despite Timrok's best efforts. Elric positioned himself between Jesus and the incoming soldiers. The soldiers approached, and one motioned to the other and pointed toward Joseph and Jesus. The other soldier nodded. They came to a stop on the trail just in front of the house. Elric held his stance between them and Jesus. Timrok stood behind and searched the area for enemy forces.

"Boy," the first soldier called out.

Jesus stopped with a plank of wood in His hand, straightened up and turned around. From the back of the wagon Joseph looked up.

The soldier pulled a large water skin he had slung around his shoulder by a leather strap and tossed it toward Jesus. It flew through Elric and landed in the dirt with a flap of dust.

"Fetch us some fresh water," the soldier said.

The second soldier flung his water skin, which also passed through Elric and landed next to the other. Jesus looked back to Joseph, who answered with a terse nod and concerned eyes. Jesus laid the wood down and gathered the two skins. Joseph jumped down off the wagon. Jesus made His way to the street, being careful to keep a safe distance from the soldiers, and the soldiers helped each other lower their packs from their backs. The packs landed in the dust with a thud.

Jesus ran down the path toward the village well. Elric nodded to Timrok, who followed close to Jesus.

Joseph stood with his hammer hanging limp in his hand and stared at the soldiers. His meager peasant clothes looked insignificant next to the brass and leather and iron of the soldiers. The soldiers looked away, eying the people on the streets and the pockets of gathering neighbors. The villagers spoke to each other in whispers and shielded their mouths with their hands. Joseph straightened the pile of wood planks, never taking his eyes off the soldiers.

Joseph cleared his throat and said, "Staying long in Nazareth?"

The ranking soldier grunted.

"Our goal is Sepphoris by nightfall," the second soldier said. "We require only a fresh supply of water."

The ranking soldier elbowed the other. "These people do not need to know our plans." He turned to Joseph. "Where is your boy? How long does it take to draw water?"

"Not long. I'm sure He'll be back shortly."

Elric, still positioned between Joseph and the soldiers, watched down the street for another minute. Finally, Jesus and Timrok reappeared. Jesus ran with hurried steps, but Timrok's long gait looked smooth and effortless.

"Finally," the senior soldier said.

Seconds later, Jesus handed the bulging water skins to the soldiers and stepped back by Joseph. The soldiers slung the skin straps around their shoulders and moved toward their packs.

*Zzzzztt!* A sizzling whistle zipped past Elric. He glanced at Jesus and Joseph. Nothing unusual. He turned to the soldiers. The words "take him" glowed on the black spiritual armor of the ranking soldier and sank into his spirit.

"We're under attack!" Elric shouted.

"Where?" Timrok said, pivoting all the way around. "I don't see them."

The soldier stopped reaching for his pack and stood upright. He cocked his head to the side. "Boy!" the soldier said with a commanding voice. "Come here."

Jesus took two steps forward.

Elric widened his stance.

"You will carry this pack," the soldier said.

"No," shouted Joseph. "You can't force Him to do that."

"I can," the soldier said. "By Roman law I can conscript for a mile."

"But He's just a boy. I will carry it."

The soldier paused a moment.

"Leave the Boy alone," Elric spoke. His words rolled up and bounced off the soldier's dark shell.

Two small fireballs sizzled past Elric and collided into the soldier. The words "take the boy" and "do it now" absorbed into his spirit.

Elric turned toward the origin of the fireballs and pointed.

"There!" he shouted to Timrok. "Rooftop!"

"I see him!" With a powerful stroke of his wings, Timrok shot toward the attacker.

A stream of fireballs sizzled inward toward the soldiers. Timrok barreled directly through the barrage, slashing some with his swords. Dozens made it through. "Take the boy!" "Take him now!" "Use force!" "Kill him!" "Take him!" Elric blocked most with his shield, the energy ricocheting off into shattered bits of plasma. Still, both the soldiers received multiple hits, which sank into their spirits.

The soldiers both appeared agitated at Joseph and advanced. The second soldier reached for his sword. The first reached toward Jesus.

"Enough of this insolence!" the ranking soldier said. "I said the boy will carry this pack, and if I have to strap it to his back myself, he is going to carry it."

"No!" Joseph shouted, moving to block the soldier's way to Jesus. His left arm extended toward the soldier. His right hand still held his working hammer.

Just before Joseph's left hand touched the soldier, Elric's forearm caught the soldier across the middle of his chest and knocked him flat on his back.

Kylek appeared and positioned his foot on the downed soldier's chest.

Jesus rushed toward Joseph, reaching for the back of Joseph's shirt.

The stream of fireballs from the rooftop stopped.

Joseph stumbled forward, his right hand raising for balance.

The second soldier lunged forward, lifted his sword over his head, and slashed downward with a dreadful shout.

His blade caught Joseph's right arm just above the elbow and sliced clean through the flesh and bone. Joseph's forearm dropped like a lifeless piece of meat, and Joseph careened backward. He tripped, spun, and crashed to the ground hard, his head smashing against a large stone. He didn't move. Blood gushed from his severed arm and gashed head and pooled in the thirsty dirt.

"What have you done?" the ranking soldier shouted. He tried to stand back up, but with Kylek's foot on his chest, he couldn't seem to get to his feet.

"He was going to attack you with his hammer," the second soldier said.

Elric knelt next to Joseph and put his hand on Joseph's chest, speaking words of strength. A flash of light from Timrok on the roof signaled he had the attacker under control. On the street, the passersby and neighbors bunched into groups and gathered around. Jesus flopped down and draped His arms over Joseph with His head on Joseph's chest.

He wailed between sobs, "No! No! No!"

Elric lifted his hand from Joseph's chest and placed it just above Jesus' back. He paused. *Do I touch Him? Do I dare? Do I . . .* He lowered his hand directly upon His back and spoke, "Strength. Peace. Strength. Strength."

"Ima!" Jesus screamed. "Ima, come quickly!"

Mary emerged from inside the house with little Rachael and Jude peeking out from the front door. The gathering crowds pressed in.

"Joseph!" Mary squealed. She ran toward the scene. "What happened? What happened?"

Jesus sat up long enough to point at the soldiers. His hand dripped with Joseph's blood.

The ranking soldier called out to the other. "Quickly, get your pack. We need to get out of here."

"But he was attacking you," the second soldier said.

"Look around," the first soldier said. "We are going to have a riot here shortly, and we have no reinforcements." He tried to sit up.

Elric nodded to Kylek, who stepped back. The soldier scrambled to his feet. The two soldiers hoisted their packs with one arm while holding their swords out toward the incoming crowds. The soldiers backed away toward the street and made a hurried retreat. The people rushed inward toward Joseph. Mary tore a strip of cloth from her dress and made frantic attempts to stop the bleeding from Joseph's arm.

In the midst of all the screaming and mayhem, a shimmering white angel appeared from above and alighted next to Elric. Elric stood and gave him a small, sad, smile. He crossed his arms, stepped back, and waited.

A moment later, Joseph's spirit stood up. Joseph looked at Elric and the other angel, then down at his broken shell of a body. A swarm of people gathered all around, yelling, crying, wailing—and paying no attention to the three of them standing there. Joseph looked dazed and confused.

"What happened?" Joseph said. "What's going on?"

Elric stepped forward and leaned down to put his arm around Joseph's shoulder.

"Am I dead?" Joseph asked.

"Joseph, it has been my true honor to have served the King alongside you. You have been a faithful steward of the gift entrusted to you. We still have a long way to go, but you have completed your course. Your work on earth is finished, and now it is time for you to enter your rest. I want you to go with my friend here."

"But what about Jesus?"

"He is exactly where He should be. You have provided well for Jesus as an earthly father. Now He will know the provision of the heavenly Father. Come, it is time for you to go. There is work here I must attend to."

Joseph and his escort left. Elric motioned to Timrok on the rooftop. A moment later, the stout lieutenant had his prisoner at ground level in front of Elric. Elric still watched Jesus and Mary, who now realized Joseph was dead. They wailed uncontrollably.

"Captain," Timrok said. "I present Tumur."

Elric turned and faced Tumur with stern eyes and clenched teeth. Timrok had Tumur pinned with his arms behind his back and his feet dangling just above the ground. Timrok muscled him forward. Elric stood with a tight jaw and his sword hanging tip-down.

"What's the matter, captain?" Tumur said. "Can't find the words for the moment?"

Timrok tightened his hold.

Tumur's bulging eyes didn't flinch. "Admit it—I won the battle here today. I may not have reached the Son of Man this time, but I did get His father. Ha! You puppets think you are so superior. Admit it—I bested you all. And what's more, I know where the Son of Man is. I will come back with my lord and there is nothing you will be able to stop us."

Elric's sword began to glow blue. Elric looked down at it, smiled, and looked back at Tumur. He lifted the flaming blade high above his head. He brought it crashing downward.

"Noooo," squealed Tumur.

Elric's sword sliced through Tumur from the top of his head all the way down his torso, rending the spirit in half. By the time Elric finished his swing, nothing remained of Tumur but a dissipating yellow vapor. Timrok's hands held nothing but smoke. He rubbed his hands together as though wiping away the filth. Elric turned back to the scene in the Physical Realm.

Jesus and Mary clung to Joseph's dead body and sobbed. The men from the village pulled at them from behind, urging them to let go so they could get in and move the body.

"I'm sorry, captain," Timrok said. "He was just outside our perimeter. But still within range to strike. We will expand our radius and double our efforts so this can never happen—"

Elric cut him off with a raised hand and a half smile. His left eye twitched twice, and he hid his twitch from Timrok behind his hand. He took a deep breath. "Make a full sweep of the area. Make sure there are no others. Make sure no one else saw this. Then send word to Zaben, Jenli, and Lacidar—we will meet here tonight. Tell Lacidar to bring his resonar."

Timrok flew off, and Elric stepped over to the place where Joseph had fallen. From the pool of blood, the energy of the innocent life rose from the earth and formed a large spiritual stone in the Middle Realm. Elric picked up the stone and placed it next to Joseph and

Mary's house. He stood with his back to the house and closed his eyes. *One day. One day.*

* * *

Elric and the four lieutenants gathered in the corner of the main living room of Joseph and Mary's house. By the dim light of one oil lamp, Mary and her children wept. The raw shock of the afternoon had turned into a deep well of pain that fed an unending stream of tears.

"A man of sorrows and acquainted with grief," Elric said. "This was foretold of Him by His prophet Isaiah."

Jenli looked at Jesus and shook his head. "It is strange to see the King in such pain. I am used to sensing it from the Throne. But seeing Him like this is like nothing I could have ever imagined."

"Yes," Elric said. "He now has felt the sting of death in a way none of us can never know."

"I wonder," Timrok said. "Will this be enough to cause Him to launch His campaign?"

Elric shook his head. "I think not. Just the opposite. Jesus is now the man of the house, and all the weight of providing for the family will be on His shoulders."

Zaben nodded. "I believe you are right. There is no way Jesus will start His campaign until He has fulfilled His responsibilities to His family. That means He will probably be here until little Rachael gets married."

"She's two and a half now," Jenli said. "That means we have at least another thirteen to fourteen years."

"The time is getting close," Lacidar said.

"Mmm," Elric said, rubbing his chin. "Tell me, who was this Tumur?"

"We know little about him," Timrok said. "He was not among any of Molech, Asherah, or Yarikh's inner circles. Low rank. He appeared to be acting alone."

"Tumur . . . Tumur," Lacidar said. "I may have seen him in Judea, in Zacharias's synagogue, stirring up dissension against Zacharias."

Timrok stroked his beard. "Perhaps he had discovered John and eventually found his way here."

"This attack tells us two things," Zaben said. "First—they are still seeking Him. It has been so quiet here for so long, I was beginning to wonder."

"They are concentrating on Egypt," Timrok said.

"And Bethlehem," Jenli said.

"Second," Zaben said, "the King remains hidden from Marr's main forces. If Tumur had not been acting alone, we would have certainly seen legions."

Elric crossed his arms and lifted his chin. "This attack tells us a third thing—we are still very vulnerable. Let us not lose focus. Compared to the millennia we have waited, the revelation of the King is close upon us. But we still have much to accomplish. Beyond our primary goal of keeping the King hidden, we must see to the prophet John and we must help prepare the King's twelve generals for His army."

Jenli motioned with his hand to the human occupants of the room. "And now, we must also minister to a hurting family."

"Yes," Elric said. "Thank you. Lacidar, this is why I asked you to bring your resonar. You are the most skilled among us to minister peace and restoration. I want you to stay here and help Mary and the children through this difficult time. Timrok and I will continue to focus on the military details."

Lacidar's eyes welled up with tears and an enormous smile covered his face. "It would bring me no greater joy."

"It may be a while—six months or more," Elric said.

"A century to minister to the King is not long enough for me." Elric smiled.

Lacidar moved to the corner of the room nearest the family and strummed his resonar. Waves of peace filled the room and washed across Mary and the children. Within minutes, the youngest ones became quiet and fell asleep in the older ones' arms.

# 57

## OVERBOARD

### Baptism minus 13 years

Six months after Joseph's death, Elric and the lieutenants gathered in John's cave over the war map. Zaben drew near the end of his report. "And the final updates on the inner twelve are about James and John, sons of Zebedee. My warriors Christov and Carothim are growing concerned about a situation there. As you know, Zebedee is a fisherman who works out of Capernaum. Several years ago, a young man named Daniel hired on, but we know he is possessed by the enemy. We monitor the enemy's activity closely, and so far, he has not had any direct impact on our mission. Daniel is only near Zebedee while they are on the boats and working. While on the water, the enemy mostly releases control to Daniel. When he is off duty, the demon becomes more controlling. To quiet the enemy's voice, Daniel stays drunk and sometimes sleeps outside the synagogue at Capernaum. Our concern is Zebedee has started bringing James and John out on the boats, and they are having direct contact with Daniel. As Zebedee continues to teach the boys the fishing trade, contact with Daniel will become frequent and difficult to control."

"Do you know the name of the demon?" Elric asked.

"A lieutenant named Vorsogh," Zaben said.

"Vorsogh?" Lacidar shouted. "Vorsogh is the one who attacked the prophet John in the temple and shot words of death into Zacharias and Elizabeth."

Elric's eyebrows raised, and he crossed his arms. "Disturbing to cross paths again with this one. Does he know our mission there with James and John?"

Zaben shook his head. "I don't think so. We keep our distance and leave him alone."

"It is time to separate Vorsogh from the sons of Zebedee," Elric said.

Zaben bit his lip and nodded. "Yes, sir."

"Lacidar," Elric said.

Lacidar turned his head. "Captain?"

"Your ministry to Mary's family has been excellent. Jesus, of course, receives every word you speak and sing, and He draws great strength from the Father. I feel, though, that the others still need your ministry—especially Mary. I would like you to continue your work with them a while longer."

Lacidar smiled and bowed his head.

"It will not be much longer, though," Elric said. "I believe John is going to need you soon."

* * *

From the hidden moonlight shadows across the plaza from the synagogue at Capernaum, Zaben, Christov, and Carothim watched Daniel fight the voice of Vorsogh within his mind in order to get a night's rest. Daniel finished the last of his wine and passed out, crumpled against the synagogue's outer wall. The restlessness of Vorsogh twitched within Daniel's limp arms and legs.

"Do you have a plan?" Christov asked with his voice low and muffled.

Zaben bit his lip and nodded. "Nothing elaborate. We only need to put distance between Daniel and Zebedee's family. If Daniel leaves, Vorsogh leaves. I think we simply need to convince Zebedee to dismiss Daniel from his business."

"Some of the other men on the crew have seen Daniel stealing from Zebedee—fish and money, both," Carothim said.

"And he often comes to work impaired from wine," Christov said.

Zaben nodded. "You two speak to the crew. It's time they share their observations with Zebedee. I will speak to Zebedee so that his eyes will be opened."

Christov and Carothim answered, "Yes, sir."

"Do not be seen directly with James and John until Vorsogh is gone. He mustn't become suspicious of a larger plan. I will stay with Zebedee—in the open—to protect him in case Vorsogh becomes violent. If Zebedee brings the boys out on a fishing trip, I may require your support, but stay hidden unless needed."

Two men passed by Daniel on the path. An elzur warrior walked with them, shimmering and white. As they passed, the angel never took his gaze off Daniel.

"Look," Zaben whispered. "Look how quiet and still Vorsogh became. I can see why Daniel likes to come here."

"If only we could free Daniel from his bondage at the same time that we drive Vorsogh away," Christov said.

"I agree. But we have no authority. This one has given himself over to the enemy."

\* \* \*

Tall, knobby clouds piled up in the south as three fishing boats left the shores at Capernaum. Squawking birds circled around the masts, and the water lapped along the graceful wooden hulls. Zebedee stood at the tiller of one boat. Six crew members of his boat tended nets and prepared for another night of working the lake. Zebedee surveyed the other two boats gliding along to his left—with their crews hard at work, and he raised his bearded chin into the breeze. His crew tonight included his sons James and John—teenagers, but carrying their weight. Zebedee smiled.

He eyed one of his other crewmembers, and his smile turned flat. *Levi. Such a strange young man. I don't know what it is about him, but he always makes me feel uneasy.* Zebedee had been hearing disturbing reports about Levi from the other crew members over the last week. *I need to watch Levi close this trip.*

Levi worked the nets with the others without much conversation. He kept glancing up at Zebedee with a strange look in his eyes. The men finished with the nets, and Levi moved all the way to front of the bow, the farthest point away from Zebedee. Even from there, he continued shooting nervous glances back toward the tiller.

The evening brought a gentle breeze, which they bridled and rode south. They planned to start south and work their way back north along the eastern side. They had made it almost half the way down the lake when the breeze gave out and they slid to a stop. The night felt eerie with no moon, and the glow of lanterns hanging from each boat mast revealed a lake surface black and glasslike. A handful of lamps in the windows from the nearby town of Gergesa, just a few miles inland to the east, reflected off the water and provided the only other distinguishable reference in the dark.

"Time to go to work, men," Zebedee announced from the back of the boat. "Let down the nets."

Sounds of action cut through the stillness—knocks on the wooden hull, swooshing of nets, and splashes in the water. The same sounds from the other two boats echoed across the water. It became still again, and they waited. The other men talked in the calm. Levi retreated to the bow alone. After an hour, all the men worked together and hoisted the nets back in with their catch. They wrestled the nets into the boat and pulled them back, dumping the fish into the bottom of the boat. Not a big catch—maybe a few dozen—but the flopping fish around their feet made it challenging to get the nets back into the water. With the nets down again, they waited for the next haul.

The men talked and laughed amongst themselves, and Zebedee looked past them at Levi up at the bow. *I suppose I should go talk with him.* His stomach balled up in a knot. Lately, the unexplainable uneasiness he felt around Levi had become even stronger. *I need to confront him about the allegations of theft and drunkenness and decide what to do about it.*

Zebedee tiptoed through the fish and steadied himself with the mast, and with each step, the dread about the impending conversation grew stronger. The weather remained calm, but Zebedee had seen the clouds before the sun went down. He looked upward into the starless sky. *Feels like a storm building. Can't help but wonder if we're in the calm before the storm.* He took another step and glanced forward at Levi, who was hunched over and facing forward as if hiding something. *The calm before the storm . . .*

The first breeze of a night storm sent warning ripples across the waters.

Zebedee reached the front of the boat. "Levi, we need to talk."

Levi startled to Zebedee's voice, and he sat upright with a half turn. He fumbled to stash something beneath his tunic.

"What is that? What do you have?" Zebedee said. He caught Levi's arm before he could get his secret concealed.

"A flask? What's in here?" Zebedee smelled the open top. "This is wine! You are drinking on the job?"

Levi looked up at Zebedee with vacant, glassy eyes and grunted. His voice sounded unearthly and sent a sharp chill through Zebedee's bones.

"You are drunk! I can't believe it. I needed to talk with you about some disturbing things I have been hearing about you. I was hoping

you could convince me they were all misunderstandings, but now—
now, this is too much. I can't have somebody on my crew who I can't
trust, and I certainly can't have somebody on the crew who is a drunk.
This is your last fishing trip. When we get back into port, you are
going to have to find employment elsewhere."

Levi's face contorted like a vicious animal. "You can't do this to
us." His voice growled like nothing Zebedee had ever heard. A gust of
wind came up and ruffled the hair on both of their heads.

"What do mean 'us'? " Zebedee said. "I don't understand how
you could do this to me. I took you in when you had nothing. No
skills. No money. And I trained you up like you were my own son.
I gave you a good job and taught you the tools of the trade. I knew
you were having some problems, but I've given you so many chances.
And how do you repay me? You steal from me. You come to work
drunk. You—"

Levi reached into his cloak and pulled out a long knife. The
silver blade flashed in the light of the lantern.

"What's that?" Zebedee squeaked. "What are you doing?"

"You can't just disown us," Levi said, his voice low and guttural.
"This is even worse than what my father did to us. I hate you. I hate
you all. I'm going to kill every one of you and take this boat for
myself. We don't need you." He started to stand up with the gleaming
silver of the blade pointed at Zebedee.

The sail gave a loud crack. A huge gust of wind took hold of the
ship. The boom from the sail swung around hard, and the entire boat
listed in a tight turn. Zebedee fell backward. Levi reached for the side
of the boat, and his knife tumbled out of his hand.

A flash storm from the south was upon them, and within moments the boat was engulfed in heavy seas and driving rain.

"Captain!" the men called.

"I know," Zebedee called back. He clambered to his feet and rushed toward the tiller. "Quickly—get those nets back in the boat! You—drop the sail! Move, everybody move!"

The crew scrambled. The boat heaved and rolled, and waves crashed in over the sides. Zebedee fought the tiller to keep the boat turned into the wind, and through flashes of lightning he watched the crew struggle for their lives against the raging elements. James and John pulled on the nets with all their might. Another crewmember pulled on mast ropes. Two others bailed water. All battled to stay upright and not get thrown overboard or be swept away by a crashing wave. During one lightning flash, Zebedee spotted Levi, still on the bow of the boat, swinging his arms like a wild man and jumping around as though fighting someone.

For half an hour the squall tested Zebedee and his crew. With each flash of lightning, Zebedee witnessed the courage and strength of his men. If they were to go down tonight, it wouldn't be for lack of effort.

As quickly as it hit, the storm subsided. The wind continued strong enough to create a rough ride over white-capped swells, but the rain stopped, and the dire danger to boat receded. Someone relit the lantern.

The first glow of the lantern flickered across the deck. There sat James and John, drenched and exhausted atop the fishing nets.

"Did you two bring those nets up by yourselves?" Zebedee called out.

"Yes, sir," James yelled. John nodded.

"But how? There's no way you could—"

"Captain," one of the other crewmembers yelled. "Look!"

The lantern from one of the other boats lit up.

"Good," Zebedee said. "That's good."

A moment later, the lantern from the third boat flickered on.

"Yes," Zebedee said. "We're all still afloat. Let's keep bailing that water. How is everyone? Is anyone hurt? Is everyone—where's Levi?"

Everyone looked around the boat.

"The last time I saw him, he was up on the bow," one of the men said.

"He must have been swept overboard," Zebedee yelled. "Signal the other boats. Hoist the sail. We're coming around."

"Captain, with that storm, there's not much hope we can—"

"All eyes on the sea," Zebedee shouted. "He's out there, and we need to find him."

A half an hour of desperate searching passed, and they saw no sign of Levi.

"Captain," a crewmember said, "with the speed we were being driven by those winds, even if we had turned around the moment he fell off, we would have left him far behind."

"Keep looking," Zebedee said.

Another half hour passed.

"Captain, by now all hope is lost. We need to concentrate on getting ourselves home safely."

The whole crew turned and waited for Zebedee's response.

Zebedee's face remained stern and determined. He looked out over his tired crew. He looked out over the water.

"You're right," he said with a defeated tone. "Signal the other boats. Let's go home."

The boat came about, and the sails propelled them northward at a vigorous pace. All the while, Zebedee kept watching behind their wake—scanning the black waters and seeing nothing. A quiet sadness settled in over the crew during the journey.

They made it back to port that night—sail tattered, nets torn, catch swept away, and a man lost.

* * *

Daniel screamed for help between each crashing wave, but his voice became lost in the uproar of the wind and the rain and the waves. The boat sped past him, driven by the strong winds; and even swimming as hard as he could, he had no hope of catching it. Within only a few minutes, the bouncing mast lit by the flashes of lightning disappeared, leaving Daniel alone in the deep.

Alone. Alone in the darkness—bobbing over the wave crests and tumbling between the swells. Even though he had become a proficient swimmer since joining Zebedee's crew, the buried memories of his childhood encounter with the sea seized his mind. Panic gripped his whole body. He flailed and fought to stay afloat. He gasped and sputtered and tried to catch his breath between plunges. He lost all sense of direction.

At the top of one swell, he caught a glimpse of the lights of Gergesa. *Need to swim toward the lights.* He tumbled under another wave and couldn't tell which direction was up. He felt dizzy. He flailed some more, got tumbled again, and then everything went black.

# 58

## STARTING OVER

### Baptism minus 13 years

Daniel awoke early in the morning on the rocks of an unknown shore. He lay on his back. He blinked and squinted in the daylight. A steep cliff rose to meet him from the east. He sat up and looked west. The lake appeared calm and beautiful. A few clouds floated above. The entire scene seemed so quiet and picturesque that it left Daniel confused.

*Where am I? What am I doing here? How did I get here?*

He tried to remember the previous day, and although it seemed dreamlike, he could remember that he had been on the fishing boat at night and there was a terrible storm. He remembered falling in the water and then . . . then there was nothing.

"Levi?" Daniel whispered. "Levi, are you here?"

"Of course, little brother," the voice answered in Daniel's ear. "I am always here."

"I was drowning last night. It's not possible that I could have gotten ashore by myself. Did you save me?"

"Yes, I did not want to lose you."

Daniel sat for several minutes and watched the ripples of water slide into the shore just beyond reach of his feet. He thought about his life and the hopeless place in which he now found himself—again.

"I wish you would have let me go," Daniel said. "Besides, you wouldn't have lost me. We could have truly been together."

"You don't understand, little brother, I need you as much as you need me."

"What do you mean?"

"In the spirit world, I would just wander around without a body. You have given me a new chance at life. With the two of us working together, I get to see and smell and feel all the tangible reality of the physical world. We are more together right now than we could ever be. You wouldn't want to lose that, would you?"

"No, I suppose not. But what are we going to do now? I've lost my job, and we're in a strange place."

"Worry not. There is a town nearby. We shall find another fishing job, or maybe even become pig ranchers."

Daniel cringed. "Pigs? Unclean, defiled creatures."

The voice said, "And delicious. Just think of what Father would say if he saw you working swine."

Daniel smirked with a rebellious glint in his eye.

* * *

## Baptism minus 11.5 years

The midmorning sun warmed the stone canyon walls around John's wilderness cave. Cheerful songs of the birds floated on the breeze. Elric and Lacidar stood in the opening of John's cave looking out.

"You have been back in the wilderness a year now," Elric said to Lacidar. "Are you glad to be back with John?"

Lacidar gave a sly grin. "Come, captain," Lacidar said. "You need to see this."

Elric and Lacidar leapt down to the ground below John's cave, walked up the canyon, and turned hard right into a smaller ravine, which opened up into a small alcove. It felt to Elric like a small courtyard in a temple—flat, smooth ground and towering walls of stone all around. Some of the rock formations looked like pillars in a palace. Near one side of the alcove, a deposit of large boulders had sheared from the walls and sat arranged like century–old pieces of art. The prophet John sat on one boulder and leaned forward on his elbows over a large, flat, table-like slab of stone. Rays of sunlight beamed in through the open roof of the courtyard and shined down on a scroll of parchment stretched out on the stone table.

"What is he doing?" Elric asked.

"Reading. From the book of Psalms this morning, I think."

Jaeden overlooked the courtyard from a stone perch two-thirds up the sheer wall. Elric turned and looked up the wall behind him. Ry stood guard from his own high perch.

Lacidar motioned around the courtyard with his hand. "This has become his favorite place."

Elric nodded and smiled.

"As you know," Lacidar said, "the first year in the wilderness was the hardest for John. He was broken, filled with pain, and terribly alone. We spent many hours strengthening him, singing to him, keeping him going. The Spirit of the King spoke to him constantly, although I think he heard little of it. He rarely prayed. He didn't read. His thoughts were empty."

"He suffered much trauma. We've seen this response thousands of times," Elric said.

Lacidar nodded. "When we established our war room in his cave, it seemed to help. He was still unable to hear in the spirit, but the continual presence of so many elzurim provided strength when there was none."

"And now?"

"Several months ago, he began reading his scrolls—mostly out of boredom, I think. And now, his ears are beginning to open. The veil over his eyes is starting to lift."

"I sense he is still disconnected," Elric said.

"Yes—disconnected from people, disconnected from everything in the outside world, disconnected from himself. But I think his disconnection from the King is starting to close."

Elric crossed his arms and nodded. "Actually, the disconnection from the world is probably a good thing right now. He doesn't need to know Annius Rufus is the new Roman procurator of Judea or about the political unrest and uprisings throughout the land. He doesn't even need to know the King himself just spent the last two years working through personal tragedy of His own."

"This is a good start for the prophet," Lacidar said.

"Yes, it is. And it means our time draws closer every day."

\* \* \*

## Baptism minus 10 years

Daniel rolled over on his bed mat and groaned. The morning sun pounded on his aching head. He reached up to wipe the sleep from his eyes but stopped. Blood—all over his hands, up to his elbows. He flopped over onto his back and let his arms drop onto the dirt.

"Not again," he mumbled. "Levi!"

The voice in his head remained silent.

Daniel dragged himself out of bed and stumbled toward the pigs' watering trough, squinting at the unforgiving sun.

"Out of the way," he said to a pig, pushing it away with his leg.

He submerged his arms in the water and scrubbed, muttering to Levi the whole time. "Why do you do this to us? I liked it in Gergesa, but because of you, we had to leave there. Then, in Kursi—I don't know what you killed, or who—but we almost ended up in prison there. Now we have to leave Hippos. We're running out of places in the Decapolis to live."

He finished washing and sat on the ground with his back to the trough. He looked out over the small herd of swine and winced.

"It's just as well. I'm tired of this. Three years of working swine is too much. I hate pigs. They are filthy, disgusting beasts. I want to get back out on the water. Let's move down to Ein Gev. They have fishing boats there. Levi? Levi?"

"Ein Gev," a voice said in his right ear.

* * *

## Baptism minus 9.5 years

Elric stood by himself against the back wall of John's cave and watched the other captains work. The ten of them pored over the war map. Elric observed and listened. In the middle of the meeting, John entered the cave with two scrolls tucked under his arm. Elric followed him with his eyes. *John's two years of focus on the Word is beginning to show.* John now had a solid layer of light wrapped around his spirit, and his spoken words and prayers had created a wall of glowing bricks of light all around the war room. He passed through the middle of the map and laid his scrolls next to all the others, and the captains paid no notice to his presence in the Physical Realm. Elric smiled.

"It looks like it's going to happen," one of the captains said, pointing to a region on the map, "despite our best efforts."

Elric strained around the captains to see the map.

"The Egyptian false prophet has amassed a force of four thousand followers and led them into the wilderness. He plans to take Jerusalem by force starting at the Mount of Olives and liberate it from Roman occupation."

Elric shook his head. *An unknowing tool of the enemy, this one is.*

One of the other captains said, "And the Roman army is already on its way to intercept them."

*Another unknowing tool of the enemy.*

Swirling black clouds, flashes of light, and mixing layers of color dominated one small portion of the war map. Elric covered his mouth with his hand and shook his head.

*So much destruction. So much pain.*

"I know your day is close, Lord," Elric whispered behind his hand, "but could it not be closer?"

* * *

## Baptism minus 9 years

Daniel stepped off the fishing boat onto the shores by Capernaum for the first time in four years. The fishing company he worked with in Ein Gev had just opened a new trade market here at the far north end of the lake, and they would be in port for the day, spend the night, and then head back out before sunrise. Daniel looked up and down the shore and in toward town. He reminisced about his days on the fishing boats with Zebedee. It felt like a lifetime ago since that night he fell off Zebedee's boat, but here on the shore with the smell of fish and the squawking birds, he knew not much had changed—not for Capernaum, not for himself. Capernaum felt like home, although a lost and distant one. He already decided what he would do after finishing his duties on the dock. He would find some wine, get good and numb, and go sit outside the synagogue where he hoped he could find some quiet inside his head.

He passed through the streets, listening to people's conversations. Most of the talk revolved around the death of Caesar Augustus in Rome and the new Caesar, Tiberius. Valerius Gratus had been appointed the new procurator of Judea by Tiberius. None of people seemed better off under the new leaders. Daniel caught little bits of people's conversations as he wove through the streets.

"I swear there is corruption at every level. Just the other day, I actually had to pay a city official just to get my . . . "

"Does it seem like there is more sickness these days? Every family I know has lost somebody to some strange disease. Did you hear about . . . "

"And you know, the religious elites are not helping matters. Sometimes I think they make the problems worse by the way they . . . "

"Then he killed her. Of course, the officials don't believe it, and he is going to get away with it . . . "

"Tax collectors. I hate them. They are filthy extortionists, every one."

Every conversation had the same dark tone. Daniel shook his head and pretended not to hear. The talk didn't sound any different in Ein Gev. *These are trying days everywhere.*

Daniel decided he would get extra numb today before heading back to Ein Gev tomorrow.

# 59

## THE WORD SPOKEN

### Baptism minus 6 years

*E*lric stood beside Lacidar at the entrance of the secret reading place near John's cave. Elric's mouth dropped open, and his eyes widened. "Look at this place," he said to Lacidar.

What used to be only an alcove with high stone walls in the Physical Realm had transformed into an impenetrable fortress of light in the Middle Realm.

Elric crossed his arms. "I thought the stronghold around his cave was impressive—but this . . . this is remarkable."

Elric lifted his chin and took in a deep breath through his nose. The sweet fragrance of the Spirit from the courts of the King made him smile.

"The Spirit of the Lord is free to operate here unhindered," Lacidar said. "His presence is very strong."

Elric looked over at John, deep in thought over a scroll containing the prophet Isaiah's writings. His uncut, sun–baked hair looked out of control, and a short scruffy beard covered his cheeks and chin. He appeared rough and weathered on the outside, but the armor around his spirit pulsed with light.

"This is not the same naïve fifteen–year–old boy who fled from the misfortune he experienced in his home in Judea nine years ago," Elric said.

"No, he is not," Lacidar said. "His daily reading in the scrolls has become serious studying. He devours them. He can't get enough of them. He reads them all day. Then he meditates on them most of the night. Every waking moment is spent memorizing, contemplating, rereading."

"He is no longer detached," Elric said.

"Good observation, captain. He is in the middle of the heartbeat of the Kingdom. The King speaks every word on the written page directly to him."

"Does he hear His voice?"

"No, but his spiritual ears are open. John asks the King questions, and He answers plainly from the scrolls or speaks directly to his spirit. Deep things—about His nature, His ways, His plans—they all well up through the words into John's spirit. The young, confused, angry, and lonely John is gone. In his place is this hairy young man, filled with joy, peace, and an intense hunger to know the King Himself."

"Look," Elric whispered to Lacidar. "John is praying for the temple and for righteous leaders."

"Just yesterday, in John's cave, the regional captains were discussing the new high priest, Caiaphas. He looks to be a powerful instrument of the enemy, close to the Roman leadership and hungry for political gain. The captains were discussing ways to counter his influence and potentially raise up a different man. John must have perceived it in the spirit."

"Kai said he would eventually have discernment as deep as Hannah," Elric said.

"He is far beyond that. In fact, I think I have not seen anyone with so strong an anointing since—Elijah."

"I agree. We are close now. I believe John is almost ready to receive his assignment from the Lord."

\* \* \*

## Baptism minus 5 years

Raziel sipped wine from his goblet and leaned against the outside wall of Mary's house. With the house so packed with family and friends, the wedding celebration had spilled outside. Raziel found a spot in the shade and watched the party. A musical group plucked lively songs, and dozens of laughing, spinning dancers kicked up a cloud of dust.

Mary bounced around the guests like a spirited puppy. "Did you try the lamb? Wasn't the bride beautiful? Be sure to get some wine."

Raziel laughed, glad to see her so happy. Jesus caught his eye. He was almost as animated as Mary. Even though only twenty-five, He filled the father–of–the–house role, and seeing His sister Elizabeth getting married brought huge joy and pride. James and his young wife laughed together with some other family members. Little eleven–year–old Rachael floated around and twirled with the music. Raziel could see in her eyes the dream of the day when she would get married like her big sister. Jesus approached from the side and surprised him just as he took another sip.

"Thank you again for doing the ceremony," Jesus said. "It was a beautiful wedding."

"Oh, I wouldn't have missed it. This family is like a second family to me."

"Are we still meeting for a lesson tomorrow?"

"That is up to you. With all the festivities here today, I would understand if you should need a day off."

"I do not wish to miss a single day. I will already be up before sunrise to pray. And I like to meditate on the lesson all day while I work."

"Very good. I will be here first thing in the morning. In the meantime, I think I am going to go steal a dance with the bride."

"Maybe I will do the same. After you, of course."

* * *

**Baptism minus 2.5 years**

Elric met with his lieutenants over the war map in John's cave. They all gazed into the map, and Jenli finished his report on the progress of his six assignments of the inner twelve.

"But, overall, I would say that these six are similar to Zaben's six—they seem to have a heart for the King, but they do not appear to be warriors. If they are to become generals in the King's army, they still have a long way to go."

"I am not worried," Timrok said. "We have all seen the King use the most unlikely servants to accomplish His purposes."

Zaben pointed to a spot on the map. "Captain, what do we know about this new procurator of Judea?"

"His name is Pontius Pilate," Elric said. "Another puppet of the enemy. He is no friend of Herod Antipas, but it appears he and the high priest, Caiaphas, have formed a close alliance already."

"A dangerous coalition," Zaben said, biting his lip.

"No more dangerous than Valerius Gratus and Caiaphas," Jenli said.

Elric nodded. "Caiaphas has been in place for a long time now. The enemy has found one who serves their objectives."

The sound of sobbing from across the room caught their attention. Elric turned. *That's John.* Elric motioned with his hand, and the war map faded away.

"What is happening with John?" Elric asked. "The last few times I have seen him, he has been weeping." Elric paused a moment and watched John. "And this is not the weeping of emotional sadness. There is something deep at work."

Lacidar smiled and did a little hop. "Twelve years in the wilderness has marked another turning point for John. It is amazing to watch. I am so thankful to have this assignment."

He did another little hop. "I have never seen a person draw so close to the King. I know Moses and David did. But I have not seen one like this since Enoch. John is completely caught up in knowing the King. Not His power or His works or His blessings. He just wants to know Him. It is a complete abandon. And, of course, when an earthly man draws that close to the King Himself . . . "

Jenli said, "He becomes acutely aware of his own sinful state."

"He weeps like this for hours," Lacidar said. "At first it was just for himself, but lately he has been weeping over Israel, the temple, the priests. Sometimes it seems like he feels the weight of the entire world."

"We are so close," Elric said.

\* \* \*

## Baptism minus 2 years

Six months later, Elric raced from his post in Nazareth to John's secret alcove. He blasted through the fortress of light and landed in the center of the courtyard. His wings folded away, and he said, "Grigor brought word for me to—" He stopped and looked around. Lacidar pounded out a jubilant melody on his resonar. The sound bounced around the walls of light and formed visible waves of joy in the spiritual air. All five of Lacidar's warriors danced to the tune, leaping high into the air, spinning and flipping and laughing and shouting.

"Captain!" Lacidar said. He stopped playing, set his resonar aside, and stood up.

"Grigor said I should come quickly," Elric said.

"We believe the Lord is about to commission the prophet," Lacidar said with a beaming smile. "John has come to a new place. For the last several years, he had been so focused on simply spending time with the King that he had buried the lessons of his father along with pains of his memories. But then, the Lord reminded him of things Zacharias had told him in his youth, and all those lessons came flooding back. John dove back into the scrolls, this time looking specifically for signs of the Messiah. For the last six months, John has searched the pages, and everywhere he looked, there was only one thing he could see—the Messiah is coming. He is so caught up in thoughts of the Messiah that—"

Waves of light boomed through the roof of the fortress. The air became thick with the sweet fragrance of the Spirit. Elric, Lacidar, and the five warriors dropped to their knees. The waves coalesced into visible words and rolled over John. His spirit absorbed them like a sponge.

"The Messiah is coming," the words said. "The time is *now*."

"Now? Now?" John cried out. "But have you seen your people? They're not ready. Their hearts are hard and filled with evil. They are not ready."

"They need someone to prepare the way. That someone is you, John. I am sending you before my Son to prepare the hearts of the people."

"Yes!" John shouted, "Yes, Lord, send me. Something has to be done. You cannot walk amongst us in your holiness when our hearts are so far from You. I will deliver whatever message you have for your people."

"Teach them what it means to repent. Call them to turn away from sin. Tell them the Kingdom of God is near. I will be with you. I will put my Word in your mouth."

The air became quiet. The Word of the Lord had finished.

"Yes!" Elric shouted. He unfurled his wings and shot straight up, spinning and shouting "yes" all the way to the high ceiling of the fortress. Lacidar resumed his song, and his five warriors bounded into a dance. Elric swooped back down and locked arms with the other dancers. While John sat in quiet prayer, the angels danced and sang with wild abandon.

* * *

Elric joined the meeting of the regional captains the next day. Rather than standing alone in the back and listening to the proceedings like he usually did, he stepped up to the war map and turned around to face the others. The other captains stepped back and crossed their arms. One motioned with his hand, and the war map disappeared. Twenty lieutenants lined the walls in rows, and the ones in the back strained their heads around the ones in front. No one moved. No one made a sound. Elric could feel every anxious eye on him. He knew they knew he worked a secret mission for the King, and the anticipation of what he might have to say could be seen on every one of their faces.

"Friends, I bring exciting news that I know you have all been waiting for." He paused a moment, heavy with the enormity his message. "The King is going to be revealed soon."

The room erupted in celebration. Every angel in the room leapt and shouted. Unrestrained dancing filled the room. Elric stood motionless in the middle of the cave, and the captains and lieutenants spun around him and did flips over him. He laughed and let the festivity continue for several minutes, but then lifted both hands in the air and raised his voice over the mayhem.

"However," he shouted. He waved his arms to get their attention. Some started to settle down.

"But we do not know exactly when, yet," he said.

Most of the dancing stopped. Everyone became quiet. Bright smiles covered every face, and they all continued to bounce with excited energy.

"What I do know is this. The prophet John has just received his commission to begin his campaign. He will move out immediately. I suspect we have about a year to prepare. John's charge is to deliver a message of repentance. Our job—your job—is to get people out to hear him. Spread the word across the whole region as quickly as you can. We must reach at least as far as northern Galilee and, of course, all of Judea. We will begin with some outlying villages around the Jordan, and once he starts gathering some disciples and word starts to spread, we will settle in the wilderness by the Jordan."

One of the other captains stepped forward. "Will the people we bring in become the army for the Lord that we will lead into battle against the enemy?"

Elric looked down at his foot and used it to scuff some dirt around. His voice became low and serious. "There is much about my mission that continues to remain a mystery. I would have expected by now that we would have identified the valiant men to be all the generals and captains. We do have a dozen men we are preparing for His inner circle. But unfortunately, beyond this, the King has remained unusually quiet about His plans. I have no instructions about an army."

All the warriors in the room stared at Elric and waited. Elric could see their hunger for more details. He remained quiet and waited another minute to see if they had any other specific questions.

"Just bring them in," he said. "They all need to hear John's message."

# 60

## THE WORD RELEASED

## Baptism minus 2 years

*J*ohn didn't know how to begin. He had no people around to give his message to.

*I obviously need to find a city. Maybe I should go directly to Jerusalem. Maybe I should go and preach in the temple itself.*

The thought of preaching in the temple felt a little unnerving, but the Word of the Lord had lit such a fire inside that he knew he could stand on the steps of the inner courts and declare his message before the chief priests and rulers if given the chance. John looked around at the empty wilderness outside his cave. He laughed to himself at the irony.

*I have the most important message in the world and nobody to tell it to. First, I need to find a city. Any city.*

He gathered all his belongings, the scrolls, and started out. He stopped and looked back at his cave, his only home for almost thirteen years. He looked down the canyon toward the Jordan and back again. Then, he took a deep breath and started walking toward the Jordan.

He wandered for two days, staying within an easy walk to the water. On the third day, he saw the first sign of civilization. A small village.

*They probably don't even have a synagogue. Still, I should stop here first. If nothing else, maybe these people could point me toward Jerusalem. There are several houses over there. I wonder how I am to know where to go.*

\* \* \*

Lacidar approached the town by the Jordan with John walking beside. Lacidar spotted Ry on the trail by a modest earthen house and gave him a high wave. Ry waved back and gave a thumbs up.

"It looks like our man is in place and ready," Lacidar said. "Today, you will meet a man named Lon and begin your mission."

Lacidar turned and spoke directly to John, "Turn up this trail and pass by this house here on the right."

\* \* \*

"Hello, stranger," Lon called out to a hairy man approaching on a trail by his house. Lon was an older man with a peppery beard and calloused hands.

"Hello," the man called back. "My name is John."

"Shalom. I am Lon." He eyed this strange looking man with long wild hair, a camel skin garment with a leather belt, tough weathered skin, and covered in dust, "You look like you could use refreshing. Could I offer you some water?"

John fidgeted with his belt and rubbed his hands through his matted hair. "Yes," he said without making eye contact. "That would be very kind."

Lon paused a moment to look at John. His wild appearance and tentative mannerisms gave Lon the sense that he might be the first person this stranger had spoken with in a very long time. "I'll be right back," he said. Lon backed away and turned toward his house.

Lon re-emerged from his front door with a large cup filled with water. "What brings you to our little town?"

John looked down at the ground and shuffled his feet. He tried to straighten his hair. He took a drink of water. "I am, uh . . . traveling around to, uh . . . people need to know that . . . "

Lon cocked his head and examined this stranger from the wilderness, trying to decide if he was just a crazy vagrant.

John continued, "The Messiah is coming. The Kingdom of the Lord is at hand."

Lon cocked his head the other direction. "Are you some kind of prophet?"

"Oh, I don't know about that. I just know that the Messiah is about to be revealed, and we all need to get ready."

This wild–looking man certainly looked like a crazy vagrant. But something burned on the inside of Lon that he couldn't explain. Something told him he needed to hear more of what this man had to say.

"Go on."

"The Messiah is the Son of God Himself, awesome in holiness and righteous in judgments. Before He arrives, we need to prepare ourselves. We need to repent from our evil ways and turn to Him. This is the Word of the Lord to our generation."

Lon's heart became ablaze. He never thought of himself as an "evil" man. In fact, he always believed himself to be a basically good person. He knew he didn't live as righteously as the priests and Levites, but he worked hard for his family, never stole or defrauded anyone, and attended synagogue fairly regularly. But something within his inner being knew that if he had to stand before the righteous Judge and account for his every thought and deed, he would surely come up short. The thought that the Messiah Himself was drawing near shook him to his core. His hidden sins—times that he had lied, had impure thoughts, had occasional angry outbursts—flashed across his mental ledger and left him feeling dirty and exposed. How could this stranger have known all these things about him? How could he have known that, under his façade of decent normalcy, there hid an incomplete soul that longed to be truly clean? Why was the very presence of this man unraveling his whole existence? He needed to hear more.

"This is," Lon said, struggling to get his heart out of his throat. "A strong word. You must be hungry. Why not come into my home and tell me more? We will prepare supper."

Lon's wife worked on the meal while stealing glances of the conversation over her shoulder. Lon offered John some wine.

"Please do not be offended," John said, "but I must regretfully decline. You see, I have taken the Nazirite vow."

"Oh." Lon nodded. "That would explain the—"

"Hair? Yes, it has not been cut from birth. I suppose I do look a little—"

"No, no, not at all."

They both laughed.

John surged like a fountain all evening. His initial apprehensive conversation turned into a torrent of spiritual water. Entire passages of Scriptures stitched together into a story of the coming Messiah, the holiness of God, and need for His righteousness. He taught about what it means to repent—how true repentance starts with brokenness and remorse, an honest admission of guilt, a turning away from the sin, and a turning toward God for mercy. Every word he spoke pierced deep into Lon's heart.

"Seek the Lord while He may be found," John urged. "Call upon Him while He is near. Let the wicked abandon his way and the unrighteous person his thoughts. And let him return to the Lord, and He will have compassion on him, and to our God, for He will abundantly pardon."

* * *

Lacidar, Jaeden, and Ry knelt at the other end of the room of Lon's house while John and Lon talked. The angels hadn't lifted their eyes once from the time John started speaking. The presence of the King rested so strong in the room, the warriors would have thought the King Himself spoke the words.

By the time John finished, Lon and his wife wept tears of true repentance. John prayed with them, and their tears became tears of joy.

Lacidar turned to Jaeden and Ry and said, "Salvation has come to this house tonight. I can't wait to see what will happen tomorrow."

# 61

## JOHN THE BAPTIZER

### Baptism minus 2 years

The next morning, John poked at his breakfast and smiled at Lon's nonstop conversation. The meal the night before was heavy for John's palate, and although he found it interesting to eat real food again, his stomach wouldn't allow him to eat more than half the portion. The fish for breakfast seemed a little better, but even still, John only nibbled at it to be polite.

Lon bounced around and chattered like a man just released from prison. "And the first thing we'll do is gather up all the men from my village—you can wait here and relax—and then you can tell all them the same message. And then we will go to another village. There is one very close. I know many of the men there. They need to hear it, too."

"How far are we from Jerusalem?"

"Oh, not too far. Good heavens, there are at least five towns within an easy walk from here. We should travel to all of them. They all need to hear this. You sit here and finish your breakfast. I'm too excited to eat any more. I'm going to go now and get the men from my village. No, no—sit down. I will be back in less than an hour."

Lon returned with no less than thirty men ranging from a bright–eyed teenager to the senior elder who needed help to make the walk. With the small group gathered outside his house, Lon stepped up next to John in front of his house. "And here he is, the prophet I told you about. His name is John." He turned to John and said, "Go ahead, go ahead."

*This is more people than I've seen in over a decade.* They all stared at him as though they expected some kind of show. *How do I just start talking to a group of people I don't even know? I don't know what to say. I'm not ready for this.*

Something within him stirred—just deliver the message. Take a step of faith. Just start.

"The Messiah is coming," John blurted out. "He is very near. We need to prepare our hearts to receive Him."

Passages of Scriptures flashed into his mind, and words came bubbling out as though a river flowed out of his belly. He spoke the words as they came, and the more he spoke, the more they came. *What is happening? These men are truly being moved!* Most of them were weeping. *I don't have eloquent speech, but . . .* But somehow the message cut through and laid the men's hearts bare.

"What do we need to do?" they cried.

"Repent. Confess your sins. Turn to God."

"Yes, yes!" they all said.

*There needs to be something more. A sign to demonstrate that they have made a change. Some kind of physical act they could do to commemorate their commitment.*

He paused. He looked around. *The Jordan. I have an idea.*

"Everybody, follow me," he shouted. He stepped through the group and headed toward the Jordan.

They made the short march to the river. John gathered them beside the bank, and he waded in up to his waist. He called Lon in to join him. He smiled and put his hand on Lon's shoulder.

"If you have truly repented and want to be cleansed, we are going to do it right here in the river. I will immerse you under the water as a sign that you have repented of your sin, and as you come back up out of the water, it will be a sign that your sins have been washed clean. Remember, it is not me who forgives sin, and it is not the water itself. So, as you do this, pray to the God of Heaven for mercy, for it is He alone who can forgive."

Turning to Lon, he said, "Are you ready?"

"Yes, yes. I can't wait."

\* \* \*

The men outside Lon's house were awash in light in the Middle Realm. Every word from the prophet John's mouth broke over the men like tidal waves of light. Beams of light from the Throne shone down and mixed with the spiritual energy. Lacidar and his team stood to the side and watched with amazement.

"Everybody, follow me," John shouted. He started walking.

"He's headed for the Jordan," Lacidar said. "Ry, go find Elric and bring him here. The rest of you, move out to the river."

Within moments, Elric alighted beside Lacidar on the bank of the Jordan. A moment later, Timrok, Zaben, and Jenli showed up. Lacidar's five warriors stood in a line on the opposite side of the river, watching John and scanning for enemy activity. Elric and the four lieutenants watched John in the river without saying a word. Their mouths hung open, and their arms hung limp.

The last man came up out of the water.

Elric crossed his arms and said, "It has begun."

\* \* \*

## Baptism minus 1.5 years

Six months after John's first baptisms, Elric and Lacidar positioned themselves on an overlook north of the Dead Sea at Bethany beyond the Jordan and gazed over the activities below.

"This is a perfect location for John's home camp," Elric said. "Easy access to the river, and these surrounding hills are like an amphitheater for the people coming to hear his message."

Lacidar nodded. "Yes, and the people are responding in droves. Hundreds are being baptized in the Jordan every day. From all over Judea, Jerusalem. People are coming in from as far away as Galilee."

John stood at the banks of the river and preached to the crowd sitting and standing on the hillside. His booming voice echoed off the hills and resounded up to Elric and Lacidar. "'Do I take any pleasure in the death of the wicked,' declares the Lord God. 'rather than that he would turn from his ways and live? Repent and turn away from all your offenses, so that wrongdoing does not become a stumbling block to you. Hurl away from you all your offenses which you have committed and make yourselves a new heart and a new spirit! For why should you die, house of Israel? For I take no pleasure in the death of anyone who dies,' declares the Lord God. 'Therefore, repent and live!'"

"He speaks with great power," Elric said.

"He has the Word of the Lord. The authority of his message is like nothing any of these people have ever seen, and it is causing thousands to travel here to hear this man in the wilderness."

"I know John had his heart set on preaching in Jerusalem," Elric said. "Did you have difficulty leading him to stay here in the wilderness?"

"No, sir. It was easy. I only needed to suggest that Lon take John to the other local villages, and Lon took charge. He was already excited about doing it. They went to the first village with Lon and ten others from his village. The reception there was dramatic. When they left that village for another, another ten men joined the group. By the time they made it to the fifth town, word had begun to spread, and John had an entourage of nearly a hundred men. After preaching in two more towns, it became clear to John that he needed to set up a home base and let the people come to him. We have been here since then."

"Is there any indication that these who are coming can be mobilized for the King's army?"

"Most come and hear and are baptized—and then return to their lives. They leave with a fresh start and anticipation about the coming

Messiah. Many, though, stay with John and become his disciples. At night John teaches them in depth about the King who is coming and who will deliver them and judge the nations of the earth."

"Is John, then, preparing their hearts for battle?"

"No. His disciples do update him on all that is going on in the world since he entered the wilderness. The state of things is worse than he knew, and it adds fuel to the fire in his message. He speaks out against corruption in the government and the temple. He lambasts the hypocrisy of the Pharisees and priests. He even condemns the evil deeds of Roman rulers. But in all of it, he is after the *hearts* of the unrighteous, not a revolutionary army."

"I see *our* battle is heated," Elric said, looking out over the hillsides.

A fiery battlefield spread out before them. Open skirmishes covered the entire area in the Middle Realm. The elzurim fought to drive away the determined demons, but it was a never–ending struggle.

"There are so many beaelzurim," Elric muttered. "And they're as unrelenting as flies."

One demon cupped his leathery hands over a man's ears. Another spoke a stream of lies to a group of men. Another put heckling words into the mouth of another man. One by one, the elzurim chased the demons away, but they returned again and again, clouding the minds of the people and disrupting John's message to them.

Lacidar said, "Yes. My team stays around John to protect him. The other warriors have their own assignments and are fighting hard."

A group of Pharisees gathered and listened to John. They talked amongst themselves, stroking their beards and shooting derisive glances at John and the crowd. Several lying beaelzurim worked in their midst.

Elric said, "These Pharisees are not here to receive the Word of the Lord, but to test John and promote themselves."

"Yes, sir. But John usually has a strong word for them."

John's voice echoed across the hills. "You brood of vipers, who warned you to flee from the wrath to come?"

"Here it is," Lacidar said.

John pointed at the group of Pharisees. "Therefore bear fruits in keeping with repentance, and do not begin to say to yourselves, 'We have Abraham for our father,' for I say to you that from these stones God is able to raise up children to Abraham. Indeed the axe is already laid at the root of the trees; so every tree that does not bear good fruit is cut down and thrown into the fire."

The rest of the crowd cried out, "Then what shall we do?"

He answered, "The man who has two tunics is to share with him who has none; and he who has food is to do likewise."

Some tax collectors who came to be baptized said to him, "Teacher, what shall we do?"

And he said to them, "Collect no more than what you have been ordered to."

Some soldiers questioned him, saying, "And what about us, what shall we do?"

And he said to them, "Do not take money from anyone by force, or accuse anyone falsely, and be content with your wages."

Many of the people came forward for John to baptize them. Elric smiled. "Even with all the enemy resistance," he said, "when the Word of the Lord is spoken, the hearts of men respond."

"Expectations are growing," Lacidar said. "People are beginning to wonder—could *this* man actually be the Messiah?"

Elric crossed his arms and took a breath. "Once the King is revealed, there will be no question."

# 62

## THE SON REVEALED

### Baptism minus 0.5 years

The wedding party at Mary's house drew to a close late at night. Many had come to celebrate her youngest daughter Rachael's marriage, and most of them stayed until the very end. Raziel stood by himself against the wall and watched the family and all their friends. His eyes sparkled, and a proud grin spread across his face. *I feel such a connection with this family. I am proud and honored to have officiated the marriage of six of Mary's children now.*

Before the ceremony, Raziel thought Mary seemed melancholy and disappointed that Joseph didn't get to see Rachael grow up and see how radiant she looked on this special day. But now, Mary smiled

and laughed and carried on with cheerful small talk. Raziel smiled.
*Jesus, though, seems more preoccupied and introspective. I wonder what is going on with Him.*

Jesus said goodnight to some departing guests, joined Raziel, and watched the others still milling about.

"What's the matter?" Raziel asked. "It is an exciting day for your baby sister."

"Yes, it is," Jesus said with a smile. "I am very happy."

"What is it, then?"

Jesus paused and looked around at the guests who still lingered.

*His thoughts are in another place—a weightier place, a place of destiny and purpose.*

"I am thirty now. And the last of my mother's children are on their own. My responsibilities to my family are complete. The time has finally come for me to begin my real work."

"I knew this day would come." Raziel said. He paused a moment. He looked Jesus in the eyes. "I know who you are," he said in a secret whisper.

This was the first time this had been said out loud. Raziel had always distanced himself from the subject and concentrated on doing his best to teach Jesus everything he could, to protect Him from inquisitive eyes, and to be a good mentor. In the latter years, it had become more and more difficult because the student had far surpassed the teacher.

Jesus smiled and looked deep into Raziel's eyes. "I know you do. You have given me much. Your reward will be great in my Father's kingdom."

"How will you begin? Where will you go first?"

"There is a prophet preaching in the wilderness by the Jordan."

"I have heard of him. His name is John?"

"Yes. He has been preparing the way for me. I must go there first."

"What about your mother?"

"She will stay with James for a while. Eventually, though, I will come back and bring her with me."

"I know I'm too old and not skilled with weapons of war—but when you build your army, will you let me serve with you? I have a strong heart and a great zeal for the Kingdom of God."

Jesus laughed out loud and grabbed Raziel by the shoulders. Out of the corner of his eye, Raziel caught the festive sight of the bride and groom opening a wedding gift. Jesus looked over at the gift opening and then back at Raziel.

"The Kingdom of God is like a precious gift that is wrapped. A man does not know what he has until the gift is completely opened."

"Ha!" Raziel said with a satisfied grin. "The student speaks to the teacher in riddles. I shall take that as a 'yes.'"

\* \* \*

## Baptism minus 1 day

Timrok stepped up from behind Elric and stood beside him on the hill overlooking the prophet John's base at the Jordan.

"Captain, the King has set up camp just behind us. It appears He intends to wait until tomorrow to reveal Himself to John."

Elric continued his gaze over the area where John worked his mission.

Timrok said, "My team is in place around the Lord's encampment. Zaben and Jenli's teams have an outer perimeter. All is quiet."

Elric continued his gaze without a single movement.

"The King's generals?" Elric asked.

"Simon and Andrew, James and John, Philip, Bartholomew—they have been here for weeks, being discipled by John."

Elric continued his gaze. "This is it," Elric said. "This is the place. Tomorrow is the day. We have waited a long time to see this day." A tear welled up and rolled down his cheek. He didn't reach up to wipe it away.

Elric and Timrok stood in silence and watched the battlefield below. Warriors in white fought relentless demons over the minds of men while John preached the good news of the coming Kingdom of God.

Elric and Timrok's attention turned to a group of priests and Levites from Jerusalem who approached the river's bank to challenge John.

"Who are you?" one of the priests called out. "Are you the Christ?"

"I am not the Christ," John said.

"What then? are you Elijah?"

"I am not."

"Are you the Prophet?"

"No."

"Who are you, so that we may give an answer to those who sent us? What do you say about yourself?"

"I am a voice of one crying in the wilderness, 'Make straight the way of the Lord,' as Isaiah the prophet said."

"Why then are you baptizing, if you are not the Christ, nor Elijah, nor the Prophet?"

"As for me, I baptize in water for repentance, but He who is coming after me is mightier than I, the thong of whose sandal I am not worthy to untie. He will baptize you with the Holy Spirit and fire. His winnowing fork is in His hand, and He will thoroughly clear His threshing floor; and He will gather His wheat into the barn, but He will burn up the chaff with unquenchable fire."

Timrok's hands moved to his swords' handles.

"Tomorrow," Elric said.

\* \* \*

## Baptism minus 0

The sun stood directly overhead on the day of the King's revelation. Elric's team moved onto the battlefield near the banks of the Jordan. John finished his morning message and stood waist-deep in the water. Elric led the march, followed by Zaben, Timrok, Lacidar, and Jenli in two columns. Behind the lieutenants, in two columns, followed their teams—twenty gleaming warriors in white. Each angel had his sword out resting against his shoulder in parade array. All combatants in the Middle Realm stopped and turned their attention to Elric's march. The spiritual air became silent. Every spiritual eye, elzur and beaelzur, fixed on them. Elric reached the water's edge. He halted. The squad behind him halted in step. The two columns faced inward and took two steps back, forming a corridor between them.

In the Physical Realm, the day appeared to be like any other. Men milled around on the hillsides and talked about John's message.

Some men made their way toward the riverbank to be baptized. Those preparing to be baptized removed their outer tunics.

From among the crowd Jesus stepped forward toward the river. He walked straight toward John, through the lane formed by Elric's warriors. Halfway down the lane, He stopped and reached for the bottom of His protective cloak, the outer tunic made by Mary from Elric's cloth that He had worn every day. He pulled the garment up over His head and slid it off. The instant He removed the cloak, His divine spirit became visible to all the beaelzurim. He flashed like the sun, and every spirit—angel and demon—fell on their face. Elric's team stayed at attention but bowed their heads.

In the water, John gasped for air and grabbed his heart. He looked up, and his eyes met Jesus'. His knees buckled, and he almost fell over. Jesus stepped into the water and stood before John.

John struggled to breathe. He swallowed hard and said with a cracking voice, "I . . . have need to be baptized by You, and do You come to me?"

"Permit it at this time; for in this way it is fitting for us to fulfill all righteousness."

"Yes, Lord. At your word."

John reached his hand out toward Jesus' back but then pulled away and averted his eyes.

Jesus smiled and said, "John."

John lifted his eyes and reached out with his hand again. Again, he hesitated. Then he touched Jesus' back. No explosion happened— no sparks, no flash of light, no sound. He paused a moment and took several breaths. In one swift motion, he submerged Jesus under the water and pulled Him back up.

Jesus emerged from the water, and the sky in the Middle Realm split from horizon to horizon. A blast of light from the Throne room exploded over the area. The Spirit of God descended through the light in the bodily form of a dove and alighted on Jesus.

Booming across the heavens, a voice from the Throne said, "This is My beloved Son, in whom I am well pleased."

Every demon in the area shrieked. They all scrambled to their feet, bolted like frightened rabbits, took to the sky, and fled as fast as they could. The angels all lay prostrate before the King.

The men in the Physical Realm continued talking and milling around.

The dove remained on Jesus. In a brilliant flash of light, the dove merged into Jesus' spirit, and He became even brighter in the Middle Realm.

A moment later, the sky closed up, and silence fell over the valley.

Elric turned with squinting eyes, and there in the river stood two men, John and Jesus. Jesus' spirit blazed with light, but in the Physical Realm, He looked no different. Jesus smiled at John and grasped his shoulder. He turned and walked back to the shore. He passed through Elric's columns of warriors, picked up His tunic, and continued walking toward His camp. Without an order, Elric's twenty warriors did a facing maneuver and marched off with Jesus, surrounding Him as they went.

The lieutenants gathered around Elric.

"Captain?" Jenli said.

Elric stood motionless with his eyes to the heavens. "Where are His Mighty Ones? Where is Michael?"

"Had you received word to expect them?" Jenli asked.

"No, but I thought . . . "

Zaben bit his lip and said, "Even now, His full plan remains a mystery."

Timrok scanned the horizons for incoming enemy forces. "The King has been revealed. Every spirit on the planet knows where He is now. If Michael and the Mighty Ones do not appear soon, I think we shall not be able to withstand the attack."

"I don't think they are coming," Zaben said.

"Who?" Timrok said with a puzzled look.

"The enemy."

Timrok gave an incredulous scowl.

"You saw them when His spirit was revealed," Zaben said. "They cannot withstand the glory of the King, and they know it. Before, when His spirit was hidden, they may have deluded themselves into thinking they could reach Him. But now . . ."

"I agree," said Elric. "I do not know the enemy's next move, but a frontal attack seems unlikely."

"What are our orders, then, captain?" Timrok said. "Until now, our objective has been to keep the King hidden."

Elric rubbed his chin and looked upward. His left eye twitched twice. "Until we receive a new word from the throne, we continue our present course."

He put one hand on Lacidar's shoulder and his other on Timrok's shoulder. He clenched his jaw and took a deep breath. "Nothing has changed. We protect the King. We protect the prophet John. We develop the King's inner twelve. Only now, we do it in full view of the enemy."

Timrok smiled and put his hands on his sword handles. "In His service."

# APPENDIX

## References to quoted passages.

## Chapter 5

Micah 5:2 (NASB):

> But as for you, Bethlehem Ephrathah,
>
> Too little to be among the clans of Judah,
>
> From you One will come forth for Me to be ruler in Israel.
>
> His times of coming forth are from long ago,
>
> From the days of eternity.

## Chapter 10

Luke 2:29–32 (NASB):

> "Now, Lord, You are letting Your bond-servant depart in peace,
>
> According to Your word;
>
> For my eyes have seen Your salvation,
>
> Which You have prepared in the presence of all the peoples:
>
> A light for revelation for the Gentiles,
>
> And the glory of Your people Israel."

Luke 2:34–35 (NASB): And Simeon blessed them and said to His mother Mary, "Behold, this Child is appointed for the fall and rise of many in Israel, and as a sign to be opposed—and a sword will pierce your own soul—to the end that thoughts from many hearts may be revealed."

## Chapter 13

Genesis 1:1 (NASB): In the beginning God created the heavens and the earth.

## Chapter 15

Matthew 2:2 (NASB): "Where is He who has been born King of the Jews? For we saw His star in the east and have come to worship Him."

Matthew 2:5–6 (NASB): They said to him, "In Bethlehem of Judea; for this is what has been written by the prophet:

'AND YOU, BETHLEHEM, LAND OF JUDAH,
ARE BY NO MEANS LEAST AMONG THE LEADERS OF JUDAH;
FOR FROM YOU WILL COME FORTH A RULER
WHO WILL SHEPHERD MY PEOPLE ISRAEL.'"

Matthew 2:8: And he sent them to Bethlehem and said, "Go and search carefully for the Child; and when you have found Him, report to me, so that I too may come and worship Him."

## Chapter 17

Matthew 2:9 (NASB): After hearing the king, they went on their way; and behold, the star, which they had seen in the east, went on ahead of them until it came to a stop over the place where the Child was to be found.

## Chapter 19

Matthew 2:13 (NASB): Now when they had gone, behold, an angel of the Lord appeared to Joseph in a dream and said, "Get up! Take the Child and His mother and flee to Egypt, and stay there until I tell you; for Herod is going to search for the Child to kill Him."

Matthew 2:12 (NASB): And after being warned by God in a dream not to return to Herod, the magi left for their own country by another way.

## Chapter 35

Flavius Josephus, *The Wars of the Jews*, William Whiston translation:

Book 1, 31, Verse 5: But Herod Stretched out his hands, and turned his head away from him, and cried out, "Even this is an indication of a parricide, to be desirous to get me into his arms, when he is under such heinous accusations. God confound thee, thou vile wretch; do not thou touch me, till thou hast cleared thyself of these crimes that are charged upon thee. I appoint thee a court where thou art to be judged, and this Varus, who is very seasonably here, to be thy judge; and get thou thy defense ready against tomorrow, for I give thee so much time to prepare suitable excuses for thyself."

## Chapter 36

Matthew 2:20 (NASB): "Get up, take the Child and His mother, and go to the land of Israel; for those who sought the Child's life are dead."

Exodus 7:16–17 (NASB): And you shall say to him, 'The LORD, the
God of the Hebrews, sent me to you, saying, "Let My people
go, so that they may serve Me in the wilderness. But behold,
you have not listened up to now." This is what the LORD says:
"By this you shall know that I am the LORD: behold, I am going
to strike the water that is in the Nile with the staff that is in my
hand, and it will be turned into blood.

## Chapter 47

Psalm 143:2 (NASB): For no person living is righteous in Your sight.


Isaiah 6:1–5 (NASB1995): In the year of King Uzziah's death I saw the
Lord sitting on a throne, lofty and exalted, with the train of
His robe filling the temple. Seraphim stood above Him, each
having six wings: with two he covered his face, and with two
he covered his feet, and with two he flew. And one called out
to another and said,

"Holy, Holy, Holy, is the Lord of hosts,
The whole earth is full of His glory."


And the foundations of the thresholds trembled at the
voice of him who called out, while the temple was filling
with smoke. Then I said,


"Woe is me, for I am ruined!
Because I am a man of unclean lips,
And I live among a people of unclean lips;
For my eyes have seen the King, the Lord of hosts."

Leviticus 17:11 (NASB): For the life of the flesh is in the blood, and
I have given it to you on the altar to make atonement for
your souls; for it is the blood by reason of the life that makes
atonement.

## Chapter 49

Isaiah 13:9–13 (NASB1995):

> Behold, the day of the Lord is coming,
> Cruel, with fury and burning anger,
> To make the land a desolation;
> And He will exterminate its sinners from it.
> For the stars of heaven and their constellations
> Will not flash forth their light;
> The sun will be dark when it rises
> And the moon will not shed its light.
> Thus I will punish the world for its evil
> And the wicked for their iniquity;
> I will also put an end to the arrogance of the proud
> And abase the haughtiness of the ruthless.
> I will make mortal man scarcer than pure gold
> And mankind than the gold of Ophir.
> Therefore I will make the heavens tremble,
> And the earth will be shaken from its place
> At the fury of the Lord of hosts
> In the day of His burning anger.

Isaiah 61:1–2 (NASB):

> The Spirit of the Lord God is upon me,
> Because the Lord anointed me

To bring good news to the humble;
He has sent me to bind up the brokenhearted,
To proclaim release to captives
And freedom to prisoners;
To proclaim the favorable year of the Lord
And the day of vengeance of our God;

## Chapter 50

Luke 2:48 (NASB): When Joseph and Mary saw Him, they were bewildered; and His mother said to Him, "Son, why have you treated us this way? Behold, Your father and I have been anxiously looking for You!"

Luke 2:49 (NASB): And He said to them, "Why is it that you were looking for Me? Did you not know that I had to be in My Father's house?"

## Chapter 56

Isaiah 53:3 (NASB1995):

He was despised and forsaken of men,
A man of sorrows and acquainted with grief;
And like one from whom men hide their face
He was despised, and we did not esteem Him.

## Chapter 60

Isaiah 55:6–7 (NASB):

Seek the LORD while He may be found;
Call on Him while He is near.

Let the wicked abandon his way,

and the unrighteous person his thoughts;

And let him return to the LORD,

And He will have compassion on him,

And to our God,

for He will abundantly pardon.

## Chapter 61

Ezekiel 18:23 (NASB): "Do I take any pleasure in the death of the wicked," declares the Lord GOD. "rather than that he would turn from his ways and live?"

Ezekiel 18:30–31 (NASB): Repent and turn away from all your offenses, so that wrongdoing does not become a stumbling block to you. Hurl away from you all your offenses which you have committed and make yourselves a new heart and a new spirit! For why should you die, house of Israel? For I take no pleasure in the death of anyone who dies," declares the Lord GOD. "Therefore, repent and live!"

Luke 3:7–14 (NASB1995): So he began saying to the crowds who were going out to be baptized by him, "You brood of vipers, who warned you to flee from the wrath to come? Therefore bear fruits in keeping with repentance, and do not begin to say to yourselves, 'We have Abraham for our father,' for I say to you that from these stones God is able to raise up children to Abraham. Indeed the axe is already laid at the root of the trees; so every tree that does not bear good fruit is cut down and thrown into the fire."

And the crowds were questioning him, saying, "Then what shall we do?" And he would answer and say to them, "The man who has two tunics is to share with him who has none; and he who has food is to do likewise." And some tax collectors also came to be baptized, and they said to him, "Teacher, what shall we do?" And he said to them, "Collect no more than what you have been ordered to." Some soldiers were questioning him, saying, "And what about us, what shall we do?" And he said to them, "Do not take money from anyone by force, or accuse anyone falsely, and be content with your wages."

## Chapter 62

John 1:19–23 (NASB1995): This is the testimony of John, when the Jews sent to him priests and Levites from Jerusalem to ask him, "Who are you?" And he confessed and did not deny, but confessed, "I am not the Christ." They asked him, "What then? Are you Elijah?" And he said, "I am not." "Are you the Prophet?" And he answered, "No." Then they said to him, "Who are you, so that we may give an answer to those who sent us? What do you say about yourself?" He said, "I AM A VOICE OF ONE CRYING IN THE WILDERNESS, 'MAKE STRAIGHT THE WAY OF THE LORD,' as Isaiah the prophet said."

Matthew 3:11–12 (NASB1995): "As for me, I baptize you with water for repentance, but He who is coming after me is mightier than I, and I am not fit to remove His sandals; He will baptize you with the Holy Spirit and fire. His winnowing fork is in His hand, and He will thoroughly clear His threshing floor; and He will gather His wheat into the barn, but He will burn up the chaff with unquenchable fire."

Matthew 3:13–15 (NASB1995): Then Jesus arrived from Galilee at the Jordan coming to John, to be baptized by him. But John tried to prevent Him, saying, "I have need to be baptized by You, and do You come to me?" But Jesus answering said to him, "Permit it at this time; for in this way it is fitting for us to fulfill all righteousness."

Matthew 3:17 (NASB1995): and behold, a voice out of the heavens said, "This is My beloved Son, in whom I am well-pleased."

# NOW WHAT?

The primary angelic characters in this story are fictional, and the specific actions they carry out are the simple musings of a single man. However, the underlying battle for the throne of the universe and the individual souls of mankind is real. Whether we know it or even believe it, we are embroiled in a perilous struggle that stretches from ancient times to the present day. All around us spiritual forces struggle for the hearts of men. The good news is that the King is and always has been working His plan for the redemption of man. This is the amazing story found throughout the Scriptures.

Because of sin, man is separated from God and enslaved to spiritual forces of darkness. The only payment for sin that will satisfy the righteousness of God is death. This is the primary issue facing every person who has ever lived—how can we ever hope to stand before a holy Creator with any, even one, sin on the ledger of our life? If we were left on our own, our situation would be desperately hopeless indeed.

But God did not leave us in our impossible condition. According to His plan, He Himself entered the world, lived as a man, and lived a sinless life as only He could. Then, He took all the sins of all mankind upon Himself and paid the price to satisfy the law of sin and death. The spiritual forces of darkness did not win a victory by killing Him—rather it was always His intent to take our place in death so He could offer us life while still satisfying His holiness. This is the greatest story of good news imaginable. Instead of facing the eternal wrath of God, He has provided a way for us to be set free from the bondage of sin, enter His Kingdom as beloved children, and live with Him in glory forever.

So how do we step from darkness into light? The scriptures make it clear that there is no work we can do to earn His righteousness. Only His perfect blood can cleanse us. All we need to do is simply believe with our heart that Jesus' death and resurrection provide the way to God and confess with our mouth that Jesus is Lord, and we will be saved. When we put our faith in Him, our spirits that were dead because of sin become alive to God, His very Spirit takes up residence within our mortal bodies, and He transfers us into the Kingdom of light.

If you're not sure what you believe about Jesus, I challenge you seek the truth. Get a Bible and read it for yourself. Start with the Gospel of John and ask the King of Heaven to reveal Himself to you.

Angels are fun to think about, and hopefully my story provides a different view of Jesus' life and work on earth, but do not focus on the angels themselves. The real story is about how God Himself came to make a way for us to reach Him. He accomplished His intent. Now you need to decide what you are going to do about the cross.

# ABOUT THE AUTHOR

Scott Wells' journey in His service began with missionary aviation—a private pilot license and some Bible college. It continued with an Air Force career, spanning twenty-one years, during which he earned a Masters and PhD in aeronautical engineering, specializing in feedback control theory. He taught aero engineering at the Air Force Academy, where he reached the academic rank of Associate Professor and served as an adjunct instructor at the Air Force Test Pilot School. In 2008, he retired as a Lieutenant Colonel and took a senior engineering position serving an aerospace company. His analytical and military background, combined with his lifelong studies of the scriptures, form a unique canvas for his speculative world of multidimensional realms and angel physics.

Dr. Wells lives in Arizona where he designs flight control systems and writes. He married his high-school sweetheart in 1983 and has three children. He enjoys playing saxophone on the worship team at church.

CPSIA information can be obtained
at www.ICGtesting.com
Printed in the USA
LVHW112300120522
718473LV00004BA/1036